MARGOT MERTZ FOR THE WIN

CARRIE McCROSSEN & IAN McWETHY

VIKING

CONTENT WARNING: sexual harassment and revenge porn

VIKING
An imprint of Penguin Random House LLC, New York

First published in the United States of America by Viking,
an imprint of Penguin Random House LLC, 2022

Visit us online at penguinrandomhouse.com.

Library of Congress Cataloging-in-Publication Data is available.

Printed in the United States of America

ISBN 9780593205280

10 9 8 7 6 5 4 3 2 1

BVG

Edited by Kelsey Murphy
Design by Monique Sterling
Text set in Mercury Text

Stanford admissions essay draft #36

What do you think is your greatest weakness? How has that weakness affected the trajectory of your life?

Hi, Stanford. Nice to meet you. Margot Mertz here. I love the Gates Building renovation you recently completed! Looks amazing!

So I know a lot of people try to answer this question by pretzel-ing it into a positive story about themselves. "My weakness is working really hard!" And "My problem is that I sacrifice too much to help those less fortunate!" But I'm not going to do that. I want to be honest with you, Stanford. I have wanted to go to you since I was in the third grade, and I feel like it's important we get off on the right foot. So here it is. My weakness. My fatal flaw.

I am not a good person.

Yikes. Dark, right? What does that even mean? What did she do? Kick a puppy? (No.) Hit someone with her car? (Also no! I take the bus!) Apply to USC? (I would never.) My badness has more to do with some deeply ingrained character defects.

Yeah . . .

In fairness, I do have a stressful job. Or, I *did* have a

stressful job. (I'm currently taking a hiatus.) For the past two years, I was the CEO of a company I created called Mertz Cleans Your Filth. If you had an embarrassing pic or regrettable tweet you wanted erased from the internet, you'd hire me. I'm sure you are familiar with this type of fare. It's the kind of thing that would make you revoke a fraternity's charter or kick someone off a lacrosse team.

And for a while, it was great. I was hired by students, adults, and one time a cat. (Okay. A ninety-year-old woman hired me to erase "embarrassing" pictures of her cat. But still, basically a cat.)

I was good at the job. People needed lots of filth cleaned. And I was banking that sweet, sweet tuition money to pay for you, Stanford. Let's be honest, you're not a cheap date. But then I took on a job so big and complex and shady that I ended up hurting everyone in my life who cared about me. I bailed on my parents, I treated my best friend like an employee, and I deliberately used a boy who liked me, pretending to date him because it helped with the case. Which sucks, because, in a twist that everyone but me saw coming, I actually like him. Like, a lot.

See? Margot = bad.

There were others I took advantage of. People I went to school with. My former best friend, who now lives in Colorado. Basically, anyone who liked me and cared about me, I took them for granted and abused their trust.

But the good news is, I have a plan to course-correct! I came up with a set of rules that, if followed, should keep me on the narrow path of not being a terrible person!

Margot Mertz's Ironclad Rules for Not Being a Shitty Person

1. Don't lose friends over a job.
2. Don't lie to parents about a job.
3. No more morally dubious clients (like Mrs. Blye, a cheater I represented last year. No more cheaters!).
4. Leave time for self-care. If a job gets in the way of grades, mental health, hygiene? Walk away.

Ta-da.

If I really stick to these rules, I'll probably never work again as a cleaner. Because cleaning, it turns out, is a morally corrosive business. But I'm okay with walking away if it means I'll be a better person. I don't want my relationships to be transactional anymore. I want to value my friends and family. I want to be a *whole person*. I want to know who I am.

Anyway. Thank you for your time.

I love you,
Margot

CHAPTER 1

MARGOT MERTZ ON THE CAMPAIGN TRAIL

I was in a small, nondescript room. The kind used for office storage or interrogating a murderer. I was told it might be a while, and that I should make myself comfortable. But I'd only just sat down when the door swung open and a woman in a blazer burst in.

"Bah!" the blazer woman shouted. "I thought this room was empty."

"Uh. Sorry, I'm interviewing to be an intern, and I was told to wait here for Jim? Jim Bilwort?"

"No," she said.

"No?" I asked.

"I mean . . . sorry. He's not going to interview you, because he just got fired." She shook my hand. "Priya Deshmukh. I'm the new communications director, aka the asshole they saddled with Jim's job."

She tried to play it cool, but I could see she was proud of her new title. She couldn't have been more than a couple years older than me. But despite her youth, she radiated authority. She had light brown skin, big brown eyes, and the world's tiniest nose ring. (I think? It could just have been a mole. Hard to tell in that lighting.)

"I'm Margot Mertz," I said.

Priya squinted. "Follow me." She led me out of the room and down a long, narrow hallway. "What made you want to volunteer for the campaign? College credit? Sense of duty? Boredom?"

"All three? Sort of. But mostly Shep has some policies that I really like."

Priya raised her eyebrows. "Oh yeah? Are you, like, a policy wonk?"

"Not really," I told her. "But I'm interested in his proposed amendment to 245."

Now Priya really looked surprised. "That's very specific."

Shep Green, whose ownership of several area car dealerships made him something of a minor celebrity in North Webster, was running to be state senator for the 57th District of the State of New York. The district had been held by Republicans for years, but recent demographic shifts made it more of a toss-up this year. Shep was running mostly on expanding health care coverage, bringing jobs to Western NY, and pledging to finish construction on the North Webster "Transit Center."[1] But his platform also included

---

1 North Webster's "Transit Center" is just an Amtrak station that has been half-finished for nearly a decade. It's both an eyesore and a local embarrassment. But on the flip side, teens go there to drink!

a host of smaller agenda items like the amendment to State Law § 245, which would make the dissemination of explicit images without consent a felony. *That* got my attention. A law that would essentially make all forms of revenge porn illegal? That was worth campaigning for. And *yes*, Shep Green also happens to be the father of Avery Green, who I may still have feelings for. But Avery is *not* the reason I'm working on the Green campaign. (He *is* the reason I started applying lip gloss between periods three and four. Ugh. I know.)

"I'm surprised you even know about that. It doesn't poll particularly well, so we won't let Shep talk about it," Priya said as she reached into a mini-fridge which was, for some reason, sitting in the middle of the hall. She grabbed a cold brew. I told her I'd stumbled across an interview Shep did on the local news where he talked about Roosevelt High's revenge pornography scandal. He said he intended to bring a bill to the New York statehouse on the first day he took office.

"He seemed genuinely enthusiastic. Which is more than I can say for the other lawmakers I tried to contact."

Priya smirked. She wasn't sure what to make of me. She took a big swig of her cold brew before almost choking. "Ugh. This is sweetened. This was not what I meant to get." All the same, she held her nose and chugged the entire thing before continuing down the hall.

We were in what she and the team called "campaign headquarters." Though the building itself didn't seem like it was convinced. Three months ago it was a TAX-to-the-MAX, one of those cheesy local accounting firms that promises huge refunds.

Now it was a pop-up campaign office with folding tables, cases of bottled water, and campaign signs littered everywhere. It all felt very temporary, like when a divorced dad tries to decorate his new two-bedroom condo. We passed by a makeshift conference room and a closet labeled EVERY YARD SIGN EVER. As we walked, Priya tapped out an email into her phone, while seemingly everyone we passed had a question for her.

"Priya, I just got a call from Wellmans," a slim staffer with a ruffled shirt informed her. "They want to know if tomorrow's press conference will be held in the parking lot or in the store itself?"

"Store itself. A parking lot makes us look like we're squatting. And it's to*night*. Seven p.m. Not tomorrow."

"It is?" the frazzled staffer asked, then hurried off.

Another staffer, this one a youngish, light-skinned Black man with locs down to his waist, said, "Pri! See the *Chronicle* poll?"

"Don't freak out. We're trying to flip a Republican seat, which is really fucking hard. We knew it was going to get tight, and we planned for this," she said without an ounce of panic in her voice.

We then passed a very white, maybe-twentysomething dude with red hair, leaning against a wall, chatting up some attractive young phonebankers. "Alex! What are you doing here?" Priya demanded, adopting the tone of a toddler's mom who had just counted all the way to three.

"Shep said I could take a lunch break!" Alex said defensively, then rolled his eyes at the attractive phonebankers. (This isn't important for the story, but the girls were *not* into him.)

"Not when he has a radio interview in twenty minutes and you're his body man!" she scolded. "Do you know what being a body man means? It means you never leave his body."

"Yeah. Okay. Sorry," Alex stammered before fleeing in the opposite direction. Priya then swung open an office door.

"Interns. Here ya go. Welcome to the fold."

Inside the room were three dead-eyed twentysomethings of various ethnicities stuffing envelopes. One of them started to say, "Heyyyy . . ." but I turned to catch up to Priya.

She had already made it halfway down the hall when I said, "Wait. Sorry. I was planning to tell Jim this in my interview, but I feel like I could be a lot more useful to the campaign if I was in a position with . . . some actual responsibility?"

Priya was glued to her phone as she said, "Uh . . . okay. So what is it you want to do? You want to be campaign manager? Or maybe replace Shep and run for office yourself?"

"Haha. No," I said, not taking Priya's bait. "But I heard you do fellowships?"

"Fellowships?" Priya repeated. She seemed surprised that I had done research into the campaign. "Fellowships are paid and reserved for interns who are majoring in political science. What are you, a freshman in college?"

"No. I'm a senior," I said proudly, before adding, "in high school."

"Right," Priya said, turning away from me. "Work your way up. In the meantime: mailers, phone- and textbanking, coffee runs; believe it or not, they are a vital part of what we do—"

"Just give me a chance!" I pleaded, running in front of her. "Look, I get that I'm young and that most people my age are useless. But you don't exactly look like an elder statesman! What if

I'm one of the good ones? Like you! What if I'm a high school Jen O'Malley Dillon?"

Priya huffed. A little annoyed that I wouldn't just shut up and phonebank already. But also maybe slightly impressed that I name-checked Joe Biden's campaign manager.[2]

"You want a task? Fine," she said. "You know Wellmans?"

"Everybody knows Wellmans," I said.

Wellmans is a chain of grocery stores in upstate New York. It's where *everyone* in North Webster shops because it is *so much more than a grocery store.* Wellmans are big and well-stocked, with store-brand stuff that is often better than the name brand (i.e., Wellmans Toasted Oats™ are five thousand times better than Cheerios). Wellmans are *destinations.* Plus they give college scholarships to their employees. *Plus* they make chocolate moon cookies that are the best thing I've ever had. And yes, they're soft. And yes, I once ate four for breakfast and I *did not regret it.* It's kind of hard to explain Wellmans unless you live here, but people in North Webster treat it with a church-like reverence. It's borderline cultish.

"Here's a task for you," Priya said, interrupting my Wellmans reverie. "At seven o'clock, Shep is doing a press event at the Ridge Road Wellmans. And I want him to announce that Danny Wellman is endorsing him."

"Okay . . ." I said.

"So I need you to call Danny and get him to do that."

---

2   Jennifer O'Malley Dillon was only the second woman to manage a winning presidential campaign. The first? Kellyanne Conway. Donald Trump's campaign manager. It's your classic "first is the worst, second is the best" situation.

My eyes went large. Danny Wellman, the founder and CEO of Wellmans, is a local celebrity. He's the closest thing North Webster has to a LeBron James.[3] The odds of me (a nobody who has never met him) getting his endorsement were . . . not great.

"That's in, like, four hours?" I clarified.

"That's the deal. You get Danny, I'll make you a fellow."

Whoa. Priya was not fucking around. "Okay," I said. "Deal." Then I forcefully shook her hand, as if that would impress her.

"If you need anything, just ask Melvin," Priya said. "He's the intern coordinator." Then she disappeared into a meeting room.

I looked around for an open desk, ready to get to work, but it seemed like most were occupied. Maybe this Melvin person would know where I could set up shop. By the main entrance sat a partially bearded white guy wearing a ratty Henley and surfing his phone. Seemed like a Melvin to me!

"Melvin?" I asked.

"Blah. No," the guy said, his eyes glued to the article he was reading. "That guy sucks. I'm Nick."

"Oh. Sorry," I said, though I wasn't that sorry. I hate people who don't bother to look up from their phones when you ask them a question. "Do you know if any of these desks are free?"

"No idea."

I grimaced. What a charmer. "Well, Nick, how about a Wi-Fi password?"

"That I can help you with." He smiled and pointed to the wall where the Wi-Fi password was posted. "Enjoy! It's very slow!"

---

3 Which isn't close at all. I know.

"Awesome!" I said. And parked myself on the floor.

And then, with my back pushed against a decaying plaster wall and my butt on warped linoleum, I endeavored to track down the biggest celebrity in North Webster and convince him to endorse Shep Green for state senate.

AND LOOK, I WON'T BORE YOU WITH THE DETAILS OF HOW I GOT Danny Wellman's endorsement. About how I stalked all his social media handles. Or how I tried to befriend two of his secretaries before finally tracking down his daughter-in-law at her ceramics class. Because who wants to hear about how I bought two of her irregularly shaped "spoon rests" in order to ingratiate myself? Or how I finally convinced Meghan Wellman to put me on a conference call with Danny Wellman himself? (I know, it kind of seems like I am telling how I did it. But aren't you glad? Aren't you impressed!? It was hard!) The important thing is, I did it. And with just enough time to tell Priya in person before she left for the press conference.

"Hey, Priya. Just wanted to let you know that Danny Wellman will be attending the press conference tonight. And he will be endorsing Shep. Although he asked if the press conference could be delayed by fifteen minutes or so because he's doing a charity golf . . . something."

Priya's jaw literally dropped. I filled the silence by saying, "So should I tell him yes? Or should I tell him to fuck off and get there at seven because, unlike the North Webster Amtrak station, we run on time?"

"No!" Priya shouted, a terror in her eyes as she apparently didn't get that I was joking. "We can delay. That's not a problem. Sorry, when I gave you that job, I didn't think you'd— Well, I thought it was impossible." She shook my hand again. And this time she squeezed back just as hard.

"Congrats on the fellowship, Margot Mertz."

As I left the office a few minutes later, I felt my heart racing. It was the same rush I got when I completed an MCYF job, only this time I wasn't breaking any laws. Or doing anything morally questionable. Maybe there was hope for me after all.

CHAPTER 2

MINIMUM WAGE. MINIMAL EXCITEMENT.

The next morning, I was scheduled to work from eight a.m. to four p.m. at the dry cleaners my dad owned and operated. Normally, my shifts were busy and went by fast, punctuated by the *RING* of the bell as customers came in. We'd make some polite chitchat as I took their clothes. I'd put their money in the old-timey cash register (my dad says it's "vintage" and "has a soul"), which makes a very satisfying *DING* whenever a cash transaction is made. So that's a bonus. Then I'd *RIP* off their ticket and put their stuff on hangers or, if it was really gross, into the "soiled" pile that gathered in the corner. Then the bell would ring again, and they'd leave.

Ring. Ding. Rip. Ring. Repeat.

Unfortunately for me, Clearview Commons, the strip mall where my dad's dry cleaners is located, was being repaved that day. The smell of wet tar hung in the air, and there was no parking for our patrons. So the first hour of my shift went by without a single person stepping through the door. Which meant I had a lot of time to myself. To think. Which wasn't my favorite.

When I'd decided to take a hiatus from cleaning filth, I realized I was going to need to get a job. A real job. The problem was I'm not really "qualified" to do "anything," as my empty résumé can attest. Which is why, after months of applying to be a hostess for god-awful chain restaurants (it turns out that owning an internet cleanup business and having a problem with authority do *not* make you the best candidate for Red Robin) and one disastrous stint as a babysitter (it's as bad as you think; it involved a nut allergy), my dad threw up his hands and allowed me to "person the cash register" on weekends.[4] You can imagine my parents' surprise when I told them I got the campaign fellowship. *"But you can't do anything!"* my mom had insisted. *"I know!"* I'd said back. Then we all jumped up and down and they took me out for ice cream. They were very proud.

Still, the fellowship didn't pay very much. So for the time being, I was stuck hocking hangers at the cleaners on Saturdays. And while I was grateful for the hookup, the guaranteed income, and the chance to do something low-stress, I was finding that there were downsides to low-stress. Namely boredom. On days like today, my mind started to spin in really random directions. Like *How many calories are in an Oreo if you just eat the cookie part?* Or *Could I pull off a nose ring?* Or *Would Avery like a girl*

---

4   He said "man the cash register." But come on. We're phasing that out.

with a nose ring? Or *Is Kermit the Frog attractive? Is it just that he's comforting?*

I checked the Fury group chat, hoping for a brief distraction and maybe some updates. It was still surprisingly active, given that the only thing the group really had in common was that last spring everyone had been victims of revenge porn. The girls would share memes or gripe about the minimal sentences handed down to the offenders. Every now and then there'd be a picture of Chris Heinz's car with a milkshake or mayonnaise poured on the windshield. But it was also a way for everyone to vent. Kind of like an informal therapy group, because a lot of the girls were still suffering. Depression. Anxiety. Shame. The story of RB may have come and gone, but they were still living with it.

Today, though, the chat was silent. Not a single post to keep me busy. I did have a book for AP English, *The Awakening*, and I dove in hoping for some relief.[5]

RING. Finally! Sweet, merciful *RING*, we have a customer! It was Mr. Lumley, my former client and current AP Euro teacher.

"Do you have any experience with cat vomit?" Lumley asked as he scratched the top of his bald brown head. He was holding a set of queen-sized sheets with a big purple-orange stain that seemed to spread everywhere, like a smelly Jackson Pollock painting. "Because this is going to be a challenge."

I get questions like this every shift. *Can you get a bloodstain out of this tablecloth? Can you get superglue out of a wig? Is there a way to remove Play-Doh from this couch cushion—my child is*

---

5 Spoiler!

really aggressive. People out there are *doing stuff* to their linens. I live for these requests. The grosser the better. When customers bring these items in, eyes downcast—a rug or a shirt or a pair of pants that have been ruined by something shameful—it gives me a window into people's very weird and complicated lives.

"Certainly," I said as I took his disgusting sheets and put them in the soiled pile. "My father is an expert in feline bodily fluid removal. He actually teaches a seminar at the annual conference for dry cleaners in Albany every year. If you're ever in Albany in August, you should go!"

I proclaimed this with such easy confidence that it was impossible for Mr. Lumley to know that I was, in fact, lying for no reason. I found myself doing this more and more these days. I don't know if it was because I was bored. Or if it was a side effect of not lying to my parents anymore. (Those lies had to go somewhere!) The only thing I knew for sure was that there was no such thing as a dry cleaners' conference in Albany. *DING!*

"Wow! Well, looks like I came to the right place!" Lumley cheered as I ripped off his dry cleaning ticket. *RIP.*

"It's like we always say. If you can secrete it, we can clean it!" Again, I was lying. We don't always say that. No one says that. It's disgusting.

"Huh, okay." Mr. Lumley grimaced, not sure what to make of my slogan, then waved as he walked out. *RING.*

"Margot?" My dad poked his head out of his "office," which is not a room so much as a small desk surrounded by boxes and one of those accordion room divider things from the eighties. "I have three deliveries due in Brighton this afternoon. Want to do 'em?"

"Absolutely."

At some point during my tenure at North Webster Elite Organic Cleaners, my dad had become aware of my extreme boredom. And he'd started throwing new tasks my way, like deliveries with the Elite van or ordering the wholesale pleating pins. One day he even let me try pressing the clothes with this big industrial iron. The kind that can press a set of king-sized sheets. I don't know why we thought that was a good idea, I can barely use the iron at home. I ruined a pair of slacks so badly they caught on fire and my dad had to offer the customer a complete refund (something he never does).

"Good. Make sure you write down the gas mileage," he said, coming around to lean against the counter, "Oh, and any way I could get you to stop making up weird slogans to the customers?"

"You could try, but . . ." I gave a cute shrug, indicating that I would definitely keep doing it.

He shook his head. "I'm guessing you're not this much trouble on the Green campaign. Or you never would've gotten that fancy-pants fellowship."

"Give it time. They'll grow to dislike me too," I said flatly.

"And . . . did you happen to see . . . Avery while you were there?" he asked sheepishly. "I mean, he's the candidate's son, so . . ."

I gave my coldest, deadest glare before answering, "As I told you and Mom both, *many* times, I'm not working at the Green campaign to be near Avery."

"Okay. Okay," my dad said, holding up his hands in defeat.

"All I care about is Shep's promise to do something about revenge porn laws—"

"I know. I know. All I'm saying is that it wouldn't have been weird if you *had* done it for Avery!" Off my look, he added, "When I was thirteen, I took a weekend job cleaning toilets at a bowling alley because Becky Santucci, the prettiest girl in my grade, smiled at me once. So I'd understand if—"

"Dad, this is workplace harassment. You need to stop."

"Okay. Fine. I'll stop talking." My dad surrendered and went back to his desk. Then he popped his head out to say, "But once you punch out? Forget about it. We're getting to the bottom of this Avery stuff!"

I rolled my eyes. Unfortunately, there *is* no bottom to the Avery stuff. Because there *is no Avery stuff*.

Do I l#ve him? Probably. Is it a struggle not to think about him constantly? Yes. All I do is imagine him opening jars for me. And I know that probably sounds fun, to imagine a really hot guy wrapping his muscular fingers around a jar of nice mustard and just going to town . . . but it's actually not. Because when you really care about someone and they don't want to open jars for you in real life, it hurts. And all that delicious mustard just goes to waste.

After I bumped into Avery over the summer, cleaning up trash on I-490, he kind of vanished. Everyone assumed he went on vacation, or got really busy working for his dad's campaign. But when school started, it was clear something else was going on. Especially when rumors started flying that Avery Green, Mr. Serial-Monogamer himself, had decided he wouldn't be dating anyone his senior year.

Avery hadn't told people why he was doing this, but he had

already turned down Jenji Hopp and Christine Shaw as home-coming dates. Naturally, questions started to circulate. Did he have a religious conversion? Did he join a cult? You usually hear about sex cults, but maybe there's a no-sex one?

Whatever it was, I tried to handle the news like an adult. I told myself to stop pining after him. To stop engineering meet-cutes with him after school. If he needed space, who was I to get in the way? Just because I had many, many jars I'd like to see opened? Pickle jars. Sauerkraut jars. Applesauce, even. God, I wanted him.

RING! The front door opened. Another customer! Thank god! I looked to the door, hoping to see one of my regulars. Like Gladys, a petite, feisty woman in her 150s who walks five miles a day and hates everyone. Or Reggie Storm, the local weather-person (and former client), who always brought his adorable puppy, Thermometer (and many of Thermometer's dry-clean-only outfits. She's a fancy pup[6]).

But sadly, it wasn't anyone fun like Gladys or Reggie. It was Ainsley McKibbon. Ainsley was a junior who had moved to North Webster from New York City[7] over the summer, instantly becom-ing one of the most popular girls at school because . . . she's very attractive. By anyone's standard. Silky blond hair, wowza eyes, perfectly symmetrical face. I'm not entirely convinced she isn't Margot Robbie researching a role.

"Margot! Hi! Did you layer your hair? I love!" Ainsley said,

---

6 With over fifteen thousand Instagram followers!

7 Actually from someplace called Westchester that everyone insists is *basically* New York City.

carrying three Free People dresses over her arm.

"No. But I did wash it this morning."

"LOL. Margot. You are so funny," Ainsley said while scrolling through her phone. Ainsley has been nothing but nice to me in the brief time I've known her. But she is one of those people who says LOL instead of laughing. Which I've always found troubling.

"Okay. So . . . please don't hate me, but I actually came here because I need your help. Or, my friend needs your help," Ainsley said as she continued to scroll her phone. "See, I had this very chill little pool party last weekend and Tiffany Sparks came, even though her mom told her she couldn't go. And Tiff asked everyone not to post any pics of her, but Ray Evans did. And then people reposted it. And now Tiff's worried that her mom is going to find out. Because her mom is like an Insta-Nazi or something."

Oof. Would not have been my choice of words, Ainsley.

"And the whole thing is extra effed because Tiffany was supposed to be visiting her cousin in the hospital last Saturday. But she lied to her mom and came to my party instead. And trust me, I did *not* know this at the time, or I would've told her to go to the hospital! Margot! Her cousin has been in a coma for a week!" Ainsley said, taking out a piece of gum. "Anyway, her mom would lose her shit if she found out. And I told Tiff I'd try to help her. So can you do it?"

The problem with taking a break from your successful cleanup business is that people still come up to you asking for help. And I have to say it's very tempting to say yes. Even though this job is clearly in violation of rule #3. I mean, what Tiffany did was the definition of morally dubious. *And what is wrong with her poor cousin?* But still, the thought of having a job again, of not being tortured by idle thoughts of Oreos and Avery opening jars, there was a not-small part of me that wanted to say yes. But I held strong.

"I'm sorry, Ainsley. But I'm not really doing cleanup work right now."

"Oh. Okay. I totally get it. Glad you're doing you," Ainsley said, putting away her phone. "I sometimes feel like I should be 'doing me' more? But it's hard because I'm new here. And I feel like I have to say yes to everything!"

I felt bad. She was a nice girl. But I wasn't going to take the job.

After a few more awkward exchanges, in which Ainsley asked me questions about dry cleaning, and I restrained myself from petting her hair like Lennie from *Of Mice and Men*, Ainsley handed over her dresses and bounded out the door.

Through our big storefront windows, I watched her walk past a tall guy lumbering toward the cleaners with a load of shirts and blazers slung over his shoulder. When he saw Ainsley, he stopped to ask her a question. I assume this happens to her five million times a day. Ainsley was polite, nodding her head. The tall boy, meanwhile, was gesticulating wildly, letting his dry cleaning drag on the ground. An indicator that he was trying way too hard. I figured I had a minute before Ainsley blew this dude off, so I bent down under the counter and took a few bites of my sandwich.

RING! The door opened and a deep, bro-y voice said, "Are you guys open? I couldn't tell."

"We are," I said between bites. "Come in."

And then I nearly choked on my tuna sandwich. Because it was Peter Bukowski, aka P-Boy. Although I barely recognized him. This was a well-dressed, freshly haircutted, possibly *Queer Eye*d P-Boy.[8]

He dumped the clothes on the counter without looking at me. "Nice. Is there any way you could have this ready by Tuesday? My dad has a big . . ." he trailed off, distracted by his phone. I waited, death-staring at him while he typed one more text. He finally pocketed the phone and looked up.

"Margot? You work . . . *here*?" As in, *How could anyone work at such a shitty place? Why aren't you working at your dad's country club like a normal kid?*

I didn't miss a beat before replying, "I do." I smiled. "And what are you doing here? I thought for sure you would be . . . what is that place called? It's kind of like detention, but worse? Oh yeah, prison! I thought you'd be in prison!"

P-Boy chewed on his lip. I couldn't tell if he was genuinely remorseful or angry, but regardless, this was very strange. I was not used to P-Boy exercising restraint. Usually he just blurted out whatever petty or misogynistic fart shot into his brain. Like "Suck it, Mertz!" or "You're such a bitch!" or "Girls! Bad!" But instead he lip-gnawed before saying, "Yeah. Well, I was lucky, I guess."

Oooooh yeah he was. If Shep passes his legislation, anyone who does what P-Boy did would get a minimum of six months in

---

8 Dear god, I hope not! What a waste of JVN's time and skills!

prison. Election Day couldn't come soon enough.

I hadn't seen P-Boy since school started. He'd been keeping a relatively low profile, though his TikTok was still active, featuring highly edited vids of himself dancing drunk, peeing on things while drunk, and throwing up at parties while sober. (Jkjk. He was very drunk.) Despite his crimes, he still has over twenty thousand followers.[9]

"Anyway, I should probably take this somewhere else. I didn't realize . . ." P-Boy muttered sheepishly, looking for a quick out, which I wasn't about to give him.

"No. Please! Just because we've had our differences doesn't mean your dad shouldn't have a clean, pressed shirt!" I walked past the counter, snatching P-Boy's load of clothes from his right shoulder.

"Oh. Okay."

"We can have it ready by Tuesday. No problem." These shirts were getting shipped out for an "executive clean" and would definitely not be back until next Saturday. "We have very high standards here at Elite Organic! We clean clothes in a timely manner, while not maliciously disseminating nude images of minors! It's the Elite Cleaners way!" I ripped off his ticket and held it out so that P-Boy would have to walk back toward me.

"Right. I get it," he said, gingerly taking the ticket from my hand. "And, yeah, look, I deserve that. All the shit you're giving me. I . . . I know you'll probably never believe this, but I feel like I've changed. Or I'm trying to, anyway." My eyes were practically

---

9   More than Thermometer! Nooo!

on fire, I was so mad. *Changed?* How could P-Boy have changed? He never got punished! Not a real punishment, anyway. He never reached out to victims to apologize, to hear how his actions affected people. Changed? Because his hair was different now? Fuck him.

"Anyway. I'll tell my dad his suits and stuff will be ready by Tuesday. Thanks, Margot." P-Boy tapped the plywood counter one more time before reaching into his coat pocket. "I'm serious about the change stuff. Really." He took something out of his pocket and left it in front of me before quickly exiting.

I dug my nails into the counter and looked down at the item he had left for me. It was a sticker. Four inches in diameter. Red, white, and blue, with black lettering that said PETER BUKOWSKI FOR PRESIDENT!

From the back of the store, my dad reappeared.

"Hey, bug! The Rodriquezes said they needed their linens done by two. Did they ever show?" I hardly registered what he said. My mind was still with P-Boy, trying to make sense of what he'd left behind. My dad craned his neck to look at the sticker.

"Who's Peter Bukowski?" he asked. Like most people, he only knew P-Boy by his douchey nickname.

"A dick stain in sheep's clothing," I said, glaring at the sticker.

My dad sighed before returning to the back. "Can you please not use words like 'dick stain' in front of me? You're my daughter, and it's very disturbing."

I silently agreed. It was all very disturbing.

CHAPTER 3

PETER BUKOWSKI FOR PRESIDENT

Monday morning I went to school a smidge early so that I could take a brief detour to peruse the Board. The Board is a giant corkboard where clubs, teams, and classes put up posters, leaflets, and other random things. Located by the stairwell near the art department and next to Roosevelt's "Wall of Fame" (where they honor athletes and valedictorians and the local kid who made it to the third round of *American Idol*), the Board is an essential stop for most students. If you've got school spirit and are engaged in some sort of extracurricular, you'll probably stop by the Board multiple times a day. I think I've walked past it maybe . . . three times in my high school career.

But today, it was a must. Because on top of clubs and tutoring and sports updates, it was also the go-to place to see who was running for student government. Secretary, treasurer, vice president. Our school has a position called *Director of the Interior for*

Student Affairs—Public and Private. (Your guess is as good as mine as to what that means.) And, of course, student body president.

It's not like I was *that* worried about P-Boy. He was a disgraced former popular kid, a creep with a literal rap sheet. He was canceled and there was no way people were going to vote for him. Still, I just wanted to make sure he wasn't, like, running unopposed or something.

There was a good deal of commotion when I approached the Board. The cast list for the fall one-act had just gone up. Eager, anxious theater kids were crowded all around, crying, celebrating, and just being *a lot.* I watched several of them go up to the Board, look at a sheet of paper, and become so full of pure glee it made my teeth hurt.

"I got Willa! I'm Willa Loman!!! AAH!!!!" Gabby Alvarez screamed, jumping up and down and hugging her friends. Ms. Corman was still taking full-length plays and musicals and adapting them into compressed, confusing one-acts. This year she'd turned *Death of a Salesman* into *Saleswomyn.* A feminist-revised "gender-swapped" one-act adaptation that was "updated for our times."[10]

I scanned the Board, doing my best to avoid *the drama.* There were leaflets, stickers, and posters for an array of candidates. Justin Chen was running for secretary. Melissa Foley and Cheryl Graham were duking it out for vice president. Charlotte Sheffield and Sophia Triassi were both running for the office of DISAPP, and both had taken their campaign photos with dogs. I

---

10 There's no way the Miller estate signed off on this.

finally saw P-Boy's red, white, and blue poster plastered in the middle of the Board, like the straight white man he is, splaying his legs out in the middle of a crowded bus. And . . . no other signs for president? I was starting to get worried. Was he really running unopposed? Was it possible no one else wanted to be student body president?

"I know you're not here for the cast list,"[11] Kelsey Chugg said, appearing next to me in her signature terrifying fashion. My sometime-henchwoman was now a sophomore.

"Jesus, Chugg!" I said.

"So. What are you doing here?"

"Nothing," I said, shrugging. But she could see that my eyes were still searching the Board.

"Nothing?" She raised her eyebrows. "I thought you might be on, like . . . a job or something?"

"I told you. I'm not taking any jobs right now."

She furrowed her brow in disappointment. "Yeah, yeah, I know. But if you *do* take a job, I'd be more than happy to help."

"Noted." I rolled my eyes at her.

Kelsey was swinging her arms involuntarily. Her body language practically screaming, *Aren't you going to ask me if I auditioned?*

"How about you? Did you try out—"

"Yes!" she said, jumping up and down. "I'm Biff's subconscious! Well, there are actually five of us. We're kind of a Greek

---

11 I had considered trying out for a play this year as an extracurricular. But then I read the script for *Saleswomyn*. Yeeeesh. I don't want to spoil anything, but it *does* end with Willa Loman doing a "suicidal TikTok." It . . . doesn't work.

chorus for Biff's internal struggles as he wavers between appeasing his mother and doing what really makes him happy. But I think that's pretty good for a sophomore."

"Wow. That's great! Is Hoffman doing it too?" One could only assume that if Kelsey Chugg had auditioned for the show, then Kelsey Hoffman must have also. The two Kelseys were *already* a Greek chorus. They wouldn't even need to rehearse.

Chugg chewed on her nail before saying, "Oh. No. She's been busy. Honestly, ever since she started dating Jenn . . . I haven't seen her that much."

"Oh yeah. I heard they were dating. Good for Hoffman!" I immediately felt a little bad for saying this. For one thing, it sounded like I was saying *Good for Hoffman for bagging a hottie like Jennifer Snell.* Jennifer *is* very attractive. But I didn't want to sound like a creepy uncle. Also, I could tell Chugg felt a little abandoned. It's always tough when one party of an inseparable-best-friend duo starts going out with someone. The other is inevitably left behind. I wondered if that was why Chugg auditioned for the play. Maybe she was trying to forge her own path.

"Yeah. She seems happy," Chugg said, staring up at an old picture of some guy from the aughts on the Wall of Fame (who apparently won a hot dog eating contest), before quickly adding, "So. Why are you here then?"

"I just wanted to see who was running for student government." Chugg cocked an eyebrow, because this did not even remotely sound like something I'd be interested in. So I clarified. "I heard that P-Boy was running. And I just had to see for myself if it was true."

"Oh. Right. I can't believe that bastard is even allowed to run!" Chugg complained.

"It does seem like if you're convicted of a crime like 'dissemination of underage pornography,' then maybe you should be barred from running for student government,"[12] I suggested.

"Well, whatever. Melanie's going to crush him," Chugg said.

I looked back at the Board and finally saw it. At the bottom right corner was a poster with purple lettering. It featured a cartoon drawing of an owl, and said WHOOOO? MELANIE DAVIS FOR PRESIDENT! THAT'S WHOOOOOO!

"Hm," I muttered to myself. If I had to pick a candidate to run against P-Boy, Melanie wouldn't have been my first choice. She was a little . . . odd. I mean, she certainly had a lot of good qualities, but they were often overshadowed by her weirder ones. She was smart, *but* she also had a habit of raising her hand in every class with a strange intensity, like she was hand-wrestling God. She was nice, *but* every time she laughed it was so loud and high-pitched I was worried she was going to kill me in my sleep. And she was cute. *But*, most of her wardrobe featured creepy cartoon animals. Tees. Sweatshirts. Jeans. And I didn't put this together until I saw her poster just now, but I think it was mostly owls. So yeah, she's Roosevelt's owl girl. You expect owl girl to be president of mathletes or vice president of sitting alone at lunch. You don't expect her to run for student body president.

"What?" Chugg asked, sounding slightly defensive. "Melanie's nice. We had gym last year. She's funny."

---

12 Seems like something DISAPP should look into? Maybe? What *is* their purview?

"What's with the owls?" I asked, suddenly getting a chill. Chugg shrugged.[13]

"Yeah. I asked her about that once. I said, 'Do you like Harry Potter or something?' and she said, 'What's Harry Potter?'"

"Oh, god," I said, suddenly feeling woozy.

"Dude. Relax. She's running against P-Boy. Everyone hates him. I mean, if he didn't have such a good lawyer, he'd be a registered sex offender."

"True. But he's smarter than he seems," I said, cracking my knuckles. "I mean, he's lazy and he sucks. But he was capable of pulling off RB, which required ingenuity. I just want to make sure he's, like, definitely going to lose."

Chugg nodded. "So what are you going to do?"

I exhaled. "Not sure. Maybe I'll talk to Melanie."

I DIDN'T HAVE ANY CLASSES WITH MELANIE. SO I PLANNED TO track her down during my independent study. Ah, independent study! My senior year schedule was way easier than my rigorous junior year one. It was made up of cake classes, study halls, and just a couple APs. But perhaps the smartest thing I did over the summer was sign up for an independent study during first period (on "The Wives of Henry VIII," a class I'd selected from a dusty book in the guidance counselor's office). Technically, a teacher was supposed to supervise me. But I'd picked one who would be as hands-off as possible: Coach Powell. His commitment to

---

13 Chrugged? Is that something?

the JV baseball team and his surprisingly well-curated book club (this month they're reading *Klara and the Sun*) left him little time to care about me.

He had given me the code to his office,[14] a tiny cubby in the athletic department warren just off the locker rooms that always smelled of socks. It wasn't swanky, but since a classroom shortage had converted my usual tech booth haunt into a remedial English classroom, Powell's office was often the best I could do.

I dropped my bag, cracked open my laptop, and signed in to Roosevelt's teacher portal as an admin. (I had access to several teachers' logins, but today I decided to be "Sonia Gushman.") I just needed to know where to find Melanie.

"Hey, Coach—" The door burst open, and a giant net bag of soccer balls walked into the tiny office. From behind the balls I heard, "Where do you want all these?"

I looked up. I'd know that voice anywhere.

"Avery?" I said as I closed my laptop.

"Margot? Uh . . . hi." In his shock, Avery dropped the bag of soccer balls (which turned out to be two bags of about thirty soccer balls). The balls bounced in opposite directions but were caught in the mesh bags, making the whole thing move with a wild intensity. Avery swore and then just repeated, "Aw man aw man aw man" as he tried to regain control. It was funny watching him struggle like a human for once—he cared so much about not wrecking the office, and everything he did seemed to make it worse.

---

14 Huge mistake.

"Damn it! Sorry," Avery said when the balls had finally lost their bounce. Then added, "I'm supposed to get these to Coach Powell. JV wanted them. They're varsity's . . . old balls."

"Makes sense" was the cleverest thing I could think to add.

Avery looked down at me and scratched his prominent—and sexy!—jawline. "Wait. What are you doing here? You don't do sports now, do you? Is the world ending? Is this the purge?"

"Haha. No," I said. "Coach Powell is supervising my independent study."

"Oh. Sure. But I . . . feel like he's doing a bad job? Because you don't seem supervised at all right now?" Avery smiled.

"Oh yeah. Coach Powell does not care. Which is why I picked him." I smiled back. "Anyway, what are *you* doing here? Aren't you supposed to be in class?" *Health class? Your first period class after homeroom and before AP Comp Gov? I know your entire schedule, please marry me?*

He held up his hands in defense. "I was helping Coach Swanson. He pulled me out of class to clean out the storage room."

I stood up. "Well, maybe he should be supervising *you* a little more. You're clearly . . ." The office was pretty small, so when I stood, I was suddenly close to Avery. Like, I could smell his hair butter, I was so close. And the pull of him was stopping my brain from working. Which is why I finally finished with the unremarkable, ". . . You clearly need supervision . . . too."

Avery looked at me but didn't say anything. Then he sighed. "Yeah. Probably."

We were headed into an awkward silence. And that's when I

noticed how weird Avery was being. Shifting his weight and looking away. I would've said he seemed nervous, but Avery's never nervous. Was he still mad about last year? When we "dated"?[15] Was that why he had been avoiding me?

"Well! I gotta run!" He hoisted the soccer balls up, nearly running into the door and threatening a repeat of the ball chaos we'd just experienced.

"Wait!" I shouted, and took a step toward him. But I had nothing to follow it up with. My brain had just spasmed: *Don't let him leave! He smells too good!*

"Yeah?" Avery asked expectantly.

"I . . ." *Come on, brain! Do that thing where you make words!* ". . . Do you know Melanie Davis? Or, do you know if she does any extracurriculars?"

"Yeah. Mel's the best! I . . . think she has Photography Club after school today?"

Oh right. When I had attended Photography Club last year with Avery, I'd seen her there. I should've remembered. "Cool. I just . . . need to talk to her," I mumbled. "Maybe I'll see you there?"

"Sorry, no. I quit photography." Avery clarified, "I'm trying to pull back on extracurriculars this year."

"Really?" I couldn't contain my surprise. Mr. Extracurricular himself? "Maybe this *is* the purge."

He laughed. "Nah, no. It's just something I'm trying . . ."

He looked down at his feet for a moment, then suddenly back

---

15 And by "dated," I mean when I ruthlessly used him in the course of my work.

at me. Right into my eyes. And I felt his pull again. It was the same look and same feeling I had when he first tried to kiss me last spring. That brooding, sexy look that meant he was about to make a move. Of course! That's why he was nervous. Not because he hated me, but because he still had feelings for me! And wanted to act on those feelings by pulling me in for a—

"Well, see ya round, bud!" Avery said, before he playfully punched my arm and left Powell's office.

Nope. I read that wrong. Clearly, I don't understand people and I'm going to die alone. *Arm punch?* I was at best a platonic "bud" friend. Ah well, at least now I knew where to find Melanie!

THE MINUTE THE BELL RANG AT THE END OF EIGHTH PERIOD, I left class and proceeded directly to Photography Club. I was not a member, but that had never stopped me from attending before.

"Margot? Are you in this club?" Ms. Gushman asked. She was the random teacher assigned to supervise Photography Club that day.

"Just for today!" I said cheerily. As though I had permission to attend a club for just one day. As though that were a thing. But Ms. Gushman didn't press it.

I spotted Melanie Davis in the third row, seated next to her BFF, the fast-walking overachiever Abby Durbin. They were talking animatedly, so I plopped my bag down, waiting for the right moment to butt in when Melanie said, "MARGOT MERTZ!" She was one of those weirdos who called people by their first and last names. "How's it going? Are you joining photography?"

Melanie was wearing a huge goofy smile, and, yes, an owl shirt. She was quite tall, with a short brown bob and olive skin. Her face was angular, with some residual scarring from middle school acne. But you could barely tell any of this because she slouched and allowed her hair to swing in front of her face all the time.

"Hey, Margot. Want a Skittle?" Abby offered. Abby was short to Melanie's tall, and had long blond hair to her short. She was like a "photonegative" of Melanie, if you're into photography parlance, which I am not. Abby was one of the girls featured on RB, and one of the few who agreed to press charges last spring. And ever since then I think she considered me an ally. I took a Skittle.

"Oh, sorry," Abby said, pouring half the bag into my hand by mistake. "Can I get the orange ones back? Mel likes the orange—"

"It's okay," Melanie said apologetically. "I'll take whatever colors Margot doesn't want."

It had never occurred to me to have a color preference.

"Cool. So, Melanie, I heard you're running for—" But before I could finish my sentence, Harriet Boyle, a white girl with glasses and curly blond hair, leaned over and started talking.

"Hey, did you guys hear Avery quit? That's like four clubs in two days!"

Harriet was a sophomore. I didn't know her too well. Last year, she'd just seemed like your average self-conscious quiet girl. But this year, apparently, she was aiming to be Roosevelt's Gossip Girl. Minus the fashion sense.

"Do you think he quit because of Margot?" she said, weirdly

referring to me in the third person though I was sitting right there. "Did he know she was going to be here?"

"Sorry, Harriet. But I am not the reason he quit," I said.

"Oh. Okay. So you must *know* the reason. Interesting," Harriet said, nodding her head for way too long before adding, "I was just thinking, because, you know, you and Avery were together but then you broke up at prom. When you had a breakdown or something. And then everyone says you went to his house and, like, hid in his bushes? So I thought maybe it had something to do with that."

I had so many follow-up questions. How did Harriet Boyle know all this? Who was the *everyone* in *Everyone says I went to his house?* And, perhaps most urgently, *Why the fuck am I talking to Harriet?*

"Well, that's an interesting theory. Maybe you should blog about it?"

Harriet nodded. Like *Yeah, maybe I should start a blog.* It was like she thought of me and Avery as people you read about on TMZ or something. I knew people did that with other popular people like Ainsley McKibbon or Nia Reid. But I never thought anyone would care who *I* was dating.

Ms. Gushman divided us into pairs and I, once again finding myself partnerless, tacked on to Melanie and Abby's pair. Which was perfect. Without Harriet there to interrupt us, I could finally get some intel out of Melanie. All I wanted was to make sure she had a plan for her campaign and was taking it seriously. Then I could go on with my life and forget all about P-Boy running for president.

"So," I began as Abby and Melanie did the lion's share of setting up a light box. "I saw your poster. I didn't know you were running for student body president! Melanie, that's so cool!"

She beamed with excitement. "It's wild, I know. But I found out Nia wasn't running and neither was Avery. And I just thought, if none of the really popular people are running, maybe I have a chance?"

At the table behind us, I saw Harriet's ears perk up at the mention of Avery's name. She was hungry for more relationship goss.

"Well, you have my vote," I told Melanie.

"Awesome! Thanks!"

"So what's your game plan?" I asked.

She paused for a second, then looked to Abby for support. "Game plan? I mean . . . I'll do a speech? And, like, posters?"

I took a deep breath. "Yeah, but, like, everyone has to do a speech? I'm talking about your . . . strategy. How are you going to win this? How are you going to get people to vote for you? And what are you doing to remind everyone that P-Boy sucks?"

"Oh," she said. "Um, well, I was just thinking, like, be true to myself? And be nice. And hope I win?"

I took a deeper breath and let it flutter out my lips. This was worse than I'd thought. She seemed to have no plan at all. One sad owl poster was not going to cut it. "Well, do you feel like you have a good chance, then? Do the people you talk to seem excited to vote for you?"

Again Melanie looked to Abby for support. Abby just shrugged.

"Sorry—" I said, though I wasn't. "I just— I really, really don't want P-Boy to win."

"Neither do we!" Abby said emphatically.

I turned to her. "Abby, you and Melanie are friends; do you—"

"*Best* friends," Abby corrected.

"Best friends," Melanie concurred.

"Right." I politely held back an eye roll. "You're best friends. So you'll be honest. Do you think Melanie has this in the bag? What's your sense of how she's, like, polling?" I asked.

"Polling!" Melanie snorted. "Ha, you sound like CNN!"

Abby hesitated. "I mean . . . it's P-Boy. Do you really think people are going to take him seriously?" She tightened some kind of clamp on what I'd heard Melanie call a "C-stand."

I sighed. "I don't know. Probably not. But this is P-Boy. You may want to run a nice campaign, but I can't imagine he will."

Melanie stared at me, doe-eyed. I could tell she lacked my cynicism. "You really think he'd, like, attack me? Or . . . what are you saying?" she asked.

"I don't trust him. And . . ." I forced her to meet my eyes. "I just want you to be in the best position to win."

Melanie looked concerned. Like I was finally getting through to her. But then a huge smile came across her face as she said, "Well, if you're so worried, why don't you help us? Join the campaign!"

I put a hand on the light box to support it. "Oh, I didn't, uh . . ."

"You must have, like, a million good ideas," Abby said.

I thought about it. Did I? "Uh . . . How about a poster that just says 'P-Boy is a sex offender'?"

Abby laughed. "Oh my god! Yes!"

"No!" Melanie said, immediately killing the brainstorming sesh. "I know P-Boy is the worst. He's *bad*. But I'm running this race for myself. I'm not looking to 'take him down' or anything."

"Okay . . ." I said, refraining from my forty-five follow-up questions like *Why the hell not?* And *What the hell is the difference between beating him and "taking him down"?* And *WHY THE HELL NOT?*

"It's just—I don't want to run a dirty campaign. Or a negative one. Like, at all. Okay? It's a long story, but I need to be proud of myself at the end of this. Win or lose." She allowed her sharp little eyes to peek out from her hair, and I immediately sensed how serious she was.

I thought for a minute. Our reasons for wanting to work on this campaign seemed very different. But I decided that my being involved in Melanie's campaign was far better than my not being involved. Even with Melanie's "I want to be proud of this" rule, I could still help her. I mean, at the very least, I could replace those damn owl posters.

So I looked right into her hopeful eyes and said, "Okay. I'm in. I'll help. And I promise the whole thing will be on the up-and-up. Even if we lose." And I meant it. If that was the campaign she wanted to run, then that's the campaign we'd run.

And then that intense little bird[16] reached out and shook my hand. And just like that, I was working on her campaign.

"Awesome. Wow. Okay. Psyched to have you on board, Margot

---

16 YES! BIRD! That's what she reminds me of. A crane I saw once.

Mertz! You'll be like my campaign manager or something! Go, team!" She giggled. "I've never been part of a team before! I have a slightly shorter left leg, which always made soccer difficult. You guys wanna make posters this weekend?"

"Uh . . . I'm not sure. I have to check," Abby answered.

"Check! Because you do not want to miss this! POSTER PARTY!" With the light stand fully assembled, Melanie snapped a photo of us. The flash made us blink. Then she flipped around the camera's screen to show us the photo. "Check it out! My team!"

She threw her arms around us in a way-too-tight hug for way too long. Oof. Far too intimate for where we were. Not ideal. But hopefully we'd work out the kinks once we got to know each other.

CHAPTER 4

TOO MANY EGGS

"A little splash of white vinegar makes the whites stay together," my dad was saying, bent over a pot of boiling water.

"I don't even *like* poached eggs," I responded. "They're too slimy."

My dad shook his head. "That's not the point! You can't get all the way to Stanford without knowing how to poach an egg!"

It was seven a.m. on a Wednesday, and I'd be leaving for school in twenty minutes. It was not an ideal time for a cooking lesson. But my dad was really going for it. He gently lifted the eggs out of the pot.

"Tomorrow we'll do over-easy. Then you'll have *options*!"

"So then every day I have to wake up and figure out what kind of egg I want? Sounds stressful. I'd rather just have cereal," I told him.

He set down a plate in front of me. Two poached eggs, three

strips of bacon, buttered toast, and a strawberry cut into what I think was meant to be a flower.

"Life is nothing but tough choices. Get used to it, bug."

The food was pretty good. But I wasn't going to tell him that. "You know Stanford has dining halls, right?"

"Yeah, yeah."

Both my parents have been a little weird lately. I guess they've started to realize that I'll be leaving for college next year. I'm not sure why it's hitting them so hard now, when they had eighteen years to prepare for it. *I'm* the one who should be going through separation anxiety. *I'm* the one who's leaving!

My dad was coping by hustling to teach me everything he thinks adults should know. Today it was eggs. Last weekend it was how to read a tire gauge. The week before that, he insisted on making me fill out a W-4. It was annoying, but sweet. And what he considered "need to know" was very random. He made me call the library *on the phone* to ask them their operating hours. Why?

My mom, on the other hand, was taking a different tack. Her fun new thing was that she was being weirdly overbearing.

"Margot," she called as she flew into the kitchen, "I thought you were going to send me your application essay."

"I'm still tweaking," I told her, and bit into my toast. (I was on draft thirty-seven, and still not done.)

My mom huffed as she refilled her coffee. "How many times do I have to remind you? The deadline is November first."

"And it's September. Jesus." I didn't appreciate the lecture.

"Jesus yourself, Margot. You need to have someone read it before you turn it in! No one's immune from spelling errors. Not even you," she said while taking a sip of coffee. "Now hurry up. You're gonna be late for school."

Never before had my mom asked to check my homework or see an assignment for class. As far back as kindergarten![17] My parents never hovered. They just let me do my thing, and it always worked out fine. But this year was different. My mom was all over me: *Have you been working on that essay? Did you do your computer science homework?* She even suggested timing me on my mile run to prepare me for gym class. Gym class is not a thing you study for!

"Mom, I understand that you're feeling anxious because I'm leaving soon. And that means you and Dad will need to . . . get a life. But don't you think all this micromanaging stuff is unnecessary?" I asked as I took one last bite of egg.

"Margot, I realize therapy isn't covered on our insurance," my mom said. "But I'd still rather you didn't psychoanalyze me."

She broke the yolk of her egg and released a gooey yellow pool.

"I don't know." My dad smirked. "Free therapy sounds like a bargain. That other guy wanted a hundred and fifty bucks an hour."

I was always a little harder on my mom than I was on my dad. But it wasn't like we fought all the time. It was just that, since the beginning of this year, both my parents had been a little extra. And it was getting harder to stay patient with them.

· · ·

---

17 And why should she have? I sure as hell knew when show-and-tell was.

ON THE WAY TO SCHOOL, I GOT AN EMAIL FROM PRIYA. AND IT was a *personal* email, not one of the automatically generated campaign ones. She wanted to know if I could come to HQ a little early. Apparently the "advance team" was having some sort of crisis, and she asked if she could loan me to them while she worked on Shep's new campaign ads. I said sure, even though it meant I'd have to skip out of school a mite early. I didn't think that would be too hard. Mr. Cooke usually spent the entirety of AP Comp Gov getting the class to help him update his Instagram. He wanted it to look more "fun" and "casual." Mr. Cooke had recently gotten divorced and was dating again so . . . we all did our best. (Though I don't know how much a Clarendon filter could really accomplish when all the pics were selfies taken in his backyard.)

When I got to HQ, there was a crowd of people milling around in the vestibule. I wasn't sure I could even get in. I saw Nick, the surly guy who I mistook for Melvin, smoking outside.[18]

"Look smart," he said to me as I approached. "Shep's here. And Marion."

That explained the crowd. I peeped in and saw volunteers standing around as Shep gave a little pep talk. Dammit. I really didn't want to see him. Or Marion. They were so polished and intimidating. And I was so . . . me. What if they judged me for not washing my hoodie in the last three days?[19] Or what if they judged me for cruelly pretending to date their son? (Which seemed more likely.) I decided not to go in.

"Thanks for the heads-up. Nick, right?"

---

18 Smoking? Come on. Gross.

19 Okay, fine. Weeks. I never wash my hoodies. It's bad.

"Yeah." He squinted. "Do I know you?"

Ugh. I was only trying to be polite. And now I was in the awkward position of reminding this smoking beard that he had met me before.

"Margot. You helped me with the Wi-Fi?" I looked at him blankly.

"Right. Margot. Yeah, cool," he said, blowing a plume of smoke away from me.

"Do you know if Priya's here? She wanted me to do some work for the advance team," I asked, though I wasn't sure what an "advance team" was.

Nick looked up, squinting. "They're putting interns on the advance team now? I didn't think we were that desperate," he mused. *Rude.*

"First of all, I'm not an intern. I'm a communications *fellow.* And secondly, I happen to be very good at . . ." [Thinks what an advance team might do.] ". . . logistics," I told him.

"Oh. Okay. Well, congrats on having a special skill," he said in between drags. "So where'd you get logistics experience? You work at Wellmans or something?"

The way he talked, it was honestly hard to tell if he was just a sardonic person or if he was negging me for no reason. Either way, it wasn't my favorite!

"No. I actually ran my own internet cleanup business for two years," I said coldly, hoping it would end the conversation.

"Internet cleanup?" He sounded intrigued.

"Yeah. I erase people's bad tweets and pictures and stuff."

"Got it. Huh. That's interesting," he said, tapping the ash on his cigarette before continuing. "Well, if you need any work, I know many people who could use your services. Both of my suitemates, a couple of uncles . . ."

"Unfortunately, I'm kinda taking a break from all that. Sorry." I cut him off, then peeked in the door again. Shep was still going strong. Dipping into the familiar hand gestures I'd seen him use in his speeches. "Well, it's been great inhaling your secondhand smoke, but I'd better get in there."

"See ya round," Nick said.

"Sure," I said. He gave me a little nod as I walked past and I felt a shiver. *Really? Him?* I wanted to say to my hormones. *He's a dick who smokes. What could be appealing about that?* Sadly, my lonely girl libido didn't really care what looked good on paper. And it didn't care that a guy was nice or showered or was even legitimately hot. Hormones do what they want. Sometimes all it takes is a well-timed nod or a smile. Plus, since Avery put me (along with the rest of the world) in his friend zone, these random feelings for strangers seemed to pop up more and more. Annoying.

I entered HQ surreptitiously and tried to blend in. Shep and Marion had both been nothing but nice to me the few times I'd met them. But I still didn't feel like having an awkward chat with my ex's parents.

"The only way we win this thing is if *everybody* turns out. And *everybody* takes ownership," Shep said to the group. "This race isn't about me. It's about— Who is it about, Joni?"

He turned to an elderly, white volunteer, "Joni," who perked up when she heard him use her name. (Shep was apparently very good with names.) "It's about us!" Joni said, taking the prompt.

The crowd let out a big whoop.

Shep turned to a middle-aged Hispanic volunteer who he also remembered. "Oscar?"

The man shouted, "IT'S ABOUT US!"

Another big whoop.

Shep clapped his hands. "Now let's go out there and cold-call strangers till our ears bleed!"

The group laughed, then clapped. Shep and Marion then made their way through the cluster of volunteers, each taking a different clump—shaking hands and thanking them. Offering everyone a flash of their personal charisma. Marion especially could make every interaction feel like you were with your best friend. And she was funny, eliciting genuine laughs out of everyone she talked to. They were such a power couple.

While they were locked in their receiving lines, I started to creep along the back wall toward Priya's office, hoping to slip by unnoticed. Especially now that I'd realized my never-washed hoodie had a sizable hummus stain on it. But the next thing I heard was, "Margot Mertz! My guardian angel of endorsements!" Shep had spotted me. Shoot. I slowly turned around to greet them.

"Heeeeyyyy" was all I said.

Shep marched over to me, shaking my hand with both of his hands for a perfectly acceptable three seconds.[20] Marion appeared next to him, all warm smiles.

"I owe you big-time. Danny Wellman? How on earth did you get him with four hours' notice?" Shep asked.

---

20 Handshakes three seconds or shorter are appropriate contact between strangers. Every other type of contact is not.

Then Marion jumped in. "Do you know how many times I've tried to get Danny's endorsement over the years? For four different candidates! But five minutes on the phone with you, and he's shilling for this no-name?" She playfully mussed Shep's hair. "Honestly, I'm a little jealous!" Marion was so cool.

She looked perfect as always, wearing a cream silk blouse and loads of tiny gold jewelry. Her full, bouncy hair was in natural coils, framing her flawless light brown skin. She made everyone else around her (including me, I'm sure) look like a toad.

Everyone except Shep. Shep was the kind of man often depicted in Roman statuary. He was tall, white, and rugged-looking. He would've looked at home holding a bow or wrestling a wild animal or carrying the world on his back. He was wearing a crisp oxford with the sleeves rolled up and tan khakis. It was the uniform of the suburban white businessman.

Neither one of them looked like they belonged in North Webster. They should have been in Hollywood or Ibiza or something. And somehow, Avery got the best genes from both of them. It really wasn't fair.

"Shep, did you tell Margot about the consent bill?" Marion asked.

"Yeah. I heard!" I interrupted. "That's actually why I'm here."

He smiled. "It's not my most popular issue," he confessed. "But I'm serious about it. I don't know if Avery told you this, but we had a niece who went to Hanover. Mandy. She graduated last year. And they had a similar problem over there." He looked at Marion, unsure of how much to share. It was clear this was personal for them.

"We thought you might be interested," Marion said. She seemed proud of him, of this thing he was doing. "After everything you went through last year. That was— You really did a remarkable thing for all those girls." She squeezed my arm. God, it felt *amazing* to earn her praise. I was this close to inviting her to a girls' weekend when Priya approached us. She was more than a little surprised to see me so chummy with her candidate. But she didn't look mad or anything.

"Priya! Tell me you've already met Margot!" Shep boomed.

"Priya gave me the fellowship," I told him.

"Oh, good," Shep said. "Margot here is a whiz with computers and— Well, she's just a very capable young woman. Make sure you really challenge her!" I definitely could not imagine my own parents saying something like this these days. They'd be too busy saying, "Make sure she gets home by nine!"

Priya nodded. "We'll do our best. I'm sorry, Shep. You need to be at Belasco's by five." She held up the watch on her wrist.

Shep turned to Marion. "Mare, I have two fundraisers followed by two hours of fundraising phone calls, so I won't be home—"

"Until November second," she said, giving him a quick peck on the cheek. Shep whipped on his sport coat (I think? What *is* a sport coat?) and waved goodbye to everyone as he headed out the door. Marion called out to him, "Go get that money!"

Priya then whisked Shep away to his car, while Marion floated around, thanking more volunteers until she herself made a graceful exit. *So this is what charisma is?* I thought to myself. I get the appeal! What must it be like to have cool parents like this?

The hubbub died down, and people returned to their work.

At the entrance, folding tables were set up with bottled waters and snacks for the volunteers. And there were about a million clipboards with various paperwork piled everywhere. Volunteer phonebankers made calls at two large tables in the center of the room, and interns moved about in one of two ways: slow and dazed, like they were walking to a brunch before their reservation was ready, or in a hyperventilating rush, like all our lives hinged on them completing their photocopies. There was no in-between for interns.

There were a couple other fellows like me who seemed engaged in tasks and didn't look up from their computers. So far I hadn't spoken to any of them. Above us in the hierarchy were the random staffers who were actually salaried. (Unlike me, who was just getting a stipend.) And above them were the bosses: Gail, the campaign manager—she was everyone's boss; then Priya, and a couple others who held positions like "grassroots coordinator" and "field director," as well as some finance people I would never meet.

I watched Nick reenter and help himself to a coffee. All the campaign workers were told we could bring our own coffee mugs to cut down on paper cups. We were supposed to write our names on the bottom. But Nick didn't bring his own mug. Instead he drank out of other people's. Today his mug said "Sharon:)" on the bottom. That's how much of a dick he was. What part of me thought he was shiver-able?

Just then, Priya returned to the bullpen with Gail, each holding a big box of cupcakes.

"We made our fundraising goals!" Gail announced. And a bunch of the more-informed-looking people cheered. "We just wanted to say thanks for bearing with us. We're getting a new printer tomorrow!" Another cheer.

Priya waved me into her office. "I told Gail I had to be on cupcake squad. If I let Gail do it herself, she would've gotten all vanilla to save money. *Believe me.* Campaigns are weirdly cheap." She bit into a chocolate cupcake. "This is my second campaign, and I'm still getting used to it."

"Your second campaign? Sorry, but how old are you?" I asked.

"Twenty-one," she said.

I knew she must've been young. But that's pretty damn young!

"I took a semester off to do this." She sighed. "I'm a junior at Cornell."

"I guess I thought you had to be older to be a comms director."

"Yeah, well, I thought you had to be older to take down a revenge porn ring!" she responded, raising an eyebrow at me. "I googled you. You started your own . . . what would you call it? Image consulting and crisis management business?"

Well, I called it "internet filth cleaning," but what Priya said was way better. I made a mental note to put that on a business card if I ever returned to that line of work.

"Pretty impressive." She smiled.

"Thanks," I said.

"Well, Shep said to challenge you, so . . . you ready?"

PRIYA EXPLAINED WHAT SHE WANTED ME TO DO. BASICALLY, I had to find a local business where Shep could make a brief public appearance, glad-handing constituents while a TV crew just happened to be there to record the whole thing for the five o'clock news. Something authentic, locally owned, and not too cutesy. So I compiled a list of local businesses and cold-called them to see who would be willing to have Shep Green stop by. I got a lot of hang-ups, several from fans of Shep's far-right opponent, Susan Lidori. One of her followers even threatened to sue me. (Remind me never to get flowers from Tasteful Elegance florists. It was entirely *dis*tasteful to speak to them. And also inelegant![21]) But by the time I finished, I had a handful of local businesses lined up and willing to host Shep: Nick's, Jackson's Bakery, Gulf of Golf, Elite Organic Cleaners (I had an in!), and a few others.

By the time I finished my "advance team" work it was almost nine. Priya called that last hour from eight to nine "Mommy and Me," since the last volunteers to leave were always moms. They would stop making phone calls around eight thirty like everyone else. But then those dang moms would stay till at least nine, chatting *loudly*, telling stories about how their kids were terrors or how much they admired Meghan Markle.

I closed Priya's office and waved to the moms, who were too engrossed in their gossip to wave back. Then I walked out the door. It was way colder now. And as I pulled my light jacket tight, I said out loud to no one, "Fuck me, it's cold!"

"It's not that cold." I looked up to see Avery leaning up against the building like he was James freaking Dean. "It's not even October. Are you getting soft on me, Mertz?"

---

21 Plus they won't do gay weddings! Fuck them and their baby's breath!

CHAPTER 5

SECRETS DON'T MAKE BOYFRIENDS

Suddenly I didn't feel all that cold. A second ago I wanted nothing more than to go home and curl up in bed. But now . . . let it snow, baby.

"I brought the wrong jacket!" I complained, an involuntary smile creeping across my lips. "And don't talk to me about soft, Mr. Heated Pool. I bet your underwear is heated right now."

"It's not heated. It has copper coils sewn into the fabric to naturally trap body heat," Avery said, smirking.

"God, you're serious, aren't you? Just tell me. Did your underwear cost more than my prom dress?"

"I really hope not. But . . . no comment?" We both laughed. And for a moment, it felt comfortable again. Like how it used to be. Easy. Relaxed. Avery was a paradox. Sometimes being around him made me so nervous, but other times I felt incredibly calm.

"So why are you hanging around headquarters? Besides to flex about your underwear?"

"My dad asked me to come by. He wanted me to do a radio spot with him or something. But they ended up canceling it. And then both my parents left and forgot to give me a ride home. So now I'm getting an Uber." He made an exaggerated shrug and scratched his dark, perfectly-grown-out two days of scruff. And I may not be a beard woman, but I'm definitely a "few days of growth that accentuate a sexy jawline" woman.

"Aw, that sucks. You're like that kid in *Home Alone*."

"I guess so? I never saw that movie," he said, before adding, "The kid doesn't die in the end, does he?"

"No! It's a family movie. Why would you think that?" I laughed.

"I haven't seen it!"

Again, we both smiled. But then Avery's smile dropped. Like he just remembered that his parents forgetting about him wasn't actually all that funny.

"How has it been? Your dad's campaign?" I asked. "It seems like it would be . . . weird maybe? I just remember some of the stuff you said about your parents. And how they stressed you out."

Avery bit his lip before mumbling, "Uh, it's fine. Yeah." Shit. I worried that might have been too much. Bringing up his parents. I knew that he had a tense relationship with them.

"Sorry. I shouldn't have— That's none of my business," I mumbled.

"No. It's . . . not a big deal," Avery responded, not very convincingly. And suddenly it was awkward again.

"Well, okay. But if it was, I'm sorry. I'll let you get to your Uber. Uh . . . bye!" I said, turning quickly toward the bus stop. But I only made it a few feet before he jogged up next to me.

"Wait!" he said. "Can I tell you something? And can you promise to keep it a secret? Like on penalty of death? Well, not death. That's extreme. But, like, on penalty of shaving your head?"

"Uh. Yeah? I promise," I told him. "What's going on?"

"Things are not actually great with my parents. They're getting a divorce," he said quickly. Then exhaled deeply and started walking me toward the bus stop.

"Wait—what do you mean? I just saw them. They seemed so . . ."

"I know. They always seem perfect in public. But trust me. They are very, very good at hiding how much they hate each other," he said. I had known that his parents didn't always get along. And I'd known Avery had some issues with them. But meeting them? And seeing them together? They just seemed like such a . . . unit. A team. And happy. It was a shock, to say the least. And a reminder that people (and parents) are never as perfect as they seem from the outside.

I shook my head. "God, that sounds terrible."

"Oh, you have no idea. Doing a campaign is like being in your own reality show or something. There's so much about it that's fake. And, like, invasive."

"Yeah, that's gotta be weird," I offered.

"Like, a few weeks ago, this guy started coming to my soccer games and taking pictures of me. It turns out he works for Lidori."

"*What?* That's so creepy!"

"Super creepy. And yet another reason I'm in therapy."

As we reached the bus stop, I took a seat on the cold metal bench and Avery continued to talk. It was like the pressure valve on my mom's Instant Pot had been released, and Avery was letting it all go. (Which is good, because those things can explode if you don't follow the directions.) He told me how his parents sat him down in June and told him about the divorce. And how they made him swear to keep it a secret. He told me how they made him go to therapy. And how he didn't want to go at first, but now he really likes it, mainly because he likes his therapist, Gerri. (Doesn't sound like a great name for a therapist, but what do I know? I've never been to therapy.) And how, after talking to Gerri, he decided to quit a bunch of clubs.

"They were getting in the way of me, like, figuring out what I really want to do. I mean, I'm co-president of the pottery club and I kind of hate ceramics! So why am I doing that?" he said triumphantly, like just the act of admitting that was freeing him from an invisible burden. He let his body swing around the bus stop pole.

"Quit! Ceramics are for unhappy women in their thirties," I said back. He smiled. And I smiled. God, I just loved being around him.

"I have to admit, I'm kind of surprised," I told him. "You . . . well, you seem like the last person to need therapy."

"Why do you say that?"

"You're so . . . fun? I don't know." I struggled. "You're, like . . . happy all the time?"

"No one's happy all the time, Margot." He lifted his eyebrows.

I nodded. Of course he was right. "So did you have any other big revelations in therapy?" I asked. "Other than hating ceramics. Which is huge. Obviously."

Avery laughed and kicked the bus stop pole near where my feet were. "Kind of. Not really a revelation. It's more like goals. Stuff I'm trying to do this year that will hopefully make me happier. I wrote down this list—"

"You made a *list*?" I said, trying not to betray my arousal. "I'm big into lists! I have one too. But not to make me happier. Mine is just because I realized I was a garbage person and didn't want to be alone for the rest of my life. So I made a list of rules—long story, but I can't take another cleanup job if it breaks any of them . . ."

He was standing over me, this handsome Adonis and *list maker*! I'll never understand how his arms always seem to be flexing—even when at rest! This time I was certain there was something between us. I could feel it. I shivered. Not a cute "I'm a little cold" shiver, like a huge, death rattle, "Is that woman having a seizure?" kind of shaking. I stood up. It was really happening. My penance was finally paid. Avery had finally forgiven me.

"So that's why you haven't been taking any jobs," he said. I took a beat. *He knew about my self-imposed hiatus? Interesting.*

"Yeah. I made a vow. No new jobs until I can do one without . . . betraying everyone and everything I believe in." I shrugged. Then I realized this line of conversation would only lead back to the fact that I used-then-dumped Avery last spring, so I quickly added, "But anyway. What's on your list?"

"Well . . . putting up more boundaries with my parents.

That's one. Cutting down on clubs and extracurriculars is one. And hopefully that helps me do the third thing, which is figuring out what I really care about."

"Interesting. Any leads?" I asked.

"Well, when I quit every club, the only ones I really missed were Trees for Frees, soccer, and weirdly . . . Film Club. So I rejoined them." Avery shrugged.

"Great, so maybe you'll major in environmental . . . sports . . . movie-starring?" I said, giving him a playful nudge.

He smiled back before saying, "Not movie star. More . . . documentaries? I've been getting into them. And I could kinda see myself doing them. Making them. Maybe."

"I could see that. I mean, I could see you doing anything, so . . ." I told his dimple, which was the only thing I could look at. God, I just wanted to rub my face all over that dimple.

"Oh, and then I have one last goal-thing. Which is basically . . . no more relationships," he said, taking a brief pause to look away from me.

It was so weird how he punched me in the stomach without actually punching me in the stomach. The rush I was feeling from talking to him evaporated. And I realized his list, which I thought was healthy and relatable, was perhaps actually the worst fucking thing I'd ever heard of.

"Oh. Huh," I said between clenched teeth. "And that's because?"

"I just realized . . . I have *no idea* what it would be like to *not* be dating someone. I mean, I've had a girlfriend nonstop since I was in seventh grade. I think I might be terrified of being alone?

Gerri thought it could be 'illuminating,' so I'm trying it out. I'm gonna go all senior year without dating anyone."

But I'm anyone!

So that's why he turned down Christine Shaw and Jenji Hopp. Not because he was wounded. Or pining after me. Because his (I'm sure unlicensed!) therapist told him to.

Thankfully, the bus came. So instead of throwing up or crying, I quickly said goodbye and fled to the safety of the B10. I felt woozy. And so disappointed in my hormone-addled brain for getting my hopes up again when every sign had been telling me Avery wasn't interested in me.

But as the bus pulled away, I saw Avery waving to me. And his goofy, appreciative smile made me realize I was being a shithead. Avery felt comfortable telling me all his personal stuff: His parents. His therapy. His list. He saw me as a friend. And even though I wanted more, couldn't I just be that? I put a hold on all my pathetic lovey-dovey feelings and decided to just be there for him. I mean, it wasn't Avery's fault he didn't want to kiss me.

I sent him a text.

> **MARGOT:** You know you can always call me? I'm happy to listen. And you know I can keep a secret.

Avery texted back right away.

> **AVERY:** I know. Thanks. You're a good friend, Mertz.

TBH, seeing "friend" still made me feel a little nauseous. But I wasn't going to give up that easily. Avery needed a friend. And I was trying to be a better one of those.

CHAPTER 6

WORKING THE POLL

I woke up the next morning determined to stop pining over Avery. So I decided to go all in on Melanie's campaign. She and Abby wanted to sit with me at lunch so we could plan our "campaign strategy." Which I assumed to them meant deciding which owls to put on the few remaining posters we were allowed to make.

School elections are pretty rinky-dink affairs. There are only a few things the school allows you to do:

1. Make and hang ten posters (and only ten! I guess so there's not a poster arms race. Unlike his lax policy on revenge porn sites, Principal Palmer is very passionate about this.)

2. Each candidate must make a ninety-second campaign ad, which will play during the morning announcements.

3. The morning of the election, each candidate makes a speech to the school.

And that's it.

Most candidates put in a minimal amount of effort, knowing full well that the office of "president" or "vice president" or "DISAPP" doesn't really mean anything. Or *do* anything, as far as I can tell. And unlike an actual campaign, it doesn't really matter what your platform is, it's all just a popularity contest.[22]

I usually take my lunch in Powell's office or in the trash hall. To avoid the ketchup stank and clique-baiting on display in the cafeteria. But today I found a table in the back of the caf and dutifully waited for Melanie and Abby. I was trying to decide if it was rude to start eating my sandwich when Abby texted me.

> **ABBY:** I'm so sorry! We had swimming and they let us out late! We're drying our hair now.

> **ABBY:** This is Abby by the way.

It was hard to be mad at someone who hadn't figured out how to get out of swimming in gym class. I was tempted to let her borrow my prescription pad.

> **MARGOT:** It's all good.

I tucked in to my egg salad sandwich (another type of eggs my dad had insisted I learn to make) and opened up my Latin workbook. No reason I couldn't get a jump on tomorrow's homework. Unfortunately, two loud freshpeople took a seat at the table next to me and made it hard to focus.

Chloe Mueller and Sara Deitz were gossipy white girls with

---

22 Which, now that I think about it, is exactly like an actual campaign.

very dramatic eyebrows and a gift for projecting their loud, raspy voices. They shrieked and laughed and played YouTube videos at full volume. They were the kind of people who made me prefer eating my lunch in the trash hall. I stared at my Latin homework.

"I don't know. Maybe Peter?" I heard Chloe say as she took a bite of pizza.

"Really? I feel like he's crazy," said Sara. "But I guess he's cute." Sara was doing something to her yogurt, but definitely not eating it.

"Yeah. I don't know. I haven't decided who I'm voting for yet. I mean, Melanie's nice," Chloe went on.

Wait. *Melanie?*

"But what about all the owls?" Sara raised her very intense brows.

"Yeah . . . I don't know."

Were they discussing who they wanted to vote for? Forgive me for not putting this together sooner, but my brain simply could not fathom someone—a woman! Nonetheless—voting for that shitbird P-Boy. Also, were people really calling him *Peter*? I had to butt in.

"Did I hear you say you're—" *Stay calm, Margot. Don't lash out at these girls. Get all the information first before you throttle them.* "You're thinking about voting for P-Boy? For student body president?"

"Oh, well, I haven't decided," Chloe said. "I was just thinking about it. They still have to do speeches and everything."

"Yeah, and campaign ads!" Sara joined in. "I'm excited for those!"

As freshpersons, Sara and Chloe may not have heard everything that went down with RB. But still, they should've known better.

"Peter Bukowski created Roosevelt Bitches," I said bluntly. "And you're going to vote for him?"

"Oh. Right," Chloe said. "But is that even true? 'Cause he seems pretty sweet. And his Toks are *so* funny."

"I like that one where he's looking at the plant and then the plant is his head!" Sara said, laughing. "Have you seen it? I'll show you." She started tapping at her phone.

I hit the table with my palm. It was loud and more than a little rude. But I would argue that it was *much, much kinder* than the alternative: yelling obscenities at both of them until they cried. Finally I spoke. "Being funny on TikTok—or cute or tall or . . . whatever—does not erase your shitty past. P-Boy caused a lot of pain. He's mean. And he's a goddamned predator." They both nodded, then went back to poking at their lunches, which was fine by me.

I stared out the window, willing myself not to pick up the lunch menu sign and impale someone with it. How was this possible? Why didn't Chloe and Sara hate P-Boy? And were there other girls like them who didn't know about RB? Or didn't care? Was this an anomaly, or were they part of a disturbing trend? A wave of silent P-Boy support that I couldn't see or hear?

I looked around the caf and had a sobering realization about the student body. I didn't *get* these people. Not really. Sure, last year I'd made a list of every student along with a few of their most notable characteristics. But in truth, I had no fucking idea what any of them were thinking. And that was a problem.

I shot Melanie and Abby a text telling them I didn't feel well, then went home early so that I could devise a poll to find out what the plebes at my school were thinking. The Green campaign was commissioning polls all the time—testing messages for future campaign ads—and I wanted to do something similar, but adjusted for high school. I planned to pass out my poll to homeroom teachers, under the guise of my bogus club, the Roosevelt Honors Friendship Society.[23] I'd done something similar with a survey last year. And I guess because teachers' coffee doesn't kick in until after homeroom, no one caught me. My poll:

NAME:
GRADE:

WHO ARE YOU VOTING FOR?
   STUDENT BODY PRESIDENT:
   STUDENT BODY VICE PRESIDENT:
   TREASURER:
   SECRETARY:
   DISAPP:

IS A HOT DOG A SANDWICH?
PIZZA OR TACO:

I needed it to be short, so that everyone would just fill it out

---

23 To my surprise and delight, the Roosevelt Honors Friendship Society actually appeared in last year's school yearbook. I don't know why.

quickly. If it were too dense or long, inevitably someone would ask, "Wait, why are we doing this?" and then my jig was up. But even a simple poll like this would give me a ton of data. Once I got all the sheets back, I could break down everyone's potential vote by grade and gender, and get a sense of how the race was going.

I got to school early on Friday and filed copies of my questionnaire into some of the homeroom teacher's mailboxes. I chose a cross-section of homerooms, twenty-six in total. As I was leaving, one of the office administrators asked, "You're not soliciting for that yogurt place, are you?" Last year there was some hoopla over a local yogurt place, Yo-Yo-Yogurts. They put flyers in every teacher's mailbox offering free scoops if they passed them out to their classes. Apparently this was deemed by the PTA as inappropriate.[24]

I didn't really have a good excuse for what I was doing, so I simply said, "I wish!" before leaving. Wagering that the office administrator was too tired to check on what I was up to.

The school day went by, and in between periods I checked on my survey, collecting stacks of half sheets and plugging them into an Excel file. During gym fifth period, I got an email from Gail asking for additional volunteers for this town hall Shep was doing on Saturday. I normally work at the laundromat on Saturdays, but I figured it was worth asking my dad for the day off. I was eager to prove that I was the campaign's best fellow. (And if, in the process, I became best friends with Priya, then what's wrong with that?) But before I could respond, I was called

---

24 While deemed by me to be delicious!

to play dodgeball. I allowed myself to be pelted with balls, then sat back down to do more emailing. (My team hated me, and I hate dodgeball, so it all kind of worked out.) I forwarded my dad the email about the town hall. And I RSVP'd to Gail.

Surveys were trickling in, but then I got a big dump right at the end of eighth period. With the exception of Ms. Cahill (formerly known as Mrs. Blye), Ms. Nader, and Mr. Ty, all the homerooms returned their questionnaires. I went to the library, plugged in the last batch of responses, and tabulated the results. Which were . . . disconcerting.

33%—Melanie Davis
39%—Peter Bukowski
6%—Neither
4%—Left blank
18%—Swear words/drawings of penises/etc.

I checked the numbers, then rechecked them to make sure I hadn't screwed up, but the math was sound. Melanie was losing. By six points. If the election were held today, she wouldn't crush P-Boy. She wouldn't even squeak out a close win. She would lose. The student body saw a choice between a smart, hardworking woman (admittedly with a weird thing for night birds) and a doofy white guy who made a revenge porn site. And they chose doof.

My throat tightened. I had been hoping that Chloe and Sara were a fluke, that the poll results would allow me to stop stressing, and that Melanie's victory was a foregone conclusion. But now I was sweating. I had to find a way to shake up this race and get Melanie's numbers up. I couldn't just let her run this lazy, owl-heavy campaign. Especially when the consequences ended with the phrase "President Peter Bukowski."

"This has gotta be you, right?" I heard a voice say. I instinctively slammed my laptop shut to see Avery. How could someone so tall be so stealthy? He leaned against the A-M biographies directly in front of where I was sitting. In his hand was my half-sheet survey. Filled out in neat lettering.

Thankfully, I was too disturbed by the poll results to be turned on by Avery's sudden appearance. He had materialized in front of me like a ghost. Though not the horror movie kind, the sexy kind that helps you make pottery. Okay, fine, I was turned on.

"What makes you say that?" I asked innocently.

"Roosevelt doesn't have a Friendship Society. I found that out when I tried to join it last year." He smiled. "I asked Jackie in the office about it. And she told me Margot Mertz was the only student she'd seen in there that day. Which made sense to me because you're the only person I could imagine faking something like this."

He was smiling. But there was a bit of a barb to it. I had also faked our "relationship" for the better part of a month.

"All you need is a printer, time, and no social life. Feels like it could be anybody," I replied.

He dropped the survey on my table, then readjusted his backpack in a way that said he would *not* be sitting down. Rude. "So is this for a cleanup job or something? I thought you made, like, a vow not to do that. Or did you finally find a client who won't make you break any of your weird rules?"

"No. This is not for a cleanup job. I'm just helping Melanie with her campaign. And I wanted to do an informal poll to see where things stood."

He laughed, picking up *Genghis Khan Lives* and casually leafing through its pages. "Of course. Only Margot Mertz would conduct a poll for a high school election."

"It's not that unusual."

"It's extremely unusual, Margot. You know what I did today? I went to class."

"Well, you are very boring," I said, watching as he replaced the book *out of order*. I know he's great, but he's still a boy.

Avery smirked and looked over the poll one more time before giving it back to me. "Well. All joking aside, I think it's cool you're helping Mel. She's a good friend." I didn't realize he was, like, *friends* with Melanie. He occasionally posted pictures with her. And they were both in Trees for Frees and jazz band. But friends? I guess I should've figured that out. He's Avery. He's friends with everyone.

I expected him to leave, but he didn't. He continued to browse biographies, biting his lip. Fidgeting until he finally said, "Look, about the other night. And . . . everything I said. I, uh . . ." He paused for what felt like a long time, picking at his nail.

"Yeah?" I said. Did he have more to confess? I couldn't imagine anything bigger than *My parents are getting a secret divorce.*

"I don't know. I guess just . . . thanks for listening. I thought I had a lot of friends, but I actually don't have that many people I can trust with stuff like that. So thanks. You're a good friend."

The word "friend" stung. But not as much as it had the other night. Maybe after hearing it a few hundred more times, it'd feel less like my heart was getting ripped out and more just like a bunch of tiny bees stinging me over and over.[25]

"Yeah. Of course. I mean, you're the *best* friend," I replied. Yikes. What was I even saying here? I meant that he was *the best* at being friends, not that he was *my* best friend. I tried to salvage my dignity by giving him a "we're just pals" punch on the arm. If I was truly going to hide my stronger feelings and be his friend, I had to get used to the body language.

"Whatever you say, Mertz." Avery laughed and walked out of the library.

RIGHT AFTER THE BELL RANG, I GOT A PHONE CALL FROM PRIYA. I had never actually received a call from her before. I had her number in my phone because there was a group chat for all the fellows. But her calling, I assumed, must be urgent.

"Hello?" I said as I walked quickly out of the school building.

"Hey, Margot. Sorry to call you. I'm sure you're at school. Or just getting out. I just had a quick question to ask you about, uh . . . emails. If that's okay?" There was a weird nervousness in her voice, which I wasn't used to.

"Yeah. Sure. I mean, I'm really not an expert, but . . . yeah," I said, moving away from a cluster of students by the front entrance, just in case I'd need a little more privacy.

"So . . . if I got an email. And, you know, it was anonymous. Is

---

25 Though I am allergic to bees, so maybe that metaphor doesn't work.

there a way—or, how would I find out who sent it? Like, the person's real name?" Priya asked.

"Oh. Well, you could check the SMTP? If it was relayed, you could at least track that and maybe that would lead you to some identifiable information? But if it was sent from a computer with good privacy settings, and didn't use a relay? Then no. There's no way to trace it."

"Okay," Priya said. I could hear a tapping on her end of the line. Like she was nervously clicking a pen or something. "And what if there was a..." She trailed off. I waited a few seconds, but she seemed to have lost her train of thought.

"If there was a what?" I asked.

"I have to go actually. Sorry. This was super helpful! Thanks, Margot! See you at the town hall!"

She abruptly ended the call.

I had no idea what that was about, but I wished the campaign would spring for an IT person. (They could probably get Sammi for cheap! He was now attending North Webster Community College, and I was sure he was desperate for textbook money.) Priya was way too busy to be worrying about that kind of stuff.

I put my phone in my pocket and started to walk home. I had never heard her so ... distracted? Guarded? Maybe campaigns will do that to a person. I was certainly stressed about Melanie. How would she react when I told her she was losing? And more importantly, would she be willing to do what it took to win?

CHAPTER 7

MEDIOCRITY TOUR

I was planning to go to Shep's town hall thing the following day, but I was so tired when I got home I was considering bailing. Then Priya, as if reading my mind, sent an email to all the staffers. The subject was "Motivation." Inside was a link to a YouTube video featuring my least favorite politician, Susan Lidori.

Lidori was at a rally, taking questions from the crowd, when some North Webster yokel asked her about the "Roosevelt Bitches thing" and how Shep Green wanted to make it "illegal to have nudes" (not accurate, but whatever). In response, Lidori *went off* about how this violated the First Amendment, about how she has two sons and she's terrified they'll be arrested for "being normal teenage boys," about how this was all a symptom of cancel culture, and if it were up to her, § 245.01 wouldn't exist at all. *That* was all the motivation I needed.

I brushed my teeth, put on my PJs, and was staring at my

closet trying to decide what to wear to the town hall when my mom poked her head in.

"Honey," she began. (Anytime she begins something with "honey," I know it's going to end with her asking me to do something I don't want to do.) "Dad told me that you have this town hall tomorrow, but I signed us up for some college tours in the morning."

"*What?*" I whipped my head around. "The whole reason I took the day off was to work at the town hall!"

"I know, I know!" she said, waltzing right into my room and sitting on my bed. "But that's not till the afternoon! The tours are in the morning!"

"Oh good. I was worried I might have to *sleep in on a Saturday* for the first time in four months," I shot back. I was mad. Though part of it might have been residual from seeing that Lidori clip.

"Your dad and I are going to a movie at 4:05. The tours will definitely be done before then!"

I rolled my eyes. I could tell I wasn't getting out of this.

My mom gestured to my shoes. "Those are nice. I never see you in heels." Then she paused a second before adding, "Is Avery going to be there tomorrow?"

"Mom, I have no idea. But even if he was, it would have no bearing on my choice of shoes." That *may* have been a lie, and I know I'm trying not to lie to my parents. But it was also a lie to *myself*. Had I thought I might run into him? Had that factored into my wardrobe choices? Possibly. But anyway, my mom should mind her own business. I was trying to get over Avery. And it didn't help that my parents kept constantly mentioning him.

"Well, look. I'm sorry I didn't talk to you first. But I wanted you to see some of the colleges around here before you do your applications. So we're seeing NWCC at eight a.m. and University of Monroe at eleven. That'll give you plenty of time to get to the town hall."

Priya's email blast had asked volunteers and staff to arrive by three. Naturally I wanted to arrive by one to show Priya and Gail how dedicated I was (and how much better I was compared to all the other fellows). Showing up on time, when they asked, felt very pedestrian.

"Okay. But, Mom. I am going to Stanford," I said definitively.

"I know, honey. I just want you to see what all your options are—"

"You think Stanford isn't going to accept me?"

"No! Of course they will!" she insisted.

We went back and forth like this for a while, my mom assuring me that she *did* think Stanford would accept me, but why not have a backup anyway? And me saying over and over, backups are for people who don't get into Stanford. We eventually settled on a compromise, where I'd skip NWCC, a community college, and only go on the second tour to U of M. And that I'd complain the entire time. (She was not aware of that last part of the deal.)

To be clear, I have nothing against community colleges. In fact, it would be prudent for me to go to a school like NWCC for two years then transfer to Stanford and save a lot of money. But Sammi goes to NWCC. And I was mildly terrified that I might bump into him.

After Sammi came forward to help with the Roosevelt Bitches investigation—revealing his involvement in the site—he was given a light sentence of community service. But he faced other consequences, namely that Rensselaer rescinded his acceptance. Sammi felt about Rensselaer a little like I felt about Stanford. Which is to say, horny. But because of what he did, he had to settle for NWCC. And stay in North Webster. We didn't text very often. But every once in a while, I'd text him something funny that had happened to me, or he would send me a meme or tell me about some system he had finally hacked into.[26] But still, I didn't feel all that confident seeing him in person yet. Things were still weird. And I don't know if that's because I was still angry and/or hurt. Or if I was worried that he was still angry and/or hurt? The road to forgiveness for something like RB is pretty long. And I couldn't tell how far we'd gotten. So a tour of NWCC, which could include an awkward run-in, was not going to happen.

By skipping NWCC, I was actually able to sleep in, PRAISE BE TO GOD. My mom, my dad, and I were on the road by eleven fifteen. While en route, I received a new email from the campaign that said, **SPREAD THE WORD. TODAY'S EVENT STILL HAS TICKETS!** Apparently a programming glitch had sent rejection emails out to anyone who had reserved tickets on Friday. And

---

26 Sammi made it so Hobby Lobby's employees all received paychecks that read: "LOVE is between a PERSON and a PERSON! And sometimes even more PEOPLE, depending on what you're into!"

reading between the lines, it seemed like they were worried no one would show.

"You guys want to come to the town hall this afternoon?" I asked my parents.

"Uh . . ." This question took them off guard, and they did not have a ready excuse. I could see them checking in with each other.

"Maybe . . ." my mom finally said.

"We were going to see a movie," my dad said. "But, maybe?" It was definitely a maybe-no, so I didn't follow up.

We made it to the University of Monroe, paid for parking (Seven dollars! Unheard of!), and entered the campus through the main gate.

"All right, let's put our game faces on, people. I have a town hall to get to after this. So no small talk with the other parents. No asking questions of the tour guide. Let's act like Navy Seals. We're in and out in twenty minutes with no civilian casualties! Yeah?" I put my hand in for a family hand-stack, but my parents just sat there. They didn't respond to the horsewhip sound I made either, commanding them to leave the car.

"Margot, I get that these colleges aren't your first choice. But you don't have to be so— You're being pretty rude."

"I'm sorry we can't all fly to California," my dad added.

That made me feel pretty bad. I knew that we couldn't afford to tour Stanford in person. I hadn't even thought to ask them about it. If I got in, I would be going there sight unseen (except for the many, many times I'd seen it in my dreams). I wondered if my parents had insisted on this local college tour as a substitute for Stanford. So they could give me some kind of pre-college experience they thought I should have. That was pretty nice, actually. And me whining and making a show of hating it was . . . the opposite of nice.

"Maybe we should just go home," my mom suggested as my dad shrugged and turned on the car.

"No. I'm being an asshole," I said, shoving my head into the front seat. "You're right, there's no harm in looking at Monroe."

They looked at each other, silently deciding to give me one more try.

"Okay," my dad said. "But please try not to be such an asshole."

"Tom!" my mom scolded him.

"What? Her words! Not mine!"

The tension lifted a bit as we all got out of the car and made our way to the quad. I forced myself to have a good attitude. (Which I should honestly do more often.) The grounds were well-maintained, and the buildings were old, which made it feel like an institution, in a comforting way. There appeared to be some sort of Frisbee event going on, and tons of students were sitting around the quad just watching some frisbros toss a disc back and forth (and lift up their shirts to reveal their abs for no reason). Some college band was playing emo covers of pop songs from a little band shell.

Our tour guide Ray (short for Rachelle), a petite and preppy Black woman, started the tour with a barrage of stilted facts and awkward jokes that I'm sure were written by the admissions office. She made not one, but three jokes about how college students love free food. (*"What do Oliver Twist, Pavlov's dog, and a college student all have in common?"* [Pause. We all regret life choices.] *"They'll do anything for free food!"*) Yikes, Ray. She stood for a moment, twisting the perky black coils of her hair while no one laughed. And then, sensing our boredom, she went way off script and started massively oversharing about her personal college experience. Her big round eyes glowed with excitement as she told us about how many UTIs she got her freshman year.[27] About how many students die of alcohol poisoning.[28] And then she told us a rambling story about her friend who forgot her student ID but was able to get past campus security by showing her Wellmans Shopper's Club card instead. None of the parents looked charmed by Ray's ad-libs, or the knowledge that a serial killer could get into the dorms if he bought his groceries at Wellmans.[29] I was starting to understand why the admissions office had given her a script.

Three hours later (actually it was forty-five minutes, but it felt like three hours), I sensed Ray was starting to wrap things up. We made our way back to the quad and I snuck a peek at my phone to find three new emails from the campaign, each more desperate than the last: **SUBJECT: TICKETS STILL AVAILABLE**, **SUBJECT: BRING A FRIEND OR TEN!**, and **WE NEED BODIES!**[30]

I skimmed the last email from Priya. It said that, in addition to our email glitch, the venue had misstated their capacity, so while

---

27 Seven! Get that checked out, friend!

28 Any number above zero is TOO MANY!

29 I say he, because they're usually he's. Except that one time it was Charlize Theron.

30 A viscerally frightening phrase no matter what it's in reference to.

they thought it only seated three hundred, it actually seated four hundred and fifty. And since we only had eighty-nine RSVPs, it was going to look cavernous. And press would be there. It was an all-hands-on-deck situation. Everybody needed to show up and bring someone. Apparently there's nothing worse in politics than giving a speech to an empty room. Plus, Susan Lidori, say what you will about her politics,[31] always draws a pretty big (and racist!) crowd. I could just imagine the local news, showing side-by-side events with Shep's looking pathetically small.

I felt bad. I knew Shep needed today to go well. I texted Melanie and Abby, but both had family stuff. I texted the Kelseys, but they were busy with "theater" and "gf." And . . . that about did it as far as friends.

Ray left us on the quad with a parting story about how she found a bug in her shower that she thinks is a new species. (Classic Ray!) The Frisbee tournament thing seemed to be winding down. But the band was still playing, and people were still milling around or sitting in the grass.

"Margot? You want to get something from the dining hall? To try it out?" my mom asked, her arm around my dad like two college sweethearts on a Saturday stroll. The tour may have been a slog for me, but they seemed to be having the time of their lives.

"Um. You go ahead," I told them. "I'm going to take a loop around the quad here."

They shrugged, happy to continue their faux-college date without me.

---

31 They are bad.

I scanned the lawn, wondering what it would be like to actually go here. Could I see myself straight chilling on the grass? Watching some bros throw the 'bee around? I wasn't sure these were "my people." I mean, did these kids have anything in common with the coeds at Stanford? Did Stanford have Frisbee boys and smoking girls and . . . *oh, come on.* My eyes rested on a particular bro who I recognized, standing across the quad. It was Harold Ming.

Harold had graduated from Roosevelt last spring. He'd finished his sentence of minimal community service over the summer (after committing two separate crimes—sexually harassing girls over text and downloading pornographic images of minors). This left him free to continue his life as if nothing ever happened. And I guess he goes to U of M now. Cool.

Harold didn't see me, that smarmy fuck. He was too busy whispering into the ear of a tall blond girl who seemed to think he was damned hilarious. I couldn't hear what they were saying. But he had his arm around her. They appeared to be together. Ugh. I will never understand how it's possible for a shitty, predatory dude like Harold to find a girlfriend. But I guess this is what happens when there are no consequences for your behavior.

Fuck that. *Fuck that.* Fuck Harold Ming and fuck the people who gave him a pass. And fuck everyone who said he was "another teenage boy just having fun." Like my mom's hairdresser. And Susan Lidori. Who could very easily get elected if I didn't do *everything in my power* to help Shep.

I took a deep breath and surveyed the scene. Racking my brain as to how I could get more bodies to the town hall. Then I realized I was at a *college.* What *is* college if not a collection of young, bored bodies just looking for something to do with their lives?

I called Priya, and to my surprise, she picked up.

"Margot. Now's not a great time. Can—"

"I think I can get you bodies. But I'd need transportation. Could you get a bus to U of M in the next half hour?" I asked.

Priya didn't hesitate. "I can get two."

"Great. Send them both to the south lawn main entrance as soon as you can."

I ended the call. And there was a gravitational collapse in the pit of my stomach. What had possessed me to promise this? Now I had to convince a bunch of coeds to board a bus. And without a sketchy music festival to offer them, that would be tough.

I ran over to a group of students seated under a tree.

"Anyone want to go to a political town hall?" I asked.

They looked very confused.

"When?"

"Now?" I said, unconvincingly. I tried to explain the situation. How they would be vital in supporting a really good, progressive candidate for state senate. I may have even used the sentence, "You can be the change you believe in!" They all passed. Crap. I was going to have to do better, or Priya just sent me two buses for nothing. I approached another group of mostly dudes. They looked fratty, which is my least favorite type of male, but I was in no mood to be picky.

"Heeeeeyyy!" One of them spoke first, coming toward me. "I don't know you. I'm Xander." Xander shook my hand in a way that made me feel dirty.

"Hi," I said, keeping my distance. "Any of you want to go to a political town hall?"

"Hell yeah," said Xander, while a few others mumbled interest.

"Great. Buses are going to load from the main parking lot in fifteen minutes—"

"You mean fifteen minutes *from now*?" one of the guys asked incredulously. "Oh, no way. Sorry, dude. We have pretty firm plans we can't break."

"Yeah, we're gonna do shrooms and watch *Golden Girls*," Xander clarified. Wow. Okay. Unexpected. But I do like *Golden Girls*.[32]

Now I was starting to sweat. So far I hadn't convinced a single person to come.

My parents came out of the dining hall eating those ice pops that have fruit in them and told me they were ready to go.

"Just one second," I said, an idea starting to form. I strode up to the band shell. I waited for the band to finish their emo cover of "Dynamite."[33] And then I walked up to the microphone like I owned it.

"Hey! Hi! The Student Activities Board asked me to make a quick announcement. Shuttle buses are now loading for the Green town hall. Anyone who wants to go needs to be at the parking lot by two thirty." The band members smiled at me politely as though my interrupting them with this announcement was the most normal thing in the world. But I could see people

---

32 I'm a Sophia!

33 Which I loved. I love anything BTS. I'm not sorry.

in the crowd starting to look at each other like, *Did we sign up for a Green town hall?*

Come on, you dingbats. You have nothing better to do! The lead singer was about to reclaim the mic, but I knew I hadn't said enough to convince people.

"The shuttles will have you back here by six at the latest," I added. Still nothing. "And again, this is for Shep Green, progressive candidate for state senate."

Still no movement. Shit. That damn singer inched forward, angling to get the mic back. But then I remembered the bad jokes Ray kept making about college students loving the promise of free food. *Food.*

"PIZZA WILL BE SERVED. This event is free."

Bibbidi bobbidi. Those were the magic fucking words. Ray may have been an erratic tour guide, but she sure as shit wasn't lying about the "college kids loving free food" thing. I watched as at least a few dozen students rose, dusted the grass off their asses, and started moving toward the parking lot. I made my way down from the bandstand and back to my parents, along the way passing tour-guide Ray, who grabbed my arm and said, "I am so in! I'm actually really into politics. My ex freshman year, the one who gave me my first UTI, he interned for AOC!" Sure!

My parents were a bit miffed that I had hijacked a normal college tour and turned it into more of my typical chicanery. But I think they were also a little bit impressed.

"Did you do this whole tour with that in mind?" my mom asked. She must've thought I'd puppet-mastered the whole thing.

"No," I assured her. "This was completely random. I just found out this morning that they needed people."

My dad shook his head. "Student Activities Board? I don't know how you— I saw at least thirty kids get up!"

"I hate to break it to you," I told him, "but you guys have to come too."

My parents looked at each other. It was clear this was important to me, so they couldn't say no. No matter how good the reviews were for Yorgos Lanthimos's latest film. I texted Priya to let her know that in addition to the buses I would also need pizza. Lots of it.

TWENTY MINUTES LATER, WE ARRIVED AT THE LYSANDER auditorium. Me, my parents, and fifty-three of my closest college bus friends. Word of pizza really traveled. Shep was set to go in ten minutes, so I helped usher all the U of M-ers toward the volunteers who were registering people to vote and giving them signs. The moment Priya spotted me, she yelled, "You are a fucking badass! How the fuck did you get this many people to show up? Are you, like, the most popular girl in your school or something?"

"No! The opposite. Everyone hates me," I said back cheerfully.

"That's not true, Margot!" my mom objected.

Priya, embarrassed that she said "ass" and "fuck" in front of my parents, and more frazzled than I'd ever seen her, apologized and introduced herself. She then went on and on about how great I was, making my parents blush and say goofy things like "She practically raised us!" Which, you know, isn't true. I never changed their diapers or anything. Priya then offered us front row seats for the speech, which my parents eagerly accepted. They hardly ever got VIP bumps, but whenever they did, they relished it.[34] She then excused herself—and I could see that this thirty-second convo had put her thirty seconds behind on some other thing she was supposed to be doing.

The town hall itself was surprisingly fun. Music blasted through the auditorium, which put everyone in a good mood. I don't know who made the mix, but it got everyone, regardless of age, up. (I secretly love to watch old people dance.) Then when Shep finally took the stage, people went berserk. And I have to say, he's a good speaker. He really listened to people and answered their questions in a way that was both personal and substantive. How someone could know the municipal tax code for a subsection of Buckner County *and* the maiden name of a random volunteer is beyond me.

After Shep took his last question, Avery and his mom came out, mostly to look hot next to Shep. And, as before, you *could not* tell that Shep and Marion were getting divorced. They kissed, squeezed each other's hands, and smiled huge smiles. If this whole campaign thing didn't work out, they should consider careers as actors.

When Shep left the stage, I headed to the volunteer area. I thought I might see Avery, but he and his mom escaped to their car while Shep stayed to do a receiving line with all the attendees. Priya, meanwhile, was as good as her word. She had twenty

---

34 My mom once got bumped to "more leg room" on a JetBlue flight and you would've thought she won the lottery. She still talks about it.

pizzas delivered to the shuttle buses. The college kids seemed happy enough. I saw them wrapping up extra slices to take back to their dorms.

"You know that what you did today should not be possible, right? Getting fifty strangers here with no notice. You're like . . ." Priya searched for the right word, before saying, "Is there anything you can't do?"

I blushed. "Sure. I can't sew. Or cook. Or maintain human relationships!"

"All of those things, highly overrated," Priya said, smirking.

"Hey—did you figure out that email thing?" I asked her.

Priya looked at me like I'd just spoken Latin (and I'm terrible at Latin). But then she had a moment of recognition and shook her head. "Oh yeah. Yeah. Got that all figured out. Haha, I already forgot about it!"

We both laughed. But there was something awkward about it. Like Priya wished she hadn't told me about her email problem in the first place.

We were supposed to be out of the Lysander auditorium by eight, and it was already eight fifteen. So Priya got on the mic and politely asked everyone to leave and grab posters on their way out. All the volunteers grabbed posters, litter, and empty water bottles and made their way to the exits. Even my parents helped. And to my surprise, so did Shep. I saw him carrying garbage bags out of the building while continuing to talk with constituents. The media was long gone. So this wasn't for the cameras. He really just wanted to pitch in. (Or he's a compulsive cleaner. Either way, I like!)

On our way to the car, I got thumbs-ups and waves from

everyone on the team. I smiled and did my best to shrug it off when I heard, "Margot! Wait!"

I saw Shep jogging over to our car. He shook both my parents' hands and introduced himself as "Avery's dad." They were a little starstruck and started gushing over his speech, which fully embarrassed me. Then they went on about how they've "never seen me as happy" as when I've been working on this campaign. And what a "nice boy" Avery was. Woof. They're such goobers.

"Well, I've gotta run. But remember! This one," he said, playfully pointing at me. "We're all going to be working for her someday."

Laugh. Laugh. Parents laugh.

"I'm serious," he went on. "She really saved my butt today. Margot is going places!" He smiled and jogged off again.

"You can't help but like the guy," my dad said as we got in the car. "Hope he wins."

As we drove away, I watched Shep and Priya talking by his car. I figured they'd be celebrating. Or talking about how great I was for saving the day! But instead they looked . . . pained. In the middle of a serious conversation. Like there was already another fire to put out. And I was surprised by how much I wanted to help. To be in the war room, figuring out Shep's next move. But for now, these problems were not my problems. And as we turned out of the parking lot, I tried to let those feelings go. After all, today was a win.

CHAPTER 8

SURVEY SAYS

The next day, Melanie invited Abby and me over to her house to make cookies for the swim team. The cornerstone of her strategy seemed to be giving away as many cookies as possible. Abby couldn't make it. (She gave no reason. Just a *Sorry, I can't* text. Which I honestly respect.) And even though I was a little nervous to hang with *just* Melanie, like, one-on-one, I decided to go. (Which meant I'd be excused from Family Time this week, but who's keeping track?[35]) I was eager to talk strategy with her, especially now that I knew she was *behind*. Something told me cookies weren't going to cut it.

Melanie's house turned out to be a very nice condo in the arts district where she lived with her mom, her grandma, and her younger brother, Milo.

I saw Milo as soon as I entered the vestibule. He was

---

35 My parents are! Meticulously.

bouncing on some kind of giant rubber ball and had Cheetos dust on his fingers.

"Melanie says you're going to help her win president! Are you?"

"I'm gonna try," I said, doing my best to avoid this pulsating orange stain.

"There IS no try!" he said in a Yoda voice. "There is only win! The ends justify the means!" Milo jumped off the ball into a karate stance. It was moments like these that made me happy my parents stopped at one.

"Milo. Leave Margot alone. We have work to do," Melanie said, emerging from her room.

He bounced away. "Fine. I'm going on Mom's computer."

"Sorry about that. He always shows off whenever I bring friends over," she said, plopping on her bed.

"He seems great," I said, inspecting my shirt for orange fingerprints. "And impressively Machiavellian."

"That's why I'm trying to set a good example," Melanie said, throwing a pillow at me. "I want him to know he doesn't have to be a jerk to succeed." She was joking, but I got the sense she took her sisterly role modeling duty seriously. (But, like, if she really wants him to grow up good, why doesn't she tell him to clean the Cheetos dust off his fingers?)

I looked around at her room, which was very Melanie. Chaotic and innocent. Weird and confusing. There was a collage with pics of her and Abby, band medals, homemade crafts. On her bookshelves were a few stuffed owls (of course). And every surface was covered with Funko Pop! bobbleheads. Like, a disturbing amount. They were *watching* me.

I pretended to appreciate them for a bit, then thankfully we moved to the kitchen. Melanie had laid out all the cookie-making ingredients in little prep bowls, which was a little *extra*, but also appreciated, because who wants to waste time measuring? As we mixed the dough, I shared the results of my informal poll. I didn't know how she'd take it. So I girded myself to stay positive. But her reaction . . . was not what I expected.

"This is SO COOL!" she said, grabbing my laptop out of my hands. (And pulling it way too close to the messy dough area!) "A POLL? Oh my god. It's so *official*. I feel like I'm running for actual president or something."

"Okay? I'm glad you like it. But you realize it says we're losing, right?"

"Yes. I know. That's not great. But we have a month! And with actual POLLS, I feel like we have such a huge advantage. Margot Mertz, you are a super genius. I mean, does P-Boy have anything like this?"

"Well, polls require time. And effort. And an understanding of rudimentary math. So . . . no."

Melanie hunched over and took a closer look at my spreadsheet, biting her lip as her eyes darted back and forth.

"And you can break this down by grade?" she asked.

"Yep," I said, opening a new spreadsheet.

"Cooooool!" she said, squeezing my arm. "And gender?"

"Uh-huh," I said, showing her a graph that revealed women preferred Melanie by a forty-point margin. Again she said, "Cooool! Women love me!"

"And the seven students who identified as nonbinary!" I added, pointing to the graph.

"YES! They love me too!" She cheered, then cocked her head. "But the men . . . do not. *Yet!* Amirite?" She leaned in close and squeezed my shoulders before turning back to the mixing bowl.

I liked her enthusiasm, but it was careening toward annoying real fast.

"How many people did you survey again?" Melanie asked, rolling out balls of sticky dough with her hands. I realized that her apron was covered with tiny little owls. (Good lord, Melanie.)

"Like six hundred? I didn't do every class, obviously." Roughly twelve hundred kids go to Roosevelt.

"Six hundred is amazing! Margot, that's, like, such a big sample. You are an inspiration!" She did a little dance while I tried not to slap her. Then she moved her fingers like she was pressing buttons on an imaginary calculator while her little brown bob bobbed back and forth. "So if I'm down six points in a school of twelve hundred students, that's only, what, like . . . seventy votes? Give or take?"

"Yeah. Assuming the remaining votes keep to this pattern. Which, you know, they should."

Melanie stood up straight, a wild, eager look in her eyes. "Seventy votes! That's *so* doable! I mean, look at all the non-voters. Or the people who voted for 'penis'! Margot! We can convince them!"

For some reason, this hadn't occurred to me. I mean, sure, I saw that 24 percent of people didn't respond or wrote in "penis" or "Zendaya" or "President McPresidentFace." But I didn't look at that as a *good* thing. I just thought 24 percent of my respondents were burnouts or reprobates. Yet Melanie saw the same results and saw potential. Open minds waiting to be persuaded. The more I thought about it, the more I agreed.

"But how do we persuade people?" I asked out loud as Melanie placed two sheets into the oven. She was doing most of the work, but I was helping by eating the chocolate chips.

"I have no idea." She shrugged. "Maybe we do another survey?"

She was real thirsty for surveys, this one. "I don't think that would tell us anything that we don't already know," I said politely.

"Well, okay. Then hopefully cookies will do the trick? These are for the swim team and girls' JV soccer. But we could make more for other clubs and stuff?"

"That's good," I told her. *But will it really move the needle?* It seemed like such small potatoes.

We kept brainstorming. But then our productivity started to wane. We took a quesadilla break. Which led to a nachos break. Which led to us just eating shredded cheese out of a bag. During which Melanie's non sequiturs increased. (Out of nowhere: "I want Timothée Chalamet to spit in my mouth." And "Some of my dolls *aren't* virgins.") And I have to admit, I was kind of having fun. I mean, she was such a weirdo. Hers was a *showy* weird, compared to my inner, mostly concealed weirdness. She didn't seem to filter herself. Or care if what she was saying was "cool" or was being "mercilessly judged by me." She just said it. And I didn't hate that.

Melanie came back to the survey idea more than once. And pitched some completely unusable (but very fun) questions like: *If you had to, whose corpse would you rather eat for survival, Melanie's or P-Boy's? Fuck, marry, kill: Melanie, P-Boy, or Principal Palmer? If Melanie were an owl, what kind would she be? (P-Boy obviously would NOT BE AN OWL.)* And finally, my favorite: *P-Boy? Why?! What is wrong with you?!?*

We were giggling so much, Melanie's grandma came in to shush us so she could hear her Lifetime movies. Which of course, only made us laugh-talk louder.

Eventually, Mel splayed herself on her sofa and said, "I give up! I have no idea how to influence a bunch of random students who may not even know who I am."

"Yeah, I'm not an influencer—" I stopped myself short. "Oh my god. We need *influencers!*"

Melanie looked up at me. "Like . . . Emily Ratajkowski?"

"No. I mean, yeah. But, like, at our school. Who is the Emily Ratajkowski of Roosevelt? Who is so popular that they would actually *sway* people by saying they were voting for you?"

We thought for a moment. And then at the same time we said, "Avery."

"Yes!" Melanie jumped up. "If Avery came out in support of me, I feel like that would get so many people. And I know he would do it! Avery's my bud!" *Mine too, unfortunately*, I thought glumly.

"Okay. So let's say we get Avery. Do you think that gets us enough votes? What about Nia?"

"Oh my god, yes. Everyone loves her," Melanie agreed.

Nia Reid is probably the most popular girl in our school. She's tall and pretty, with dark brown skin and long black hair. She was in Support Group (I think she's pretty religious) and on varsity soccer, where she was such a good goalie, colleges were scouting her. Like Avery, she seemed to be friends with everyone and was very nice. But unlike Avery, I didn't know her at all. I had no idea what it would take to get her endorsement.

"Let's bring cookies to her game on Saturday and we can talk to her then!" I suggested.

"YES!" Melanie agreed, before asking, "And . . . who's that new girl?"

At first I wasn't sure who she meant. Then I got it. "Fuck! Ainsley!"

"Yeah! Ainsley McKibbon! She's *so* popular."

I hadn't thought of Ainsley. I guess because she was new? But like Avery and Nia, Ainsley seemed to have a lot of sway. Her influence was clear by the number of hearts and comments on everything she ever posted. And one day she wore a visor to school and three days later I counted fourteen other girls wearing visors. *Fourteen!* And visors are definitely not a thing! At least not in North Webster.

"If we could get all three, that should bring us at least seventy votes," I told her.

It was starting to get late, and Melanie's mom asked me to stay for dinner. But I felt weird saying yes. Dinner with parents is so intimate. So I said my parents were expecting me back and took the bus home. But while I was on the bus, I regretted it.[36] Maybe it wouldn't be bad to do something so friend-y. Melanie was legitimately fun. And wasn't the whole point of post-MCYF

---

36 Along with my choice to eat far more shredded cheese than the surgeon general recommends.

Mertz to have hobbies and actual relationships with humans? I decided that if her mom ever asked me to stay for dinner again, I'd say yes no matter what. Even if they were making pork chops.[37]

When I got home, I felt so great about finding a solution to Melanie's campaign that I wanted to keep that feeling going. So I wrote Priya an email,[38] asking her if I could do more for the campaign. More jobs, more crisis management. Maybe I could be doing opposition research. That seemed like something I would really thrive at. (It's kind of like the opposite of filth cleaning: find the filth and BRING IT TO LIGHT!) But whatever job she gave me, this much I knew. I wanted to be in the inner circle.

I GOT TO THE GREEN campaign office around three thirty the next day. It was pretty quiet. Some volunteers were milling around, getting ready to canvass, and Nick was asleep in an inflatable chair by the snack table. Priya and Shep were wrapping up a meeting in the conference room with a few other people I couldn't see. When the door popped open, Shep and Gail came out first, followed by a pair of be-blazered people they'd been meeting with. Behind them came Priya, speaking animatedly to . . . *Caroline Goldstein*? *My lawyer*? Well, not exactly *my* lawyer, but the lawyer who had helped all the victims of RB last year. Caroline clocked me the second she left the conference room.

---

37 Do you love chewing but hate enjoying your food? Then pork chops are for you!

38 Or, to be clear, I wrote her twenty-five drafts of an email that varied wildly in tone, before finally sending her an anodyne, basic twenty-sixth.

"Margot Mertz!" she said upon seeing me. "Fuck me. How are you?"

I smiled. Leave it to Caroline to work "fuck" into a greeting. "I'm okay."

Priya joined us, a puzzled look on her face. "You know Margot?"

"She brought me the Roosevelt case. Which is the whole reason I'm here!" she said, giving me an aggressive side hug.

"Sorry," I said, trying to catch up, as always, to Caroline. "Uh . . . *why* are you here?"

"Shep and Gail want me to help draft an amendment. It has to do with revenge porn legislation actually—"

"245.01?" I cut her off. "You're helping Shep with that? It's why I'm volunteering here."

She narrowed her eyes. "Of course it is. Margot, you are a fucking treasure. Are you treating her well, Priya?"

"Yeah. Margot surprises me every day," Priya said, studying me.

"Anyway, Priya, I have to say, I'm pleasantly surprised by all this. Usually these politicians are just looking for talking points. They call you in to talk, but they never actually listen. Or do anything. But I got a very different vibe here today. I think your guy's serious."

Priya looked over Caroline's shoulder to see that Shep had left. "Well, between you and me, he's lazy about other issues. He honestly doesn't give a shit about fishing licenses. But on this one, he's serious." They both laughed.

"Well, now all you need to do is win!" Caroline said as she left, before turning back to call out, "And, Margot, you should be interning for *me*. I have all kinds of shit jobs I could use an intern for!"

"I'll keep it in mind if this doesn't work out!" I laughed, waving as Caroline clip-clopped out of HQ.

"So." I turned to Priya. "Did you get my email? About me taking on some more jobs? With more responsibility?"

"Yes," she said thoughtfully. I waited for more, but her eyes just drifted away, distracted.

"Priya! The video unit is waiting for you," a staffer called out.

Priya stared off into space without responding. Maybe the grueling campaign schedule was finally getting to her.

"Priya?" I gently prodded. She snapped out of it.

"Yep! Sorry, Lance. I'm coming," she said, looking at me the entire time. "And yeah. Why don't you, uh, chill for a minute and I'll come find you."

"Great!" I said to her shadow as she hurried away. "Thank you!"

"More jobs, huh?" I heard a sleepy voice say. Nick, it seemed, was up from his nap.

"Nick. What's your deal? Why are you, like, randomly here all the time? Do you really work here? Because if you don't, and you're just hanging around . . . that's kind of creepy," I said as he walked over to the snack table.

"Wow. I didn't realize I came off as creepy. Is it the beard?" he said, scratching his face.

"Yes," I said bluntly. He laughed in that way you do when someone says something a little too honest.

"Okay. Wow. Well, to answer your rude question, no, I don't

technically work here." He grabbed a bag of SunChips and ripped it open. "I quit a few weeks ago and now I'm a spy."

I blinked at him slowly, before saying. "Okay. For Russia, or . . . ?"

"I volunteer for the Lidori campaign two days a week. But only so I can spy on them and leak shit to Priya. Or to the press," he said, then leaned back, evidently proud of himself. "Did you see that story the *Gazette* ran on Lidori? About how instead of putting her dog to sleep at a vet, she shot it?"

"This . . . can't be real," I said, shaking my head.

"It is. And her neighbor's kids saw. It was a whole thing. I was the 'unnamed source close to the Lidori campaign.'"

"No. I meant *you* can't be real. You working for Lidori," I said, shaking my head.

"And yet? I am. Weird, huh?" He popped a SunChip in his mouth. "Uck. I forgot these are gross. You want?"

"No thanks."

I really did not want to give him the satisfaction of being amazed. But in all honesty, I kinda was. A campaign spy? Who does that? "Did someone, like, tell you to do this?"

"No, no, no. Can you imagine if the campaign *told me* to do this and then that got out? That would be a disaster. No, I just started doing it."

"And nobody knows?"

He sighed. "I mean, Priya must know I'm getting my intel from somewhere. But she never asks."

"I bet she knows," I said, thinking of how intuitive Priya was. Then I turned to him. "Aren't you afraid they'll catch you?"

"No. I'm not. Margot,[39] the Lidori campaign is a fucking mess. Her ex-husband is the campaign manager, and her brother just stepped down as treasurer because he got arrested for shoplifting. So trust me, they're not paying attention to me." He popped open a mini tube of Pringles.

I still wasn't sure I believed any of it. But I couldn't think why he would make something like that up. It was too far-fetched. Too weirdly specific to not be true. I studied his eyes, but all I noticed was that they were very blue. Like strikingly. (His eyes were nowhere near as amazing as Avery's girlfriend-magnets. But they were still nice.[40]) Was Nick *attractive*? I was trying to imagine him without his hideous scraggle-beard. *God. Beards. Why?*

Nick looked down the hall one last time before turning back to me. "Why do you want more jobs from Priya? Are you trying to get hired?"

"Hired?"

"Yeah, if Shep gets elected. Are you trying to get a job on his staff?" he asked, trying to make it seem like he didn't care at all.

"Oh," I said. "No?"

He squinted. "I figured for sure you were. A lot of people here are."

"Nope," I told him. "I'm not planning to be in North Webster next year."

"Oh," he said. "Right on. So you're transferring. Where do you go now?" he asked. "Fisher?"

---

39 Honestly shocked he knew my name.

40 Or maybe I'm just horny for eyes?

Fisher is the name of another area college. For a split second, I considered lying to him.

"Roosevelt," I said. And waited for him to realize that I was in high school.

"Roosevelt?" he said, and straightened up his posture in a way that looked almost guilty. "I— *How* old are you?"

"Seventeen."

"Whoa. Okay, sorry. I thought—" He looked around the room as if looking for backup. "I thought you had to be in college to work on these things."

"Not if you're exceptional," I said, smiling.

"I need a coffee," Nick said as he walked off to the kitchenette. While he was gone, I replayed his reaction in my head when he found out I was in high school. Why did he look so shocked? Almost guilty? Was that because he was *interested* in me?

"Margot!"

I whipped my head around. Priya was now poking her head out of her office. "I'm ready for you!"

"Cool!" I answered as I quickly walked over, brushing away any thoughts of Nick and the weird exchange we'd just had.

"Can you shut the door?" she asked. I did, thankful that Priya wasn't Matt Lauer. She seemed flustered and grabbed a water from the mini-fridge that now lived in her office. "You want something? Water? Tea?"

"No. I'm good," I said.

"Right." She clapped her hands once. "You might want to sit down."

"Okay," I said, sitting down. "I'm not fired, am I?"

"No! God no! Sorry, I'm . . ." Priya trailed off, putting her hands to her brow. Then she continued, "So something has come up that is . . . putting the whole campaign in jeopardy."

"Okay," I said cautiously.

"So . . . I guess . . . I was wondering if you would consider taking Shep on as a client. There are some pictures . . ."

My heart sank, and I felt a well of spit rise up into my cheeks. I stared straight ahead, trying my best not to show how disappointed and uncomfortable I was. This was not going to be a promotion. Or Priya bringing me into more meetings to problem-solve. This was a cleanup job. The one thing I was trying really hard not to do.

She explained the situation.

A week prior, Shep received a mysterious email from DropOutShep@hotmail.com. There was no subject, and the body of the email just said: **some things you can't delete. drop out now.** Attached was a cache of photos. Twenty-three, to be exact.

Priya hesitated, debating whether to show me the actual photos. Maybe she could sense my strong desire *not* to see them. So instead she just described them to me. It was Shep, in a hotel room, in various compromising positions with a woman who was not his wife. She went on to explain the whole Shep/Marion divorce saga, which I mostly already knew. And when she was finished, she said, "And since the marriage was on its last legs, I don't know if you'd even call this an affair.[41] These photos are of a consensual relationship between adults. But it would create a ton of drama if they got out."

---

41 I would!

I sat for a moment, trying to wrap my head around everything. This was definitely bad news for the campaign. But what could *I* do about it? It seemed like an attempt at blackmail. Or extortion. Which was a serious crime. Why would they want me, a seventeen-year-old, to handle this? And even if there was a way for me to disappear these pictures, *should I*? Wouldn't it be better to just be up-front about things and let the voters decide? And god, what about Avery? Did he know?

"Margot?" Priya said, after giving me a few moments. "I know this is a lot to ask. But, do you have any thoughts?"

"Why not bring this to the police? Or the FBI?"

"We might. Especially if they ask for money. But once we turn this over to the authorities, the pictures will leak. They always do. And then the local news, maybe even the national news, will cover this 'sex scandal' twenty-four seven." She took a second to chew on her nail. She was right. They would never run the headline: *Candidate caught on sex tape! Sex was consensual and marriage was ending anyway! No follow-up questions! This is no big deal!* This was just the type of story that could end a budding campaign like Shep's. Plus, it was always harder for progressives when they made mistakes. Susan Lidori could probably cheat on her husband with a raccoon and her base would love her for it. (As long as the raccoon was pro-life.) But Shep was supposed to be above scandals.

"What did Gail say?" I asked.

Priya looked a little surprised. "Oh, uh, Gail doesn't know about this." She straightened up in her chair. "The only people who know are me and you. And Shep, of course."

"Huh" was all I said at first. Then, "And Shep's fine with you hiring a teenager to fix this problem?"

"Shep trusts me. And—" She took a beat, readjusting a ring on her finger before saying, "We both think you're the best person for the job. Plus the fewer people who know about this, the less likely it is to leak. And this *cannot* leak."

My thoughts went back to Avery. *Is anyone gonna tell him?* "What about Marion?" I asked. "And Avery?" I pretended the last part was an afterthought.

She took a deep breath and looked away. "Shep doesn't want to involve them," she said. Seeing my look of horror, she added, "They're already giving so much to the campaign, and he doesn't want to add to their stress. Especially if we can make it go away quietly."

I frowned. They really weren't going to tell Avery that his dad cheated and got caught? That his dad's whole campaign was in crisis? They weren't even going to tell his *mom*? I swore to myself that I'd never lie to Avery again. And while Priya was claiming it was better for him if he didn't know, I found that hard to imagine. *Not* telling him felt like a big, glaring, bad-person-type lie.

I honestly couldn't believe Priya was telling *me*, given how tightly they were keeping this locked down.

"And this was a week ago? He hasn't received any more emails? Or demands for anything?" I asked.

"No. I'm not sure what this person's motive is, but maybe it's just some kind of one-off?" Priya hazarded. "You know, just to get his attention? He sometimes gets angry emails from people who don't like his politics. But never anything like this."

I could feel my mind turning on, the part of my brain that likes the puzzle of cleanup work. And I suddenly felt the urge to make a list of likely suspects. Lidori staffers? A jilted lover? The woman in the video herself?

No. I stopped myself. I couldn't actually take this job, could I? I had rules!

I pushed back my chair. "Priya. I—I don't know."

"I know. I know, this is all so fucked up." Priya rubbed her head. "Why don't you think about it? If he gets another email, one with specific demands, then we'll take it to the authorities. But if there is a way to retrieve these pictures discreetly, I mean, we have to try."

I nodded. Not ready to put myself in the "we" category yet. I stood up and said, "I'll give you an answer by tomorrow." Then I walked out the door, closing it behind me. I sensed that Priya wanted to say more. *Thank you*, maybe. Or apologize for putting me in this position. But I felt like I had to get away from her. No matter what my decision was, I couldn't make it based on how much I liked her personally. I had to come to it on my own, based on my own ethical compass of right and wrong.

Unfortunately, my compass kinda sucks.

CHAPTER 9

I'D RALLY RATHER NOT

I hit snooze three times the next morning before ultimately deciding that I wasn't going to get up at all. I felt like I'd been hit by a truck. A truck that had been carrying a very heavy ethical dilemma. I figured the best course of action was to stay home from school, stress-eat, and spend all day mulling over the pros and cons. I needed space. And quiet. I rolled over and turned off my alarm.

The next thing I knew, my mom was shaking my shoulders. "Margot! It's 7:05!"

I could barely open my eyes.

"I'm sick!" I said, groggy.

"Let me see." She sat on the edge of my bed and whipped out her wrist, placing it gently against my forehead. "You don't have a fever—"

"I'm not, like, *sick* sick," I told her, bailing on my first excuse.

I knew there was no way to bullshit my RN mom about sickness. Still, I couldn't tell her what was actually making me feel wretched. "I just—I didn't sleep well and I feel crappy. So I need a personal day."

I rolled over, thinking the matter was closed. But then she stood and ripped the covers off my bed like a magician doing that tablecloth trick.

"*Personal day?*" She leaned over me. "You'd better get your butt out the door in the next ten minutes so you're not late for school."

This was the kind of thing that my mom had started doing. She never used to check up on me to see if I went to school on time. She never cared when I skipped class. Because she knew I always maintained my grades.

"Mom. You're being ridiculous—"

"Ridiculous?" I could see that she was getting for-real mad now. "How's this for ridiculous? My daughter thinks she doesn't have to go to school. My daughter thinks the rules don't apply to her."

"They often don't—" I was getting mad now too. Of all the times to put her foot down. Why now? When I was clearly having a rough time?

"It's not funny, Margot. I get that you're going to be eighteen soon. But you're still my daughter, you're still living under my roof, and you still have to go to *freaking* school."

My mom never says "fuck," even when she's mad. It would be cute if she weren't being so fucking annoying.

"Are you going to call the truant officer on me?" I asked, slowly sitting up in bed.

"Don't test me, Margot. Where do you think you got your stubbornness from?" She tapped her hand on the doorframe before leaving.

I got dressed, my head pounding, my eyes burning, and my conscience tormented by the Shep pictures. Was I really getting dragged back into cleanup work? To clean up Avery's dad's affair? How could I possibly do this without breaking rule #3? I was momentarily distracted by a text from Melanie.

> **MELANIE:** Do you think I should start wearing hats? Would you vote for a hat person?

This felt very friends-ish. A random text with a fashion question? I wasn't used to that at all, but I felt like I should respond.

> **MARGOT:** I'm going to say, no?

> **MELANIE:** Yeah. Good call. It feels like I'm trying too hard. LOL! THANK YOU!

> **MARGOT:** No prob.

> **MELANIE:** . . .

> **MELANIE:** You're the best Margot! Seriously!

Glad I could help out. And that we were becoming friends-ish. But Jesus, use a Tapback already.

• • •

THE WHOLE WALK TO SCHOOL, THE PICTURES WERE ALL I COULD think about. Everything about them was so strange. Gail didn't know about them? *Gail?* She was the campaign manager, for Christ's sake. And neither did Marion? And then there was Avery. I knew I couldn't take this job and not tell him. But would I have to be the one to tell him that his dad had cheated on his mom? And if I did tell him . . . I mean, god. This was going to suck so much for him.

There was so much to think about. And since my jerk mom refused to listen to logic, I now had to mull over this decision *at school*. Which meant lots of day-thinking, zoning out, and possibly even the skipping of class.

Unfortunately, school had other plans. I was three minutes late for homeroom, so Ms. Okado made me read all the announcements out loud. *Infuriating*. You can't day-think when you're reminding people not to use the loading dock entrance after two p.m. Then first period, I had independent study, which should've been great for thinking. But Coach Powell was actually in his office and in between novels, so he decided he should check all my independent study work, which was a complete waste of time, since he doesn't even grade me. And then second period, I was due to give an oral presentation on *Titus Andronicus*, which I had completely forgotten about. So I had to watch the other presentations and steal some of their ideas. And you can't zone out when you're cannibalizing someone else's *Titus Andronicus*.[42]

Finally, I caught a break. Third period, AP Euro was pretty

---

42 ALSO A SPOILER!

quiet. And Mr. Lumley was in a hands-off mood. So I was able to zone out and draw a big pro/con chart in my notebook.

Pros of taking the job:

1. It might help Shep win, sending a strong progressive to state senate.
2. The affair was consensual. So it's not like I'm being asked to cover up something predatory. I don't know if this is a *pro*, per say, but it's at least a neutral.
3. I could probably succeed in erasing the pictures. And that would feel good.

"Otto von Bismarck," I answered when Mr. Lumley called on me. I was only half listening, and my answer was incorrect (it was Wilhelm I), but I was close enough that Lumley didn't call me out for not paying attention. Back to my day-thinking!

Cons of taking the job:

1. I haven't been doing cleanup work. And my life has been pretty great without it. I have a regular job, a humane schedule, and I think I even have a friend! Plus, I've been lying way less, which feels very healthy.
2. Whenever you clean anything, you're insulating a person from the result of their choices. Sometimes that's the right thing to do, like helping the survivors of RB. But should Shep really be off the hook for his infidelity, consensual or not?

And then there were my rules. Which are pretty damn important. Rule #3 is I can't work for morally dubious clients! And wasn't Shep morally dubious? I wasn't sure. His marriage was ending, which made it a little easier to forgive the affair. And Priya had said that Marion was having affairs too. (She was apparently dating a podiatrist named Javier.) That didn't excuse Shep's *per se*, but it certainly made it less morally flammable. I don't know. It wasn't ideal, but Shep *was* working for righteous causes and, as Caroline had said, he seemed serious about the revenge porn amendment—my whole reason for helping him. Those things made him seem less dubious.

In the end, I decided the moral scales were tipped in his favor. I was pretty sure I could work for him without breaking rule #3. But I still didn't know what to do about Avery.

I did, however, come up with a whole new pros and cons list.

Pros of telling Avery:

1. Maybe Avery learns to trust me again?
2. Maybe in his sadness, he leans on me for support and eventually falls in love with me.

Cons:

1. He shoots the messenger.

The bell rang. I was late for class and nowhere near a decision.

My fourth period alternated between computer science (a class I could sleep through) and Latin. Today was Latin, and of course Ms. Gushman gave a pop quiz on *cursus honorum* that took up most of the period. I'm pretty sure I failed.

Finally, fifth period *should* have given me some time to think. Gym is almost always a complete waste of time where I sit in the corner and look at my phone.[43] But we had a fire drill, and my line ended up right next to Avery's, so I spent the whole period trying to avoid him. (Avoiding is better than lying, right? Or is avoiding the same as lying? Soon as I have a free period I'll make another list.) When the drill ended, the whole mass of students slowly moved like a big blob back to the entrance. I kept getting bumped by people. Tanya Mercer stepped on the back of my shoe *twice*. Once is understandable, but twice warrants a grisly death.

I felt like I was losing my mind. I couldn't focus on anything. I could feel my breath becoming shallow. My mom, my teachers, the North Webster Fire Department—it seemed everyone was conspiring against me.

"You okay, Mertz?"

Avery was standing over me. And I realized I had stopped walking and was kind of crouched against the bike racks.

"I'm fine," I said, trying not to look up at him.

"Want a bar or something?"

He was holding out a chocolate Lärabar.

"Yes," I said glumly, accepting the bar. It was delicious.

He squinted at me. "You seem a little pale."

I looked up for a half second and caught his big brown eyes, now sporting a look of concern.

---

43 Except for badminton week. Badminton week I come to play.

"I'm always pale. Just right now I'm a little . . . lightheaded," I said, realizing as I said it that it wasn't a lie. "Listen, Avery. I need to talk to you. Can we—maybe after school?"

I don't know what possessed me to say this. I did not have a *plan* for what to tell him or how. I just knew I couldn't keep this a secret anymore.

"Totally. Is everything okay?" he said, sensing how serious I was.

"Yeah. I just can't talk about it right now," I responded.

"I have Film Club at three, but I can talk until then. We're watching *Exit Through the Gift Shop*," he said. I had no idea what that was. Clearly, my face was conveying this, because Avery quickly said, "It's a doc. It's supposed to be wild. But, yeah, I'll meet you."

God. Now I only had three periods to figure out what the hell I was going to say to Avery. And since I wanted to explain my decision to him, I'd need to *make one by then*.

Luckily, sixth period I had lunch. I brought my lunch to the library for some privacy. (You're not allowed to eat in the library, but if you sit in the high-backed chairs near biographies, the librarians can't see you). Finally a moment alone. Finally quiet.

"Margot!" a voice from a lipstick ad said. "You are eating your lunch in the library. You just do not give a fuck, do you?"

It was Ainsley McKibbon.

Usually, I'd politely escape Ainsley before she could try to hire me for another of her heinous friends, or tell me how progressive the cheer squad is being.[44] But Melanie needed her endorsement, and now was as good a time as ever to ask. So I sat up, put on a big smile, and said warmly, "Ainsley! Hey! Pull up a chair!"

"This is a really good spot for a sneaky solo lunch! I'm gonna start eating here when I need a little me-time. Margot, you're such a trendsetter!" she said, pulling up a seat next to me.

No one has ever accused me of that.

"And I love that shirt! It's hilarious."

I had to look down to see what I was even wearing.

"This is a promotional T-shirt for a prescription drug," I said. It was a teal polo shirt that said: VAYNERA: DON'T JUST LIVE WITH RHEUMATOID ARTHRITIS, THRIVE WITH IT. "My mom brought it home from the hospital."

"It's so vintage and ironic! My mom never brings home anything from her job!" Ainsley complained.[45] She was talking so fast, I was finding it hard to pivot to the election. "I feel like I need to go to more vintage stores! That's what my look is lacking! Wait—what bronzer are you wearing?"

"I think it's just eczema," I said, before awkwardly segueing with "SO! What are your thoughts about student body president?"

"Oh," Ainsley said, seemingly caught off guard (which makes sense). "Actually, I have a ton of thoughts—"

And then the bell rang.

"Shit! I can't be late for health again or Miss Legler is gonna fail me!"

---

44 They cheered for *one* women's soccer game.

45 I found out later her mom works for a hedge fund. Her mom doesn't bring home anything BUT SHITLOADS OF MONEY, I guess.

And then that beautiful goddess floated out of the library. Ah well. I'd try again another day. Back to my Avery dilemma.

I FOUND NO MORE CLARITY IN MY LAST TWO PERIODS. I SPENT seventh participating in a particularly intense game of Art History Jeopardy. I lost. Then, in eighth period AP Comp Gov, which is usually a surefire nap class, I was put into a group project with Gabby Alvarez, who talked nonstop about *Saleswomyn*. None of that helped me make a decision.

And then the final bell rang. And somehow I found myself standing in front of Avery in the trash hallway. Just as we'd planned.

"So? What's up?" he asked.

I looked down the hall and saw only Mr. Bilsack, the custodian. He always has headphones in, but I swear he isn't listening to music—he's just eavesdropping all day long.

"Let's go outside," I said.

We went out the loading dock door and around the side of the school, where there's a little creek. It was usually quiet there.

"You might want to sit down," I said. So he sat his very nice butt down on a dirty rock.

"Okay?" Avery looked confused. Like he didn't know whether to tease me for my antics or just patiently listen because I seemed genuinely upset. I was trying not to be emotional. So I looked at his throat as I talked. His eyes were too much for me.

"So Priya wants to hire me. To do a job for her. Like, a cleanup job."

Avery got deathly quiet.

There was no good way to say this, so I just spit it out.

"Your dad had an affair. And someone took pictures of him, uh . . . in the act, and sent them in an anonymous email. And now Priya wants to hire me to clean it up."

He was silent for a moment. "Yeah . . ." he said, with the casual calm of someone who had just been read a Snapple fact. "Yeah," he repeated. Then he ran his hands through his hair, scratching the back of his head, before closing his eyes and making a weird, indecipherable moan.

"Avery?" I asked gingerly. I sat down on a dirtier, less-comfortable rock while Avery let out the world's longest exhale.

He buried his head in his hands. "Fuuuuck."

His reaction was intense—pained and miserable. But to my surprise, it was not shock.

"I'm sorry to just drop all this on you. I know that it must be awful to hear something like this about your dad—"

"I knew about the affair," Avery said, cutting me off. His eyes met mine. "My parents told me about it in family therapy. They were trying to be 'open and honest.'" He used finger quotes. The saddest finger quotes I've ever seen. I shifted my weight uncomfortably.

He went on, "My mom had an affair too, around the same time. With a podiatrist. Isn't that sweet? I guess they wanted it to be even. So they had 'his' and 'hers' affairs." He sucked in his cheeks. I had never seen him so upset, which, for some reason, was making me upset. "It's just gross. I mean, I don't care how bad your marriage is, you don't do that." He stood up from the dirty rock, pacing.

I nodded, watching him. "Yeah. I mean, I wouldn't."

He turned sharply, sat back down, and started picking at the grass. "Anyway. Now there's pictures. Of my dad and . . . whoever he was with." He shivered. And not in a jokey way. The thought of his dad and some stranger literally made him shiver. "I can't believe they didn't tell me about this. Guess they weren't being that 'open and honest.' "

"Your mom doesn't know about it," I told him. "It's just your dad, Priya, and me now."

Avery looked up at me, before returning his attention to the grass. Ripping blade after blade in half. Lost in thought.

"Look, Avery. I know this is kind of a weird request," I said after a long stretch of him murdering grass-blades. "But could you maybe not tell your dad that I told you?"

He scoffed. "Oh, I'm not talking to my dad about anything." He was so angry.

All I could think to say was "I'm so sorry."

Avery stared straight ahead with glazed eyes. Almost like the emotional overload made him drunk. Then he turned to me and asked, "Sorry, but why did you tell me all this?"

I felt a pang of guilt. Maybe Avery would've been better off not knowing about the blackmail and all this drama. But wasn't *not* telling him a lie of omission?

"I didn't want to lie to you. And I thought you should know. I'm sorry if that was a mistake," I said, before I continued to ramble, standing up. "And, also, I don't have to take this job! So if you don't want me to, I won't! Honestly, I don't even know if I should. But . . . I could probably help the campaign, so . . ." I finally petered out. This was the kind of verbal stampede that could've been avoided if I actually had *a moment to myself to think today*!

Avery nodded, now looking down at the creek. He looked exhausted, and I was almost worried he might dive in, he was so focused on what was in front of him.

"I don't know. Don't you think he should maybe just have to live with it? If the pictures got out. I mean, he fucked up, right?"

I looked down at him, sure he must be right, but surprised at how cold he could be talking about his own father. Things must've been really bad between them.

"Yeah. I mean, part of me definitely thinks that. That's part of the reason I stopped doing cleanup work. Because sometimes people *should* be held accountable," I said, before taking a deep breath. "But I also know that without your dad in the state senate, no one will be pushing for 245. I don't want to see another Roosevelt Bitches pop up somewhere because some asshole like Susan Lidori torpedoes the amendment." My voice got scratchy and my eyes even got watery. Which was unusual for me. But I guess that's because I really cared about this.

Avery nodded, perhaps persuaded by my unexpected eye leakage.

"Sorry," I said, embarrassed.

"No. I get it. I know how much it means to you." He thought for a moment before saying, "And I know that my dad— I know he really believes in it. That's kind of my problem. I love Shep Green the candidate. I'm just not that wild about Shep Green the dad."

In response I just nodded. What else was there to say? Maybe this would've been one of those times where lying, or omitting, would've actually been the more humane thing to do.

After a few moments of lip-biting, Avery exhaled and got up off the ground. "Look, Margot, I don't even know how to tie my shoes right now. So I can't tell you what to do. Sorry."

"Yeah. That's fair."

"All I ask is, if you do take this job, please don't give me any more updates. I don't think I need to know anything else about my dad's affair. Like ever. Yeah?"

I nodded. And then we slowly started walking back to the school. It was like an unspoken agreement that the conversation was over. We both just understood it somehow.

WE PARTED WAYS, AND I CIRCLED AROUND TO THE FRONT OF THE school. I didn't know where I was going. Home, I guess? I was more just moving, hoping that the motion of my legs might get me some kind of clarity.

"Margot Mertz!" I heard a familiar voice shout at me. It was Melanie, calling from the passenger window of her car. "You wanna go to the mall? My mom gave me money to buy a new outfit for the campaign commercial. She said I wasn't allowed to go on Roosevelt TV wearing a shirt with animals." *Thank you, Melanie's mom!* "Abby was supposed to come with, but she bailed on me. Again. Ugh!" she said, giving a mock thumbs-down.

This was not a wheelhouse situation. Shopping for clothes? I never do it. The mall? Not my scene. But it was either that or be alone with my thoughts. So . . .

THE MALL WAS SURPRISINGLY CROWDED.[46] MELANIE INSISTED ON parking very far away because she was still "new to parking" and was afraid to pull into a spot when there were cars parked on both sides. So we walked at least three hundred yards to the nearest entrance at JCPenney.

Entering the mall was very strange. Not just because malls are cavernous retail zombies from another era, but because I hadn't gone to the mall with a friend since Beth. And Beth and I only went one time that I can remember. My mom had given me fifteen dollars to spend, which was enough to buy one scarf from the sale rack at American Eagle. It was pretty itchy, but I still have it.

Melanie led us to Banana Republic[47] because they do tall sizes. And in between popping in and out of a dressing room in various blazers and sensible cardigans, she kept a running monologue going, mostly about Abby and how she kept ditching her for stuff. But I was having a hard time paying attention. This mall diversion wasn't working. I was completely and utterly consumed by Shep Green. And the thought of Shep's bare ass. And if it was right or wrong to keep the rest of the world from seeing it.

"Margot? Are you okay?" Melanie asked. She was wearing her sixth blazer. (This one had gold buttons. Otherwise, they all looked the same.) "You just seem really spacey. And you're lacking your usual scowl."

---

46 Even when a mall is *not* crowded, it is still the worst place on earth: consumerism run rampant, arcane 40-percent-off sales that don't actually save you money, Bath & Body Works.

47 Which is an offensive name for a store, right? How did they come up with that one? *We want our brand to reflect style, luxury, and a pejorative for unstable countries reliant on single exports.*

"I'm sorry. I'm distracted," I said, rubbing my eyes. "What were you saying?"

"Nothing. Just that Abby keeps flaking and I don't know why. Maybe she got back together with the guy she was dating over the summer? When they broke up she was, like, really upset about it. But why am I talking about Abby?" She retreated into the dressing room and shouted, "What's going on with *you*?!"

Obviously I couldn't tell her what was on my mind. "I have this big decision to make," I said. "And I have no idea what to do."

"What's it about?" she asked before returning with yet another identical blazer. Also with gold buttons. She moved her bony shoulders back and forth to model the fit.

"I can't really talk about it. It's not my secret to tell. Sorry."

"Gotcha. Super-secret stuff. No worries. I'm not nosy," she said while looking at herself in the mirror. "This one? You like?"

"Yeah. It's fierce," I said, trying to sound fashion-y and failing. Melanie looked in the mirror one more time before saying, "Yeah. This is the winner. I like the buttons." Then she turned to me and out of nowhere grabbed both my arms.

"What are you doing?" I asked, suddenly worried for my safety.

"You don't have to tell me any specifics, but this always helps me make a decision. Ready?!" And before I could say *No, I'm not ready. And stop touching me*, she screamed in my face, "DON'T THINK. JUST ANSWER. YES OR NO!"

"I don't— What are you doing?"

"YES OR NO YES OR NO YES OR NO YES OR NO!"

"Melanie, I don't think this will—"

"OKAY, JUST SAY THE FIRST WORD THAT POPS INTO YOUR HEAD!"

"COLONOSCOPY!" I shouted, genuinely rattled.

"There!" she said with a knowing smile. "Was that the answer you were looking for?"

"No. Not at all."

Melanie let go of my arms, then thought for a second. "Shoot. That usually works." She shrugged before throwing her gold-buttoned blazer over her shoulder. "Ah well. Let's get mall pretzels!"

We HAD TO WAIT IN LINE BEHIND THREE WOMEN WHO ALL AP-parently wanted to open up Banana Republic credit cards, but after that, we were on our way, with Melanie's new campaign blazer in tow. Melanie continued to prattle on about Abby. How it was unlike her to not show up, but then she suddenly stopped midsentence. "What the hell is that?"

There was a huge crowd gathered at the far end of the mall around a little temporary stage. I squinted and saw some signs.

"It's a Susan Lidori rally." I groaned. So that's why so many people were at the mall today. I walked to the back of the crowd, standing on my tiptoes as Susan Lidori walked onstage.

"AMERICANS!" she cried out. "I SEE YOU, AMERICANS!"

She was giving us real Eva Perón vibes. But the crowd seemed to love it. Susan was fit, white, in her late forties maybe?,[48] with dyed-blond hair and what could only be described as

---

48 I have a hard time telling people's ages once they're over thirty.

pageant-ready makeup. Her confounding fashion choice had been to wear a professional-looking navy skirt suit with a large buffalo-checked flannel shirt over it. Accessorized with a holster. But then she accessorized every outfit with that.

She gave a bland yet loud speech about cutting taxes and keeping the government out of our public schools.[49] States' rights and all that. Occasionally she'd interject some truly racist and nonsensical improvs into her speech. "WE'RE NOT GOING TO LET THESE SOCIALISTS RUIN OUR COUNTRY! WHEN WE EARNED OUR FREEDOM!" And "WHEN IS CHINA GOING TO APOLOGIZE? FOR EVERYTHING!" And "I GOT MY SIGHTS SET ON SHEP GREEN! YOU KNOW WHAT I'M TALKING ABOUT!" The crowd cheered every time she veered off script. With every nasty thing she said, the temperature in the mall went up. Melanie and I looked at each other like, *Who are these people and why are they so angry?*

It was almost funny to see all these red-faced white people screaming about socialists in front of Auntie Anne's pretzels. Did they really think that socialism was a threat? That it would take their pretzels away? But I couldn't laugh. Because there was also something dangerous about her rhetoric. The way she was winking at the crowd, not-so-subtly telling them that shooting Shep was okay. It was all so unnerving.

"Forget the pretzels. Let's get out of here," I said to Melanie, and turned to head back toward JCPenney. As we weaved our way out of the crowd, I heard Lidori shout, "And if they don't

---

49 Not possible by definition.

get the message, WE'RE GOING TO MAKE THEM HEAR OUR MESSAGE!"

And then she turned and flashed the gun in her holster for everybody to see. The crowd went nuts. It was like a revival mixed with a riot, and if anyone knew I worked for Shep, I was seriously worried what they'd do.

Melanie grabbed my hand and yanked me away from the roaring crowd. Our pace quickened as we walked back to the relative safety of her car.

"Was she threatening to shoot Shep Green? Or did I miss something?" I asked as we power-walked.

"That's how I took it," Melanie said. "I'm going to have nightmares about that woman."

When we got to the car, we locked ourselves in. I wasn't entirely sure about Shep. But I got a close-up view as to what his alternative would be. Susan wasn't just ignorant. Or mean. She was dangerous.

I whipped out my phone and pounded out a text to Priya.

MARGOT: I'm in.

CHAPTER 10

THE EAGLE HAS LANDED (ON MY SHIRT)

Melanie dropped me off at HQ. I went straight to Priya's office. She was on the phone, but hung up as soon as I came in. "Margot, I— Thank you so much. I think you're making the right decision! I'm going to pay you a bigger stipend! And make you assistant comms director, if you want. I—I really can't thank you enough."

She wasn't *crying*. But she was sincerely emotional. Which I found surprising. She was usually so unflappable.

"I'll take care of it. It's going to be okay," I said, feeling my years at MCYF kick in as I took a seat. Suddenly I was the confident one. The steady hand, calming my client down. "You have a lot invested in this campaign, don't you?"

She nodded. "Yeah." And she looked like she was going to say something else. But then she just said, "Yeah," again.

She instructed me to work out of her office, and to ask her for anything I needed. And then she insisted, *insisted*, on buying me dinner. She, herself, not the campaign. I felt kind of bad. I wasn't at all used to people buying me dinner for no reason. So I just ordered french fries from Nick's.[50]

"Nick's?" she said, looking at her phone. "Is that 'Nick's Authentic Diner and Burger'?"

"Priya, *how* long have you been in North Webster?"

"Four months."

"And you've never had Nick Sauce? Unforgivable," I said, lightening the mood a bit. "Nick's has the best food in North Webster!"

"I thought everyone liked Pomodoro—"

"Priya, Priya, Priya. Come down from your ivory tower and see how the *people* live." I forced her to order some eggs with Nick Sauce.[51]

I got to work, settling in at Priya's desk while she zipped in and out of the office, handling various campaign matters. I started by snooping through the backend of the photo files, seeing if there were any clues in the metadata as to who took them. They were labeled with what looked like automatically generated file names. I couldn't find any sort of digital signature that would tell me what kind of camera was used or what computer they were downloaded onto. But that didn't necessarily mean this email was sent by a hacking expert. It was possible that they

---

50 There is no relation between Nick's, the beloved local diner, and Nick, the surly campaign intern. They just happen to have the same name. And they're both a little dirty.

51 Did you think that breakfast *wasn't* available twenty-four hours at Nick's? Because then you're a goddamn fool.

just used a computer with good privacy settings or they changed the file with an editor that stripped the metadata.

I eventually forced myself to glance at the photos themselves, hoping they might illuminate something. I waited until Priya was out and clicked on the first file. The first thing I noticed was that they were screenshots from a video. Or maybe a livestream? Or maybe someone hacked Shep's laptop camera without his knowing it. That wasn't too hard to pull off. Someone like Sammi would know how to do that.

The pictures themselves were what you'd imagine. Shep and this random blond woman intertwined. I won't go into the details of each one. But thanks to where the camera was placed, I could see *everything*. I didn't know how I would look at Shep again and not think of . . . *everything*.

The pictures were taken in a hotel room. My guess was the Courtyard Marriott in Brighton. Which is not very sexy.[52] But other than that, I wasn't finding much. And there was a lot I still needed to know. When were the pictures taken? And by whom? And who was the photogenic blond woman Shep was doing *everything* with?

I tried to see what I could glean from the email itself. Normally when we send emails—like through Gmail or whatever—they go through a relay server. Anytime an email passes through a relay, the server records it. If it passes through a bunch, that can be a trail of bread crumbs for you to follow. (A relay server is kind of like if I told Melanie to tell Abby to tell

---

52 I can't even really say why. But something about a Courtyard Marriott just feels like it's for traveling businessmen who wear white undershirts and eat hard-boiled eggs from the breakfast buffet.

Avery that I l%ved him, instead of just telling Avery myself. In this case, Melanie and Abby would be relay servers.) When your email passes through a relay server, the server will record that it did. Unfortunately, the Shep email didn't go through any relays, so there was no way to track it. Maybe the sender knew how to hide their tracks, or maybe they just got lucky with their ISP's email configuration—either way, a dead end.

Eventually our food arrived, and Priya came in to join me. I let her take her first bite of Nick Sauce before I probed her with questions about the photos.

"Jesus. This is good," Priya said once the mysterious sauce hit her tongue.

"Duh," I responded, shoving a few fries in my mouth. "Sorry to be blunt, but do we know who this woman is? And do we know when and where this picture was taken?"

Priya looked at me for a moment, I think debating whether or not to trust me with the name of the woman, before exhaling. "That's Deanna."

"Deanna?" I asked.

Priya explained that Deanna Hastings was one of Shep's best salespeople at Green Automotive. She and Shep had worked closely together for years before their tryst last spring.

"It was a real low point in his marriage," Priya said, cracking her wrist. "But he felt terrible. So he ended things almost as soon as they started. And then he and Marion tried counseling for a month or so."

That got my attention. "Shep ended things? How did Deanna take it?"

Priya shrugged. "I don't know. That's all he told me about her."

"Was she upset?" I pressed.

"You think *Deanna* is the one who took the pictures?" Priya asked.

I sat back in my chair, thinking. "I don't know. In my experience, scorned exes can do pretty extreme things to get attention." I was thinking of sophomore year, when Samantha Barber poured human urine down Jordyn Barry's trumpet right after Jordyn dumped her. I swirled a fry in sauce as I went on. "Maybe she made the video herself, as, like, a sexy memento, and then it fell into the wrong hands." I may not have had a case in months, but I still had all my old MCYF instincts. I was suspicious.

"I . . . I don't know." She shrugged. "I think they were on good terms."

"Well, can you ask him?"

"Honestly, I feel like the most likely scenario is that it was someone working for Lidori," she offered.

I thought about all the lies the Lidori campaign had stoked and shared on Facebook. Negative (and false) ads ranging from the misleading, *Shep Green Will Raise Taxes on Middle Income Earners*, to the outrageous, *Shep Green Secret Owner of Illegal Sweatshop Linked to International Pedophilia Ring*. The Lidori campaign had no problem bringing any of these lies to the press, so it was hard to imagine them sitting on proof of an actual affair. Why would they wait?

"The email is so *weird*," I went on. "They don't ask for money or anything. Nothing tangible. They just want him to drop out of the race. Which he would probably do much faster if they just leaked these to the press. Right? The whole thing is so irrational."

"But that tracks with the Lidori campaign. They have no idea what they're doing. They violate campaign finance law on a daily basis. And they're cruel. So I wouldn't put it past them to do something like this. But also do it in a way that's sloppy," Priya suggested. I sighed. Maybe she was right. If anyone had a motive to destroy Shep's life, it was Susan Lidori.

After the fries, I thanked Priya and headed home. I didn't feel the need to stay late. This job wasn't going to be finished in one night.

BACK AT HOME, MY BRAIN FRIED AND MY EYES GOUGED FROM looking at the Shep photos, I saw that I had missed a text. From Sammi. Since he didn't text me very often, that was notable.

> **SAMMI:** i feel like this is what they should do to trinity towers

This was followed by a picture of an apartment building in Spain that was being demolished.

He was never like, *Hey, Margot, How are you? Let me tell you how college is going so far.* It was always a random GIF or a meme or something.

I wrote back.

> **MARGOT:** Come on! I still live here!

There was a pause on his end. Was he thinking what to type next? Something about our exchanges these days felt different from the old days. Tentative. But I guess that was to be expected after what happened last year. Still, I didn't want to let our friendship go. So I kept texting. I asked him if he had made any friends in college, which I thought was a good question, but he didn't answer. Then I tried to engage him one more time by telling him about working on Melanie's campaign. That got a big response.

> **SAMMI:** you? student government?

> **SAMMI:** hahahahahahahaha

And then . . . nothing again. I asked him how his classes were and he replied with this non sequitur.

> **SAMMI:** my school was giving these away. do we think this is malware?

He sent a picture of a small thumb drive that said: *North Webster Community College. Student learning is the goal.*

> **MARGOT:** Haha.

> **SAMMI:** im serious. do you think it's agent.btz? they're probably trying to track me

> **MARGOT:** Sammi, what the hell are you talking about? No, I don't think your free flash drive is malware.

He sent me a link to a *New Yorker* article. Apparently in 2008, Russian operatives hacked the US military's internet (the

US military apparently has their own internet? Fancy!) by selling soldiers zip drives from a kiosk near the base. Russian agents had embedded a worm called Agent.btz onto the drives prior to stocking them in the kiosk. All they needed was for one soldier to buy a drive and plug it into their work computer. And apparently, many of them did.

Sammi was like a wiki for weird hacks like this. If he had still been working for me, I could've had him hack into all the Lidori campaign emails. And he probably would've done it in ten minutes. But I couldn't ask him to do stuff like that anymore.

Still, he was so good at it. Couldn't I at least ask him for advice? Without making things weird?

> **MARGOT:** Have you ever hacked into a political campaign?

> **SAMMI:** . . .

> **MARGOT:** . . .

> **SAMMI:** nope sry! ur on ur own!

> **MARGOT:** I didn't say I was going to

> **SAMMI:** haha sry

> **SAMMI:** anyway, i got2 run now. my suitemate invited these people over.

> **MARGOT:** People?

> **MARGOT:** Did he invite *girls*? That kind of people? Are they hot???

> **MARGOT:** ???

He didn't answer. So I can only assume it was because he *was* having women over. Wow. I guess people really do change in college. Last year I couldn't imagine a scenario where Sammi would invite a girl over, let alone plural girls. Good for him, I guess.

I decided to call it a night and go to bed.

I must have been pretty damn tired, because the second I lay down, I passed out. Several hours later, I woke to the sound of ringing. But it wasn't my cell (which is always silenced). It took me a minute in my groggy half sleep to realize it was coming from my desk. From a burner phone I always forget I have. I would've wondered who could be calling, but only one person had that number.

"Sammi? What the hell?"

"Maaaargot," he said, in our old style of greeting. He sounded a little tipsy.

"You never talk on the phone. Are you drunk?"

"No. Kind of. But look, I have a few ideas regarding your thing, but I didn't want to text."

"Okay," I said expectantly.

"Campaigns are very easy to phish. *Very* easy. That's how you want to get in."

"I'm not sure I have time. I need to check the emails of everybody working there. I can't wait for each of them to click my phishing links."

"You won't have to . . ." he drawled. "If you send it from inside their network. Corporate email scanners live outside the network. If you're inside, the scanner won't even see it. The call will be coming from inside the house, mwahaha."

"Huh," I said, still sleepy.

"It's pretty easy," he said. *Sure, easy for him*, I thought. "But don't fuck up. Because if they catch you . . ." He started laughing.

"If they catch me, what?"

"It's a federal crime."

"Oh," I said, my voice dropping an octave. "Right."

"I hacked Jim Jordan once. I wanted to see if I could prove the whole Ohio State thing. But then I was like, what am I doing? It's too risky. If you leave even a trace, they'll get you. So watch your back, okay?"

"Yeah," I said, sighing.

I heard people laughing in the background. "Shit. I gotta go—"

"Thanks. Saaaaammi."

"Maaargot."

I lay back down on the bed. But now my head was swimming with ideas. It sounded easy enough to break into the Lidori campaign's email server if I went to her campaign office. But the stakes were high. Hacking a student's computer, or even a teacher's, would amount to a misdemeanor if I got caught. But this would mean jail time. From what I could tell online, two years at minimum. That gave me pause. I needed to be very, very careful.

• • •

I DECIDED TO GO TO THE LIDORI CAMPAIGN IN PERSON THAT Saturday. If I could get onto their server and send a phishing email from within their network, it wouldn't send up as many red flags. And my odds of getting responses seemed a lot higher. I'd make sure to have a good disguise (glasses, hat, maybe even a wig?!) and several exit strategies in case things got dicey.

Unfortunately, I was scheduled to work at Elite Organic. I'd need to get out of my shift, and really all my shifts for the foreseeable future. But I couldn't break rule #2. No lying to parents. So instead I heavily omitted.

"I got hired by the Green campaign! Like, officially! I'm the assistant comms director. So can I take a leave of absence from the laundromat?" It was technically true! I just didn't say *what* I'd been hired to do, or how shady it was. Luckily, my parents were still dazzled from their VIP treatment at the town hall and impressed by this "promotion." So they didn't give me a hard time about it. My dad even let me borrow his car.

I dropped him off at Elite, then made sure to pull out of the parking lot as though I were going to Green headquarters. But instead, I drove to the Jefferson Road thrift shop where I bought (and changed into) a T-shirt with an eagle and the American flag on it, ripped-up jeans, and boots. I pulled on the only wig I owned, a medium-length blond one that my dad had used to be Thor for Halloween. But I quickly abandoned that part of my disguise because it was itchy. Instead I opted for a trucker hat that said "Truck You."[53] All this new gear, plus some thick glasses

---

53 It only cost four dollars. And my dignity.

I already owned, did a pretty good job of obscuring my identity. Not even my mom would recognize M#GA Margot.

Lidori's campaign office was based in a dive bar called SHOTS FIRED. It was kinda like Petey's, the bar I used to meet clients in, except louder and less Irish. The owner had given Lidori the space as a campaign donation, and the whole operation had set up in a large back room normally used for private parties. Nick said that most of the campaign staffers stayed late at the bar drinking, so it seemed like it was working out for everyone. SHOTS FIRED was on the edge of North Webster, in a strip mall with a paintball place and a shop that sold "adult toys," according to its signage.

I parked in front of Paint Misbehavin' (what I call the paintball place—its actual name is Ridgeway Paintball, which is boring) in case the bar had surveillance cameras—I wouldn't want them to catch my license plate. I checked myself out in the mirror. Unrecognizable. Check! Then I grabbed my keys and phone, and realized I had three missed texts from Melanie.

> **MELANIE:** Hey! So what time are you getting to Nia's game?

> **MELANIE:** Do you need a ride? I can drive if you want but i don't have to.

> **MELANIE:** I don't want to be early but i do want to get bleacher seats. So . . .

Shit. I had completely forgotten our plan to approach Nia after her game. I hoped Melanie would understand. I did not want to break rule #1 (don't lose friends over a job), arguably the most important rule!

> **MARGOT:** Sorry Mel! My internship has been crazy busy and they need me to work today. I suck.

> **MELANIE:** It's totally cool. I guess I'll just go? I mean, it can't hurt to ask her myself, right?

I held my breath. Something about this made me nervous. Nia was sweet, but she was very . . . *normal*. It was hard to imagine her talking to a weirdo like Melanie. Still, I couldn't stop her from going. And who knew when I'd have time to reach out to her?

> **MARGOT:** Totally! Just make sure you're really nice. Flatter her!

> **MELANIE:** Yes okay!

I hearted Melanie's text and even sent her a happy cat emoji. (*What have I become?*) I just didn't want her to be mad at me for flaking.

She messaged back a bunch of hearts and flowers, so I felt okay. I grabbed my bag and looked over to SHOTS FIRED. The doors were open, and volunteers were walking in and out. While some of them were dressed like me (like the flag had thrown up on them), many of them were dressed similar to Shep volunteers. Hm. Maybe the "costume" I had chosen was unnecessary.

I put my hand on the car door handle. But I felt myself getting nervous. The weight of jail time kept popping into my head.

Was this too risky? My breath started to quicken. What if I got caught? That would be far worse for the Shep campaign than if I did nothing at all. The sides of my vision started to blacken. What the fuck was I doing?

I reclined my seat, took off my hat and sunglasses, and tucked up my legs. I started to do a breathing exercise when I heard "HEY!" and someone pounded on the hood of my parked car.

Had they found me already? Found what? I hadn't done anything illegal yet! I looked up at the man standing in front of my car. It was Nick. Looking like he always did, casual slacker, but with a Lidori button on his rumpled jacket.

"I didn't know you were into paintball," Nick smirked. I looked around. The lot was empty, we were alone, so I rolled down my window.

"Hi, Nick."

"What are you doing here?" he asked. "Are you trying to steal my thing? My spy thing?"

He fished a pack of cigarettes from his pocket.

"I'm not trying to steal your thing. I promise. But I can't tell you why I'm here. Sorry."

"Did Priya send you?"

"I can't tell you that either."

"Right. So I'm gonna assume *it is* for Priya. Because if it wasn't, you'd just say so," Nick said while putting a cigarette in his mouth and lighting it. "That's interesting."

"You don't know that for sure!" I said, flustered and annoyed.

"You're right. I don't," Nick said before taking a drag, with a cocky undertone that said *I really do know though*, which was *so* infuriating. "But I'm guessing you're gonna pull some shady, Karl Rove dirty trick."

"I have no idea what you're even talking about—"

"Karl Rove? Tell me you know who that is."

I paused. I vaguely remembered reading about him in AP US last year. "He was a campaign manager or something?"

"Oh, yeah!" He went on, relishing the opportunity to mansplain, "Karl Rove was this evil genius Republican motherfucker who ran really dirty campaigns. So it's nineteen-ninety-whatever, and he's working on this really tight governor's race in Texas, and a week before the vote, my man Rove puts a bug in his own office. Bizarre, right? Why would anyone spy on themselves? Because, the next day he calls a press conference and tells all the local news outlets, 'I just found a bug in my office! My opponent is spying! Whatever you do, don't vote for those cheats!' And everyone believes him! And Rove's guy wins! Isn't that amazing? I mean, it's evil. But it is undeniably brilliant too, right?"

Nick popped a piece of nicotine gum into his mouth. And yes, he was simultaneously smoking.

"Okay . . . I mean, thank you for that very long story, but that is not why I'm here," I said, throwing up my hands.

He fluttered his lips. "Bummer. I really hoped you were gonna take her down."

I tapped on the steering wheel. *Yeah, well, that makes two of us.* Something about his persistence was starting to annoy me. Or maybe I was just annoyed at myself, and it was bleeding over. "I was going to do something stupid. But I decided it's not worth it. So I'm going home," I said as I hastily buckled my seat belt.

"Whoa. Wait. Don't go!" Nick said, leaning against the car window. "What's the stupid thing?"

I sighed and waved his gross smoke out of my face. I didn't really want to tell him, but I knew he wouldn't stop asking me until I did. "I was going to sneak in and send an email from the campaign server. But I don't want to go to jail."

"Why would you go to jail—"

"It doesn't matter, I'm not gonna do it. Just trust me, it would've been illegal."

Nick took another puff, then shrugged. "I'll do it. Everybody there already knows me. So they won't be suspicious. And I don't care if they catch me. Mostly because they won't. 'Cause that place is a smoking hot mess. So . . ."

I thought about it. Nick didn't need a disguise. He was a known volunteer there. Plus, if he did get caught, it would be hard to tie him to the Green campaign. He didn't officially work there anymore.

"Nick. I don't think I can ask you to—"

He shrugged, dropping his cigarette and grinding out the butt with his shoe. "What you're asking isn't that hard, right?" he said.

"No. You'd just send an email on the campaign's network. Wait for someone to respond. Then leave. But still. If you got caught, it's a federal offense—"

Nick shrugged. "Yeah, yeah, yeah. Just tell me what to do."

"Fine. Screw it. Get in the car, and I'll explain."

Nick got in the passenger seat while I forwarded him the draft of the phishing email I needed him to send. Then

I walked him through how to delete his keystrokes and sign out of his email so that there was no way they could trace it back to me or the campaign. Nick seemed to be paying close attention. Which was surprising. He usually had a lazy, "fuck it" attitude.

"Anything else?" he asked.

"Nope. That's it," I said. Nick nodded, then opened the passenger door to get out. "But if you change your mind at any point and want to bail, bail. Do not feel bad about—"

"I'll be right back," Nick said dismissively, not looking back as he walked down the cracked pavement to SHOTS FIRED.

And then I sat. And waited. Which was a very strange feeling for me. I had never, ever sent someone else to do an in-person job like this. Not even Sammi. I was always the doer. The one taking risks. Being the waiter was awful. There was nothing to do. Sure, I tried to dull my nerves with my phone. Scanning Instagram to see if Nia had said anything about Melanie's campaign. But I kept checking the clock. How long had it been? Only two minutes. Weird. It felt like seven. How about now? Still only two minutes. Shit! Stop looking.

By the time fifteen interminable minutes had gone by, I'd convinced myself that Nick had been caught. Then I heard a distant siren and I was certain it was the police coming for me. That was, until I listened a little closer and realized it was a fire truck. And unless Nick also burned down SHOTS FIRED, they weren't coming for him.

Finally, he came out. He was chatting with someone just inside the door, then he turned and waved goodbye. He then very,

very slowly walked back to my car.

"Here you go!" he said, handing me his phone as he got in.

"Should we drive somewhere else?" I asked, realizing it might not be a good idea to do this out in the open. "There's a bar I go to sometimes where no one would bother us."

"Margot. It's fine. It's an early phonebanking shift, and there's only like two grandmas working there. And they are both very drunk."

I shook my head. I guess I didn't realize they'd be serving alcohol already. This was coffee and orange juice time! I wiped all evidence of the email Nick had just sent. "There. All done. Your phone is clean."

Nick took it back, impressed. "Wow. That's it, huh? That's cool you can do all that. Deleting my . . . phone proof or whatever. Is that the kind of thing you did in your cleanup business?"

"Yeah. Kind of," I said.

"Huh." He leaned back, then shot me a look. "I still don't get why you quit, then. Seems like you were good at it."

I closed my laptop and turned to look back at him. And for some reason, I was really noticing those damn peepers again. Just so very blue. God, did I like this guy? This surly beard who smells like ash and old carpet? Or was it that I was attracted to someone appreciating me? Seeing me at work and being impressed? Shake it off, Margot.

"I don't know. It just got too complicated," I said, putting my laptop into my messenger bag.

Nick got out of the car. But before leaving he said, "That bar you mentioned . . ."

"Yeah, I just go there because it's safe. And empty. But I already got everything I needed. So I'm done here," I said.

Nick froze for a moment before saying, "Uh. Great. So . . . good luck with your email thing." Then he shut the door and quickly walked back to SHOTS FIRED to do whatever it was he did there.

ON THE WAY HOME, I FELT RELIEVED THAT THIS WAS BEHIND ME. That no one had noticed. And that there was nothing tying me to the phishing scheme. But then it dawned on me. Was Nick bringing up the bar because he was about to ask me out? I'd been so caught up in Avery and my unrequited feelings for him that I hadn't really considered liking someone else. Let alone a smoker with a beard. In college! But then again, it's not like I run into that many guys who are interested in me. So maybe I shouldn't be too critical.

I put the thought to the back of my mind. It was just a misunderstanding. In all likelihood, now that I was doing cleanup work for the campaign, I probably wouldn't even see Nick around the office anymore. So there was no reason to even consider him as a potential . . . whatever.

Still, the whole way home, I kept thinking about those damn blue peepers.

CHAPTER 11

EMPLOYEE OF THE MONTH

I slept in the next morning and woke to find my dad eating a box of doughnuts by himself.

"I'm not eating them all myself!" he insisted, when I accused him of just that. "I'm *sampling* them. I'm taking a bite of each."

"Dad. You're eating all the doughnuts."

"If you keep saying that, I won't let you have the pumpkin doughnut *I bought for you.*"

Well, I'm not one to pass up a free doughnut. I apologized profusely.

But, as they say, there's no such thing as a free doughnut. Because the moment I sat down to eat, my dad started asking me "casual" questions about the campaign.

"So it's a pretty big promotion?"

"Yeah. I'm assisting the comms director now. Which means I'm getting a bigger stipend. But it's also a lot more work." All true statements, believe it or not.

"That's cool. Like, what kinda work?" my dad asked, fishing for more details. I started to feel a little anxious. I did not want to lie to him, but it was almost like he was trying to force my hand, like he knew I was hedging or something.

"Just . . . kinda . . . whatever Priya needs," I said. I'd made it this far without breaking my rules, I did not want to start now. Still, I was probably in gold-medal contention for all the contortions I was doing.[54]

"What are we talking about?" My mom swooped into the room and snagged a half-eaten blueberry frosted then sat between us.

"Margot's new job," my dad said.

"I wanted to ask you about that," my mom said, taking a sip of coffee. "I've noticed you seem busier. And tired."

She had probably noticed the bags under my eyes. I'd stayed up all night looking through hundreds of internal emails from the Lidori campaign. And while I did find lots of infighting and conspiracy theories about Shep—apparently Shep is a vegan communist *and* a cannibal—I didn't see any mention of Shep having an affair. Or a plan to blackmail him. The Lidori campaign didn't seem to know anything about it.

"Yeah. I had a hard time falling asleep last night," I agreed.

"You're not doing cleanup work for the campaign, are you?" my mom asked, squinting as she put a spoonful of yogurt in her mouth.

I stopped chewing. "You think a *future state senator* would hire me to do cleanup? Wow, Mom. I mean, thanks. You must

---

54 I'm told "contortions" is not actually an Olympic event. And to that I say, how should I know? *I don't sport.*

really have a high opinion of me." This was verging *real* close to an all-out lie. My palms were getting sweaty. My mom squinted, unsure whether to accept my lie.

"So just to be clear—"

"No. Mom. I'm not doing cleanup work for Shep Green."

And there it was. I lied. She flat-out asked me and I flat-out lied. Bye bye, rule #2. I tried to enjoy my doughnut, but now it just tasted like greasy bread. I looked across the table at my nice parents. They did not deserve to have a liar daughter making their lives more complicated. Why couldn't I just be nice like them? Why couldn't I be quiet and rule-abiding?

I had failed on rule #2, but this was a really important case, wasn't it? And as long as I didn't break the other rules, I was sure I'd be able to forgive myself when Shep was in the statehouse, guiding § 245.01 into law. At least I think I was sure.

Since I'd already lied to them about one thing, it was pretty easy to just add one more lie in for good measure. When they asked me where I was headed, I did not tell them I was headed to Shep's dealership to investigate his mistress's[55] computer. I told them I was going to Melanie's to plan her campaign ad. At which point the universe promptly punished me. Because when my dad heard we were going to make a video, his dormant film-nerd brain became activated.

"You're shooting a film! I could rent you a camera package from Studio Bantam. I still know a couple guys there."

"Dad, we are not going to rent equipment—"

---

55 There's got to be a better, sex positive term for this? "Out-of-wedlock sex partner"?

"You need to grab people visually. Right off the bat. Think: Michael Chapman with *Raging Bull*. Do you have a good editor? Line producer? And what about sound?"

"Dad, this is just for school—"

"Margot! Do not go cheap on sound. Sound is everything!"

"Dad, we're not even shooting this till Tuesday. We're just talking about what we want it to say," I told him in a raised voice.

My poor dad. All he ever wanted was a film-nerd child to share his passion. And this was the only time I'd ever done anything movie-related. I took pity on him and said he could edit the ad (under my strict supervision), and I agreed to use his Sennheiser MKE2 "lav mic" for "superior" sound.

"It's going to be EPIC!" He banged on the table. "SCORSESE!"[56]

"Sure, Dad," I said, grabbing my coat.

"You'll be home in time for dinner, right?" my mom called. She was a real stickler about my being on time these days, and I assured her *three times* that I would be.

"Yes, Mom. When the big hand is on the six!"

ON THE WAY TO THE DEALERSHIP, I TEXTED MELANIE. SHE WAS headed to a Roosevelt swim meet to pass out cupcakes. She sent me a GIF of an owl dancing, because Melanie is nothing if not on-brand. Though if she planned to put an owl in the campaign ad, I'd have to resign.

---

56 Martin Scorsese is a director my dad really likes. He screams his name sometimes when he's happy. This is the level of film nerd we're dealing with.

When I got off the bus at Hammond Corners, I went into the Starbucks bathroom[57] to change into some of my mom's scrubs. My plan was to enter the dealership pretending to be a potential car buyer and chitchat with Deanna. Then, before leaving, I'd give her a flash drive as a seemingly innocuous gift . . . a gift full of malware. And yeah, it's probably not great that I'm getting inspiration from Russian agents attacking our infrastructure. But a good idea is a good idea! And I couldn't think of a better way to break into Deanna's computer than to have Deanna herself do it for me. I had placed a rush order for custom flash drives. (I only needed one for the job, but I had to order twelve in order to meet the minimum. Which was very annoying. And cost $124.) The drives seemed like any other flash drive, almost a terabyte of free storage. But once Deanna Hastings plugged it into her computer, I'd be able to view her drive remotely. (It was basically a RAT that she would install herself.)

I put on a lanyard I had made myself that said, "Jacquie Rolfe, Atlas Medical Group." If I wanted Deanna to see me as a potential buyer, I figured it made sense to dress as a young professional. Meet Jacquie Rolfe, physician assistant.[58]

And then at around three p.m., I strolled onto the lot and pretended to admire a bunch of Kias. A male salesperson came up to me to ask if I needed help, but I told him I was "just looking."[59] From the lot, I could see inside the showroom. There was a

---

57 Even Starbucks can't ruin a bathroom.

58 Jacquie loves pub trivia, subscription boxes, and her cat, Fido. She and her fiancé are planning a *winter* wedding, just to be a little different!

59 I also said, "Sorry, I just came from work," and pointed to my scrubs, which felt a little unnecessary. I needed to chill.

lounge-y area with a Keurig machine, and along the back wall were four small desks, belonging to the salespeople. To the back right was the repair shop, and to the back left was Shep's office, enclosed in glass. It was dark and empty—he was probably busy with campaign stuff.

Slowly, I made my way into the showroom, pretending to seek out cars that were in my imaginary price range. I could see Deanna at her desk. She was pretty in real life; tall, blond, and sturdy-looking, with a wide jaw. And unlike the last time I saw her, she was fully clothed. The guy sitting next to her said something, and Deanna laughed like a hyena. But before I could catch her eye, that damn male salesperson appeared behind me again.

"She's a beaut, huh?" he said.

It took a moment for me to realize he was talking about a car. This dude had thinning light brown hair, waxy tan skin, and, it grieves me to say, a soul patch.

"She's not just pretty to look at, though," he went on. "She's got a V-8 engine in there."

"Nice," I said wanly, hoping he would take the hint that I was not a serious buyer and that I didn't enjoy gendering my automotive vehicles. "I'm really just looking."

He lingered. I eyed the laptop on Deanna's desk across the room. It seemed like it was a personal one, not a "work computer." Which was good news. But how was I going to get my hard drive into her hands when this other salesdude had already "claimed" me?

"Do you have any questions I might be able to answer?" he asked, reeking of commission-thirst.

"Can't think of any." I shrugged. "I'm not sure I can even afford a new car!"

This backfired. The salesdude, *Bryan*, went on to describe how, with financing, I could lease a new car for "cheaper than my gym membership." He spoke continuously, and I could not find an opportunity to tell him I did not have a gym membership. Or that it was incredibly off-putting that he had assumed I did.

Eventually I was able to cut him off with, "Good to know. Good to know."

Bryan laughed as though I'd made a joke. (He also laughed like a hyena.)

I debated just leaving my flash drive on her desk. Or several—after all, I had twelve of them. But I thought the odds of her actually using the drive would be way higher if Jacquie Rolfe offered it to her in person.

I changed tactics and tried to stump Bryan with some questions, hoping that he'd need to reach out to Deanna for help. I asked him if leases were subject to excise taxes in the state of Michigan, then how many miles per gallon I could expect to get off-road, and finally if my *Proforma Spec* brand snow chains would be compatible with the Sportage. He rattled off the answers to my questions with no hesitation: Yes. Thirty-three. And yes.[60]

I excused myself to the bathroom and prayed that Bryan wouldn't follow me into the ladies' room. When I cautiously reemerged, I was relieved to find that he was now on the lot

---

60 For the record, he was 0 for 3. There's no tax in Michigan. No one compiles data about off-road gas mileage. And there's no such snow chain as *Proforma Spec*. That is just some gibberish I made up. Bryan was bad at his job.

speaking animatedly with a young couple and laying on the hyena laughs extra thick. Deanna was still in the showroom, now speaking to an older woman who wanted to trade in her Kia Sportage. So I decided to do something bold. I went over to Deanna's computer, opened up her browser, and searched for: **SPORTAGE SAFETY RATING** and **KIA CONSUMER REPORTS** and **WHAT IS A SAFE, AFFORDABLE SUV?**

I heard her excuse herself to the woman and start walking toward me.

"Excuse me?" she called, her heels clicking their way over to me.

"Hi!" I said warmly, as though I'd done nothing wrong.

"Can I help you with something?" she asked. "You're, uh, you're using my computer."

I looked up in shock. "You mean, this is *your* computer? I— Oh my god I'm so sorry. I thought it was for, like, the dealership. So we could look stuff up. Like at the Apple store." I continued to apologize profusely. She laughed. (Hyena.) And I laughed. (My best hyena.) We were finding a rapport.

I let her show me the options on the Kia Sorento. I told her I was very interested and would come back tomorrow with my fiancé. During all this Bryan came back in, spotted us, and dropped his head like a sad cartoon dog. *Damn it, Bryan, you missed another one*, his sad inner monologue told him. (Now, *he* would've made a great Willa Loman.)

When it was time to go, Deanna gave me her card. Perfect. As I rummaged in my bag for my card, I pulled out a handful of pens, keychains, and of course, the flash drive.

"Would you look at all this crap" I asked. "The pharma reps just keep forcing it on us. Every shift I work, there's more point-less swag."

Deanna laughed. "So I'm guessing you don't want a Green Automotive keychain?"

"No thanks," I told her. "Any chance I could unload some of this on you? Want a Cialis pen? Or a Vaynera thumb drive?"

She laughed.

"Please? I promise I will *buy a car from you*."

She laughed again. But then she took several pens and two of my dummy drives. There was no guarantee she'd plug them into her computer, but I was pretty hopeful. When you need a drive, don't you just use the first one you have lying around?

With my ready-to-hack flash drive in Deanna's hand, there was nothing left to do but get the hell out of there. With my arms full of Kia literature, Deanna walked me to the front entrance and shook my hand. But as I grabbed for the door handle, it swung open. And there was Avery. My Avery. Looking right at us. My jaw dropped. I felt *sure* he was going to say, "Hey, Mertz." And my cover would be toast. I got ready to tap dance. *Oh, Mertz is just my middle name! And also my nickname! And I've never seen this man before in my life!*

But thankfully, Avery just said, "Hey, Deanna," smiling, then turned to me with a quizzical look.

I wanted to blurt out something about the Sorento's highway gas mileage. Or something about how I just needed the week to discuss everything with my fiancé, Tony. Anything to stop Avery from outing me as myself. But I was frozen. I knew it was his dad's dealership, but still. Of all the gin joints!

Deanna smiled and said, "Hi, Avery." Then to me, "Avery's dad owns this dealership." Then to Avery, "Avery, this is Jacquie Rolfe. She's interested in owning one of the new Sorentos."

Avery didn't even blink. He just said, "Nice to meet you, Jacquie," and smiled. "Can't go wrong with a Sorento."

He was so good. Of course he covered for me even though he had no idea why I was in scrubs with a fake mom purse. I muttered something about being in touch about financing and how I hoped everyone would remember to get their flu shots, and I scurried out to the parking lot.

I HAD A GOOD FEELING ABOUT MY PLAN AS I WALKED TO THE BUS stop. Having done dozens of jobs by now, I have a decent sense when things will break right for me. Sure, there was a chance Deanna could throw away the drive, or just keep it on her desk and never use it. But my gut told me she would. People usually like free stuff and don't question it. Just ask the Trojans.

I sat on the sad bus-waiting bench and looked at my phone. Eleven missed messages from my mom. This had taken longer than I thought it would—it was already past six, and my mom's escalating texts let me know that I was going to miss dinner. **Can you come a little early and help me with the salad? And ETA??? And It's 6:00 and I don't see you.** And—you get the idea. I started to text back an apology, but was interrupted.

"So. Nurse Mertz," I heard a low and, I would argue, sexy voice behind me say. I turned around to see Avery, leaning against the bus stop awning. "What the hell was that?"

"Did you follow me?" I asked with real concern. "Did she see you?"

"Relax. A family of four came in after you, and she's sweet-talking them," he said. "And I didn't *follow* you. I just knew where you'd be headed. You are at the mercy of the public transit system, Mertz."

He stepped out into the street looking for the bus. Then added, "You want a ride? My car's right over there. And on the way you could tell me the way-too-elaborate backstory you made up for . . . Jacquie, was it?"

I was dying to tell someone! Deanna never asked me how long I'd been a nurse (three years), or how long Tony and I had been engaged (ten months!). Or about how I was on day four of Whole30! But still, I couldn't. "I really don't want to risk being seen together, so . . . I think no. But thank you."

"So you decided to work for my dad, I guess?" he asked. And for once in his life, he didn't try to make eye contact with me while he asked a prying question. "And Deanna . . . is the reason you were talking to her—is she—"

"You said you didn't want to know about any of it," I reminded him.

"I did. I did." He nodded. "And I don't. I really don't."

I could tell he wanted to say more. "But?"

"But I can't help it. I mean, I've known Deanna since I was like seven. She bought me Legos once. If she's his 'other woman,' that's just very . . ."

He did a big long exhale that sounded like *pfff*. Then wrinkled his brow and asked, "Wait. Is *she* the one blackmailing him?"

"I don't know yet. It's still early," I said.

"This whole thing is just so fucked up," he said, standing over me and pointlessly kicking the bus stop.

"I know it's weird that I'm in your family's business. And I'm sorry about that," I said, looking at the ground. "Are you mad at me? For taking the case?"

"*Mad*? Why would you think that?" he asked, and he seemed so shocked that I felt a little embarrassed for asking. "I'm mad at my *dad*. For being a lying, cheating asshole. I'm not mad at you. What you're doing—breaking into car dealerships and hacking computers—that's just what you do."

"Yeah . . ." I said, wondering if "what I do" is not so great.

I saw a big vehicle coming down the street. I prayed it wasn't a bus. I wanted to keep talking to Avery. Even though nothing was going to happen between us, I just liked being near him. I breathed a sigh of relief when I realized it was just a sheriff's bus full of prisoners.

"But just so you know, I'm not doing it the way I used to. I mean, I'm really trying to make better choices about work stuff," I said, standing up. "And I know I probably shouldn't bring this up, but what I did to you last year—I'm still horrified. And I'm trying really hard to be better."

I was inexplicably pacing around him as I rambled. And the only expression I saw on his face—when I glanced a peek at it—was bewilderment.

"I mean, I'm not a hundred percent sure that people actually *can* change. Which is depressing. Because what if I'm just this horrible person forever? No matter how many rules I make?

I could be rotten deep down, and my rules are just a BAND-AID! Maybe I'm fated to be a goddamned monster who nobody wants to hang out with?"

"I want to hang out with you," he said. And in one motion, he grabbed my waist, pulling me toward him. I looked up at him, stunned. He looked back at me and kissed me like in the movies. Like in *old* movies with entrenched and problematic gender stereotypes. An MGM kiss.

Also, a choir of angels may have started singing "Ain't No Mountain High Enough" while the B7 arrived, drawn by four white horses with white doves shooting out of its windows. But in my frame of mind, I couldn't be sure. Memory is a funny thing.

When I gently pulled away and slowly opened my eyes, the bus was gone. I felt dizzy. I wrapped up my little tirade-slash-monologue with "Uh, yeah. Huh. So . . . right." I got an 800 on my English SATs. And yet one kiss from a boy and suddenly Margot talk bad like not know how. Sad.

Avery, however, looked even more stunned than me. And a wave of terror washed over his face as he said, "I'm sorry. I shouldn't have just, like, done that. I think." And even though I was thinking, *Uh, no, you definitely should have, ya dingus!* I let him talk. Mainly because my brain hadn't properly rebooted from the best kiss of my life.

"I know I've been weird! And, like, distant. And then at my dad's campaign I, like, overshared all the shitty things going on in my life! And now I'm kissing you! I must seem batshit!"

"You don't!" I said, wondering how to get him to kiss me like that again.

"I just— I couldn't help it! And now I'm hearing myself say that and it sounds really bad. I should've asked for your consent! What the fuck am I doing?"

Avery rarely swore. It seemed he was now going through a similar shame spiral to the one I had just recovered from. And I could think of only one way to help him with that.

I grabbed his face and kissed-him-slash-shut-him-up back. (A *contemporary* movie kiss, where the empowered woman takes what she wants from the neurotic man.) And then, thank the gods, we both stopped yammering for a bit and made out at the bus stop. His one hand on my face, the other around my waist. His lips, pressed against mine. My hands on his face, then his hair and neck. I felt a rush of excitement but also a weird calm. Like this was the most natural thing to be doing. Like this was where I belonged. With Avery. Kissing Avery.

"I thought you made a vow not to date anyone," I said when we finally broke our embrace.

"I thought you made a vow not to do cleanup work," he said. Then he put his arms around me. "If you can break your thing, I can break mine."

CHAPTER 12

I'm Margot Mertz and I Approve This Message

Avery drove me home. And, not to brag, but he told me that he'd started to have feelings for me again over the summer and that was the only reason he'd been avoiding me. That's why he was so weird every time I saw him, because he was sincerely trying *not* to date me. I told him that I'd had feelings for him since prom. And that I sincerely wanted to throttle his therapist for trying to come between us. *Fucking Gerri!*

"I'm sorry to just, like, leave," I said when we pulled up to Trinity Towers, "but I'm already super late and my mom's been up my butt—"

"I'll call you later," Avery said, putting his hand on my left knee. I caught a slightly roguish look in his deep brown eyes.

"I mean, obviously I'd rather be here in your fancy-ass Muskmobile," I replied, sinking back into him for a kiss as he laughed. I wanted to straddle him. And honestly, I might have, if Avery hadn't pulled away.

"You better go. I don't want your parents to be mad at me."

As if my parents would ever be mad at Avery. For the month we dated, my parents had never seemed more proud of me.[61]

"Fine. I'm only going because I don't want my first time to be in the Trinity Towers parking loop. But you—" I kissed him again. (I could do that now!) "You are making me rethink that."

I slammed the door and practically skipped to my apartment, looking back once or twenty-five times to catch one more glimpse of Avery. He kept looking at me too, grinning from ear to ear, all the way until I got through the front doors of the vestibule.

I slipped off my scrubs in the stairwell. Then I entered my apartment and found my mom sitting at the kitchen table. My place setting was still there, though my parents had both clearly already eaten. My mom looked pissed as she performatively checked her watch.

"Margot," she intoned. "We had a deal. If you were going to be late, you were supposed to text."

I was in no mood to fight. Or to continue to lie to my parents more than I already had. So I tried a different tactic. Over-truthing.

"I'm sorry. I am. But I had a hard time texting you because I was too busy . . . making out with my new boyfriend! Or my old boyfriend. Avery Green. We got back together! You remember him? Tall guy. Very handsome. Dad also kind of has a crush on him?" I downed a glass of water, wiping my lip with my sleeve before walking to the hallway. "Anyway, now I'm drowning in

---

61 And I often get straight As. Which is kinda fucked up!

Latin homework, so I really have to go! But I promise you, next time, I will extract my lips from Avery's and text you back right away so you know where I am."

I was hoping all this new info would cloud over the parts of the story I was choosing not to mention. Margot has a boyfriend? And it's Avery? And she's openly exploring her sexuality? And she's telling us about it? It was too much for them to take in in one moment. I heard my mom make an exasperated huff, probably trying to figure out if she was still mad.

"Well, obviously I'm happy for you. But you need to let us know where you are—"

"Yes. I know. I love you. I'm glad you worry about me. I worry about you too!" I called as I headed to my room and shut the door. Then opened it one more time to say, "Oh, and I'm not sexually active. But when I'm getting close, we should talk about birth control. Yeah? Night, guys." One more door slam.

I heard my dad say, "Well, okay. Uh . . . okay. Let's talk tomorrow!" after I closed the door. Mission TMI? Success. I threw my bag on the bed, pulling out my laptop.

It was already a great day because, well, Avery. But do you ever have a great day that just keeps getting better and you think, *Am I going to die tomorrow?* Well, I was having one of those days. Because in addition to the man of my dreams making out with me, I was getting a signal from Deanna's laptop. She'd used the drive. Yahtzee!

I started to dig into her files, emails, and passwords when I got a text from Avery.

> **AVERY:** I made a huge mistake. I decided I don't care if your parents hate me. Come back to the car!

> **MARGOT:** I'd say "turn that car around!" but I already started digging around your dad's mistress's hard drive. So I'm suddenly feeling debonered.

For a moment, I just got the dot-dots. I worried that joking about this was too much for Avery. But then he wrote back with:

> **AVERY:** Yep. Me too! Consider me officially de-bonered. Maybe for the rest of my life!

I laughed. And then I wasn't sure what to do. I needed to work. But I also didn't want him to think I didn't want to talk to him. I was about to suggest we FaceTime briefly when he beat me to the punch.

> **AVERY:** I know you're busy. Call me if you need a break.

Avery always had a weird sixth sense about when to give me space. Which ironically, just made me want to be around him more. Jesus. He really was perfect for me.

I stayed up late combing through the laptop. But I didn't find anything linking Deanna to the pictures. There were no copies of them on her laptop. No emails or texts about them. Plus, according to her DMs and emails, she was now in a semi-serious relationship[62] with a guy she met on Bumble. "Luca" was a white guy with a man-bun and sleeve tattoos, which isn't a look I'd choose for her, but she seemed happy. But that meant she

---

62 Her words. "Semiserious." I thought at some point we graduated from such wishy-washy relationship descriptors. Does it ever end?!

probably didn't have the motive to blackmail Shep. She wasn't wounded and pining and secretly plotting revenge. She was happily boning Luca.

Which meant I was in need of a new lead.

THE NEXT MORNING WHEN MY ALARM WENT OFF, I SHOT OUT OF bed. I'd only gotten a few hours of sleep, but I was jacked from all the . . . Avery. I bounded into the kitchen, poured myself a completely unnecessary cup of coffee, and tapped my feet against the table as my parents ate breakfast. They seemed pensive, nervous. I sipped in silence for a moment before my mom said, "Margot. We're happy that you and Avery are back together. But you still have to text us if you're going to be late. And curfew is now eleven on weekdays."

I whipped my head to look at her. "Are you kidding me? You've never enforced a curfew."

"Margot—"

"Why? Because I was late for *dinner*? It was *leftovers*."

"No," my dad answered. "Because you didn't text to tell us you'd be late for dinner."

"While you're living here, we want you to be respectful," my mom said softly.

I angry-laughed. "Wow. Okay," I said, getting up from the table. "I will make sure to be home by my curfew."

And I know it's not a great look, but as I walked out, I slammed the door to our apartment shut behind me. I know, very angsty teenager of me, but curfew? I was offended!

. . .

I TRIED TO LET GO OF MY FRUSTRATION DURING MY FIRST FEW classes. After all, my parents didn't know how stressed I was about the whole Shep thing. Or how my entire afternoon spent investigating Deanna had turned up nothing, and I now had no promising leads. I had kept them in the dark and so couldn't expect their empathy. Still. Curfew? Come on, guys.

I met up with Melanie during lunch to talk over the campaign ad. Even though I had joined her campaign solely to stop P-Boy, I had to admit that I was growing to really appreciate the weird owl girl. And I was looking forward to our meeting. It would be a welcome break from all the Shep stuff.

When I got to the caf, Melanie and Abby were already there. Melanie looked like she had just downed two Red Bulls, even though she swore she hadn't. She said she was just "high on politics." Huh boy. And Abby was almost as manic as she described their outreach at the swim meet. "We gave away all our cupcakes! Even the ten I screwed up!"

I'm not sure what that really says. Who doesn't like a cupcake? If Lidori were giving away free cupcakes, honestly, I'd probably take one.

I started out by apologizing. I felt pretty guilty for neglecting her this weekend. But the fact that I couldn't tell her about the whole Shep thing made it hard to explain. Luckily, Melanie didn't seem to mind. She went on and on about one of the swim heats they'd watched and how close it was. I'm glad she enjoyed it and everything, but that's not what we were there to discuss.

"Did you talk to Nia?" I asked.

"Yes." Melanie made a thumbs-down. "But I couldn't convince her."

My heart sank. "What happened?" I asked. Maybe there was still a way to get her on our side. "She said *no*? Flat out like that?"

"Well, it was right after her game," Melanie explained, tucking her hair behind her ears. "And they won, which was good. But she missed a save at the end, and I could tell she was still kind of mad about it."

"But Mel wasn't going to let that stop her. She went right up to Nia and asked for her endorsement. Like a total boss," Abby chimed in.

"So what happened?" I asked.

"Oh, well, basically, Nia said, *Sorry, can you get that cupcake out of my face? I can't eat a cupcake right now.* And I was like, *Totally.* And then I said, *Would you endorse me for president?* And she said, *Melanie, I'm going to vote for you. But I'm not going to, like, post about it. That's not what my Story is for.*"

"Okay, so she won't put us on her Story. But if we could just *tell* people who she's voting for—"

Mel shook her head. "She said she has friends who are still friends with P-Boy, and she doesn't want to make anyone mad. So she's not gonna say who she's voting for, like, in public." She took a big bite of her peanut butter sandwich. Oh boy. I knew I shouldn't have left any of the endorsements to Melanie. If I could get Danny Wellman to endorse Shep, I sure as hell could've gotten Nia Reid.

"Honestly, it's not like Nia's *that* popular anyway," Abby lied. "But I gotta run. Catch me up after school?"

"Sure thing!" Melanie said, giving her air kisses. "Love you!"

"Love you!" Abby said, getting up from the table.

". . . Bye!" I added. I guess I was uncomfortable saying the L-word even to a friend. Especially one who was always randomly bailing.

Melanie turned back to me. "What about you? Did you talk to Ainsley yet? Or Avery?"

Without intending to, I made a big goofy smile. "Yeah, um, Avery is in."

She raised both eyebrows at me. "Uh-huh. So are you two together finally?"

"I don't know what you mean by finally—" I dropped my phone. Twice. Before picking it up and putting both my hands on my waist. Clearly I was giving off *ohmygodAverykissedmeeeeee* vibes.

"Mar-got! Hell yeah!" Melanie shouted. "But I thought you said he wasn't going to date anyone?"

"I know! But he changed his mind, I guess," I shouted back, shrugging happily.

"So what happened?!" More shouting!

I did my best to lower the volume of my voice and recount the whole thing, including going into probably too much detail about what his tongue tasted like and my inner debate over how far I wanted to go with him the next time we were alone together.[63] If Melanie was grossed out or bored, she didn't show it. In fact, she was more enthusiastic than I was.

---

63 PRETTY FAR! ALERT THE THIRD BASE COACH! *Is* there a third base coach? *I don't sport!*

"Margot, I've never seen you this—well, I don't know if 'happy' is the right word, but you don't seem pissed off like you normally do."

I laughed. I couldn't believe I had a boyfriend. And a friend to talk about said boyfriend with. What a world!

But then I checked the clock. Lunch was almost over, and we hadn't even started talking about the campaign ad. And since we were supposed to shoot it after school, we had to get moving.

"We have to decide what we're doing for the video—"

"Way ahead of you!" she said, shoving her phone in my face. "I got inspired last night, so I took a stab at writing a script. I'm calling it 'A Better Tomorrow.'" She extended her hand upward as she said this, as though she were looking at an imagined "better tomorrow."

I took her phone and gave it a generous read. I really, really wanted to like it. I wanted to prove that I wasn't a control freak who has to do everything herself. But right away, I knew this ad wouldn't work. It was cheesy. And overly earnest. It included the bland yet confusing line, "Change for tomorrow, today," and *two* quotes by Archbishop Desmond Tutu. If Melanie were running a real campaign, like in the real world, this script *might* convince people to vote for her. But this wasn't the real world. It was high school. This aspirational message would most certainly be tuned out by 99 percent of the Roosevelt student body. Clearly my face was revealing my inner thoughts, because Melanie said, "You hate it. Don't you? Either that or you're having the world's worst cramps." She shyly took back her phone.

"I don't hate it. I just . . . I'm having a hard time believing this is going to change people's minds," I said, trying to be diplomatic while also reminding her that she was behind.

"I think it will," she countered. "It's inspiring. We'll have swelling music. Like Aaron Sorkin made it."

"So it's going to be two white guys talking really fast?" I asked.

Melanie winced. "Well, what do you suggest, then? Because I worked really hard on this and I haven't heard you come up with any ideas!"

I stood up like I had something profound to say, but alas, I did not. She was right. I didn't have a better idea for what the campaign video should be. I had been so overwhelmed with Shep that I honestly hadn't thought about it at all until just now.

"You're right. I don't have a better idea," I finally said, before sitting back down. "But I feel like I should be honest with you. And my honest opinion is that your ad won't work. Not in the way we want it to."

I picked up her phone and pulled up Instagram. "Look at the people who go to our school. The question we have to ask ourselves is, how are we going to appeal to Christine Lee and Ray Evans and . . . Harriet Boyle in a one-minute video? People from all these different groups. And different interests. I mean, how?" I asked.

Melanie took her phone back and scrolled through her grid as she said, "I don't know. They have nothing in common! Except for the fact that they all . . ." She trailed off as she continued to scan her feed.

"What?" I asked, craning my neck so I could see her phone. But her feed looked completely standard: selfies and food pics.

"Okay. What do teenagers, or what does *anybody*, always like to see? I mean, what's the one universal thing every person wants to see when they go online?" Melanie asked excitedly. I was stumped.

"Cats? Celebrities getting canceled?"

"Themselves! People love seeing themselves. If the *North Webster Gazette* did a story on you, wouldn't you go online and read it? Just to see your name in print?" She made a good point. The *North Webster Gazette* did do a story on me after the whole RB thing. And it is the only article in the *North Webster Gazette* that I have ever read. "So why don't we make the ad about everyone? We'll go around, interview people about why they're going to vote for me. And then we'll make, like, a supercut of all the best answers!"

It was a brilliant idea. I could see it instantly. I jumped out of my chair, adding, "And some of them could be funny. Or weird. And some of them could be heartfelt! We could have teachers in the middle being like, 'I can't vote!'" Suddenly we were talking over one another, adding to each other's ideas. This video would be the perfect way to contrast Melanie with P-Boy. While P-Boy's ad would likely be all about him,[64] Melanie's would be about all of us! Inclusivity! I was thrilled. And honestly a little jealous I hadn't thought of it.

· · ·

---

64 Probably peeing on something!

WE MET UP TO SHOOT THE AD AT THE END OF EIGHTH PERIOD. I took the two tiny lav mics out of their box and fastened one to Melanie's shirt (according to my dad's overly detailed instructions). Then we roamed the halls like two guerilla filmmakers, grabbing random people after school as everyone left for the buses. We shot it on our iPhones. Most of our subjects were caught off guard, so they ended up giving us fun, off-the-cuff responses. Jenji Hopp gave a really sweet anecdote about a time when she and Melanie were in Girl Scouts together. Kelsey Hoffman went on a bizarre rant that had so many obscenities I didn't think we could use it. I interviewed a cute freshman couple who said they'd gladly make their relationship a thruple for Melanie.[65] I was sure that we'd have a lot to work with.

As we were wrapping up, I got several texts from Avery asking if I wanted to come over and "hang." This seemed like a blatant attempt to continue our interrupted make-out sesh. Which I was not opposed to. But I'd promised Melanie I would bring the footage to my dad. I told Avery this, but he *insisted* that I come over anyway.

> **AVERY:** I want to see what you shot!

So I gave in and asked Melanie to drop me off at his house. But when I got there, I began to realize that his invitation was not actually a subtle pretense for making out. He really did want to watch all of the raw footage, even the outtakes, because "You never know where you might find gold."

---

65 Flattering. But not at all an appropriate response to the question I asked: "What grade are you in?"

Apparently, Avery had gotten really into editing since rejoin-
ing Film Club. He even volunteered to edit promotional videos
for Trees for Frees. He said he likes the headspace he gets in
when he edits. (Meanwhile, the only headspace editing puts me
in is boredom.) "This is really good cinematography," he said as
we sat at his kitchen island. "See all those low angles? You're
making Melanie seem larger than life."

I was pretty sure he was full of shit, but he kept insisting that
I had great "composition."[66] So I just shrugged and said, "Maybe
I'm a natural?"

Avery assured me I was, before turning back to the footage.
And for some reason my mind wandered back to Shep's illicit
photos. I thought about their "composition," and how it was a
bit odd. I mean, for a webcam, they looked like they were taken
from high above. Like on the wall. Which made me think, maybe
it wasn't a webcam? Maybe the video was taken with a pinhole
camera. Anyone could buy one; you can get them on Amazon.
But who would put a pinhole camera in a hotel room? A random
pervert? A private investigator? The NSA?

In a burst, the door from the garage swung open and Marion
came in, holding some dry cleaning.[67] "Avery? I'm just dropping
these off, but I have to turn right around and— Oh. Hi, Margot!"
Marion said. "I didn't realize we had company!"

I did a mental check of how I was dressed (fine, but not

---

66 Oh god. If my dad finds out Avery's a film nerd now, into "cinematography"
and "composition," I'll never get a moment alone with him.

67 Not from Elite Organic Dry Cleaners. But I'm not going to dignify our com-
petition by repeating their name here.

Marion-glamorous), if I'd washed my hair (I had!), and whether I had anything in my teeth (my tongue said no, but who can say for sure?).

"Hi, Mrs. Green! It's great to see you again!" I said, probably sounding much too eager.

"Avery, why are you bringing people into our *very* messy kitchen?" Marion said, poking Avery in the arm for not cleaning up. (For the record, there was one cup in the sink. It was cleaner than my kitchen has ever been.)

"We're just doing a school project," Avery said reluctantly. "Everything doesn't have to be perfect all the time."

It was clear there was some tension between them. Marion waited for a moment before saying, "Well, I have to go to another fundraiser for your father. Feel free to have anything in the fridge. But nothing from the liquor cabinet! Last thing Shep needs is a story about drunken teens gone wild in his house!"

"Wouldn't want to do anything to mess up the campaign." Avery smiled somewhat passive-aggressively.

Marion nodded. "Right," she said firmly, before closing the door softly behind her.

Marion left me completely in awe. Here she was, going through a secret divorce, in a miserable marriage (with a son who refused to immediately wash his dirty cup!), and you really would have no idea. She looked amazing. She must be compartmentalizing everything all the time. Was she even mad about the affair? Well, probably. How could she not be? He cheated on her. But I'm guessing Marion's not the type to smash windshields. Or burn all of Shep's suits. She's too put-together and practical.

My guess is that Marion would get definitive, ironclad proof that Shep was cheating on her. Something she could then bring to the best divorce lawyer money could buy . . .

Ohmygodfuck. Marion took the pictures. Or she hired someone who did. I was sure of it. Now all I needed was proof.

CHAPTER 13

PROPAGANDA

After Marion left, Avery finished watching and labeling the footage, before uploading it to the cloud so my dad could access it. Then he turned to me and said the ever-popular pre-make-out line of "Uh, so do you want to watch something? In the den?"

No. But I wouldn't mind doing something else in the den, I thought. I was so close to him, I was breathing his air. This was what I had wanted since last year's prom. Finally, Avery had forgiven me. Finally, I wasn't getting in my own way. Finally, we were alone together, in a house! With a den, no less!

And yet, all my stubborn brain could think about was Marion. Wondering if she took the pictures of Shep. Or hired the person who took them. Avery sensed my distraction. But I think he read it as discomfort, because he said, "We don't have to, if you don't want. We can just hang in the kitchen?"

I *was* comfortable though! And I would be even more

comfortable with his tongue in my mouth! In the den! But I just could not stop my mind from racing. No matter how much my body was aching for Avery. So I said, "There's no way I could just copy your mom's hard drive real quick? Then we could head over to the den to . . . 'watch something'?"

Avery's brow crinkled, the classic sign of confusion and disapproval.

"Um. I'd rather you didn't?"

I took a step away from him. "Totally. Makes sense." This was followed by awkward silence. I assume because Avery was expecting me to explain myself. Which I didn't know how to do.

"There's no way you could just forget I said anything and we could go back to the den?" I asked, then made my eyebrows do that silly "hubba-hubba" thing. Avery was not charmed.

"Okay, look, Priya told me that your mom doesn't know anything about the blackmailing email." I went on, "But it's at least *possible* that your mom paid someone to record your dad. If she suspected he was cheating, wouldn't it be natural for her to want proof?"

"Margot—" Avery said before I cut him off.

"I'm not saying she's the blackmailer. She'd be as embarrassed as anyone if those screenshots got out. But if she made that video, and then someone else got to it and leaked the screenshots . . ."

Avery just looked at the clock on his stove.

"Maybe you could ask her?" I suggested. "I'm sure she would tell you the truth. And if she says yes, then I need to know—"

"Yeah . . . I'm not gonna do that," Avery cut me off. "If I tell my mom, she'll be furious. And then I'll be in the middle of yet another fight. And I'm just not doing that anymore."

"Yeah. I get that," I said, allowing my gaze to rest on the stove clock as well. "But look, if her computer is clean, that would be good to know! I could cross her off my list."

Avery didn't respond to me. Instead, he stood up and left the room. I called after him, "But I also understand that what I'm asking is a violation . . ." I trailed off, running my hands through my hair. I couldn't believe I was doing this again, and to Avery.

But then Avery returned a few moments later with a MacBook.

"Look, Avery," I said, before he could say anything. "I don't want to violate your mom's privacy. *Or* lie to you anymore."

He pushed the laptop over to me and opened it up, revealing a neat desktop with a wallpaper image of him and Marion hugging. "Just tell me what I'm looking for," he said.

"Are you sure?" I asked.

Avery sighed. "This way I at least have some control over the situation."

IT DIDN'T TAKE LONG BEFORE WE FOUND SEVERAL EMAILS FROM A private investigator named Tamika Cole. From their few exchanges, it appeared that Marion hired Tamika to follow Shep starting in early April. Then later, when Tamika mentioned that she had proof of the affair and asked when Marion would like to see it, Marion responded with **Let's discuss over phone**. Which was the last time they corresponded via email.

Avery shut the laptop, then slumped in his chair. "Well. There you go. She hired a PI. Does that help?"

"It does. Yeah. I mean, I still need to find out what this Tamika person did with the photos. But . . . this is progress."

"Do you think it's even remotely possible that my mom blackmailed my dad?" Avery asked, staring down at the table, his head resting in his hands.

"Honestly? No," I said. "Why? Do you?"

He shook his head. "No. She really does want him to win. That's about the only thing she likes about him right now: what his campaign stands for. His policies. Everything else about him . . . not a fan."

I nodded. He looked so drained. Maybe his therapist was right. Maybe I was bad for him.

"I'm sorry, Avery. I promise this is the last time I'll ask you to do something like this."

"Sure you don't want to look at *my* laptop?" he teased. "Maybe I'm the blackmailer."

I smiled, then quickly gave him a hug. It was nice he was trying to be upbeat about it, but I could tell the whole thing made him miserable.

HAVING SUCCESSFULLY DEBONERED MY HOT BOYFRIEND FOR THE second night in a row, I left soon after. With Avery—of course— offering me a ride home.

Meanwhile, my dad had texted me several times saying he was ready to edit then got the files and starting without you

#roughcut #spliceupyourlife. By the time Avery dropped me off, he had his cut ready to show me.

"Your boyfriend organized all the footage for me!" my dad proclaimed the second I walked through the door. "He's a catch! I feel like I'm working with Thelma Schoonmaker!"

"Great. I'll be sure to tell him," I deadpanned, hoping to move on from the words "boyfriend" and "catch" and whoever the hell "Thelma Schoonmaker" was.

"You never told me he was into movies. I knew he liked basketball, but film too?" My dad swooned. "What a dreamboat!"

"I have no idea how he feels about movies," I lied. Obviously he's becoming a total doc jock.[68] "And I'm not going to ask him. He's my boyfriend, not yours. Now show me your damn cut so I can rip it to shreds."

My dad surrendered and pulled up his "rough cut," which is apparently an "industry term" real editors use. (He said Avery would know what he was talking about. I told him to shut up.) And to my surprise, his first attempt was actually pretty good. It was fast and funny, and he'd included most of the responses I would've wanted. And to my even greater surprise, he was incredibly easy to work with. When I asked him to add that freshman "thruple" couple, he didn't blink. And when I asked him to cut out the intro he clearly spent lots of time on, he just nodded and said, "You're the boss."

I expected him to dadsplain editing to me for two hours, but he actually did the opposite. "It's up to you and Melanie. I'm

---

68 A boy who loves documentaries. Is *that* something?

just the meat grinder." Getting to work on a short movie with his daughter seemed to be reward enough for him.

I sent the ad to Melanie around midnight, and she was thrilled with the cut. She had a few minor notes, which my dad could easily implement in the morning. I was relieved that Melanie and I were on the same page. And this sounds cheesy, but it was honestly pretty fulfilling to make something with another person. I was ready to call it a night, but I wanted to check in with Avery one more time. Just to make sure he was doing okay.

> **MARGOT:** I'm sorry again about tonight. I really just wanted to hang with you.

> **MARGOT:** I promise I won't make you spy on your mom every time you invite me over.

> **AVERY:** It's okay. I knew the risks of dating *the* Margot Mertz. It's what I signed up for.

I knew he was making a joke. And I was glad he was joking, rather than calling me out for being the flawed, work-obsessed harpy that I often was. But still, it hurt a little. No wonder I hadn't had a boyfriend until Avery. I'd be terrified to date me too.

I felt a little better when he texted:

> **AVERY:** Can I drive you to school tomorrow?

THE NEXT MORNING AVERY SHOWED UP IN HIS SPOTLESS TESLA at seven fifteen. He brought coffee and bagels from BlueMonday (which is where rich people get bagels. They're four dollars a freaking bagel! And they're *so* good). I was worried he'd be depressed, or maybe mad. But he seemed happy to see me. We talked about the edit. I relayed my dad's compliments, and Avery said, "Really?! He called me Thelma Schoonmaker? Margot, that's, like, a huge compliment! She edited all of—" and I told him to please god stop. He laughed. I laughed. I made a mental note not to bring up his parents again. The less we talked about them, the better our relationship would be.

As soon as Avery pulled into the parking lot, I leapt out of the car and hightailed it to the AV room where they did the morning announcements. But as I weaved my way through the crowded hall, trying my best not to run into anyone, random thoughts about Shep's case kept overtaking me. *Avery's mom hired a PI.* And *Shep had no idea.* And *Why is Avery living in a soap opera?* I would need to track down this Tamika Cole person as soon as possible. She must be able to tell me something about the screenshots. It took me full-on slamming into Danny Pasternak[69] to realize I needed to focus on my current problem: getting Melanie's commercial to the morning announcements.

Announcements were done by a different student each month. And this month it was Jenji Hopp's stint as anchorperson. I hadn't seen too much of her this year, but she had been doing some truly impressive outreach with HAH. They even got on the local news for saving an animal shelter in Brighton.[70] I

---

69 Lucky for me, Danny just said, "Whoa."

70 HAH (or High Schoolers Against Homelessness)'s outreach now includes animal welfare. And education on how to recycle plastics. And social justice. Their mission statement is a bit of a mess, but all the things they support are very admirable.

gave Melanie's ad to Justin Chen, who ran the tech. Justin took my flash drive and put it next to a smaller one labeled PETER. I asked Jenji if she'd seen Peter's.

"Yeah," she said, rolling her eyes. "It's very . . . Peter."

"I thought it was dope," Justin chimed in. "I mean. It's not his best. But it's pretty good!"

I said nothing, but arched an eyebrow, which I felt said volumes. Justin lowered his head and got to uploading Melanie's commercial.

On the way to homeroom, I got a text from Melanie.

> **MELANIE:** I know this is just a weird ad that no one cares about but I AM NERVOUS!

> **MELANIE:** Might throw up before. Or After. Or during?

Couldn't say I blamed her. I was nervous too, and I wasn't even in the ad. Abby, who was also on the thread, responded:

> **ABBY:** GO MEL! You got this! CIRCUS CIRCUS

> **MELANIE:** THREE RING CIRCUS!

> **ABBY:** THREE RING CIRCUS! YES! EXACTLY!

I had no idea what this meant. I'm guessing inside joke. So I ignored.

> **MARGOT:** It's gonna kill!

> **MARGOT:** And if you vom who cares? Isn't that like good luck?

I put my bag down on my chair in homeroom, then loitered around the back of the room. I wanted a good vantage to see everyone's responses to the video. The bell rang, and Ms. Okado told everyone to quiet down for the morning announcements. Students shuffled, moaned, whispered to each other. A day like any other, but to me, it felt like a Broadway debut. My heart was thumping as Jenji's face appeared on the flat-screen.

"Hello, Roosevelt High! Today is Tuesday, October twelfth, and before we start your announcements, we have two campaign ads to show you! This week is propaganda week, so each day we are showing you campaign ads from the candidates running for student government. Today we're viewing ads by the two students running for president."

With that, Melanie's ad played. It opened with Melanie standing in front of the school as classmates walked in and out of the building.

"Hi. I'm Melanie Davis. I'm a senior. I work hard. And I try not to be too much of a dick.[71] And if you vote for me, I'll work hard for you. But don't take my word for it . . ."

Then came the supercut of Rooseveltians. We started with Cory Sayles looking bewildered and saying, "I'm voting for Melanie . . . uh . . . 'cause she's way smarter than me." Next to me in homeroom, Ray Evans pointed at the screen and screamed, "THAT'S MY BOY! WOOO!" Cory was followed by a bunch of

---

71 I suggested she say "not a dick" as opposed to "I'm nice." Has a little more joie de vivre.

popular ninth graders who seemed to love Melanie for no reason; then Coach Powell, saying, "Ah, Jesus. Get that out of my face. Last thing I want is to be a goddamned TikTok!" He then fell out of his chair and onto his butt.[72] That got a big laugh.

As the video continued to play, I saw various students perk up. Many of them pointed out themselves or their friends as they watched. People were laughing and trying to grab screenshots. And in between all the goofy cameos, there were genuine testimonials from people who really believed in Melanie. By the end of the ad, the entire room was engaged, discussing their favorite parts. The commercial worked. As well as we could've hoped. A couple of the kids even clapped. I started typing out a text congratulating Melanie on our triumph. But then P-Boy's commercial played. And my fingers froze.

P-Boy's ad opened with a shot of his face. He was outside. Surrounded by blue sky and clouds, so it was hard to tell exactly where he was. It zoomed out a little and we saw that he was wearing a formal suit. He looked directly into the camera as he said, "Hi, everyone. I'm Peter Bukowski, and I'm running for student body president. But first I need to get something off my chest." P-Boy then ripped off his suit and ran away from the camera, revealing that he was actually on the roof of his house. The camera jogged after him as P-Boy leapt off his roof and into his below-ground pool. His body made a loud *SMACK* as he hit the water, and the whole classroom practically erupted in screams and laughter. The cameraman shouted, "Dude! Are you dead?"

---

72 Sometimes when you sabotage a teacher with no warning, shoving your phone in their face and shouting a question at them, you get gold!

When P-Boy emerged from the water, he shouted back, "I think I landed on my nuts!" All the boys in my homeroom howled, while the girls—some of them tried to laugh along, but the majority just crossed their arms and shrugged.

P-Boy's ad was, as I expected, a little light on policy.

It then cut to P-Boy coming out of the pool in a Speedo. "Anyway, I know a lot of you are mad at me for that dumb thing Chris Heinz did last year. And I get it. It sucked. So to make amends, I offer you this: I will either pay you five dollars or you can slap me in the face. Hard as you want, no judgment. That is my offer to every student at this school. Because, hey! I deserve it!"

This was followed by a montage of P-Boy getting slapped again and again. Scored by a rap song P-Boy composed himself called "Slap! Slap! Slap!"[73] Again, the boys in class ate it up. And again, I was livid.

As soon as the bell rang at the end of homeroom, I marched myself right over to Palmer's office. I found Melanie already waiting there. He let us in, and I lit into him about P-Boy, demanding to know why that video was allowed to play: P-Boy clearly wasn't taking it seriously! He went over his allotted minute! And he was effectively bribing voters!

Principal Palmer gave an audible sigh of annoyance. He and I were not on the greatest of terms. After the Roosevelt Bitches scandal came to light, Principal Palmer was placed under an ethics review and nearly lost his job. But in this case, I think our past was working in my favor. He had a healthy fear of me and

---

73 Despite its title, the song did not slap.

knew I would follow up on what I said. He suggested arranging a time after school to speak with "Peter" so that the issue could be resolved.

"I'd like to resolve it *now*," I said. "*Peter* clearly violated the terms of the election and he should be expelled. But we'll settle for ejected from the campaign. So please do that right now."

Melanie looked a bit horrified at the tone I was taking with our principal.

"Can I say something?" she asked, looking at me. "I am not here to get Peter expelled. But I did have a problem with the video. And I don't think it's right for him to pay people. That's buying votes."

Palmer looked annoyed. He glanced at his phone. Then he made another big, melodramatic sigh as he called into P-Boy's classroom.

MELANIE AND I WAITED OUTSIDE HIS OFFICE WHILE PALMER spoke with P-Boy. I tried to eavesdrop, but all I could hear was the kooky office ladies talking about why gel nails are bad for you. When P-Boy emerged—head down, tissues in hand—it looked like he was . . . crying? Jesus, had Palmer finally grown a backbone and doled out an appropriate punishment?

"I've just had a chat with Mr. Bukowski. And he has given, what I feel is, a sincere and heartfelt apology. Which he would now like to give to you. Peter?" Palmer looked to P-Boy, teeing him up for his, I guess, prerehearsed apology.

When P-Boy turned to us, I could tell that he was actually

sorry. Which, honestly, kind of sucked. I came ready for war. Armor on. I wasn't expecting a little Charlie Brown/puppy. It threw me.

"Fine. Let's hear it," I said.

P-Boy wiped his eyes. Blew his nose one more time before turning to face Melanie and me. "I know you have a reason to hate me, Margot. I know I messed up last year. But I'm telling you, I'm different now. I have nothing to do with Chris Heinz anymore. And all I have wanted to do since all that went down is just, like, help people. And make art. And make people laugh. Which, since I do that on Tok, I thought being president would do it too."

He seemed sincere. Even though what he just said was a grammatical atrocity.

"But every time I try to do the right thing, I screw up. I'm such an idiot and . . . I'm sorry. The video was supposed to be funny. But also, like, a real apology for what I did. And also, like . . . my presidential vision? And the whole five dollar thing. I saw it as a joke and not, like, bribing people. But now I feel like some vote-buying scumbag. It sucks."

He looked at Melanie in the eyes to really drive his last point home.

"Obviously, I'll retract the offer to pay people. I'll cancel everything. And just so you know, Melanie, I think you'd make an awesome president. I really do. And I would, like, love it if you won. So if you think I crossed a line with my video, then I'll drop out."

"Great. He's dropping out. Can we leave now?" I said while making hate-eyes at P-Boy. I was not at all swayed by P-Boy's sincere but utterly vapid and hard-to-follow apology. But Melanie shot me daggers, clearly not appreciating my speaking on her behalf.

"If that's what you want," he went on. "I will. No hard feelings."

"Great. Melanie won. Let's go!"

"No!" Melanie stopped me. "Don't just drop out. I accept your apology, so—you can stay in the race."

Steam blasted out of my ears. "He can stay in the race?! He's a fucking cheater!" I practically shouted.

"Ms. Mertz! That kind of language is unacceptable!" Principal Palmer projected over me. Of course he doesn't mind when P-Boy publicly bribes voters, but when I use a little colorful language, that's when he lays down the hammer! God, he's worthless.

"Margot? Can I speak to you for a moment? In private?" Melanie said, leading me out of the room.

"We'll be right back," I promised. "And then I'm dying to hear more about Peter dropping out!"

Once we stepped out of the office, I whisper-shouted at her. "Melanie, what are you doing? If he drops out of the race, you win by default!"

"Yeah, well, I don't want to win like that," she whisper-shouted back.

"Why not? P-Boy did something wrong. He should be punished!" I pleaded. This was the same guy who traumatized half our school last year with RB. The girls on Fury were *still* in pain from his bad choices. I couldn't figure out why no one was talking about that. "Why are you letting him off the hook? That's what always happens! He does something shitty and doesn't have to pay for what he—"

Melanie threw up her hands. "I can't win that way, Margot. Because then everyone will say it doesn't really count. And I'll just be the bitch who made super-fun Peter drop out! It would make the whole thing suck," she pushed back.

I could kind of see her point. Everyone would probably think of Melanie as a wet blanket and blame her.

"But isn't the point of this to win? Who cares if people don't like you?" I said, raising my voice involuntarily.

"I care. I'm sorry, but I'm not you," Melanie said, shrugging. And with that she pulled away from me and went back into Palmer's office.

I stood there stone-faced as she accepted P-Boy's apology with grace and they shook hands.

"Great. Well now that that's settled, I look forward to your speeches and the final votes. It's been a spirited campaign thus far," Palmer said, adding his typical useless "closure" to an unresolved conflict.

I stormed out of the room. I couldn't stand enabling P-Boy. Giving him a pass just because he showed remorse? And cried? For fuck's sake. If a woman cried, she'd be told to "get it together." But crying boys get *listened to*. And *empathized with*. And their sentences shortened. I was so sick of guys like P-Boy getting the benefit of the doubt. He may have won today, but I was gonna make damn sure he didn't win anything else.

CHAPTER 14

WHO INVESTIGATES THE INVESTIGATORS?

The following morning, I felt a wave of regret. I imagine it's kinda similar to when somebody goes on a bender and wakes up the next morning thinking, *Did I shit in an ice bucket last night?*[74] I had let my enraged feelings get the best of me, and even though it felt momentarily good to yell at P-Boy, it wasn't what Melanie wanted. And I tried to remember that this was her race. It was her name on the posters, not mine.

And even though I should have been prepping for my mission that afternoon—to surveil Tamika Cole at her PI office—I instead sat down for breakfast (which this morning was a cold, semistale bagel I found in the back of the fridge) and texted a nice apology to Melanie. She didn't text back right away, which

---

74 My uncle Richard gave a detailed apology to the housekeeping staff of the Hyatt Regency during his fourth-step apology tour. And he wanted to practice on me first.

was unusual. So I proceeded to text her a bigger apology. Then text her again. And again. Until finally she texted back saying she took so long to respond because she was driving her brother to a dentist appointment and that she was not actually mad. Still, I doubted her. Melanie usually texted back no matter where she was. She said that if it would make me feel better, I could buy her two Grandma's cookies from the vending machine. (Two *packages*, each containing two cookies. Four cookies total, she clarified) and that'd make us golden. I said sure, hoping that this was just her being silly and not that she had residual anger or annoyance.

Once I had promised to purchase the cookies (and more than two packages if she wanted them! She did not), I started texting her about campaign strategy.

> **MARGOT:** Tomorrow Avery's going to do a story about who he's voting for and why. And he's going to make it funny and stuff.

> **MELANIE:** That's amazing! Thanks for hooking up with him just to get him to endorse me! Jkjk

> **MARGOT:** And I'm gonna ask Ainsley today.

> **MELANIE:** How many followers does Avery have again?

I opened Instagram to check (though Melanie easily could've checked herself). And what I saw made my bagel taste worse than the days-old fridge bagel it already was. A picture of Ainsley and Peter. *Together.*

I scrolled. It wasn't just one shitty photo on her Story—of the two of them wearing each other's hats, which is now burned into my retinas—it was also on her grid. They were grid-official or "grid-icial," a word Avery coined but failed to bring into popular usage. I won't describe the pic further, but the caption included the word "bae." It was a gut punch to Melanie's campaign.

I literally spit out my bagel, I was so shocked. My mom, late for work, noticed me for the first time that morning.

"Ew. Margot? Don't spit your food on the kitchen table." Like I meant to. It was an involuntary response to seeing something gross! She grabbed a yogurt out of the fridge. "I can't believe I have to tell you that."

I ignored her and dove back into Insta. The hearts were coming in fast. People seemed to like them as a couple. Including many, many girls. Fuck. If there was one person who could help Peter with female voters, it was Ainsley. I could imagine the thoughts going through people's minds as they voted: *Hmm . . . Peter . . . I heard some bad stuff about him. But how bad could he be? He's dating Ainsley McKibbon! And I love Ainsley, she's so pretty and nice! Maybe he's changed. You know what? I'm voting for him. Fuck you, Margot!*

I sent out frantic texts to Melanie and Avery. This was an emergency, all-hands-on-deck situation.

THEY MET ME AT LUNCH, CONCERNED BY THE NUMBER OF EXCLA-mation points I had used in the texts. I assumed once I showed them Ainsley's posts that they'd join me in freaking the hell out.

They did not seem to think this was a big deal.

"*This* was the emergency?" Avery asked, laughing. "I thought someone was dying!"

Melanie added, "I don't think this is going to make a big difference, Margot. I mean, it would have been nice to get her endorsement. She's very sweet. Plus, she told me she likes bay owls. And you know I love a bay owl girl."[75]

"You two are proving my point. This is why it's a big deal. *Everyone* likes her. She's Teflon-popular and she's going to put P-Boy over the top."

"Margot," Avery said in a tone that told me he was for sure about to gaslight me, "you don't *honestly* think people care who P-Boy's dating, do you?"

I glared at Avery. Oh, to have been popular since the sixth grade.

"Do you know how many people offered me a seat at their table today? Just today?" I said, while gesturing at the noisy cafeteria surrounding me. "Five! From the time I entered the caf to the time I reached this table, five different people asked me if I needed a seat."

"Okay . . ." Melanie looked confused.

"Now. Do you know how many times I was offered a seat in the caf before Avery posted a picture of us on his grid?"

"You mean before we were *grid-icial*," Avery corrected with an impish smirk.

"No. I don't," I assured him. "The answer is zero! *No one*

---

75 If you were curious what a bay owl is, it's an owl with black beady eyes and a face more squirrel than owl. [Shiver.]

ever asked me to sit at their lunch table until we started dating. And now, all of a sudden, I'm freaking avocado toast. Everybody wants me!" I said, taking a big sip from my water bottle.

"So, okay. People like Ainsley," Melanie said. "But it's not like she's as popular as Avery or something."

I nodded in agreement. "Yeah. That's true. It's honestly too bad *you* guys aren't dating. Avery could probably win this thing for you."

I knew the minute I said it that it was a mistake. In one sentence I had demeaned Melanie by suggesting she needed Avery to win, while also pimping out my boyfriend just to win a high school election. Plus, they were just friends, it was weird to ship them to their faces. The table was suddenly thick with awkward tension, and I now understood why no one had asked me to sit at their table before.

"I'm *kidding*!" I said, way too late. "Anyway, I'm sure you two would be a weird couple anyway. Or maybe a great couple? Avery and I are kind of a weird couple, so I don't know!"

"Margot, this is very uncomfortable," Avery said, making a huge understatement. "Do you have a point? Besides that you want us to date?"

"I just want Melanie to win!" I blurted out. "And now—I don't know what to do!"

"We'll figure something out. A different strategy," Melanie said before taking another bite of her sandwich. "I want to win this too. Not enough to date *Avery*, but . . ."

She punched Avery in the arm, and he laughed. I sighed, grateful they were able to laugh off my weirdness. They were both so much nicer and better than me. I hoped that with practice I'd improve at this whole socializing thing. I really didn't want to be the one making things weird all the time.

I TOLD AVERY I COULDN'T HANG WITH HIM AFTER SCHOOL BEcause I had to stalk his mom's private eye. (Which was a very strange thing to say out loud.) I wanted to stake out her office and get a sense of her habits. When she came in. When she left. That sort of thing.

Avery asked if I wanted company. I did, but I knew what would happen if he came along. We'd make out. Furiously and awesomely. And I would not focus on my stakeout.[76]

So I sat alone in the Elite Organics Dry Cleaning van across the street from the office of Tamika Cole, Private Investigator. I had persuaded my dad to allow me use of the van on a *trial* basis, if I promised to pay for any gas I used. (I *suspect* he thought I'd be using it to visit Avery. And I didn't bother to correct this useful assumption.) It was a pretty fair deal. My previous "stakeouts" were usually just me finding reasons to linger in public places, acting like I was lost or on my phone, until I could catch sight of my target. This was cushier. And allowed me more anonymity. No one would notice a dry cleaning van.

While I waited, I decided to do some background research. Tamika Cole was fifty-seven years old, Black, and short, with dark brown skin, freckles, and a series of pretty phenomenal

---

76 Never bring a make-out to a stakeout.

wigs. Her website claimed "Fast Results," "No Funny Business," and a "Deep Abiding Love for Bruce Springsteen, a.k.a. the Boss," which seemed unrelated to private eye-ing.[77] Further internet research told me that Tamika was president of the North Webster branch of the NAACP, vice chair of the League of Women Voters, and held the record for longest ride on the SusieCue's House of Bar-B-Que mechanical bull. She was certainly colorful, and completely upended the straight-white-male-problem-drinker PI stereotype that all noir movies have shoved down my throat.

I got a text from Avery.

> **AVERY:** I can't believe you're doing all this for my dad and I am sitting at home doing homework.

I felt like I had to respond.

> **MARGOT:** You should feel bad! It's very boring!

> **AVERY:** Should I be there though? Helping?

> **MARGOT:** I told you. You would distract me.

> **MARGOT:** Just thinking about you distracts me.

> **AVERY:** Just thinking about you gets me very

> **AVERY:** . . .

> **AVERY:** distracted

---

77 Her website insists it *is* related.

God, he was so hot. I don't know what was hotter. Being with him, or texting about being with him.[78]

A *knock-knock-knock* jolted me from my phone. Tamika Cole was standing at my driver's side window. Eep. I froze. Too shocked to do anything.

"You want to come inside?" she yelled through my window. "I have coffee and a toilet."

"What?" I asked, sincerely confused. "I don't—"

"I've been on enough stakeouts to know. You must want a toilet, honey."

I *did* have to pee. *But how did she know that?*

I got out of the car and followed her, kicking myself. How had I gotten so sloppy? I was texting with Avery when I should have been alert. I was stalking a PI, for Christ's sake!

"How did you know?" I asked her.

"Your van. Elite is on the other side of town. Everybody over here gets their dry cleaning from Rose [sic]."[79]

"Not necessarily. I've made deliveries in this neighborhood," I told her.

"You asked me how I knew. That's what tipped me off," she said unapologetically.

She unlocked a large padlock and led me into her office. It was cozy and looked more like a place where you'd get your palm read than where you'd hire a private eye.

---

78 Okay, it's definitely being with him, but you get my point. It was all pretty hot.

79 "Rose" is not the accurate name of our competitor, but I'll be damned if I'm going to print the actual name here.

"Coffee?" she offered.

"Uh . . . Yes?"

I looked around her office. It wasn't dirty per se, but it was very cluttered. There were pictures of her with clients and tons of tchotchkes. There was a kitchenette teeming with half-full snack bags and boxes. Behind her desk were four framed mug-shots of Tamika at various ages (and in various wigs).

She noticed I was staring at them. "Those are just the glamour ones. I've been arrested *twelve times*," she said proudly. It turned out that Tamika had a tendency to get arrested during protests and social justice marches. She told me all about lying down in the street to protest Guantánamo and taking a knee in the middle of DeWitt Square to protest systemic racism. Tamika was the real deal.

All this made me wonder how Marion had found her in the first place. Marion Briggs-Green was a polished socialite. She belonged to the North Webster Country Club and didn't even do her own grocery shopping. (Something Avery told me in strictest confidence.) I couldn't imagine her hanging out with a woman who brewed Bustelo in a Mr. Coffee and counted among her tchotchkes one of those ducks that bobs for water.

"All right," Tamika said. "Enough about me. Who the hell are you and why are you following me?" She peered at me over her coffee cup with a look that said, *Don't lie to me.*

So I didn't. I told her the higher power's honest truth. All of it. From getting hired by the Green campaign, to being asked by Priya to kill the pictures, to dating Avery, to how I had tracked down Tamika.

When I finished, she was quiet. But instead of addressing my concerns about the photos, the first thing she said was, "Hmm. It's strange that they hired you. *How* old are you?"

"I'll be eighteen in December."

Quiet. "Yeah. If they're hiring you, something isn't right." She bit her lower lip and started tapping her foot on the ground.

"That's a little insulting," I told her. "But okay."

"Sorry. But seventeen is *young*," she said, before taking a sip of coffee.

"Well, just so you know, I started my own business as an image consultant and crisis manager," I told her indignantly. Tamika looked confused. "I clean up internet mistakes. You know, nude pics, embarrassing screenshots. I find them and—"

"That's confusing," she pontificated, like she was giving me notes. "Just tell people you're a *fixer*. People know what that is."

"Okay." I shrugged. I guess everyone has opinions about my job title. "My point is, I'm highly sought after."

Tamika leaned in. "I'm sure you're a great fixer, Margot. But it would've been strange if they hired *me* on a case like this. They should have gone to the police. Or lawyers at least. Hiring you is . . . odd."

"Well, it's a very sensitive matter," I told her. "And they wanted someone they could trust."

She didn't seem convinced. Thankfully, she dropped it and finally said, "Well, that's just my two cents. So! Ms. Fixer. What would you like to ask me?"

Why beat around the bush with a no-bullshit woman like Tamika?

"Look. I know you probably have a confidentiality agreement with all your clients. Marion especially, I imagine. So I get if you're reluctant to talk to me about her," I said, taking a breath before barreling ahead with my pitch. "But it's in both our interests to find who did this. I imagine that if these pictures got leaked to the press, it wouldn't be great for your business."

I hoped this might rattle Tamika a little, but she only gave me the pokeriest of poker faces.

I went on, "Unless, you know, you're actually the one who's blackmailing Shep. In which case . . ."

"You're in trouble. Because I'm about to kill you and bury your body in the woods," Tamika said, with a slight lilt that I *think* meant she was joking? But it was very hard to tell.

"Relax," she finally said. "I'm not going to kill you."

"Great. I didn't think you seemed like the blackmailing type," I added.

"Like you said, blackmailing my client's husband would be very bad for business," Tamika said, walking over to her kitchenette.

"Would you mind if I did a quick scan of your hard drive—"

"I *would* mind, actually," she said, laughing. "But there is something I can give you. I'm pretty sure I know where the pictures were stolen from."

Tamika poured a giant lump of powdered creamer into her coffee, and over the next thirty minutes, she told me how Marion Briggs-Green got in touch with her (via an aunt who had hired Tamika in the past). And how, after Tamika took the photos of Shep, Marion insisted Tamika take them to her divorce attorney for safekeeping. Once Tamika turned them over, that was the last she ever heard from Marion.

"Why did she insist on giving the photos to her lawyers?" I asked.

Tamika returned from her kitchenette with a bag full of popcorn and plopped it on the desk.

"I guess she figured her two-hundred-dollar-an-hour lawyer had better security than I did. Which is bullshit," Tamika said. I reached over to grab a handful of popcorn, but she quickly pulled the bowl away. "I'm not sharing this. This whole bag is only two points, and I need it."[80]

"Oh. Sorry," I said, pulling my hand back.

"I told her I could keep the pictures safe here. There's no reason to send them to a third party. But she said"—in Marion's uptight voice—"*I just think they'd be safer with a lawyer. They have protocols.*"

I nodded.

"I wanted to say, *Bitch! I have protocols!*" She ate a big handful. "But I'm trying not to say the word *bitch* anymore."[81]

"So," I said, drumming on the desk, "you think the lawyer's office leaked the pictures, then?"

"I sure do," Tamika answered. "The minute I went in there, they were looking down their noses at me. But I could tell they had big holes in their security," she said, tossing in another clump

---

80 I was familiar with the antiquated Weight Watchers point system because my dad had tried the diet a few years ago. He ate a ton of popcorn for three months but then got diverticulitis and had to stop.

81 Even though she wasn't sharing her popcorn, I liked her.

of powdered creamer. "I even tried to warn Marion. I told her the office had tons of people moving in and out all day long. And that they asked me to leave the flash drive with the receptionist."

"The *receptionist*?" I shrieked. "No!"

"Yes! When *I* have someone's pictures, I'm like PricewaterhouseCoopers! I would never, ever leave pictures with a receptionist." She looked around her small office. "Not that I have a receptionist."

I leaned back in my creaky chair, playing out various scenarios in my head. "This is going to sound cynical, but . . . you don't think Marion *wanted* the pictures to leak, do you? Like, was this her way of getting them out there? Without doing it herself?"

For the first time, Tamika looked at me with a hint of respect. "Your instincts are not bad. It's worth considering," she said while dusting off her fingers. "But no. I don't think she wanted them to get out. Marion is a snob. The way she dresses, the names she drops. Hell, even the lawyers she hired. Huge waiting room. Everything all glass. Marion Briggs-Green is one of those people who think that expensive equals better. And that outward appearances are everything. And those pictures? They wouldn't make her look great."

Tamika was probably right. But if Marion hadn't done it, who did she think had?

"Do you think the lawyers leaked it?"

"Well, not necessarily on purpose." Tamika casually tapped her fingers on the desk. "But yeah, they're the source of the leak. For sure. My guess is, some shithead that works there either stole the pictures or didn't lock them up properly. And here we are. And there was a lot of other stuff on that drive—call logs, receipts, things like that."

I tapped my pen a few times. What she said made sense. And my gut told me she was trustworthy and careful. Even though she had played coy and acted tough, and even though she hadn't *shared her popcorn*, she had integrity. Which meant my next stop was Marion's high-priced attorney's office to poke around and maybe even get a look at that drive. Woof. I really wanted this to be over.

Tamika looked at me. "I feel bad about the popcorn thing. You want me to make another bag?"

As I was heading home, Avery texted to see if I wanted dinner, suggesting Noodle Town, despite its being "only okay." I said fine, though I would describe it as even less than okay.

> **MARGOT:** I'm starting to think you actually *like* Noodle Town.

> **AVERY:** I like it because we went there.

> **AVERY:** Before.

> **AVERY:** Remember? Last year? When you were using me?

> **MARGOT:** Yes. Yes.

When I got to NT,[82] sure enough, Avery was seated at the same table where we'd eaten six months ago. The first booth on the left. I looked at him sitting there. Handsome, impeccably dressed, eyes studying the menu, probably deciding between two equally awful noodle choices. I had to pinch myself. I had to *assure* myself it was real. He likes you, Margot. And you like him. *More than like* even. L*ve. God, you could tell he was tall even when he was seated.

The Noodle Town vestibule was crowded with people waiting for tables. I told the hostess I could see my party, and I was walking through the foyer to meet him when I almost bumped into Abby Durbin.

"Abby!" I said. "Hey!"

Abby did that thing where instead of making eye contact, you look over the person's shoulder to see who they're with. "Margot . . . hey . . ." She seemed a bit lost.

"I—" I began.

"Are—" she began.

"No, you go," I said.

"Are you here with Mel?" she asked, again looking around.

"Oh, no. I'm meeting Avery," I told her. She seemed surprised.

"Avery? Oh." She spun around to look at the dining room and spotted Avery in his booth, still glued to his menu.

"Is he here with his family or . . . ?"

"No. Just me," I said, wondering why she was so surprised by my being there with Avery. We're not *that* weird as a couple. I

---

82 Noodle Town! It's what the cool kids are calling it these days. JK. No one cool goes to Noodle Town.

decided to make nice. "Hey, listen! Melanie and I are staying after school on Monday to work on her speech. It's not, like, ready or anything. But she said it would be helpful to practice in front of people. You should come!"

God, I wished my parents could see me. Having social engagements, inviting other people to social engagements. I was so goddamned *normal*.

But Abby didn't look interested. "Oh. Yeah, Mel told me about that. Maybe . . . I'm kind of busy though, so . . ."

I nodded okay. But I couldn't help but notice that Abby seemed weird. She kept looking over her shoulder and fidgeting with her Apple Watch. "Well, I just thought I'd let you know. I know you guys are good friends—"

"BEST friends," Abby snapped. "Mel and I are best friends, and I don't really need you to explain our friendship to me. So . . ."

"Whoa. I'm sorry?" I felt bad that I pissed her off. But also, why the hell was she snapping at me? What had I ever done to her? Was she jealous that I was friends with Melanie now?

Her eyes narrowed and she crossed her arms. "You think you're so important because you're working for the Green campaign?"

I momentarily lost my breath. "What? No I don't."

"Well, guess what? I know a lot about campaigns too." She stepped closer to me, her cheeks red with anger. "And what you're doing? Doesn't matter. And no one cares. Okay? So don't think that anyone cares."

Thank god Noodle Town was packed, because Abby was being kind of loud. I shot a glance over at Avery, who didn't seem to notice anything. Where was this *coming* from?

I tried to deescalate. I didn't want to fight and I didn't want to mess things up with her and Melanie. "Abby, I'm sorry if I did something wrong. Me and Melanie—"

"You don't even know Melanie!" she shot back. Then she stopped herself, looking around the restaurant again, seeming to catch her breath. "I have to go. I think they called my table." They had definitely *not* called her table.

I stood there for a moment. Had I done something wrong? Was I really, like, "stealing" Melanie from Abby? Abby never seemed jealous before. Why now? Could this still be residual stress from being on RB?

I sat down with Avery and filled him in on my little adventure with his mom's private eye. But I decided to leave out everything with Abby. It was just too strange and weird. I worried he'd think less of Abby. Or worse, that he'd agree with Abby that I was stealing her best friend. And that he'd think less of me. Which is the last thing I wanted. So instead, I asked him how his day was, and listened as he told me in way too much detail how brilliant the Up! series is, since they'd watched *Seven Up!*[83] in Film Club. And while I still don't care at all about documentaries, his enthusiasm kind of made me want to watch it. His energy was contagious, and soon I forgot all about Abby and my other problems and just enjoyed my middling noodles.

---

83 It's not about the pop. I know. Disappointing.

CHAPTER 15

EYE ON THE PRIZE

When I walked out of the emergency room and into the waiting area, my mom and dad stood up.

"There she is!" my mom said as they both came in for a big hug.

"I'm fine," I reassured them. I looked over their shoulders to see Avery standing sheepishly with a big hospital cookie that said *Get well*.

"You called my parents?" I asked.

"Of course he did! You were in the hospital!" my dad said.

"Yeah . . . I thought they'd want to know . . ." Avery shrugged.

"You did the exact right thing!" my mom told him.

"Well, this is a circus," I told them. "We don't need to make such a big deal out of it."

My mom shushed me and went to confer with Roz, the nurse on duty.

My dad gave me a squeeze. "I'm going to get the car, bug. You stay right here."

"I can walk to the car—" I protested.

"No. You sit. Save your strength."

I turned to Avery. "How bad is it?"

He looked at me and scrunched up his face. "If anyone could pull off this look, it's you. It's very badass."

I looked in the mirror. My new eye patch was not "badass." It was a big, bulky surgical patch that was going to be living on my face for the next three months. Avery was lying.

"It's very *pirate*," I said.

"It suits you."

"It suits me? What does that mean? I had two ugly eyes, and now you only have to look at one of them?"

"No! You have amazing eyes. So amazing that you can pull off an eye patch," Avery said. "It's honestly kind of hot. Like you're an assassin or something."

"Arrrrr," I said. "Well, I hope you also think it's hot when I run into doorframes, because my depth perception is shit."

My mom returned. "Okay, Dad's outside with the car."

So this is how I got here. On the way home from our romantic but tastewise mediocre dinner at Noodle Town, there was construction on Ridge Road. So Avery had opted to take backstreets. He turned down Fulton Lane, a street name I only recognized because it is where Chris Heinz lives. (And I once had to memorize Chris's address in order to hack into his hosting accounts. Once I commit something like that to memory, it's like I can't *forget* it. On my deathbed, I'm sure I will be able to recite

Beth's phone number, all the colors of Joseph's Technicolor dreamcoat, and Chris Heinz's address. And the names of his first three dogs.)

I wasn't sure if Avery knew we were passing Chris's house. And I didn't want to make a whole thing out of it. So I just casually glared at it as we drove by. Chris's house was a big, ugly McMansion among many big, ugly McMansions, all squeezed into lots a little too small for their square footage. His could be distinguished only by a wooden sign that read HEINZ and by the folksy ornamental flint corn hanging above the entry.[84] But as we drove by, I noticed something even more disturbing than the suburban blight that was Chris's house: a red Toyota 4Runner with the custom license plate PPPPBOY.

I made Avery slam on the brakes. *P-Boy was hanging at Chris's. After he claimed he never saw that guy anymore. What a fucking liar!*

I took a picture of the car and sent it to the Fury chat. Avery was ready to drive on, but I was still too pissed. I told him to hold on and got out of the car. (In retrospect, this is roughly the moment that I crossed a few lines.) I crept toward the house, peeking in the front windows. I'd hoped to get definitive photographic proof that P-Boy and Chris were indeed still friends. But I couldn't get a good view into the vaulted living room. So I attempted to climb a drainpipe. And no, I do not have the requisite upper body strength to do that. And yes, I slipped and fell into a hedge of barberry bushes. And *yes*, great question,

---

84 Corn décor is . . . wait for it . . . décorn. Okay. *That's* something.

barberry bushes *do* have thorns. And yes, the thorns did leave me with dozens of minor scratches all over my body, and one *major* scratch, on my cornea, which required immediate medical attention. And now, eye patch.

My parents freaked out when Avery called. They hadn't even changed out of their junky/holey/lounging-around-the-house clothes in their rush to the hospital. But the doctors told them there wouldn't be any lasting damage as long as I wore my patch and came to all my follow-up appointments to monitor for infection. Once they heard that, they relaxed, and then spent the ride home saying things like, "Aaarrren't you glad we came!" and "We should get you a parrot!" etc. Real dad jokes that I'm sad to say my mom participated in. (My mom, who for two years worked as a nurse in an ophthalmologist's office before moving to the hospital, and who I believe would never make jokes like this to an actual visually impaired person, felt perfectly fine making jokes like that to me. Her daughter.) I was not on board.

SO WITH MY ONE GOOD EYE AND THESE HUGE, CUMBERSOME goggles I now have to wear in the shower (like I'm a snorkeling addict who just doesn't know when to stop!), I went about my life. I called the law offices of Forsythe & Mahn and tried to arrange an appointment. They were, as Tamika had warned, pretty snooty, with a phone manner that could only be described as "butt-clenched." They said they wouldn't give me an appointment until Tuesday because "Ms. Forsythe doesn't ordinarily take meetings with children." Unnecessary. But, whatever. What was more annoying was that I was basically in a holding pattern until then. That meant five days where I had nothing to do for Shep's case but wait.

I decided to swing by HQ after school the next day. The election was less than three weeks away, and it had been a while since I was officially on-site. I figured I could help out by doing a more legitimate/less clandestine task like stuffing envelopes. When I entered the office, everyone was celebrating.

"What's going on?" I asked a pale blond intern with stars tattooed on their hands.

"Shep just got booked on Anderson Cooper!" they replied breathlessly.

"Whoa." National media was a pretty big deal. "How did he manage that?"

"Priya found out Anderson was doing something on down-ballot elections and snagged Shep a spot." The intern shook their head. "She called CNN like seventy-five times. She's amazing."

Just then Priya emerged from her office, and the whole place erupted in a chant of "Pri-ya, Pri-ya!" I joined in out of respect, even though chanting is not my thing. Priya laughed and tried to be gracious. Then to my surprise, her eye caught mine in the crowd, and she blanched. I wondered if that was just due to the eye patch, but this seemed like something else. She tried to hide the look of horror spreading across her face as staffer after staffer pushed in to give her a high five or fist bump. Eventually she made her way over to me.

With a big fake smile plastered on her face, she took my

arm. "What are you doing here? And what the hell happened to your eye?" she whispered. When I explained about my eye, and about how I couldn't get an appointment at the law office but still wanted to help the campaign, she said, "Margot, I really just want you focused. The stress of those pics being out there . . . it's weighing on Shep." She took a breath. I wondered if she was going to tell me more. But instead she just walked me back out of HQ the way I'd come in.

"Okay. No big deal," I said. "But can I at least get my paycheck?" It had been about two weeks since I'd started my "new role" at the campaign, and I hadn't been paid yet.

Priya froze. "Right. Uh . . ." She turned us back toward her office. "Come with me."

I couldn't help but roll my eyes. She was acting so weird. She swung open the door to her office and stuffed me inside. "I got you."

Then she opened up her purse and took out a wad of twenties. I stared at her.

"All right. What's going on here? You're paying me out of your purse?"

Priya shook her head. "This is from the campaign. I just have to fill out a form later . . ." She trailed off. What she was saying was so clearly a lie.

"Priya," I said in a tone firm but worried. The kind my mom uses on me when I pull all-nighters. "There's no way the campaign is throwing around petty cash like that. What is going on?"

She sighed, then gave a "fuck it" kind of laugh before saying,

"Um. Okay. What's going on is that . . . Shep doesn't know. About any of this."

I clenched my jaw as I tried to understand exactly what she was telling me. "He doesn't— Sorry. He doesn't know that you hired *me*—"

"He doesn't know about any of it. The email. The threat. I manage his email, and when I saw the one from DropOutShep I just hid it in his junk folder."

My jaw almost dropped, but something about it all started to click. There's no way Shep would have kept a secret like this from Gail. There's no way he would have left it up to Priya to hire someone like me. If Shep had known about it, he'd be managing this himself.

"Right," was all I said, pissed I hadn't caught on sooner. It would've been a *serious* campaign finance violation if she'd paid me, a fixer, to cover up an affair.[85]

"Look, I get that this is news to you. And I'm sorry I didn't tell you. But is anything really different, Margot? You still believe in his platform. And all the stuff he would do if he got elected," she said, picking up her laptop and throwing it in her bag. "And won't the chances of that happening be almost zero if those pictures get out?"

I ran my fingers through my hair, catching a bunch of snarls. "Maybe, but—"

"I can still give you the title of assistant comms director, if that's what you're worried about. And pay you in cash," she said,

---

85 Or not. Some people get off scot-free for doing that and still get elected president LOL God bless America.

throwing up her hands as if this were a no-brainer. "It's from my savings."

This was anything but a no-brainer for me. "I don't like being lied to!" I was forced to say.

Priya looked down at me like I was a petulant child. And I guess I looked like one, compared to her with her perfectly fitted blazer and her manicured nails. "Look, if you're going to quit, quit. I'll find someone else if I have to. But if you still believe in this campaign, then go figure out who sent that email. Find the person who's trying to bring Shep down, or all this work is for nothing."

At first this pissed me off. I was mad at Priya for talking to me like this. At Shep for creating this entire situation. At politics for sucking so much. At the blackmailer. At Chris Heinz and P-Boy. And basically everyone who was making my life so difficult.

But I had to admit Priya wasn't wrong. For Shep to win, they still needed me. Damn it.

I nodded. I had never been on the receiving end of a Priya-tough-love scolding, but it was surprisingly effective. I somehow felt shamed and inspired. How the hell did she do that? "Okay, fine," I finally managed to say, and Priya shoved some cash in my hand. "But no more surprises. I need to know about everything from here on out."

"Deal." She shook my hand, as if ending any other meeting. "I really think you're making the right choice. Shep is going to win this thing. And help a lot of people. And that really matters." For a second she dropped her tough facade, and I got a glimpse of the Priya beneath the comms director spin. Earnest. Hopeful. Fully believing in the mission.

"Congrats on Anderson Cooper," I called over my shoulder as I left.

I debated whether to call Avery with this news. He'd asked me not to update him about the case. But wouldn't he feel better knowing that his dad didn't even know about the email? That he wasn't hiding it from Avery, because Priya hadn't even shown it to him? So I told him. His response: **Great. Now all I have to be mad at my dad for is cheating on my mom. And, you know, being a bad dad.**

EVEN THOUGH I HAD JUST RECOMMITTED TO SHEP'S CASE, AND even though that case remained extremely urgent, there still wasn't much I could do until I could see the tight-asses over at Forsythe & Mahn. So I dove into my other pressing concern: Melanie. Since Ainsley blew up my plan to go after female voters, I had to think of something else. The student government election was only two weeks away. And we needed a big, bold idea to persuade voters.

That night, I pulled up the informal poll I had done a few weeks ago. Then I broke down the results by grade. I was curious to see if the undecided/penis-doodlers were in a higher concentration based on age/class. The results were, in retrospect, pretty obvious.

Freshperson Undecided—58%
Sophomore Undecided—17%
Junior Undecided—14%
Senior Undecided—11%

Of course! Freshpersons![86] They probably didn't know who the hell Melanie or Peter even were! If we could get inside their bubble and tell them that Melanie was great (and P-Boy sucked), we should be able to convince them pretty easily. Hell, when I was a freshperson, I would've done anything anyone asked! I was very lonely!

I texted Melanie my findings, and we started to brainstorm. Should we hound them at lunch? DM them on social? None of these ideas seemed big or cool enough. What we needed was a big group event that was fun. Like an assembly, but less formal. And maybe not even at school.

> **MELANIE:** You realize that what you're describing is a party?

Right. A party. We could throw a party. What freshperson wouldn't be delighted to be invited to an upperclassperson's party?

> **MELANIE:** And you realize that you're dating Avery? Who loves to throw parties?

Right again. Not only did Avery have a big house, but he threw parties fairly often. I'd never actually been to one, but people spoke highly of them. I wondered if he'd consider throwing one on Melanie's behalf.

---

86 Fresh*men* feels a touch patriarchal to my ear. But I don't know if this is *the one*. I experimented with several substitutes: freshpeople, freshhumans, fresh-dividuals, freshfolk, freshfucks. Going with "persons" for now. But I may keep playing.

MARGOT: How would you feel about throwing a party this weekend?

AVERY: Is this Margot? Did someone hack your phone?

I gave him a call, and did my best to explain to Avery that, no, I hadn't been hacked. And yes, I was of sound mind and body, requesting that Avery throw a party. Even though going to parties is my seventh circle of hell.

"Uh. Yeah? Possibly. My parents won't be home this weekend. But, uh . . ." He hesitated. "I was going to ask if you wanted to go see a movie this weekend?"

A movie in a darkened theater with reclining seats and Avery? Yes please. "I mean, that . . . sounds fun too?" I said in a soft voice that I hoped sounded sexy.

"There's this new doc out called *Dead Lie* about this doctor who over-prescribed opioids in the early 2000s. It's supposed to be brutal. But so good."

Okay, my voice must not have been very sexy. "It sounds . . . informative," I offered.

He laughed. "I just thought it would be cool to watch it with someone. Well, with you. But it's not a big deal if you're not into it."

His first instinct was to abandon his thing and act like it didn't matter. But I know he wouldn't have mentioned it unless it was something he really wanted to do. "No! We should totally do your thing. The party was just a thought."

"No reason we can't do both. Party on Saturday, then see *Dead Lie* Sunday," he said, upbeat. "So how many people are you thinking?" Avery asked, likely confused as to how I would find more than two friends to bring.

"Like . . . fifty? Or a hundred? Would you break up with me if I invited a hundred random freshpersons that I don't really know at all?"

Avery paused.

"You can say no!" I squeaked. "I realize I'm being a complete asshole! But it's not just for me! It's for Mel's campaign!"

"So you're being an asshole for *her*," he said.

"I'm the worst girlfriend ever, aren't I?" I tried to explain my plan to woo their lonely, awkward freshperson hearts with the promise of a better tomorrow full of friends and pool parties. "You can still say no! If I'm making you do something you don't want to do, I—"

"Nah. It's cool. Invite whoever you want," he said. Had I somehow forced him? Manipulated him? I hoped not. I hoped this was a genuine, independently-arrived-at yes.

"Are you sure?"

"Yeah. I wanna help out Mel, and you make a good case," he said. "At least I think you do? I like you, so I'm probably compromised."

"I like you too, Avery. Like . . ." Suddenly I was shaking. Jesus, was I going to tell him I l#ved him? *Now?* I hadn't planned for this at all! I hadn't done the pros and cons! But I felt an L-word coming from the back of my throat so I instead said, "L-like a lot. Thank you for this. You're doing me a big favor. So I owe you! But not like a sexual favor. I would never trade sex stuff just because you did something nice for me! Get your head out of the gutter!"

"You're the one who said 'sexual favor.' I never—"

"I know. My point is, you did me a favor. Nonsexual in nature. And I will do something nice for you. Maybe like leave you a note in your locker or something. The end."

There was a long pause on the other end. Until finally Avery said, "I think that was a Margot way of saying thank you. To which I say, you're welcome, ya weirdo."

THE NEXT DAY DURING LUNCH, I ENLISTED THE KELSEYS TO HELP me invite as many freshpersons as possible. After the requisite "What happened to your eye?!" conversation that I now have fifty times a day, they surprised me by being less than enthusiastic.

"Margot, we're not, like . . . automatons you can just pick up whenever you need help," Hoffman said, while biting into a banana. "You never call us unless you need something."

Chugg piped up a bit cautiously, "And then you always expect us to be together. Which we're not really anymore."

Hoffman looked taken aback, clearly registering the hard feelings. But she didn't respond.

"That's fair. Sorry. I shouldn't expect you to just drop everything when I summon you," I said, before grabbing both of their hands. "But hear me out. I'm trying to stop P-Boy from becoming our student body president. I figured you would want to help, given . . . everything."

The Kelseys nodded. They may have been annoyed at me, but they utterly loathed P-Boy.

But I knew I had to give them more. Because they weren't

my minions. They were my friends. So I told them, "Going forward, I promise to be a better friend. How can I support you? Name it, and I will do it."

They looked at one another, not sure if they could trust me. But then they caved. Hoffman asked if I would go to her girlfriend's birthday party at a bowling alley (I do not like bowling,[87] but there are worse things), while Chugg made me promise to attend opening night of *Saleswomyn* (like that!). But, lucky for me, I now had a BF who I could drag to these things. Who, knowing him, would probably be excited to go.

Fragile truce brokered, the Kelseys helped me fan out across the cafeteria and invite all sorts of random freshpersons to Avery's party. Robot Club kids. Techies. Stoners. Animal Appreciation Club (which seemed to be overly focused on playing Tails of Time[88]). Thanks to the Kelseys, word spread quickly that Avery was throwing a big, raging, no-parents-at-home pool party. Now all we had to do was throw the damn thing.

ON SATURDAY, MELANIE AND I WENT OVER TO AVERY'S HOUSE TO help with party prep. We brought plates, cups, drinks, snacks, and trash bags. She wore heels, which made her height even more striking, and a dress that—besides the little owls on the collar—was pretty normal. Melanie and I asked Avery not to supply any booze for the party. Which I know sounds weird, but we

---

87 OTHER PEOPLE'S SHOES!!!

88 Tails of Time is a magic/strategy card game with sexy cats. I would argue that no one who plays it comes out a winner.

decided that plying froshies with booze would be no better than what P-Boy had done. So Avery ordered pizza from Carbone's and agreed to be a bad host and make the party a BYOB affair. (Because he is the damn nicest/coolest boyfriend ever.) Then he gave the pool a thorough skimming[89] before people arrived promptly at eight p.m. Because of course nearly every freshperson, ever bored and lonely, showed up *right* at eight p.m. Just like my aunt Sarah.

The party itself was not as awkward as I feared. Well, that's not true, the first forty-five minutes were awkward as hell. People came with their friends and talked only to the people they knew in small, three-to-four-person clumps. I pulled Avery aside to apologize.

"I'm sorry. This is the weirdest party ever. I never should've made you invite all these randos."

He laughed and said, "Everybody just needs to settle in." Then he kissed me a very casual bf-kiss and said, "Hey, can you hold my phone for me for a sec?"

I was momentarily dazed from touching his lips, an effect that didn't seem to be wearing down the more I did it, but I managed to say yes. When I came to, I saw that Avery had climbed onto a tiny ridge at the edge of the infinity pool. He shouted, "HEY! HEY!!!"

The second he spoke, all the outside lights went out, except for the ones in the pool. Everyone was suddenly illuminated by a

---

89 I never really understood the whole "pool boy" fantasy. I figured it was just for cougar divorcees and trophy wives. That was until I saw Avery skim a pool. And now I get it. I really get it.

blue, shimmering glow. Avery, silhouetted by the pool, now had everyone's attention. "I just wanted to say, thanks for coming. Everybody looks great. And look, I don't care *how* you do it. You can change into a bathing suit if you want. You can strip down. Or you can do like me. It really doesn't matter. All I'm saying is this: THE LAST ONE IN THE POOL MUST GO HOME!"

And with that, he jumped off the ridge and into the pool with all of his clothes on. Everyone just stood there for a moment, dazed by his confident splash. And then one by one, every single damn person at this party started jumping into the pool. And thank god it was heated, because it was freezing out. Most jumped in with their clothes fully on. Everyone was shrieking. If he'd had any close neighbors, we for sure would've gotten a noise complaint. (But of course he had two and a quarter acres, because rich.)

By nine p.m., the pizzas were cold and some ninety or so people were crammed into Avery's pool. You couldn't really *swim*, everyone was packed in so close together. And yes, I got in too. I had to strap on my ridiculous medical goggles first, but I did it. I had to. I didn't want to go home! The last person in turned out to be Cory Sayles, who had been "in the bathroom" (read: shotgunning beers in his car), but instead of making him leave, Avery made him appeal to the "party gods" by performing a song-and-dance routine from his favorite musical. Cory shocked us all by singing "Younger Than Springtime" from *South Pacific*. It was terrible.[90] But he did know all the lyrics by heart and really committed, so was allowed to stay.

---

90 And *not* a dance number!

In the pool, the social divides all went away. Groups started intermingling. There was ample splashing. It was like everyone was in elementary school again. Happy to be floating and playing Marco Polo.

"How did you know everyone would get in the pool?" I asked when I finally floated close enough to him. Avery shrugged.

"It's just one of those things. Everyone likes pools." Simple. Yet seemingly true. I draped my arms around him and looked into his eyes. They were so warm. So deep. Of course everyone jumped when he said jump. I certainly did.

AROUND TEN P.M., JUNIORS AND SENIORS (AVERY'S ACTUAL friends) started to arrive. Kim Carpenter and Anthony Capuzzi from jazz band. Tara Good and Maria McConville from Photography Club. And of course all his soccer bros (Traydon Reed, Craig Layton, etc.) and all their girlfriends (Tiffany Sparks, Megan Mills, you get the idea, they all had girlfriends). The upperclassfolk were all a little cold to me. They probably knew I had nixed the idea of Avery buying all the booze. And that put a cramp in their night of debauchery and drunken soccer-ball juggling. What made it worse was that I was feeling a strong urge to make them like me. I was hearing the voice of a 1950s housewife inside my head: *A good girlfriend must make sure her boyfriend's friends like her.* I told the voice to shut up, as it wasn't helpful. But I had a hard time tuning her out.

"Come on in! Everybody's in the pool! The last one in the pool had to— Never mind. You had to be there. Avery did a thing,"

I said to the cool kids as they mostly ignored me. Some of the soccer girlfriends took pity on me and asked me to join their selfie.[91] And after snapping the photo, Alli Pough said, "I *love* your shirt," which everyone knows is girl code for "I'm not sure I hate you anymore." The 1950s housewife within me was thrilled. *Honey, your friends loved me! No crying into my aspic tonight!*

As the cool kids fanned out across the party, I ducked into the kitchen to take a break from being so *social*. I went straight for the fridge, which was, as rumored, stocked with every flavor of LaCroix, even some I'd never heard of. (Spicy coconut? What?) I stood there mesmerized for a moment, then Navion Wilson came in from the patio, followed by a group of freshman dudes. Navion was a Black junior, and the best pitcher Roosevelt's baseball team had ever had. He was popular, and it wasn't unusual to see him surrounded by a bunch of fans. But today he and his froshbros weren't talking about baseball.

"Tasha Ahmadi?" one of them asked.

"Yes," Navion responded.

The group exploded. "Aw!" "Shit!" "No way," etc. Apparently, none of them saw me behind the fridge door.

"Megan Mills?" asked another eager bro.

"Yup. She was on it too! *Very* on it."

"FUCK!" The group exploded again.

"Both boobs. Plus butt," Navion clarified. "That's a triple threat."

My skin crawled. I realized that they were talking about

---

91 Goggles and all!

girls who had appeared on RB. But with nostalgia. Like RB was a favorite canceled TV show they were hoping Netflix would revive.[92]

"Dude, I can't believe I was in eighth grade when that went down! How did Taft Middle miss it?" a freshman with a rat face asked sadly.

"I feel for you," Navion said. "I mean it was wrong. It was. But also . . . so right?" He weighed his hands like scales. The boys laughed. I guess anywhere can be a locker room if you don't respect women!

"I can't believe Peter did that. That guy's a stone-cold legend," Ratface said with reverence.

"Yeah," echoed Zits.

P-Boy was a legend? I wanted to scream at the world. I wanted to hurl pop cans at them. But I managed a little self-control. I couldn't murder a bunch of people at my boyfriend's pool party. That seemed tacky. So instead, I slammed the fridge door shut, causing the freshboys to jump.

"What happened to your eye?" Ratface squealed.

"I ran over a freshman, and his blood got in my eye," I said back. They looked terrified, except for Navion, who groaned.

"Are you going to put me on a billboard again, Margot?"

"I don't know. Maybe?" I turned to the other guys. "Tell you what, why don't you all show me your dicks? Just so I can take a quick pic? Come on! Do it and I won't ruin your lives? Whip 'em out. Let's go."

---

92 And Netflix probably would. Those bastards greenlight everything!

They were frozen.

"No? You don't want to? Hmm. Okay. I guess I won't *force* you. You're in charge of your own bodies and *I* respect that. *So how 'bout you fucks try and do the same*?" I turned and stormed out of the kitchen.

I needed some air. Outside by the firepit, I spotted the Kelseys talking to Tasha Ahmadi. I considered venting to them about what I'd just heard, since they were all on the site, but I figured it might be too triggering. And besides, once I approached, I realized they were having their own venting sesh.

"—piece of garbage like that. Because you know every time I have to look at it, my soul dies a little," Chugg was saying. Then, acknowledging me, "Did *you* know that Chris Heinz is on the Wall of Fame?"

The Wall of Fame, like the Board, is not something I've spent a lot of time looking at. It's mostly full of dudes who did sports things.[93]

"For what? Being an asshole?"

"It's so fucked up!" Tasha chimed in. "Like, how has no one taken it down?"

Hoffman poked the fire with a stick. "I wrote 'predator' over his face in Sharpie a couple days ago. Because I just couldn't stand looking at it anymore. But someone came and cleaned it."

That was pretty messed up. Keeping it up there was one thing. But maintaining it? And cleaning it when it got defaced?

---

93 Despite the fact that our school's alumni include scientists, doctors, a Tᵣ Award–winning actor, and a veteran who saved three children from dr⸍ ing. But please, let's celebrate the ball-throwers!

That took some effort on Palmer's part. Why was the school continuing to celebrate someone who should be a registered sex offender?

"We're gonna start a petition on Monday," Hoffman jumped in. "I'm messaging Fury right now. If Palmer doesn't agree to take down his fucking plaque, we're gonna blow up his office. Or kidnap his kid or something."

We all agreed that *that* was probably not the right way to go about it, but we felt we should do *something*. As we started to brainstorm, I clocked Navion making out with his girlfriend, Missy Reed, in the hot tub. They were draped over each other and she was giggling, completely unaware of all the shitty things Navion had said just moments before. In my mind, assholes like Navion, and Harold Ming, and Chris Heinz, and—I could go on— didn't deserve girlfriends. They should be dying alone, jerking it to free porn. It's times like these I almost consider alcohol.

Instead, I took five *very* deep breaths and found Avery. I did my best to suppress my anger and be a friendly, sociable-ish girlfriend. The least I could do was not ruin the party that I made Avery host. Luckily, I found navigating on his arm to be a hell of a lot easier than doing it solo. Avery had the gift of talking to people for the perfect amount of time. He would ask them how they were doing, talk for a few, then find a reason to move on before it got boring.[94]

It seemed like everyone was having fun, even without booze. (Though plenty of people had brought their own.) The pool

---

94 Without him, I would've been trapped talking to Phoebe Skinner all night as she listed her 375 TikTok followers aloud.

remained a *scene* where people who loved their bodies seemed keen to show them off by stripping down to their underwear. And let's be real, underwear is barely opaque when it gets wet. There were the requisite chicken fights. (Always an abomination.) Some doof had a guitar and was playing it on the patio, and another doof had a guitar by Avery's firepit. Inside the house, music was blasting and couples were trying in vain to grind to completion.[95] And all the fresh-faced freshpersons looked pretty damn happy. So I'd say the party was a success. *Vote for Melanie*, I thought.

EVERYTHING STARTED TO WIND DOWN AROUND MIDNIGHT, WITH most of Avery's friends leaving before then to "go to someone's basement or something." I had told my parents that I'd be staying the night at Melanie's. I didn't know how late the party would be, and I didn't want to cut out early and leave Melanie and Avery with a mess just because my parents now had a "curfew."

I was about to ask Melanie if she was ready to clean up when she abruptly said, "Well, I hate to leave y'all with this, but I have to get up early tomorrow. It's my cousin's birthday, and we have to drive to Poughkeepsie. And I need at least six hours of sleep before a road trip or I get very carsick." As always, it was way more information than necessary. She waved at Avery, who was across the pool picking up cups. "Avery! You are amazing. Thank you for doing this! Prayer hands! Prayer hands!" He gave her a cute wave.

---

95 Honestly, I don't know if it was in vain. Maybe they finished.

"Don't thank me. It's a campaign contribution," he said. "I hope to be awarded with a good ambassadorship if you get elected."

"Will do." She laughed. I would have laughed too, but I was distracted.

I followed Melanie inside the house. "I thought I was sleeping over? Should I leave now too, or . . ."

Melanie looked at me like I was playing a practical joke on her. "Oh. You're serious. No, Margot. Stay here. Help Avery *clean up*. In his empty mansion with no parents." She grabbed her purse from the front hall closet.

"But I told my parents I was staying with you."

"And if they call, I'll lie for you." Melanie turned around before leaving and scolded me, "Jesus, Margot. You are so smart about some things and so clueless about other things."

My mind was spinning. What did *Avery* think was going to happen tonight? Did he think this was all part of my plan? Did he go along with my party request because he knew we'd be *doing it* after? I wasn't on the pill. I didn't bring condoms. And I was pretty sure that I didn't even want to have sex tonight. At least, I didn't think I did. But did *he*? And why was I thinking about sex anyway? Did that mean I was ready? And also, did Melanie just neg me? *Melanie?* Did that mean she was more sexually experienced than I was? Was Melanie now the cool one? *WHAT WAS GOING ON?*

"Haaaaaave fun." We hugged, and Melanie left. As the door clicked shut, it echoed in Avery's grand, cavernous front entrance. The house suddenly felt so much bigger. And my chest so much tighter.

. . .

HERMAN, A SWEET NERD WITH SOME INTENSE ORTHODONTIA
who always stayed too late at parties, finally left at twelve thirty.
I thanked him for coming, then found Avery in the basement,
picking up empty bottles from the wet bar.

"Life finds a way," Avery said.

"What?" I asked, picking up an empty garbage bag to help
him.

"I just think it's funny. People find a way to drink. I didn't put
out booze, but look at all the stuff people brought."

I surveyed the empties. It was quite a cache. And now poor
Avery was tasked with cleaning it up. God. Why do I always do
stuff like this?

"I'm so sorry I forced this on you. Now your house smells
like freshperson BO, and there's trash everywhere and—"

"Whoa, Mertz. Don't apologize. I'm not mad," he said, drain-
ing the dregs of a can into the sink.

"You're not? But what if your parents find out?"

"My dad is doing some fundraiser in Albany. And my mom is
staying at the podiatrist's. They won't be back till Monday. So we
have time to erase all the evidence," he said, tying up a full trash
bag, then reaching over to get a new one.

"Oh. Well . . . great," I said, suddenly hyperaware of how
alone we were.

"Yep. There are perks to having self-obsessed parents who
don't have time for you!" he said, before slinking his arms around
my waist. And suddenly we were holding each other. Looking
into each other's eyes. Or . . . eye, in his case.

"What's wrong? Is my patch crooked? Did it get wet?" I said, readjusting.

"It looks good to me," he said, guiding my face to look at his, such that I *could* look with my injury. "I know you think I'm bullshitting you. But the patch is a turn-on."

"Avery. No."

"It makes no sense!" he said. "And yet . . ." He cupped my face and gently kissed me. I smiled and kissed back. Then he kissed me harder, and the next thing I knew we were on the couch, and I was rethinking some previous comments I'd made regarding my readiness for sex. I climbed on top of him, straddling him as he put his fingers in my hair.

"Is this okay?" he managed to get out between kisses.

"Yes."

Then we were grabbing and fumbling and doing a lot more than just kissing.

WE DIDN'T HAVE SEX. BUT WE DID OTHER STUFF. AND IT WAS *WAY farther* than I'd ever gone before. Like, before this, sexually speaking, I'd only ever gone to the 7-Eleven on the corner near my house. But tonight, suddenly, I'd gone as far as . . . I don't know, Cleveland?[96]

And it was all way different than how I'd imagined. In my fantasy it was all biceps flexing and soft kisses and then, some-how, me having an orgasm. But this—while very fun—was way

---

96 Still in the contiguous US, but pretty far for me! Across state lines!

more awkward. Upstairs petting is all fine and good. Pretty self-explanatory and not too much you can mess up. Particularly on a guy. But downstairs, that was *fraught*. I had no idea what I was doing. Penises are not intuitive. But even with all the awkwardness and all the *Is this okay?*s from both of us, it didn't really matter. Because I was with Avery. Who made me feel safe. And who, the more time I spent with him, was all I wanted.

CHAPTER 16

SAFEKEEPING

The next day, I accompanied Avery to the Little Theater, where we saw *Dead Lie*. Avery found it "inspiring," while I found it "depressingly depressing." Then we went to Target to buy a new phone charger because his was disgusting. And he bought me some grapes (from Target! I know, but they actually looked good). And even though none of this helped Melanie or brought me any closer to Shep's blackmailer, I still felt good. Like it was time well-spent. And that for a few days at least, I was actually being a pretty decent, non-selfish girlfriend.

But by Tuesday I was back to the grind. I arrived at the offices of Forsythe & Mahn fifteen minutes early for my three o' clock appointment so that I'd have plenty of time to observe/surveil. I was meeting with one of the firm's founders, Karen Forsythe, under the guise of profiling her for *The Roosevelt Gazette*. You'd be surprised how often this cover works. People, it turns out, are always eager to talk about themselves, even for a rinky-dink high school rag like the *Gazette*.

I had two goals. One, learn more about the firm's security. Specifically their surveillance cameras and how to break into them. If I could hack them and see the footage, I should be able to tell who took Tamika's drive.

And two, I needed to get that flash drive the hell out of Forsythe & Mahn. Tamika had put the fear of Tamika into me. And I wouldn't feel safe until those pictures were in a more secure location.

The law office was as fancy and glass-forward as Tamika had said. Behind the reception area, I could see what I assumed were various lawyers and paralegals toiling about in the open-format office space. They all looked very tall and stylish, and very much like an ad for J.Crew. And at the corners of the space, large enclosed offices that I could only assume were the domains of "Forsythe" and "Mahn."

When I approached the pretty blond receptionist, she greeted me with the always unpleasant "Can I help you?" simply oozing with disdain. She evidently assumed I didn't belong there, like chocolate chips in an oatmeal cookie. (Get out of there! Raisins or bust!)

I told her I had an appointment.

She scoffed, "With *who*?"

"Karen Forsythe."

She double-scoffed before checking her calendar and seeing that I wasn't lying. She then commanded that I take a seat, refusing to make eye contact with me for the rest of the afternoon.

I waited. The only time she dared speak to me was to inform me that it was a "very busy day" at the office. Even though it did *not* seem that busy.

By three thirty p.m., I was still waiting. There wasn't really much to see. I watched a mail carrier drop off some letters on the desk, which the receptionist very quickly stashed away. Not much to glean. And no sight of a file cabinet or safe where they might have stashed Tamika's drive.

By three forty-five p.m., I was still waiting. And no one was making restaurant-hostess apology eyes to me, as if to say, *I'm sorry this is taking so long, we'll seat you in a second.* But then a suited, brown-skinned law bro stormed into the waiting area. He was followed by a short, white intern-type. The first man called out to the receptionist.

"Casey, I need you to open the safe."

He turned to leave when the mean-to-me receptionist, Casey I guess, responded, "J.B.? Sorry. But I need you to sign the log. And you need a partner to sign too."

J.B. whipped his head up from his phone. Beyond furious that Casey was making him look at her face. "The fuck, Casey?!"

Seeing an opportunity to ingratiate himself, the short intern piled on, "Casey. Come on."

But she held firm, squeaking, "I'm sorry!"

"I don't have time for this shit!" J.B. exclaimed.

Casey wilted. All the snobbery and disdain she had served me were gone. She knew her place in the food chain. She was at the bottom, with only couriers and pesky teens to talk down to.

Now she was all nerves and grovel. "I'm sorry. But Ms. Mahn said only partners can sign things out now."

"Jesus Christ. Why in the world would they make *you* the only person who can open up the safe? You went to *Ithaca*!" He went back to his phone, I assume to like tweets by Tom Brady.

"I'm sorry . . ."

J.B. scoffed. "Eliza Wellman is coming in tomorrow at seven a.m. to sign divorce papers. I spent months negotiating with her prick of an ex-husband to get her engagement ring back, and if you don't have it by the end of the day, I will make your life a living hell! You feel me?"

Casey nodded vigorously as J.B. stormed off and screamed "Fuck!" to no one in particular.

I was starting to feel uneasy about meeting Ms. Forsythe, based on the David Mamet play I'd just witnessed in the lobby. This kind of toxic atmosphere always comes from the top down.

At 3:55, Casey told me that Ms. Forsythe was finally ready to see me. I awkwardly gathered my belongings and followed her through the open-format office, past the J.Crew fall edit, to the corner office on the right. As soon as I entered, Ms. Forsythe stood up to greet me. She was a slight figure, with curly reddish-brown hair tamped down into a tight bun. She wore a visible amount of ivory foundation, which did the thankless work of covering up the age spots.

"Karen Forsythe," she said, lunging forward with a handshake. "You must be Kelly Marshall! Welcome! So! You're doing a story for *The Roosevelt Gazette*. You know, I think Sylvia Mahn's niece goes to Roosevelt! Do you know her?"

"I might. What's her name?" I asked.

"Haha, I have no idea! Allie? Tammy?" She threw out several more random women's names until I regained her attention by kissing her ass.

"It is so amazing to meet you," I said. "Thank you so much for seeing me. I'm such a fan!"

"Well, thank you!" Karen took a seat behind her desk. I followed suit, sitting in one of the two leather chairs in front of her desk. "Believe it or not, this is the first time a student has asked to interview me."

I feigned shock. *"Really?* You were the youngest woman in your graduating class to make partner at a firm! You did George Matriciano and Linda Salvia's divorce!" The Matriciano-Salvias are a wealthy local couple whose ugly divorce was chronicled with excruciating detail on the WNBB five o'clock news.[97] Karen saved George from paying any real damages, even though he cheated on Linda with their son's tutor. *That's* the kind of law she practiced. "You were the first person I thought of to interview. But then, I've always been kind of a law nerd."

Karen leaned back in her chair as she said, "Well, to be honest, George is an old friend, and Linda was a huge bitch. So between you and me, I knew she wouldn't be a very compelling 'victim'!"

"Haha, yeah. I bet!" I smiled. *Linda stood by George throughout his chemo for testicular cancer and now she's left with nothing. But you know, you "won," so good for you.*

---

97 While things like the passing of the school budget and the firing of two police officers for being racist did not get covered at all. WNBB has a real interesting editorial formula for what makes something "newsworthy."

She went on about how she left her previous law firm. (They didn't value her enough!) How she tries to be "a role model to women" by "being extra tough on them." (Yikes.) And all about the firm's most valuable clients, like Marion Briggs-Green and Eliza Wellman, spilling all kinds of tea that must have broken confidentiality rules.

"Eliza's divorce literally bought me my lake house!" she confided with a wink. Karen was having such a fun time that she offered me a drink, maybe forgetting that I was a minor. (I declined her scotch, Karen poured herself a glass.)

Once I felt the vibe was suitably relaxed, I started in with my questions about who ran the firm's security.

"Oh—" Karen seemed taken aback when I asked. "We have a private contractor. It's my nephew, actually."

"Oh really?"

She smiled with aunt-pride as she explained, "He's actually saved us a ton. We used to use AFT, but they were gouging us. Jeremy installed all the cameras himself and now I can— here—" She clicked something on her desktop computer and whipped the monitor around to face me. It was the home screen of a very simple Ring cam setup. The screen was divided into six, with views from the six cameras fanned out across the office. One of these cameras was monitoring the file room, where it looked like the infamous safe was sitting. I found this out later, but apparently it's standard operating procedure for law offices to surveil their own file cabinets at all times. (Who knew?)

Karen laughed to herself. "I can access this whenever I want.

Sometimes I sign in just to make sure the staff is working! We don't pay them to check Twitter!"

"That's so funny!" I said, even though what I thought was, *That's so creepy!*

"Though I'd prefer if that didn't end up in your article!" she added. I assured her it wouldn't end up in the article. (Because there would be no article!)

Karen rambled on about how in law school she got the nickname "the arsonist" for getting so many TAs fired. But I wasn't really listening. I was too busy thinking about how *Ring cameras are notoriously easy to access.* My dad uses one for the dry cleaners, and I'm always begging him to upgrade because they get hacked all the time. It's a *little* harder if people used two-step verification. But honestly, it's still not that hard. I could use Fuzzword or find a Ring Video Config to try logins. It wouldn't take me long.

"So, is it basically just the cameras then? For security?"

"Well . . ." She thought. "Whenever we handle client valuables, we use an *iso-metric* vault,[98] which we keep in the file room, just down the hall there." *Thank you, Kar, now I know the location of the safe.*

"File room," I repeated, pretending to make a note in my "journalism notebook."

"You know . . . no one has ever asked me about the firm's security before." There was a slight tinge of suspicion in her voice.

I pretended not to notice. "Oh well, the article is about the power and responsibility you have as a partner. And a woman.

---

98 She meant biometric, but I wasn't going to stop her.

So I was curious to know how you're involved in all the different aspects of the firm."

Karen nodded knowingly. "I *do*. I do have a lot of power. And it's a lot of responsibility, but that's what I signed up for." She sighed, pleased with herself.

I checked the clock in her office. It read 4:45. In fifteen minutes, the office would close. Crap. All of Karen's humblebragging had made me lose track of time. I knew where the safe was, but I hadn't figured out a way to get into it yet.

I made an excuse to leave, to which Karen replied, "Me too. I'm having drinks at Ja Livy, and you *can* print that. I'll walk you out." She picked up her bag and coat and walked me out of her office. I then asked to use the bathroom, hoping to shake her so I could circle back to the safe.

Once I was in the bathroom, I did a quick mental inventory of what I knew. I knew that the vault was in the file room, twenty feet away. I knew that the safe had video surveillance, but I also knew that I could erase the security footage once I hacked the company's Ring account. The only thing I hadn't figured out was how to get into the biometric vault itself. And without a severed thumb at my disposal, I'd have to rely on the greatest hacking tool in my kit: human error.

And thanks to my forty-five minutes of sitting in the waiting area, I had a pretty good idea of which human's error to exploit. Casey. Underpaid, stressed, and in charge of a security protocol she hadn't quite mastered. Perfect.

I texted Chugg.

MARGOT: I need a favor.

MARGOT: And I know what you're going to say! I only text you when I need something.

CHUGG: Yup that's what I was going to say.

MARGOT: But hear me out because there's a reason I'm asking you. I need your specific expertise and honestly I think you might have fun?

MARGOT: It involves acting.

CHUGG: Fine. What is it?

MARGOT: When I text you, can you call this number and pretend to be an angry divorcee named Eliza Wellman?

CHUGG: Oh! Cool! Okay. Anything I should know about her? Is she bitter? Depressed? Do I need to cry during the call?

Actors always have a lot of questions. I probably should've texted Hoffman.

MARGOT: All you need to know is that the receptionist has your engagement ring, and you are coming to the office in person to pick it up in two minutes.

MARGOT: Try to really scare the shit out of her! My plan won't work if you don't. Be a real monster.

CHUGG: Oooh! Playing against type! How exciting!

I hoped her enthusiasm for acting matched her talent for acting. Otherwise, this wasn't going to work. But I didn't have a better plan.

I made my way slowly to the reception area, pretending to be so immersed in my phone that I forgot to leave the office. Casey, sensing an opportunity to kick a dog, sniped, "Are you having trouble finding the way out?" I looked up from my phone to see Casey's self-satisfied mean smirk. Then she mock-frowned before saying, "It's that way. And unfortunately, we don't validate bus passes."

I was about to say something really cutting when her phone rang. She picked it up, giving me the unnecessary "one minute" finger and without breaking eye contact said, "Forsythe and Mahn."

I heard yelling on the other end of the phone. I couldn't catch it all, but it sounded like an angry, belligerent woman with a Brooklyn accent[99] screaming at the top of her lungs. Casey eventually responded with "Absolutely, Ms. Wellman. I'll have the ring for you tomorrow, first thing—"

More yelling. More Casey fidgeting. Until she said, "Wait. I'm sorry, Ms. Wellman. You're . . . outside?" And then I heard even more yelling. So loud I could distinctly hear, *Get me my ring, or I will strangle you with the handles of my Birkin! They're very strong!*

Casey dropped the phone and scooted past me to the filing room. Chugg's "Ms. Wellman" had put the fear of God into her.[100]

---

99 I didn't ask her to have an accent, but Chugg was making a choice.

100 I was impressed. Maybe Chugg should've been cast as Willa.

I quietly jogged down the hall after her, trying not to draw too much attention to myself. She swung the door to the file room open wide in her haste, and it was still floating to a close by the time I made it there. I caught it with my toe. And then I did a little acting myself.

"I'm so sorry. I know you're busy, but—" I said, pretending to be out of breath.

Casey, who was now bending over the open safe frantically rifling through various clients' valuables, shouted at me, "You're not supposed to be back here! Go! Leave!"

"Sorry, it's just— I was leaving the building and I saw this messed-up-looking truck smash into a car in the parking lot."

"Okay?" Casey said, still rifling.

"It was a black BMW. Parked by the front. I just thought you might want to—"

Casey stood up, petrified. "That's Ms. Mahn's car! Shit! Shit! Shit!" A client's wrath is one thing. But if someone on either side of the ampersand gets mad at you, that's a whole different level of fear.

Casey bolted out of the file room as fast as her three-inch heels would take her. Leaving the safe still ajar as she left.

And that, ladies and gentlemen, is what you call human error.

I pulled the door to the file room shut behind me and bent over the safe. I rifled through a few items before I saw something small enough to be a drive. There it was, in *a sandwich bag,* just hanging around next to someone's deed of ownership and a box of jewelry.

And Eliza Wellman's engagement ring.[101] I took the drive out of the bag and slipped it into my pocket. Then I placed a Vaynera thumb drive into the baggie (Why not? I had ten of the damn things!), zipped it up, and put it back where I found it, closing the safe that turned out to be not-very-safe at all. I cracked the door open to make sure the coast was clear, then discreetly exited through the back stairwell. I managed to avoid Casey, who was still in the parking lot wondering why the BMW didn't seem to be damaged.

On the bus ride to HQ, I felt strange. I was getting the same rush I'd gotten on previous MCYF jobs. My heart was pounding. I was sweating. I was pumped. But I also felt like I needed a shower. Carrying photos of a congressional candidate's affair in my backpack? It felt more than a little shady.

When I got to the office, Priya was in a strategy meeting with Shep. I sent her a text saying I was there, and that I'd wait in her office for her. I was eager to look at the thumb drive to see if it had any clues about who copied the photos.

I closed the door behind me, helped myself to one of her cold brews, and opened up my laptop. When I clicked open the drive, it was full of folders labeled RECEIPTS, STAKEOUT LOGS, TRANSCRIPTS, etc. And to my surprise, there were *two* folders labeled PICTURES. One said APRIL 8TH and the other MAY 30TH. That was strange. I thought all the photos were screenshots from one video. I called Tamika on my cell.

---

101 I wanted to like it. But it was tacky.

"Hi. It's Margot."

"Hello, Margot," Tamika said, dry as ever.

"I just wanted to let you know that I got the drive. So we don't need to worry about any additional leaks coming from the law office," I told her. With a tinge of pride.

"The lawyers just gave it to you?" she asked, confused.

"Well, they didn't exactly *give* it to me," I said, then paused.

"I knew I liked you," Tamika said.

"I just wanted to verify something with you," I said, clicking open the April 8th file. I started scanning through the thumbnails. Each graphic photo, and all the unspeakable positions Shep and Deanna were attempting, appeared before me as we talked. "The pictures that were leaked were from an encounter on April eighth, right? They're screenshots from a video taken by a pinhole camera. But I see another folder here for May thirtieth. So does that mean you followed Shep and Deanna on multiple occasions?"

"Well, I followed him for two months. And I saw him with Deanna Hastings on several occasions. But I only caught them in the act once. In the Marriott. On April eighth," she said, while fumbling for something on her desk. "May thirtieth. I think those were photos from a different liaison. With a different woman."

I froze. Fucking Christ. *Another woman?* How many side-pieces did Shep have?

"Sorry. Another . . . You're saying Shep had affairs with multiple women?" I asked, feeling a lump settling in my throat like it was just going to live there for the rest of my life. I couldn't believe this hadn't come up in our last meeting.

I could hear her creaky desk chair moving, like Tamika was leaning back in her chair as she talked. "I only caught him with the second woman that one time. I was working to identify her, but that's when Marion ended my contract. I guess she and Shep had started therapy, so she didn't want to hear about what I found."

I thanked Tamika and hung up. My mind was reeling. Why had the blackmailer only sent the April eighth pictures? Maybe they were saving the others for the press? Or maybe adulteress number two, the one in the May thirtieth pictures, *was* the blackmailer?

I closed the April eighth folder and moved my cursor to May thirtieth.

There were only about twenty JPEGs. And in thumbnail form, you could see the whole movie play out. Shep and the second woman meet by his car. They talk. Hold hands. Then they kiss. Then they grab each other. And then they're in his back seat. The camera moves to a closer vantage. They're on top of each other. I could tell that the woman was not Deanna. She had dark hair and brown skin. And . . .

I felt a terrible pressure under my tongue. The kind I get before I throw up.

I enlarged the first picture.

It was Priya.

CHAPTER 17

THE BULL MOOSE

I pushed the puke back down my throat, all burny and hot. But I'm not sure why. It was so gross. Why didn't I just throw up and get it out of my system? Priya? And Shep?

I heard a voice outside the door, followed by the doorknob turning. Someone was coming. I stood up quickly and tried to look as normal as possible. But the second I stood, I got a wave of lightheadedness. The corners of the room got really dark, and I felt my chest getting tighter. I tried to breathe.

The door swung open, and it was Priya. Of course. It was her office. Fuck.

"Just have him call me," she was saying to someone on the phone before registering me. "Margot! Hey, I— Margot? Are you okay?"

She closed the door and came over to me, taking me by the shoulders. "What happened?"

I walked to the other side of the room the second she

touched me. I had no desire to be hugged or consoled by her. I needed distance.

"I'm—I'm—" I tried to reassure her, but the word "fine" just refused to come out of my mouth. And it didn't matter, because Priya's eyes were now away from me, trained on the computer screen. Where there was a picture of her and Shep, holding each other in an embrace.

"Where did you get this?" Priya demanded, any hint of concern for me now gone.

I think she expected me to say something here. But I was still just focusing on not letting my heart jump out of my chest.

"Margot. Seriously. Where the hell did you—"

"Marion's PI. The same woman who took the video of Deanna. She followed you and Shep on May thirtieth," I said, now making strong eye contact with her. "So does that answer all your questions? Because I have, like, five thousand for you."

"Margot, look—" Priya said, before I talked over her.

"Did you know about these? Because if DropOutShep@ hotmail sent these to you and you kept them from me—"

"No! This is the first I've ever seen them!" she sputtered.

"Are you sure?" I said, studying her face.

"Margot, you saw the email! The pictures were of Deanna. I . . . I didn't know these existed . . . *Oh my god.*" Priya paced around the room, aware of what photos like this could mean for her budding political career. Her shock made me think she was telling the truth. But it was hard to trust her now.

For a brief moment, we said nothing. Priya went to the computer, studying the photos of her and Shep. Her breathing getting heavier with each picture.

"Priya. What the *fuck*?"

"Margot. It's . . . complicated."

"It's complicated?!" I shot back. "Carbon capture is complicated. This is pretty simple, I think. You fucked your way-older, married boss and didn't tell me about it!"

"Let me just say a couple of things. Okay?" She took a moment to calm herself. "Shep and I hooked up *one time*. We both knew it was a really bad idea because of the campaign and everything. It was after his first public appearance and we were both just . . . swept up in the moment."

I stared at her, making sure she was hearing all the bullshit coming out of her mouth.

"I know that sounds corny. But it's true. It was consensual. And I don't regret it."

"Priya, you are . . ." I was struggling to respond. "So much younger than him."

Priya looked at me the way I'd look at anyone who questioned my age. Or rather, questioned *my ability* based on my age.

"Margot, come on. I didn't expect *that* argument from you." She shook her head in disappointment. And despite how pissed I was, I almost wanted to take it back.

But I held strong. "He's twice your age."

"So?"

"So . . . that's a little weird. Why did you—"

"Because I wanted to! Margot. Be real. You're almost eighteen, right?"

"Yes."

"Okay. So you're almost an adult. And once you become an adult, you're an adult. It doesn't matter if you're twenty or forty or fifty. Everybody is just . . . kinda the same." She sat down in the folding chair across from me and leaned back.

"But Shep is your boss. Doesn't that—"

"Margot, what are you saying? You think he forced me into it or something? Believe me, if anything, it was the other way around," she said, crossing her arms. "I think I'm old enough to choose who I sleep with."

I sat there expressionless. *Was she?* The whole thing seemed weird to me. But then, I'd never had sex. So maybe I couldn't understand. Certainly no one could look at Priya and see her as a victim. She was so confident. She knew who she goddamn was. But if this affair was so harmless, why didn't she mention it before now?

"So this is why you hired a high schooler to handle Shep's problem," I said. "And why you never told anyone? Because you didn't want anyone to find out you were fucking Shep," I said. Priya winced as if I had just thrown a dart at her chest.

"Once. We . . . once. And no, Margot. I hired you because I thought you could do the job," she said sadly. "Honestly."

I was furious. "Then why keep things from me? I can't do my job if you keep things from me!"

"I'm sorry. You're right." She added, "I truly didn't think it would matter."

"I am going to spend the next half hour scouring your laptop. To make sure you're not the blackmailer."

Her eyes widened. "You think *I* did this?"

"No." I gave an exasperated shrug. "But now that I know about you and Shep, you clearly have a motive. So I need to check you off my list before I move on. *If* I move on."

Priya nodded. "Well, there's my computer. The same one I've given you complete access to for the past month. Use my iCloud. It's all there." She stood up to leave. "So have fun reading a lot of bitchy texts from my sister."

She picked up her purse and her coat, giving me space to do my work. But just before she left she said, "And when you're done, and you realize that I'm not lying to you, I hope you can move past this. Because I still need you to do your job."

Then she shut the door behind her. Leaving me alone with her computer and a sudden piercing silence.

PRIYA'S LAPTOP WAS CLEAN. THERE WERE A BUNCH OF TEXTS BE-tween her and Shep, but nothing inappropriate. And there was no indication she'd ever seen the photos of herself, or had anything to do with DropOutShep@hotmail. Fine. So Priya didn't do it. But was I really going to keep working on this case now that I knew all this?

I forced myself to consider Priya's argument. Was there any version of this where Priya was right? Was there really nothing wrong with her and Shep hooking up? Every time I thought about it, I just got so mad. She lied to me. Twice! And sleeping with her boss just seemed so tawdry. Not the kind of thing you expect from your cool, capable role model / future BFF.

But as angry as I was with Priya, I was even angrier with Shep. He was sleeping with a subordinate! Could I really still help him knowing that? And what if there were more women? Was this a pattern? It felt like a drip-drip that could very easily turn into a downpour. There was no way to deny that if I kept working for him, I'd be breaking rule #3. I wasn't supposed to work for a morally dubious client, and Shep was looking pretty dubious. God, this whole thing was such a mess.

I got the hell out of her office and rushed through the bullpen toward the exit. My body was on autopilot, while my brain had turned the Priya pictures into a nightmarish GIF that I couldn't stop watching over and over again in my mind. I swung open the HQ door and almost tripped over Avery.

"Hey! Ready to go?" he said, as if he'd been expecting me to tumble out of HQ at that very moment.

Fuck. What was I supposed to do about Avery? Was I going to tell him? He told me he didn't want to know any details. But wouldn't he want to know this? Priya was only a few years older than us.

"Sorry . . ." I said, taking a moment to collect my thoughts. "Go where?"

"We said we'd go to Jenn's birthday. Bowling? Remember?" He looked at me more closely and probably noticed the stress veins bulging in my forehead. "Are you okay?"

"Yeah. I'm good." Double fuck. I'd completely forgotten that, in my attempt to be a "better" friend to the Kelseys, I had agreed to go to Hoffman's girlfriend's birthday. Bowling? Kill me now. "Just—uh, it's been a really long day. I don't think I can bowl."

"Ya gotta, bud," Avery said, putting an arm around me and leading me toward his parked car.

"Just tell them I'm sick or something," I said, pulling away. "You're more fun than me anyway."

He stopped in front of his car and turned to me. Then began pacing like a TV lawyer making their closing arguments. "Margot. We have to go. For one thing, I am an amazing bowler and I want you to witness it." Doubtful. This sounded like one of his mini golf boasts. "For another, Penny Lanes has a two-for-one corn dog special, and I cannot let myself eat both. And for my closing argument: you love the Kelseys. So I don't think you should bail on them."

I wanted to come up with a retort, but I couldn't. And I definitely didn't want to tell him about what was weighing on me. Avery sensed that I was stuck and gestured toward his car, unlocking it with Bluetooth and making the mirrors unfold. "You can't work *all* the time, Mertz. Ya gotta work hard, bowl hard." I then had to text my parents to obtain permission to be out on a *school night*, and that was about as quick and painless as a game of Catan.

"Do you have any cash?" Avery asked, interrupting my thoughts, once we were on our way.

"I think I have like twenty bucks?" I told him, digging in my purse.

"Oh good. You're going to need some cash once you see how good of a bowler I am."

"Why would I—"

"So you can THROW IT AT ME! Money, flowers, teddy

bears. You're going to want all that stuff," he said, stopping at a red light.

"You're not a *figure skater*," I said. Avery was forcing a smile to creep its way across my face. "Nobody sees a good bowler—and I do not believe that you *are* good, by the way—nobody sees a good one and thinks, *Let me throw money at them*. They think, *This activity is depressing*."

I did my best to sound light and breezy. Which in some ways, I was. Avery naturally put me at ease. And he was never more attractive than when he was being an ass like this. I just hoped his dad didn't come up too much tonight. If he asked me point-blank, I was sure I'd tell him the whole truth.

"You seem like you're in a good mood or something," I observed, hoping to focus on him instead of me.

Avery always seemed like he was in a good mood. But right now he *really* seemed like it.

"You are looking at a guy who just finished his last college essay," he said proudly. "And tomorrow I'm sending in all my applications."

"You're so early!" I said, shocked and jealous. I hadn't even sent mine in to Stanford yet (and that was the only application I was putting any effort into).

"I know. I know," he said. "I just wanted to be done. And honestly, the thought of being away from here, from my parents, was all the motivation I needed."

Avery was exuberant, tapping the steering wheel as he shared his happy news. But I suddenly felt like my stomach had dropped all the way down to my butt. I hadn't really thought about the fact that, come next fall, Avery and I might be headed to totally different corners of the globe. And it stung more than I thought it would. I didn't want to be the clingy girlfriend who made him apply to Stanford. But I also *kinda* wanted him to apply to Stanford.

"Where are you—"

"Did you—" He laughed. "You go."

"I was just going to ask where you're applying?" I said, trying to sound casual.

"A bunch of places," he began. "NYU, Columbia, Berkeley, USC. A lot of places have good doc programs, if I decide that's what I want to do. Let's see, Yale, but there's no way my grades are *that* good, North Carolina School of the Arts . . ."

Come on. Stanford. Stanford. Stanford.

"Um . . . oh, and Stanford. They actually have a really good doc program. I hope that's not weird. I know Stanford's kinda your thing."

Do I tell him that I want him to go to Stanford? We just started dating, I shouldn't be thinking that far ahead. I'M NOT THINKING THAT FAR AHEAD. I'M NOT A PSYCHO, YOU ARE!

"Well, yeah. But that doesn't mean you shouldn't apply," I said, raising my voice more than I intended. It was thirty-eight degrees outside, and yet I still had no chill.

"You wouldn't, like, mind if I ended up going there too?" he asked.

Move into my dorm. I l#ve you.

"No! I mean, I don't want to tell you where to go or anything. But I . . . definitely wouldn't mind if we both ended up going there," I said, biting my lip until I could see a clear reaction.

Avery looked relieved. "Oh. Great. Okay. I was afraid you'd think I was a stalker if I applied. Or a serial killer."

"Oh, you're *definitely* a serial killer. I've been saying that for forever!"

I smiled. And he smiled back. And then I just stared at his damn dimple and his perfectly symmetrical face, and marveled at how this guy, for some reason, seemed to like me as much as I liked him.

Avery parked in the Penny Lanes parking lot, and we made out in the car for the next twenty minutes, and I did not think we were actually going to enter the bowling alley. In fact, for most of it, I forgot there *was* a bowling alley. But then Avery insisted we get it together so we could at least make an appearance. So that I could admire his "backswing"?[102]

Penny Lanes was loud, smelled of wet carpet,[103] and was disappointingly *not* Beatles-themed. Jenn's party was taking up the first three lanes and was louder than everyone else in the alley combined. I saw Hoffman, Chugg, Melanie, and several freshgirls I'd talked to at Avery's party and whose names I had completely forgotten. There was also Mike Gibbons and Jason Pizzarello and a few guys I didn't know.

The two lanes next to ours were for "league bowlers" (read: old white men with beer bellies, and one woman named Maggie who held her own and had an impressive smoker's cough). Our party brought the median age in the alley down by thirty.

---

102 Bowling has something called "backswings"? Sure.

103 Even though the floors were wood. Explain that!

Avery insisted on paying for my shoe rental and my game and my half of the two-for-one corn dog special. I still hadn't figured out a good way to refuse him. I didn't want him to pay for everything. But his family did have so much money. And it wasn't like he was saving up to pay for college or anything. But I don't know. It still felt weird.

Melanie greeted me with a hug. "Hey, you!" Then under her breath, "You never texted me after the party. *How did it go?*"

I smiled sheepishly and gave her a shrug that meant, *It was fantastic. Thank you for being a good wingperson.*

"FUCK YOU!" Hoffman yelled when she saw me. She climbed over a couch, pointing at me until she reached me. "I had a bet with Chugg that you were going to bail!"

She gave me a somewhat painful but very good hug. Then she whispered, "I told Jenn we were friends, but I don't think she believed me. So thanks for actually showing."

I draped an arm around her shoulder and said loudly, "Love this girl!"

I wished Jenn a happy birthday and pretended to remember the names of her friends. (Unlike Avery, who actually did remember their names. And their parents' names. And their favorite hobbies.) I put on my rental shoes, while doing my best impression of someone not completely grossed out to be sharing foot space with the, I don't know, five thousand people who came before me. And even though a huge decision should have been weighing on me, I felt myself getting swept away in birthday fun, and just being with Avery. Soon I was singing "I found love in a hopeless place" with everyone else.[104]

A game was already in full swing, but Avery and I were able to tag in for Mike and Jason, who preferred to play the strip poker video game at the bar.[105] I knocked over four pins on my first try and was getting ready to shit-talk Avery. But as I opened my mouth, I saw him jog lightly toward the line on the floor, curve his foot behind him, and let loose a stunningly confident ball. I thought it was headed for the gutter, but it *spun* as though he were controlling it with his mind and came back to the middle of the lane. He got a strike. Or a spare. I don't know anything about bowling. He knocked down all the pins.[106]

"So you actually do know how to bowl?" I asked.

"I told you I did."

"I thought it was like mini golf. Complete bullshit."

"No. I could actually qualify for a bowling scholarship." He laughed. "Not that I want to bowl in college."

Apparently Avery did bowling camp for one summer and realized he was something of a savant. He soon made our team unbeatable, despite my below-average scores. And that was great, because we had the birthday girl on our team. And we love to see a birthday girl win.

The birthday girl's girlfriend, meanwhile, was in rare form all

---

104 Everyone in our party. All the bowling league people hated this. But Hoffman found the jukebox, and that's how jukeboxes work. For $1.50 you can subject a crowd of people to your whims.

105 I'm certain you were supposed to be eighteen to play this game, but it wasn't being policed.

106 Apparently, at the end of the game, you get bonus turns if you knock down all the pins, which is cute.

night. Ever since Hoffman came out to her parents last year, she had become bolder, more fun, and a little wild. She was getting a rep as someone who would take any dare at any time. Tonight alone, she bowled blindfolded one round. Then the next, she spun around three times before each turn, like she was playing pin the tail on the donkey. At one point I thought she was going to get into a fistfight with the league bowlers next to us because she kept throwing balls in their lane.[107] But then she and Maggie sang a loud duet of "I'm Every Woman" by Whitney Houston, and it seemed to mend fences.

When the first game ended, Melanie asked if I wanted to go to the bathroom with her. Another sign that *I have arrived in the world of female friendship*. I said sure, and together we took our purses to the gross Penny Lanes bathroom to pee and touch up our makeup. I'm not big into makeup, so for me that meant looking in the mirror, shrugging, and reapplying my clear lip gloss.

The conversation, per Melanie's nudging, went back to my night with Avery. I was trying to explain in nongraphic terms what we did.

"So . . . he fingered you?" she asked after I rambled to her about "crossing Ohio's state line." "Was it good? Or did it hurt? Did you come?"

"Mel! I thought you were, like, a goody-goody prude. I did not expect you to be all 'Did you come?'"

---

107 Her ball knocked over a bunch of their pins, messing up their score (and gave someone an unearned strike). Hoffman then climbed into the other lane and attempted to manually replace the pins . . . which can't be done and is honestly dangerous? Then one of the league bowlers rolled his ball *toward* her, and things got really ugly.

"Why did you think that?" she asked.

"I don't know. Because you're . . ." I didn't know how to finish that sentence without offending Melanie.

"You were going to say something about owls, weren't you?" she said, raising an eyebrow.

"Not necessarily!" I said back. But yeah. I was. Owls are not sexy.

Melanie shrugged, before applying some kind of glitter powder to her eyes that would soon be hidden by a flop of hair. "Well, I'm not a virgin. Did you know that?"

"No," I said, utterly taken aback. Melanie seemed *so* virginal.

She then went on to tell me all about her first time, with this guy Roland. They were both counselors at nature camp the summer before last. He was apparently very nice. But when the summer ended and he went off to college, they ended things.

"College? So he was an older guy?"

"He wasn't *that* old. He was eighteen." Melanie shrugged. I wondered what the age difference was between Priya and Shep. Twenty years? Thirty years? But maybe I was the only one in town bothered by a May/September romance.

"Margot. Can I ask you something?" Melanie asked, finishing up her face.

I braced myself for more sex questions. "Sure." [Gulp.] "What?"

Melanie looked down at her purse, almost like she was embarrassed. "Is there any chance I'm going to win this thing? Against P-Boy?"

"Of course there is!" I shot back. "It's tight, for sure, but your speech is going to seal the deal. I know it."

Melanie nodded. Not entirely convinced. And that was probably because she could sense my lingering doubts. The party had
been good for freshperson turnout. But I kept thinking about
Navion and his crew. And how they viewed Roosevelt Bitches as
P-Boy's *accomplishment*. As a reason to vote for him. It made me
think that P-Boy, in some circles at least, was still popular. And
now that he was dating the beloved Ainsley, I just couldn't figure
out a way to pierce his armor.

I was about to tell her some of this, hopefully in a way that
wasn't too discouraging, but then Hoffman poked her head in the
bathroom door and shouted, "We're singing happy birthday, you
twats!"

Hoffman can get away with language like that.

She dragged us by our arms over to the lounge, where there
was a big cake that said JENN, QUEEN, YOU'RE FIFTEEN! Hoffman
had somehow wrangled everyone, including the league bowlers,
over to the lounge. And everybody sang.

I really marveled at Hoffman. She had Avery's skill for getting people to warm up, plus this bonus X factor of being fearless
and scary bonkers. I mean, who else but Hoffman could almost
hit you in the head with a bowling ball, then get you to duet a
Whitney classic?

"Oh my god!" I said out loud as everyone was dirge-ing
through "DEEEAR JENNNNN!"

Avery turned to me. "Are you okay?"

"I'm fine," I whispered. "I just figured out how to beat P-Boy."

I pulled Melanie aside before the cake was even cut. I know,

I know. Few things are > cake. But I felt like this was.

"I know how to beat him! For real. In fact, I think I figured out a way to really bury Peter Fucking Bukowski!"

"Great! How?!" Melanie said, eyes wide at the possibility.

"We get Hoffman to run for president!"

"What?" she said, raising her eyebrows. "*Hoffman?* Are you drunk?"

"No! Think about it! We get her to run as a third-party candidate! She's not going to *win*. But she'll appeal to the same voters who think P-Boy is 'so funny' and 'so random.' She'll be the chaos candidate!" I said, waving my arms as I spoke. I clearly could not contain my excitement.

"So you're saying we use Hoffman to pull votes away from P-Boy? That sounds shady, Margot." Melanie looked skeptical, standing up and putting the brakes on my plan. "I told you, I want to run a campaign that I can be proud of."

"But this is legitimate, Melanie! I promise," I said, putting my hands on her shoulders like I was a person comfortable with this level of human contact. "I mean, this is what democracy is! Anyone can run! For any reason! And believe me, even if Hoffman isn't running 'to win' per se, she'll still be doing it for a very good reason."

"To sabotage a campaign?"

"No," I said, looking around to make sure we had some relative privacy. "You remember that Hoffman was on RB last year?"

"Um, I think so," Melanie said, straightening her back. "I knew that Chugg was, but I never, like, looked at all of them."

"Well, she was. And even though everyone's 'moved on' and

no one talks about it anymore, the girls who were on that site, they're still dealing with it."

"Yeah, I mean, I know Abby's still struggling with it," Melanie said quietly, then turned to face me. "So you're saying it's okay for Hoffman to run just so she can get revenge?"

"No," I said, although I *did* believe revenge was a good reason to do pretty much anything. "What I'm saying is, if P-Boy wins, it's not just disappointing. It's dangerous. Because then all the freshboys who see him get elected six months after he committed a legitimate sex crime will think, *Hey! Cool! No punishment! I should do that too!* So if Hoffman wants to run to try and stop him, well, that would be her right."

Melanie nodded, bouncing her knee as she thought. It seemed like maybe this argument made sense to her.

"Okay. I guess. If Hoffman really wants to run . . . she can," she said. "But, Margot, this is as far as I'm willing to go. Some people think winning is all that matters, but I'm not one of those people. Okay?"

I nodded vigorously, even though I didn't appreciate the implication that I *was* one of those people.

"Yes! Squeaky-clean from here on out! A campaign you can be proud of!" I said, giving her a big hug before I ran to ask Hoffman if she would consider running. Before I could fully get the question out, Hoffman interrupted me with "FUCK YEAH!" Then she made everyone at the party recite the pledge of allegiance to her. And then she took requests for what her platform should be. Everyone at the party had ideas: "No more football!" "Clothing should be optional!"

"Beer Tuesdays!"[108] etc. I sat down with Avery, still glowing from his win. He put his arm around me as we watched the Hoffman show.

We left around nine, even though the party and Hoffman in particular showed no signs of slowing down. (She was organizing a game she called "Hunger Games Karaoke," which somehow made karaoke competitive and dangerous.) Avery and I were ready to call it a night.

We got in his car and I felt giddy from the night's revelations. Getting Hoffman to run felt like a game changer. Plus I was sitting next to the boy I liked, excited about a round two make-out sesh.

But as we got into the car, Avery checked his phone and let out an exasperated "Goddamn it." He turned to me. "Sorry, Margot, I gotta call my dad. Or . . . Priya."

"Priya? Why?" I asked, turning to face him.

He took a deep breath and gave me his phone. It was a headline on the local conservative blog *Nation Builders*, which was run by a few Lidori cohorts. The headline read, "Candidate's Son's Troubled History with Drugs and Vandalism Threatens Campaign."

"*What?*" was all I could say. "Is this like an *Onion* article or something?"

"I wish."

It was an almost completely fabricated article about Avery that accused him of having been arrested for vandalism. (As Avery explained to me, this was misleading. He was *questioned*

---

108 That last one was from Maggie. Who, even though she wasn't a student, had a lot of thoughts about Hoffman's campaign from the bar.

in connection to an act of vandalism at the YMCA because he had witnessed someone tagging the door.) It also intimated that drugs may have been the cause for his "aggressive and irrational" behavior. And, as you might have guessed, there were plenty of racist dog whistles, including the use of the word "thug." It was reprehensible.

"This is disgusting! It's obviously racist. And not only is it not true, you're a minor. I mean, aren't the candidates' children off-limits?"

"Guess not?" He shrugged, like he was used to this kind of thing, and shot off a text. "I'll tell my dad, he'll shit a brick, and they'll take it down. I mean, it's not a great strategy. But they keep doing stuff like this, so . . ."

"What do you mean? They've done this before?" I asked, furious.

"A few times over the summer. Any time they start to slip in the polls. It's desperate."

This made me so mad I could see stars. I guess because I was clenching my whole face so hard? "Avery. This is . . . We should have them disbarred. Or what's the journalistic equivalent of disbarment? We should do that! Besides, you're such a freaking goody-goody who never does anything wrong. It's not fair!"

"I'm not *that* good," he argued, placing a hand on my thigh. My pulse quickened as he leaned in and kissed me. But all the time I was thinking, *How is he not angrier?* The Lidori campaign was trying to troll Avery? *My* Avery? The sweetest, kindest, most amazing person in the fucking world? No. Do not fuck with Avery Green.

I had made up my mind. Shep had made bad choices, and working for him was definitely a violation of my "no shady clients" rule. Multiple affairs were not great. But the alternative? A world with Susan Lidori in charge? Someone whose campaign targets minors? That was fucking untenable.

Goodbye, rule #3. Hello, moral ambiguity.

I was finally ready to get my hands dirty.

CHAPTER 18

COLLEGE GUYS

Hoffman dove into the campaign with her characteristic intensity. After getting the fifty signatures she needed to run (which she impressively did in half a day to beat the deadline), her first official act as a candidate was to march over to P-Boy's lunch table in the cafeteria, slap the sandwich out of his hand/ mouth, and yell, "You just got presidented!" Which didn't make sense, but got a big reaction from the caf. She then turned to Jenn, who was recording the whole thing on her cell, and screamed to the camera: "I'M KELSEY HOFFMAN AND I APPROVE THIS MESSAGE!" Jenn uploaded it to Tok, and it went Roosevelt-viral by the end of the day. Then Jenn and Kelsey made out until the lunch lady came over and told them to cool it.

Hoffman was perfect. For the rest of the week, Melanie and I ran our boring/normal campaign (reaching out to undecided voters, passing out buttons) while Hoffman went full Joker. Her campaign poster was an extreme close-up of the crease between her forearm and bicep, with the heading, IS THIS MY ARM, OR MY BUTT? YOU DECIDE! And then in tiny letters: VOTE HOFF-MAN. She got a group of people to run onto the football field in the middle of a game[109] and use their bodies to spell out VOTE HOFFMAN.[110] Johnny Spatz, the head of the athletic department, removed her from the field. But then she turned the tables on Johnny by secretly filming him and uploading it to Tok. It also went Roosevelt-viral.

Basically, Hoffman was doing exactly what I had hoped. Kicking ass and sucking the oxygen out of P-Boy's campaign. The following week, I heard an array of rando dudes say they'd vote for her. Traydon Reed and Jason Pizzarello said they were thinking about it. And *John Pfeiffer* said he was definitely going to vote for her because, and I quote, "she has balls."[111]

So now, with two "let the world burn" candidates duking it out for the slacker vote, Melanie was sure to clean up the rest. People liked that Melanie was the only one who seemed to care. I did an informal poll on Instagram, which showed Melanie with an almost double-digit lead over P-Boy. The Hoffman candidacy was working.

This was a relief. And it meant I could take a step back from the school election and focus on the much bigger, much more complicated, *actual* election.

---

109 Not only during a game, but during an actual play. She prevented the opposing team from getting a touchdown, which made her surprisingly popular with a group of jocks.

110 They ended up spelling VOIE HOF^^AN, but people knew what they were going for.

111 John found a way to make voting for a woman somehow sound sexist.

• • •

THAT WEEK, I BROKE INTO THE (ONE-STEP-VERIFIED!) FORSYTHE & Mahn Ring account using a Ring Video Config I sourced on Reddit. After that, any free moment I had, I barricaded myself in my room and started digging into the security footage. Eventually, I was able to narrow my search down to the time between when Tamika first dropped off the drive and when Shep received his email. From watching hundreds of hours of Ring cam footage on five-times speed, I zeroed in on three employees who accessed the safe during that period, and therefore could've taken Tamika's drive. They were Casey Price (the mean receptionist), Orson Fischer (the gross intern I'd seen in the lobby—I was able to find his name on LinkedIn), and, believe it or not, Karen Forsythe herself! So I looked into each of their socials and did some further snooping into the Forsythe & Mahn payroll (thanks, Fuzzword, for the sign-in). I needed to figure out if any of them had any possible motive for blackmailing Shep.

I followed dead end after dead end, every moment I wasn't at school. I was over an hour late to dinner Wednesday night. And Thursday, I missed a follow-up appointment with my ophthalmologist because I forgot to check my calendar. Which sucked, because my right eye was starting to hurt whenever I stared at a screen for too long. This was something I'd planned to ask the doctor about before I skipped my appointment. (I did not tell my parents. But as I had already broken rule #2, I made peace with it.)

At any rate, I was learning about my suspects. Casey Price, my *favorite* receptionist, loved to complain on social about how "broke" she was, almost always while sipping $18 mixed drinks with her friends (?) who looked like Rainbow High dolls. Maybe she was blackmailing Shep for money? But the email to Shep hadn't explicitly asked for cash. And payroll showed that Casey was making $23 an hour, which is pretty good.

As a partner at the firm, Karen Forsythe certainly had easy access to the safe. But despite being a total shark who helped men avoid paying alimony, she actually seemed to be a liberal? She regularly donated to Democratic candidates—including Shep—and showed up at their galas. Plus if it ever got out that she had betrayed her client by leaking those pictures, it would probably ruin her practice. So that seemed unlikely.

Which left only Orson. Orson's posts weren't overtly political, but he did post about women's looks a lot. (That doesn't make him a suspect per se. More just an asshole who's living it up in the patriarchy.) But according to the payroll, Orson started his internship at Forsythe and Mahn *just one week before the threatening email was sent out.* Coincidence? Methinks not! Of the three people caught on camera accessing the safe, Orson had the least to lose and the most to gain from taking the drive.

But was this enough to go on? I wasn't sure. Orson, a junior at U of M, seemed pretty blah on the surface. Until I dug a little deeper into his Twitter and realized he had liked *several* of Susan Lidori's posts. This was before she declared her candidacy. It was broadly libertarian stuff: a picture of her wearing a tight T-shirt that said FREEDOM in bright red across the boobs, a picture of her kissing a gun, a picture of her eating a hamburger with the caption **Libs can't take this from me**. Did Orson have a thing for sexy conspiracy theorists? Did he think Lidori would kiss *his* gun if he helped her win?[112]

So the offices of Forsythe & Mahn had a secret Lidori-head working for them? That was all the motive I needed. Now all I had to do was get on the dipshit's computer to prove his involvement.

I hatched a plan. On Saturday, Avery and I would go to U of M, posing as students. Orson belonged to something called the "Fantasy Freaks," which was a semi-school-sanctioned fantasy football club. Avery's job would be to chat up Orson while I snuck back to his dorm and copied his computer. Obviously, I still needed to iron out some of the specifics. Like how to break into a dorm room. And how was I going to pretend to like fantasy football?

I reached out to my only college-aged friend for some advice.

> **MARGOT:** Hey. If I wanted to break into a dorm room how hard would it be?

> **SAMMI:** my school is mostly commuters

> **MARGOT:** I know that. But you have that one building.

> **SAMMI:** i don't know. nobody really closes their doors. unless they're hooking up and then they sometimes do.

Huh. Maybe this would be easier than I thought. Come to think of it, all the doors had been left open at the dorm I visited during my tour of U of M.

---

112 His gun would be his penis in this metaphor. Guns are often stand-ins for penises, I've found.

I called Avery, and he was a little ambivalent at first. He was usually game to help me, but anything involving covering up his dad's affair was a lot more complicated. But when I told him more about my plan, he said he'd help. And apparently he was in a number of "leagues" and so would have no trouble talking fantasy sports to random strangers. Which was good for this job, but bad for how attractive I thought he was.[113]

But then, two hours before Avery was supposed to pick me up, he called with some rather disappointing-for-me news. "M? I think I have to bail on you. I'm sorry. I have to go to New York City with my mom."

"Oh. Okay," I said, both impressed by his last-minute jaunt to NYC and bummed that he was ditching me.

"There's this hospital in New York that really wants my mom to come work for them. So they invited her to come tour it. She wasn't gonna go because she doesn't want to work there. But I think she feels bad about all the campaign stuff I've had to do and wants to make it up to me." He was trying not to show it, but I could tell he was excited. "Plus it's the last weekend of the New York Film Festival. Mertz, *Ezra Edelman* is doing a Q&A after his film. Maybe he'll even A my Q?"[114]

"That's amazing," I said, trying to hide my annoyance.

But I probably didn't do a great job, as Avery responded with, "No. What am I doing? I can't bail on you like this! I'm just gonna tell her I can't go." I was about to hang up, but I stopped myself.

---

113 I mean, he's still a ten. But he used to be a twelve.

114 Ezra Edelman was Avery's current doc-maker crush. Thankfully, he didn't go around screaming, "EDELMAN!"

This didn't feel great. I could see that it was something Avery really wanted to do. And it was very Margot 1.0 of me to ignore that.

"No," I said. "You have to go. You can't miss an opportunity like this. Go to New York City with your mom."

"Are you sure? 'Cause I really could—"

"Go!" I said. "I'll be fine. I honestly just wanted you there because you're nice to look at."

"Thanks. I think?" he said. "I'll make it up to you. In a nonsexual way. Of course."

I laughed and we made a plan to meet up when he got back. And then I hung up and got to work on my Avery-less plan B.

AROUND SEVEN P.M., I TOOK A PARTICULARLY ODOROUS BUS TO the U of M campus.[115] On the way, we passed a billboard for a new TV show called *KEENE*, based on the Trudy Keene books. It featured a brooding twenty-four-year-old who I assume is playing the teenaged titular character, a fixer who helps clean up messes in her small town. The books are dated and problematic. By the looks of this ad, the TV show would be current, and every bit as problematic! Just below her cleavage it said, *Keep it Keene*, God, I hope it's not a hit.

IT TOOK FORTY-FIVE MINUTES, BUT I FINALLY GOT THERE IN ONE smelly piece. Once at the campus, I made my way to Crosby

---

115 It smelled of feet *and* bubble gum, and now I'm pretty sure that's what hell smells like.

Hall, apparently named after a pharmaceutical magnate who gave beaucoup bucks to the university. And lucky for me, Crosby Hall was just two buildings down from Tiernan Hall, Orson's dormitory.

When I got to Crosby, I joined a clump of undergrads as they entered the building, hiding myself in the herd as we passed the security guard, flashing our IDs. (Thanks to my otherwise unnecessary college tour, I knew I could use my Wellmans Shopper's Club card. I just held my thumb over the part that said WELL-MANS.) The security guard barely looked at any of us. I was in.

I headed to a large multipurpose room where about forty or so students were already mingling. I heard the phrases "approximate value" and "Josh Allen's hamstring," which meant nothing to me. So I assumed I was in the right place. I parked my ass by the door and tried to scope out Orson. I just needed to make sure he was there doing his weird sports shit, so that I could go break into his room without fear of him walking in on me.

After a minute or two, I spotted him. He was dressed for a daytime golf game, wearing seersucker *shorts*,[116] a turquoise vest, and hair slicked back with way too much gel. I watched him drift from group to group, talking to people who did not seem to particularly know or like him, his bro-y veneer not doing much to hide his loneliness. Then he homed in on the women in the room, chatting them up, touching their arms, offering them drinks, and inevitably getting shot down. The outfit, the handsy-ness, it told me Orson was looking to get laid. And also that his odds of success were quite low.

---

116 The high that day was forty-six degrees.

This presented both a threat and an opportunity. If I snuck off to his room to copy his computer and he arrived shortly thereafter with a woman he planned to bed, well then, game over. But . . . what if *I* were that woman?

It had all the trappings of a terrible idea. And yet, the more I thought about it, the more viable it seemed. I had never been confident I'd be able to break into his dorm. I was betting on his door being left open—but that left so much to chance! I had a 100 percent chance of the door being open if he *took me there himself and opened it*. I could stall him with small talk,[117] giving off the vibe that we were about to hook up, while my program got the time it needed to copy his drive. Then all I had to do was get out of there without him getting handsy with me. And how hard could that be? The only real danger was if he recognized me from the law office. I was wearing an eye patch after all.

I overcompensated for the unsexiness of my patch by unbuttoning two more buttons of my shirt, scrunching up my hair to give it a little body (it fell limp immediately), and applying another round of lip gloss. I had a fleeting thought that maybe I should run this by Avery. I'd never had a boyfriend while attempting a honeypot for work. *Would he mind?* I wondered. But Avery wasn't the jealous type. So I was relatively sure he wouldn't object to some meaningless flirting (besides, the whole reason I was doing this was because he'd ditched me for New York).

I pulled myself out of my day-think and spotted Orson by the big-screen TV. I threw myself into his path and pretended to look

---

117 "Wow, you have such a cool shot glass collection" or "Wow, you and your dad have played at a lot of golf clubs." Small man small talk.

at my phone. He spotted me like chum in the water and made his way over. Clearly I shouldn't have been worried about the eye patch. Orson seemed to be looking exclusively at my chest.

"They say looking at your phone releases dopamine," he said, leaning over my phone. "But looking at you seems to have that effect on me too."

What? Was that supposed to be a line? I gagged. Like, I literally gagged in that moment, because of how gross he was, and it almost blew the whole damn thing.

"Oh my god. Are you okay?" he asked, putting his arm around my shoulders. "Want me to get you a water?"

I guess he assumed I was drunk or something. And I didn't correct him. "I'm fine," I said, smiling the biggest smile I could manage. "I'm Heather." I put out my hand for him to shake, and he held it for like eight seconds. Finally found someone with a grosser handshake than my dentist!

"I'm Orson. Pre-law. I work at the top firm in town. And I came in second in the league last year because I didn't let J. C. Campbell's off-field conduct cloud my judgment."[118]

"Cool!" I said, even though clearly this was the least cool thing anyone had ever said. "This is my first time."

"Well, don't worry. I'll be gentle," he said grossly. "Seriously, though, I *love* when women come to these things. It's like, hell yeah. Anyone can play fantasy. That's the thing about it . . . it's fantasy."

---

118 J. C. Campbell was supposed to be suspended for six games for a credible domestic abuse complaint. But then his team started to lose, so they reinstated him after one. See why I don't like sports?

I will not describe in detail how he intoned the word "fantasy," because maybe you just ate.

He went on, "Honestly, and this is me, but I don't think there's anything hotter than a girl who's into sports."

He was so casually offensive, while trying *so hard* to be appealing. It boggled the mind. I basically hadn't said anything, but I felt I had him right where I wanted him. I was about to steer us toward his room when I heard, "Whoa! What the fuck are you doing here?"

And I turned around to see Nick, holding a Solo cup and looking truly shocked to see me. Shit. I forgot he went to U of M. This was not good. At any moment he could say my real name and throw a wrench in the whole thing.

"Oh, you know me, *your girl Heather* is always down for some football."

"Your girl Heather?" he asked, looking confused.

"NICK! Meet Orson. Orson, Nick. You both already know me, *Heather*." I made a pleading eye at Nick. Nick didn't look like he entirely got it, but he at least stopped talking.

"Hey, man," Orson said, giving Nick a 'sup nod.

"Oh no. I don't have a drink!" I said all cutesy. And thankfully Orson took the bait, leaving to get me one.

I pulled Nick to the side.

"Okay, what's going on? Why are you Heather?" he asked.

"I'm here for work. I'm doing a . . . cleanup thing. So tonight my name is *Heather*. Got it?"

He leaned in, and I could smell his leather jacket. It covered a (probably dirty) T-shirt that said PEARL JAM. "I thought you were 'retired' from that." He smirked and took a confident sip of his beer.

"What I said was that I was taking a break," I shot back, staring straight ahead. "And the break is over."

"All right. So what did that little golf dandy do?" he asked, gesturing to Orson, who was getting two drinks from the makeshift bar.

Even though Nick had helped me earlier with Lidori, I wasn't about to tell him the truth. For one, I didn't trust him. At least not enough to tell him the whole truth about Shep. So I lied. "His exgirlfriend hired me. Baby Tucker Carlson over there has nudes of her that he refuses to erase. So tonight, I'm gonna do it for him."

"Yikes. Well, if you'll excuse me, I'm going to punch him," Nick said, moving toward him.

"No! No." I grabbed his arm, pulling him back next to me. "Just, pretend my name is Heather and do everything in your power not to punch him, because that will fuck up my whole thing."

I gave Nick my most commanding stare as Orson returned with our drinks.

"Vodka cranberry for the lady," Orson said, presenting it. Nick looked at me, as if to say, *Are you sure I can't punch him?*

"Oh shit! I should have said. I'm allergic to cranberries!" I pouted.

"Cranberries?" he asked, annoyed.

"Yeah, it's the enzymes," I lied, tossing my hair over my shoulder. "My body just can't handle it."

"I get it." He looked me up and down. "I'm going to find

something your body *can* handle." [Gross smirk.] "Besides me."
Aaaaand that's when I almost punched him myself. Blah. I was
having some serious second thoughts about going back to this
guy's room alone.

As Orson left to get me a "cranberry-free beverage," Nick immediately turned to me. "Well, as fascinating as this is, I'm not
sure I can keep talking to that creep and not kick him in the dick,
so . . . I'll leave you to it."

"Wait," I said. "Maybe you can help me. Could you talk to
him? For like thirty minutes? That should give me enough time
to break into his dorm room and mirror his laptop. Just, make
sure he stays here at the meeting for the whole time, okay?" The
meeting was supposed to start any minute.

"What dorm is he in?" Nick asked.

"Tiernan."

"Hahaha." He shook his head. "You cannot break into
Tiernan. It has hand scanners."[119]

God. This whole thing was devolving fast.

Suddenly a guy with a gavel got up and called the meeting to
order by having everyone there take a shot. Across the way, I saw
Orson approaching with some noncranberry beverage that I sure
as hell was not going to drink.[120] I had to think of something else.
But I was blanking.

"You sure I can't just punch him? I mean, that's also a
distraction."

---

119 They didn't mention that on the tour. Thanks a lot, Ray!

120 The only scenario where I drink something handed to me by Orson is if it
were hermetically fucking sealed. And even then, I'd have my doubts.

"No. Just—let me think." I stopped him. But nothing was coming to me. And Orson was already headed back with the same awful smirk, holding my drink out to me.

"One cranberry-free sex on the beach. I hope it's good for you."

Wow. He was like a walking, talking roofie. I was sure Nick was just going to slug him, because clearly I didn't have a plan. But instead, he forcefully said, "You play the new LandBlast?" He was smiling and acting . . . friendly? Like he and Orson were buds.

"Fuck yeah, man. It is [gross chef's kiss sound]," Orson replied, and for the first time he wasn't staring directly at my chest.

"It's beautiful, right? You ever play, Heather?" Nick asked. Then he gave me a look like, *I have a plan, so play along.* Which wasn't ideal. I'm usually the planner, but what choice did I have?

"I—I haven't," I said. In truth, I had played up to season six, when it got boring. But I figured it would pay off to play the noob with Orson. "I'm not much of a gamer . . ."

"You get past the tunnelers?" Orson asked Nick.

"Fuck no!" Nick laughed. "That shit's impossible."

"I think I'm really close," Orson bragged. "If you put C4 in their helmets, they don't regen."

"Really?" Nick seemed very interested. "God, I kinda want to go play now."

Orson looked at Nick, then at me.

"Let's fucking do it!" I said like a cheerleader. "But I'll just watch! I love to watch."

"Fuck it. Let's go." Orson high-fived Nick. And just like that, we were headed to his dorm. "I heard after the tunnelers, there's a planet where gravity is optional."

LandBlast is, of course, this very popular first-person shooter game on Xbox. A new season had just been released and, as Nick would later tell me, everyone at U of M was obsessed. So much so that it was threatening people's grades, and the school started warning people about it. Nick placed an educated guess that Orson would be as into the game as everyone else. And it paid off.

So the three of us headed to his room, where he told us he had "some really good whiskey" and Nilla Wafers because "girls love Nilla Wafers, and I try to keep the ladies happy."

I know I'm not actually in college yet. But I was starting to gain some understanding of its disappointing social norms. It seemed perfectly acceptable to make a girl you want to hook up with watch you play video games. And to serve whiskey and Nilla Wafers. Gross. I prayed Stanford was more evolved.

En route, Orson prattled on about LandBlast cheats and I sent Nick secret text messages outlining my elaborate but foolproof new plan. Basically, once Nick and Orson started blasting some land, I'd excuse myself, say I wanted to get drinks from my dorm and that I'd be right back. But I wouldn't be right back. I would be going into the hall to flood the communal bathroom sink. Then I'd start screaming and hopefully everyone on the floor would come out and make a commotion about the leak. Once there was a crowd, and once Orson came out of his room, I'd sneak back in and copy his hard drive. If I needed more than fifteen minutes, I'd simply lock the door. Or something. I guess I hadn't figured that out, but Nick would be with him, so he could always stall for me too.

Anyway, I was in the middle of relaying my master plan via text when Nick cut me off.

> **NICK:** Too complicated.

I gave him a look like, *No it's not*. I pointed to my phone and mouthed, *We're doing my plan*. He waved me off.

> **NICK:** He's going to be gaming and probably drunk.

> **NICK:** Just go over to his computer. He won't even notice.

This seemed too simple. But Nick insisted that he knew college guys better than I did.

We signed in and made it up to Orson's dorm. (After waltzing past the hand scanners as his personal guests. Solutions!) It was a single (of course, who would want to be his roommate?), clean, and his shelves were organized and alphabetized like a frat Marie Kondo. Orson offered us his whiskey. Nick had some, but I declined. Several times. Though he kept saying, "It would be more fun if you joined us. Just saying." [Shudder.] Then he and Nick settled on the couch and started LandBlasting. Apparently they were playing on the same side, because they kept shouting back and forth. Things like, "I'M GOING IN!" and "ON YOUR LEFT" and "IN THE HOLE!" Nick hated Orson. But get them in front of a video game, and they were instantly teammates. Strange.

I took a seat next to the couch in Orson's clean but disgusting beanbag chair[121] and pretended as best I could to be the type of

---

121 Because all beanbag chairs are disgusting.

girl who likes watching other people play video games. Saying things like, "You guys are really good at this!" and "Wow! This seems really hard." And even though this was all for show, I did die a little inside.

While they were playing, both Nick's and Orson's backs were to me. I waited, biding my time. I wanted to be sure Orson was truly engrossed in his game (and would therefore not notice me snooping). But Nick kept turning around, nodding his head in the direction of Orson's desk and mouthing, "Go!" To which I mouthed back, "Not yet!" And I guess Nick got fed up because eventually he said, "Hey, do you mind if Heather uses your computer? She needs to check something." *Check something* was Nick's brilliant excuse. Why not just ask if I could steal his hard drive?

But Orson, now on his third whiskey, didn't even turn his head as he said, "Oh yeah. Should be open. But if not, my password is orsonatlaw. All lowercase." He waved his hand back at me, not willing to unglue his eyes from whatever small genocide he was committing on screen.

And . . . that was it. Easy. Just like Nick predicted. I've said before that most of the "hacking" I do is in-person, exploiting human error—but it was rarely *this* easy. Not once did Orson stop his game to come check on me. After twenty minutes, his drive was copied. I unhooked my external and signaled to Nick I was done, at which point he abruptly stood up and said, "Okay. We gotta go. You play like a noob and you suck. Believe women. Never call me. Bye!" Nick then walked out of the room. I stood for a moment, shocked. Then I gave an awkward wave and followed Nick out of Orson's room as quickly as I could.

Nick led me out of Tiernan and into the campus night. After the warmth of the dorms, the cold was bracing. I needed a rideshare. So Nick walked with me down a tree-lined path across campus toward the pick-up spot. The path was lit with giant floodlights every twenty-five feet, presumably to make us feel safer.

I was a little pissed he blew our cover on the way out. What if Orson put it all together after we left and called campus security? I had erased my keystrokes, but still! I was about to smack Nick when he said, "I know I just blew your cover. But hanging with that Matt Gaetz in training made me want to stick a pen in my ear. Did you hear him ask me if having one eye made you 'extra willing'? Very classy," he said, shuddering.

"You know you're the only person who hasn't commented on my eye patch?"

"I figured you're probably sick of explaining it." He shrugged. "Why, is there a good story or something?"

I paused. I mean, I *was* kind of sick of explaining it. "No. Not really."

"I hope you got what you needed tonight," he said as we walked.

"I copied his drive. So, yeah." I tapped the external hard drive in my pocket.

Nick nodded, then smiled to himself. He seemed impressed, or, at the very least, amused. He stuck a piece of nicotine gum in his mouth. "Well, I'm happy your hiatus is over. You seem like you're pretty good at this."

I let out a sigh as we kept walking. "Well, I don't expect you to understand. But . . . it's not just about being good at it. If the thing you're doing makes you a shitty person. And makes all your friends hate you. Then it might not be worth doing."

"Oh, fuck that." Nick scoffed, stopping underneath one of the floodlights. The lighting was not good for either of us. But hey, it prevented assaults! "If it's getting in the way of friendships, fuck those friends. They don't get you. Because believe me, they'll fucking forgive you the minute they need your services."

He said it so firmly. Like no part of him thought friends could be more important than a job. I bristled.

"Yeah, well. Anyway, thanks for helping me," I said, hoping to change the subject. "You were right. He was dead to the world playing that game."

Nick pulled his jacket a little tighter. It had gotten colder. "So you wanna get a drink? Celebrate your big heist? Or a coffee?"

I was tongue-tied for a minute. Was Nick asking me out? Drinks seemed like a date thing? Or was this a normal friend thing to be doing? Gettin' drinks with a pal? That's what you do in college, right?

"I have to get back. Sorry. I'm—" I stammered.

"Hey. No problem." He nodded as if that was the response he was expecting. He started walking again, but I didn't follow him.

"I'm dating Avery," I blurted out. I was flushed and confused, and it just kind of plopped out of me.

"Avery *Green*?" he asked, turning back to me. And smiling.

"Yeah. Sorry." I shrugged. *Why did I say 'sorry'? I don't know. I was confused.* "I don't know if you were asking me out—"

"I was." He smiled. And then he started walking again, facing me and walking backward. "Dating the candidate's son, huh?"

I didn't like the look he was giving me. It was almost like he thought I was dating Avery to help my own political career or something. Dating him to get ahead.

"It's not like that. Avery and I used to date before. So this was like a getting-back-together thing. It doesn't have anything to do with, like, the campaign or—"

"Sure." Nick nodded, looking away for a moment and then back to me. "I . . . apologize. I would not have asked you out if I knew you were with someone," he said, making some very unnecessary prayer hands, pivoting to face forward and turning up his collar in a way that was very on-the-nose but also very attractive.

"It's okay. Really. It's totally fine," I said, not at all sounding like it was totally fine. What was going on in my brain and body?

"Cool," he said. "You want a ride home or something?"

Given how awkward that would be (and the fact that he had been drinking, which he didn't seem to think was a dealbreaker), I opted for a Lyft instead.

Nick stayed with me until it arrived. And when I got in, he leaned over the open door and said, very matter-of-factly, "Let me know if it doesn't work out with Avery Green." Then he slammed the door shut and walked back to the dorm as my driver pulled away.

Who *says* that? *If things didn't work out with Avery?* Of *course* they would work out. I l#ved him! The arrogance of Nick to even— What was he trying to pull?

My shock gave way to a buzzing feeling in my face. I felt

flushed. Did I actually *like* what Nick had just said? (Gross, Margot.) I'm not someone who gets asked out a lot and it was, in a weird and shallow way, validating. Nick didn't seem to mind that I was in high school. And he didn't seem to think there was anything wrong with Margot 1.0 and the way she treated people. Whenever I thought about my old cleanup work, I felt ashamed. But Nick thought I *should still be doing it*. Where was Nick last year, when I was alone, having alienated all my friends? When I hated myself and doubted everything I'd done with MCYF?

I put it all in the back of my mind. Maybe when this was all done, I could sort out whether liking this attention from Nick made me a bad person or not. For now, all that mattered was the hard drive in my purse. I had a job to finish. I had to keep moving.

CHAPTER 19

SPEAKING THE SPEECH

I woke up the next morning, no closer to knowing who was blackmailing Shep. Orson's hard drive, while loaded with pornography and plagiarized college papers, did not seem to contain Shep's pictures. Nor was I finding any evidence linking Orson to the email.

But while this was an annoying step back in my Shep case, I was one giant step closer to knowing one very important thing: that I fucking loved Avery. No more l#ve. Or l%ve. I loved him, full stop. And being hit on by Nick only crystallized these feelings. Sure, Nick had nice blue eyes. And yes, I'd been flattered when he asked me out. But the only thing I cared about when I woke up that morning was Avery. And now I wanted him to know how I felt. Like, right now. Even though he was still in New York and likely busy hailing a cab or watching a rat eat pizza or something.

"Hey, Mertz!" Avery answered the phone after one ring,

shouting over the throng of pedestrians and honking cars. "You called! You must really like me!"

"Haha. I mean, yes, I do. How's your trip going?"

"So good. The screening was incredible! Margot. I asked two questions! But I can't really talk. I'm about to meet this film professor from NYU. Informally. Not like an interview or anything. But my mom knew his wife, so—"

"Right. Well, I'll be really quick, then. I just wanted to tell you . . . and I know this may make me sound irrational. Or pathetic. But I kind of just realized something and I felt like I should tell you."

"Okay. What's up? Are you okay?" Avery said, an undercurrent of worry in his voice.

"Oh yeah. I'm fine. I just . . . love you. I love you. And I know that's a weird thing to say. Over the phone. But . . . fuck it. I love you, you handsome, suspiciously kind person. I . . . yeah."

And then there was a pause. Because of course there was. We had only been dating for a month, and who the hell knows if they're in love after a month? Juliet?

"And you don't have to say anything. I know this is so weird and—"

"I love you, Mertz," Avery said, mercifully cutting me off. "You're a force of nature and you have a cute butt."

I was smiling so hard I thought my cheeks might break. "Okay. Well. Great. I'm— I guess it's good that I'm not alone in this. And I know this is probably something you've said to, like, a bunch of different girls because you are experienced, and I am a troll who lives under a bridge, but—"

"I haven't," Avery said bluntly. "I had a few girls say it to me. But I've never said it back. But look, if you're really dying to talk about my ex-girlfriends, I can tell you—"

"Nope!" I said quickly. "I'm good."

And then I just stood there, moving up and down on my tippy-toes, happy to just hear the New York City street noises in Avery's phone for the rest of my life. But eventually Avery said, "Well, I gotta go. This guy is doing my mom a favor, so—"

"Right, go have your meeting. Have fun!"

"Thanks! I'll call you later!" Avery said, before ending the call with, "I love you."

My heart jumped into my throat, and my fingers got hot. But that didn't stop me from replying, "I love you too." And I guess we were already an I-love-you-as-goodbye couple, because we both hung up after that. After five to twenty-five minutes of squealing and jumping (I know, I'm the worst), I sat down and forced myself to focus on the case. Shep. The blackmailer. I still had to figure this out.

Without any promising leads, I decided to go back over Orson's emails one more time looking for *anything* suspicious. It took the whole day. I went through thousands of his god-awful, typo-riddled emails and I still couldn't find anything. Which in retrospect makes sense. Why would Orson have been so blasé about my looking at his computer if he had the illicit photos sitting on his hard drive?

As soon as I got home from school on Monday (which, sadly, was Avery-less since he was still in New York), I signed back into Forsythe & Mahn's Ring account. Since Orson was a bust, I decided my next course of action was to rewatch the footage. At two-times speed this time. Maybe I missed something? Maybe something was blocking the camera, allowing someone else to slip in. The answer had to be on this security footage, I was sure of it. I was only an hour into my very boring and monotonous security viewing when I heard a knock on my bedroom door.

"What song is that?" my dad asked as he leaned against the doorframe.

"What?" I asked, snapping out of my footage-watching fugue state. There was no music playing as far as I could tell.

"You were humming just now. Never known you to hum. Or sing. Or make any kind of music with your mouth. You seem very . . . chipper."

"Oh. I didn't even know I was. Sorry." I shrugged.

"No, no, no. It's nice!" my dad said, before asking, "So . . . how's Avery?"

"He's good," I said, looking back to my screen. But my dad kept standing there, picking at the doorframe. God, he was being awkward. What was he doing?

"Are you okay?" I asked. But my dad just looked at nothing for five seconds before abruptly saying, "Ooh, I think I left the kettle on!" Then he left. I did a quick google to make sure Rachel McAdams hadn't died or something before putting on my headphones. But then I heard another knock on the door.

"Got a minute?" my mom asked. I nodded and pushed away from my desk.

"Sure. Is Dad okay? He was being really weird just now."

"Oh, he's fine," my mom said. "He thinks that you're either in love. Or having sex. Or both. But he's a coward, so he asked me to find out."

"Mom!" I groaned.

"Look, I told him it's really not our business! But I said I'd bring it up in case you *wanted* to tell us."

"Just because I was humming!" I said.

"Well, you have to admit, Margot. It's a little unusual for you," my mom replied. Was I really that much of a grinch? I never hum?

"I . . ." I said, then had nothing else to say, 'cause I didn't particularly feel like talking about any of it.

After a moment or so, my mom said, "Okay. I don't want to force you to talk to me. But I made an appointment at my ob-gyn for next week."

"Mom!"

"What? You're the one who said we should talk about birth control!"

Well, that really came back to bite me.

"You need to see a gyno anyway. And if you wanted to ask about the pill while you were there, then that would be up to you!" she said, shrugging. "And we're here if you ever want to talk. About anything. I know I've been hard on you lately. But— that doesn't mean I'm not here to listen, okay?"

I rolled my eyes at her, but I smiled. "I know. Thanks, Mom." For all the head-butting my mom and I had been doing, this was the one time I was actually glad she took control of the situation. I didn't feel ready to have sex today. But the next time I saw Avery, who knows? Better to be prepared.

"Open or shut?" she asked, gesturing to the door.

"Shut, please."

My mom gingerly shut the door, and right as it was closing she said, "And always use a condom. Even if you're on the pill! I know guys say they don't like it, but it's honestly not that different. Your dad doesn't mind them."

From down the hall, my dad sputtered, "I'm going for a run in the park! See you at dinner!" and I heard him scramble out the door.

The election was a week away, and I was running out of time. If I didn't find the blackmailer by Tuesday, November 2, all this would be for nothing. I mean sure, so far they hadn't released the pictures. But what if they were just waiting to get closer to Election Day? When a bombshell like this would do the most damage? The stress of it had become so overwhelming that I almost forgot to turn in my Stanford application. (Thankfully, I got it in with a week to spare. Eye on the ball! Even if there are several balls, like in juggling.)

It took me the next four days to go over all the Ring footage. Mostly it told me nothing. Except that on Wednesday and Friday nights a zaftig cleaning woman in her fifties entered to dust the room and sometimes she would, seemingly accidentally, knock into the Ring camera, making me lose sight of the safe for a few minutes. This was troubling. Because anyone could have slipped into the safe while the camera was askew. And I had no way of knowing. I scanned every side corner of the screen for a hint of someone's shoe or hair or anything that could lead me to a new suspect. But I didn't notice anything!

While Shep's case felt like an endless run on the treadmill of hell,[122] at least Melanie's election had become a lot less stressful. In fact, it was feeling like a foregone conclusion, thanks to Hoffman joining the race. The only thing left to do was for the candidates to give speeches, and for the school to vote.

I got to school early Friday morning and headed to the auditorium to meet Melanie. As I walked through row after empty row of velvet auditorium chairs, I was struck by how quiet it was. There was a very weird energy as the sixteen candidates all milled about the stage, nervously practicing their speeches in their heads. And then the energy got even weirder when I got a notification from the Fury chat. It rang through the cavernous room like a tiny gong. *Doooonnng!* I picked up my phone to see a message from Tasha Ahmadi.

> **TASHA AHMADI:** Hey FC! Finally got an answer back from Palmer and you're not going to believe. He says he can't/won't take down CH pic because he has "no jurisdiction" over WOF. It's student-run. Chris is a registered sex offender what the fuck!

> **TASHA AHMADI:** Who wants to send a petition to student government?

I could feel my hands squeezing into fists. This school was such a joke. They were letting a garbage human stay on the Wall

---

122 Though to me, any treadmill is a "treadmill of hell."

of Fame? Because Palmer claimed it's the student government's job? *What?* I looked up at the stage, where P-Boy was practicing his speech. And something made my stomach churn. With somebody like P-Boy on student government, Chris's precious little ball-kicking accomplishment would probably be enshrined on the Wall forever.

I marched up to the stage and found Melanie in the wings. But before I could tell her about the Wall of Fame, she gave me a hug. (This is, I had learned, how girls must greet each other.)

"I'm sooo nervous!" she squealed.

Abby was there too, brushing cat hair off Melanie's blazer.[123] She regarded me coolly. But when I gave her a shrug and a smile, she moved in for the world's most reluctant girl hug.

"I stayed up all night working on the speech," Melanie said, a nervous energy to her voice. "I tried to put most of your jokes in, except that one about Palmer's car. I think he truly loves his Nissan, so that seemed a bit harsh." She showed me her note cards, and they were covered with strikethroughs and hastily scribbled phrases.

"Are you going to be able to read this?" I asked.

"I think so? I don't know. Should I have printed it out? Shit. Abby, can you type this up for me?" Melanie said, now frantically cycling through her note cards. Abby shot me a look.

"Mel. You're gonna be great. There's no need to second-guess yourself," she said calmly. I saw Abby's point. My input was clearly stressing her out. As Priya once told me, sometimes

---

123 No, Melanie doesn't have a cat. Your guess is as good as mine.

working on a campaign means showing up and shutting up. (Not that I should be using her advice without a big grain of salt.) And today was definitely a shut-up day. "I'm going to give you some bobby pins." Abby slid some pins next to Melanie's temples, and they held her hair back.

"Yeah. Abby's right. You're gonna kill it. Just have fun," is all I should have said. But I couldn't help myself from trying to add one more thing.

"And, uh . . . hey, what if you mentioned something about the Wall of Fame? Did you know that student government is in charge of it? Some of the pictures on it are a disgrace. Like Chris Heinz's."

Melanie stuck out her chin. "Oh. Um. I don't know, Margot. That seems a little negative . . ."

"It isn't negative," I insisted. "It's a fact! Plus it would give you a chance to remind everyone about last year! About P-Boy's involvement in RB and—"

"I know how much you hate P-Boy!" Melanie sputtered. "I hate him, too. But even if I call him out now, it won't erase what happened. I—I just want to give the speech I wrote. I worked really hard on it. So that's what I'm going to do."

She seemed like she was trying to convince herself as much as me. But it didn't matter. She was right. It was her speech, not mine. I bit my lip.

"Okay, I just . . . No, you're right," I said. "You're gonna do great! You've got this!"

Melanie nodded.

At that point people were filing into the auditorium, and

Palmer called all the candidates into the "greenroom."[124] As I left the backstage, I tried to remind myself that Hoffman's candidacy basically assured Melanie's victory. My job was done. Now there was nothing left to do but vote, and wait for the inevitable.

I made my way to the back of the auditorium where Avery was standing. This was the first time I had actually seen him since we both said the big Ls. Would I be awkward? Would he? Or, in a twist, would I actually act normal because he said he loved me, so what was there to stress about anymore?

Turns out it was answer C. The moment I got to him, I gave him a quick peck on the cheek before sliding my fingers into his and leaning against his shoulder. He looked at me, a big smile on his face. I guess that's a nice thing about being in love. Finally, with at least one person, you're not an awkward goon all the time.

"You nervous?" Avery asked.

"No. Why?"

"You're just squeezing a little hard there," Avery said, motioning to his hand. His fingers did look a tad purple. Even though I knew this was in the bag, I guess I was still nervous for Melanie. More than anything, I was just praying that she didn't trip or something. Or, like, fart really loudly.

Onstage was a row of folding chairs all labeled with the names of the candidates for treasurer, secretary, DISAPP, vice president, and president.

I let go of Avery's hand and took a step forward. I felt a knot in my stomach tighten up. "Where's Kelsey?" I asked.

---

124 A janitorial closet with one full-length mirror mounted on the wall.

He turned his head and saw what I saw. All of the candidates' names were on their seats. Except Hoffman's.

"I don't— Huh," Avery answered.

Jenn Snell, who was seated in front of us, looked up from her phone and said, "Kelsey just texted me. Palmer's making her drop out of the race. That asshole."

"What? *Why?*" Avery whispered.

Jenn shrugged. "He said that her signatures were fake and she's disqualified." She chewed her lip. "I mean, a lot of them were fake. But still!"

"Fuck!" I said too loudly. Ms. Gushman shushed me.

"Yeah, I know," Jenn agreed. "And you should have heard her speech. It would've been *epic*."

I felt all the blood in my body rushing into my ears. And heat growing behind my eyeballs. The good one *and* the bad.

"I'll be right back," I told Avery, and ducked out of the row. I marched directly to the "greenroom" and opened the door. Inside I found Palmer talking to Melanie, Hoffman, and P-Boy. It was basically shouting and cross talk until Palmer, like a gavel-less judge, started hitting the door with his palm.

"Okay! Okay! Okay!" he said, finally giving the poor door a break. "One at a time."

I barged in first. "How the hell did this happen?!"

"Language!" Palmer glared at me. "And this meeting is for candidates only!"

"I'm Melanie's campaign manager, and I want to know how this happened," I spat back. Palmer looked like he was ready to gavel my face.

"We received an anonymous complaint last night. It questioned the legitimacy of the signatures Ms. Hoffman used to qualify for the race. Upon closer examination, we discovered that many of the signatures were . . . not real names." Palmer reached into his coat pocket and pulled out a crumpled sheet of paper. "Here we go. We've got Peppa Pig. Tyler Perry. Tyler Perry presents Tyler Perry. And, uh, I think this just says 'Dr. DogHorse.' See for yourself. The last ten signatures were just 'Kelsey Hoffman.'"

I gave Hoffman an exhausted look. *Come on, buddy, you couldn't have tried a little harder?* Hoffman just shrugged and said, "Are we sure Dr. DogHorse doesn't go to this school? 'Cause I thought *she* was in my biology class last year." She looked around the room before declaring, "That's right! Dr. DogHorse is a woman! *That's why she was at the hospital!*"

I did my best to ignore Hoffman as I said, "Who sent the 'anonymous email'? Did you even think to ask that?"

There was a knock on the greenroom door.

"Ms. Mertz," Palmer cautioned. "You need to watch your tone!"

Another knock, and a quiet voice called out, "Peter, it's time for your speech!" Everyone ignored it.

"I think we have a right to know who sent the email!" I said. "I mean, someone was clearly trying to get Kelsey out of this race! Who would do that? I thought you'd at least—"

"I did it!" came the voice from behind the door. Ainsley cautiously poked her head in. "I sent it in. Okay? I did it! And I didn't send it anonymously. I sent it as myself."

"Great. Ainsley. Anyone else like to join this meeting?" Palmer moaned.

"Sorry," she muttered. "Ms. Cahill told me to get Peter for his speech. And I heard you talking."

I scoffed at Ainsley before turning my ire back to Palmer. "And you don't think that's messed up? That P-Boy's girlfriend is trying to take Hoffman out of the race? She's clearly got an agenda!"

"Let's not point fingers, everyone wants their candidate to win," Palmer said, looking directly at me. "I'm surprised you're not more angry about the fake signatures yourself, Ms. Mertz."

I was not interested in explaining my third-party wedge strategy to him.

Ainsley, meanwhile, got defensive. "I'm not trying to be mean, but Kelsey was bragging about how she made up all her signatures. She was, like, flaunting it in gym. And Peter worked really hard to get all of his on time, and she cheated! It wasn't fair!"

I felt like my head was going to explode. "Fair? You—fair?! You know what's not fucking fair—"

"Margot! *STOP!*" Melanie commanded. I turned around slowly.

"Stop what? Are you serious? You—you're just going to let them get away with this?" I asked, flabbergasted.

"Let them get away with what, Margot? Kelsey cheated. She got caught. That's it," Melanie said, glaring at me. "And honestly, it's a little weird that you're getting this upset. Kelsey's not even that mad."

Suddenly I felt lightheaded. And completely tongue-tied. Melanie was calling me out in front of everyone. Making me look petty when the only petty one here was P-Boy. And Ainsley!

And then, the prodigal son himself decided to chime in, meekly adding, "Look, I didn't tell Ainsley to do that. But I believe in a woman's right to choose. So, like, since that's what Ainsley chose to do, then it's like . . . her body, her choice, ya know?" My god, there was something so disturbing about hearing P-Boy co-opt these slogans out of context. He was like a parrot who flew by one pro-choice rally. "But just so you know, Hoffman, I thought your campaign was dope. And I'm sorry you got DQ'd, because I just wanted this to be fun."

I couldn't listen to this bullshit anymore. My face felt hot as the words spilled out. "Liar! Why should we believe a word you say?" I turned to Palmer. "He told us he wasn't friends with Chris Heinz, but then guess what. I saw his car in Chris Heinz's driveway *last week*."

P-Boy looked surprised. "My car? Were you, like, following me?"

"His car was at Chris Heinz's house, because he's *still friends* with that predator. And who knows what kind of toxically masculine bullshit these two are cooking up for their next big hate crime—"

"Language, Ms. Mertz!"

P-Boy was getting defensive. "I'm *not* friends with him! I swear! The only reason I went to his house was to tell him that to his face! He keeps texting me and I had to be like 'Dude! Take the hint! I'm not like that anymore!'"

I put my finger right up to his face. "Peter. If you say another goddamned word while I'm in this room, I will rip your fucking throat out. Okay?"

"Okay. That's it. Detention after school, Ms. Mertz!" Palmer shouted.

"Great! I'll see you there!" I shouted back before I stormed out of the greenroom and slammed the door.

I walked away from the auditorium as fast as I could. I had no desire to talk to anyone. Even Avery. I just had to move away from where I was and to anywhere else.

I stormed past the gym hallway, its usual sneaker squeaks noticeably absent, past the trash hall, tempted for a moment to just sneak right out of school and be done for the day. But then I realized where I was. A few feet more and I'd be at the Board. Then the trophy case. And, finally, the Wall of Fame. And even though I had never even glanced at the Wall before, today I knew I had to see it. To see Chris's face again. It didn't take long for me to find him. He had a primo spot: center left, right at eye level. Jesus, they weren't even trying to hide him.

I stared at his picture, his chiseled jaw and vacuous eyes staring back at me. Then I leaned over and put my hand over his face. Momentarily erasing it from my view.

In the spring, I would graduate. And in a few more years, everyone I knew here would be gone as well. And everything everybody ever did would be forgotten. Everybody except him. He'd be here forever. Smiling. Looking down at all the incoming classes. For as long as this school stood, so would Chris.

I removed my hand so that I could really look at him again. Then I leaned in and said, "You. Don't get. To win."

CHAPTER 20

FULL ROVE

"I need to speak to Principal Palmer. *Immediately*," I said a few hours later. The bell had just rung, and students were filing out of school, all their votes cast and ready to be tallied.

"Margot? Are you okay?" said either Helen or Jackie. I get the two office ladies confused.

"I'm . . . fine," I said, holding back tears. "I just— I need to talk to him right now?"

"Of course, honey," she said, full of matronly pity. "Have a seat. I'll see if he's available."

Tell him to get his ass available. This is important, I thought. But luckily she waved me in a moment later.

And I'm not proud of what I said next. Partly because it was a lie, and partly because it was born out of desperation, but *mostly* because it was loosely inspired by Karl Rove. (Who even a Machiavellian like *Nick* called an "evil genius Republican motherfucker.")

"I've been hacked!" I said upon entering his office. I collapsed on a chair in front of his desk, holding my laptop like it was my suckling babe.

Per usual, Palmer was not pleased to see me. But my fake tears made him a little warmer, or at least a little more cautious, toward me. He handed me a tissue. "What are you talking about?"

I meekly handed him my laptop. "Look for yourself."

Palmer sighed and asked Helen to get him a cup of coffee, even though I'm almost positive that's not her job.

"During fourth period, I was looking at my computer—I take computer science, and we're allowed to bring our laptops to class," I added because I could tell that he was going to complain. "And Ms. Drexel was showing us how to do a full system diagnostic. It's like doing an MRI for your computer, to see if you have any viruses. And when I did mine, I realized I had been hacked." I sniffled. It would've been a great place to break into sobs, but I was limited by my acting ability. I'm no Kelsey Chugg.

Palmer looked at the screen. It did indeed show that my computer had been "hacked," though I didn't think Palmer could actually read and identify code. "Ah, okay . . ." he said, pretending to understand what he was looking at. What a weird choice for him. Why not just ask me to explain further? Or to point out where the code had been hacked? I guess the answer is . . . ego.

"Ms. Drexel thinks it probably happened like a month or so ago?" I added. I thought it would strengthen my case if Ms. Drexel were included in my story. So I brought it to her attention during class. She hadn't shown us "full system diagnostics" today, but I doubted Palmer would think to verify that. Drexel really did understand code, so I had to make that part look believable.

"It's a zombie patch." (There's no such thing as a "zombie" patch. But I thought that sounded more nefarious than just a plain patch.) "Once installed, an outsider can access every bit of data on my computer. They can even turn on the camera and use it as an illegal recording device."

Palmer looked at the code and squinted. "I see. Hm. But, I'm not sure what you want me to do about it?" Palmer said. He never was. That was basically Palmer's slogan. He should make T-shirts!

"I've only seen this specific patch once before. Last spring. On Tasha Ahmadi and Kelsey Hoffman's phones. They were the two girls who showed up on Roosevelt Bitches even though they'd never sent nudes. Because their phones were hacked."

Palmer's eyes widened, now getting where I was going with this.

"So you're saying . . ."

"P-Boy used the patch then. And I think he used it again on me."

Palmer walked around his desk and sat in his chair. His brow furrowed as he thought what to do. "That's quite an accusation."

"It's not an accusation. I have security protocols installed in my computer. And they traced the patch to the IP address 24.134.73.228. Which, I know from my interest in the Roosevelt Bitches case, is P-Boy's home IP." I pushed my laptop forward like it was definitive proof. Even though it definitely was not. I put the patch on my computer at lunch and made it look like it was placed there a month ago.

"Jesus," he said, rubbing his cheek. Then he punched a button on the intercom. "Helen, can you pull Peter Bukowski out of athletics and tell him to come to my office?"

He then sat back in his chair and stared at me. "He hacked your computer. And you didn't notice it until just now? In computer science class?" Palmer said, a new skepticism in his voice.

"Yep," was all I said.

It wasn't like this was a foolproof plan. I was relying on Palmer's ignorance of the technology to make the whole thing work. But I also knew what a bind Palmer had been in since last year. The superintendent was watching him, and if Palmer let P-Boy get away with hacking a female student, he'd surely be fired.

"You said his IP address comes up? Can you show me that?"

I pointed at the screen. It had been easy to engineer. Palmer thought he was looking at a page of actual coding, but really it was a PDF of a page of coding, one that I had messed around with a little.

"Well . . ." Palmer finally said, after much chin stroking, "I don't think it gets more definitive than that. Thank you for bringing this to my attention. I will deal with it, and Mr. Bukowski, immediately." And I could tell by the tone of his voice that he was serious, for once. P-Boy was done. Before I left, I asked Palmer one last question.

"Just out of curiosity, who won?"

"Mr. Bukowski and Ms. Hoffman are both ineligible. So Ms. Davis wins by default," Palmer said while turning on his computer.

"Okay, but I mean, who got the most votes?"

"Does it matter?" Palmer said, shooting me daggers. He was in no mood to keep chatting with me. And even though I was worried my brain would implode if I didn't know the outcome, I just nodded. "You're right." I let him take a few pictures of my laptop for "evidence," then left.

AS I WALKED OUT OF SCHOOL, I SAW A MISSED TEXT FROM Melanie offering me a ride home. I told her to pick me up at the drop-off loop.

When she arrived, I dumped my backpack in the back seat and climbed into the front. "I have to go pick up Milo, if that's cool. But it's on the way to Trinity Towers."

"Totally fine," I assured her.

"Aghhhhhhh, what a day!" She sighed. "I was so nervous for the speeches this morning. And then during second I took a huge dump in the freshman bathrooms and *that* was stressful because I was afraid someone would come in and smell it. And then Mrs. Alawi gave us a pop quiz, which I'm sure I failed!" She slumped forward on the steering wheel as if she were dead. I know we were only in the parking lot, but I wished she'd keep her eyes on the road.

"Well, it's all over now," I said.

"It's not! This weekend is going to be AGONY while I wait for the results! You know they're probably just sitting there on Palmer's desk!"

I tried to sound emphatic. "I know!" Then I quickly looked out the window.

Melanie turned to me. "Margot? Do you *know something*?"

I couldn't help it. I smiled a little. And she became even more insistent.

So I asked, "Would you want to know? The results? If I could tell you them right now?"

"YES! NO! Wait! Wait for Milo. He's more invested in this campaign than I am."

Four minutes later we pulled into the Walt Disney Elementary School drop-off loop, and Milo hopped into the back seat. He was, as ever, a giant ball of energy and crumbs.

"Did you win? Did you win?" he asked, hurling his backpack into the back seat. Upon seeing me, he added, "What's she doing here? Is she sleeping over or something? How come you get to have people sleep over and I don't?"

"I'm just giving her a ride home! And Margot was about to tell me who won. So shut up," she said playfully.

Milo then clammed up with comedic vigor, pursing his lips together to keep from talking. But his eyes just made a huge, pleading, *Wellll? Tell me?*

"Okay, yes. Results of the election . . ." I said, trying but failing to match their enthusiasm. "You won. You're going to be president," I said without drumroll or fanfare.

"AHHHHH!!!" I'm not sure who screamed louder (or more shrilly!), Melanie or Milo. She laid on the horn for a good long beat. And then they both got out of the car and started running around, leaving their doors wide open in the drop-off circle. I sat there helplessly as the poor crossing guard tried to guide traffic around Melanie's car.

She was so happy. After she got back in and started to drive, she banged her long fingers on the steering wheel. And for a few moments, all felt right in the world. The good person won. There was balance in the universe. And Milo was happier than I've ever been in my life.

Several minutes later, when we were en route to Trinity Towers, Melanie started asking questions. Thus far, we had avoided the unsavory details of *how* she'd won. But I knew it was only a matter of time.

"So was it close? How many votes did P-Boy get?" Melanie asked at a red light.

"I bet it was a landslide!" Milo offered, almost unintelligibly, his mouth full of Starburst. "Haha. And you told me you weren't going to win!"

Melanie smiled and looked at him in her rearview. "What I *said* was, it doesn't matter if I win. What matters is if I run a clean campaign."

"So how much did she win by?" Milo asked. Although it was more like, "Howmussiiwiiibyy?" with all the Starburst.

I smiled a tight smile. "Well, actually . . ." But at the first sound of my explanation, Melanie whipped her head toward me. She sensed that I didn't know how to continue.

"What?"

"Well, it's a little underwhelming actually. P-Boy is being disqualified. So . . . it's just you!"

"Disqualified?" came a garbled voice from the back seat. "How come?"

"Yeah, sorry," Melanie added with a note of concern. "What?"

I hadn't really thought through this whole thing when I made the rash decision to frame P-Boy. And how that would probably mean lying to Melanie. This did not feel good. But here I was, in too deep to back out.

"Well, it's really messed up actually. But, uh, P-Boy hacked my computer. A month ago actually. But I only found out about it today. So I went in and told Palmer about it and now . . . P-Boy's out." I was getting more nervous with every passing word. Again, it was just silence.

"How did you find out?" she asked, a subtle but powerful sense of doubt in her voice.

I told her my story about computer science class and the patch. And how I was able to trace it to P-Boy's IP. I was a little less convincing than when I told Palmer. But I got it all out without too many "um"s.

She stared ahead at the road. "You told me you log every outbound program and if something weird is running, you'd be alerted."

Hm. I'd forgotten that I mentioned that to her. I looked out the window. "Yeah, but it disguised itself as another program, so I just missed it . . . It's wild . . ."

"Yeah," Melanie finally agreed, her voice flat. "That is wild."

"But still! You won! You're going to be class president!" I cheered.

It seemed Milo could sense there was some awkwardness, because he, too, stayed silent.

"Yeah. I just didn't want it to go down like that," Melanie said, biting her lip. "But I guess you were right. P-Boy's an asshole."

"Huge asshole!" Milo piped in. "Huge, *huge—*"

"Okay, Milo, we get it," Melanie said, rolling her eyes.

I got out of the car and thanked her for the ride. The last thing I saw was Melanie staring out the window. She did not look like a winner. In fact, she looked like she'd just lost something.

No one was home. I had some of the old coffee left in the pot and a couple of animal crackers. The school campaign was over. I'd beaten P-boy. I'd won. But I didn't feel like it. Was I burnt out? Exhausted? I didn't know. I should've been happy. Melanie would be president, and she'd be a good and just president. But I didn't feel happy at all. I felt dirty.

My phone pinged. Then pinged again and again. The Fury chat was blowing up. Apparently word had spread that Peter had dropped out. Multiple people asked if I had anything to do with it, but rather than stir the pot, I just turned my phone to silent. I couldn't think of anything clever to say and I was tired of lying. Instead, I tried to get some work done. But half an hour into security cam-watching, I felt a migraine coming. So instead of working, I ate an Almond Joy and lay down on my bedroom rug.

I started to wonder if I was feeling so shitty because I'd lied to Melanie? Had I done that only to avoid her wrath? That was pretty cowardly. And I am many things, but not usually a coward.

I decided I would tell her the truth. In a few days. Once things were a little quieter, then maybe she'd understand. She might not approve of my tactics, but she'd have to forgive me once she was president.

• • •

WITH THE SCHOOL ELECTION BEHIND ME, I SPENT THE REST OF the weekend port scanning all of the Shep campaign IP addresses. I don't know what I really hoped to achieve, other than finding some loser still running an old OS from the nineties that would be easy to crack. It wasn't just a long shot—it was an impossible shot. My odds of winning the Powerball were better. (And I never win anything.[125]) But at least it let me pretend that I wasn't staring at another dead end. I did most of my work in bed, wearing cozy pants and speaking to my parents only when spoken to.

I should've been feeling that last-ditch, MCYF-crunch-time stress, the good kind of stress that makes you ACHIEVE and SCORE WELL ON STANDARDIZED TESTS. But instead I just continued to feel crappy. And no good ideas were coming to me.

Priya was texting every few hours with messages like, **Hey!** and **Checking in!** and **How's it going?** but I stopped responding. I had nothing new to report, and every new text from her just needled my anxiety.

But then Sunday night, she sent an urgent text and followed up almost immediately with a phone call. I got out of bed and answered.

"Priya! Hi. I was just about to call you," I said, even though I wasn't. "I got a mini break in the case. Well, it's kind of a setback, but I at least know—"

"Margot. We're taking this to the police," Priya said. Wow. Okay. Hello, gut punch. But before I could respond, Priya continued. "The election is in two days. And Shep just got another

---

125 At Field Day in fifth grade, everyone got a ribbon just for participation. Except me. Because I was sent home early with bad allergies.

email. With more pictures. First thing tomorrow morning, I'm telling him everything and we're going to the authorities. I'm sorry, Margot. But—"

"I get it," I said before giving a long exhale. "I took too long. I know I did. I . . . I'm sorry I couldn't—"

"It was a hard ask. Too hard. And I know you gave it everything you had."

I didn't feel like crying, so I made an unconvincing excuse about dinner and hung up. Then I plopped my body on the bed and just lay there. I assumed it would be momentary. That soon I would get up and see what my parents were doing. Or get something to eat. Or literally do anything other than not move. It was only eight fifteen. But the more I lay there, the heavier my body felt. And the more muddled my thoughts became until I gave in and went to sleep. And why not? What else was there to do?

HOURS LATER, I WOKE UP IN A COLD SWEAT. "FUCK!" I SAID, OR dreamed that I said. There was one last thing I needed to check—something that would solve our little email mystery, if I got very lucky.

CHAPTER 21

RELAY RACE

I stumbled toward my computer in the dark. My good eye wasn't ready for the brightness of the screen, so I squinted, momentarily seeing nothing but a pale white glare. But a few seconds later, my eye adjusted, and I logged into Shep Green's personal email.

I'd never signed into Shep's account before. But I'd found his email password when I did a thorough search of Priya's computer. I didn't intend to ever use it. But I had no other way of viewing this most recent email. So here I was, using it.

I opened his account and quickly found the new email from DropOutShep. Like the first, it was cryptic. It was hard to discern what the blackmailer even wanted.

YOU'RE GOING TO LOSE. YOU'RE A LIAR AND A CHEATER. YOU KNOW WHAT YOU DID AND SO DO I.

Still no mention of money. And this time it didn't even mention him dropping out of the race. And voting started in something like thirty-six hours. It was like the email was purely to fuck with him or get in his head.

But the content of the email wasn't what had woken me up in the middle of the night. What I needed to see was the backend. It was a total long shot, but I realized I could check the new email's server path. With the prior email there'd been no relays, but my gut told me there was a *chance* the sender hadn't been as careful this time around.

So I opened the second email, closed my eye, and said a little hacker's prayer. When I opened it, I got my answer. The email was sent through a standard relay and even better, it ran through several hops. Maybe I *was* a winner! I was able to see each hop and reverse the IP addresses as it bounced around servers in North Webster and Syracuse, originating from an IP address of 17.176.54.413.

That sounded familiar, I thought as my middle-of-the-night brain stared at it. I know most people don't pay attention to IPs, but if you look at traceroutes all the time like I do, you start committing them to memory. 17.176.54.413. Was it the North Webster community library? It wasn't my parents' laptop or Sammi's home IP. Why was it ringing such a bell? What other IP did I see all the time?

And then it hit me like my fourth cup of coffee. Holy shit. It was Roosevelt High. The email was literally coming from *inside the building*!

I called Priya and crawled into my closet—I didn't want to

wake up my parents. It rang for a while. It was three a.m., after all.

She didn't pick up. But after a minute she texted back.

> **PRIYA:** Did you call me on purpose? Did something happen?

I told her to call me right away. I didn't know when Priya and Shep were planning on turning over the emails to the authorities, but I didn't want to risk being too late.

"Margot. I know you're dedicated and all. But even for you, three a.m. is a bit much," Priya said.

"I know where the email was sent from! I traced it to a server at my fucking school," I whisper-shouted.

"What?" Priya asked, and I could hear the sounds of sheets rustling as she sat up. "Your school? Like your high school?"

"Yeah. Which means I can figure out who it is! I just need a little time—"

"God, Margot. I don't know. I just told Shep everything and he's freaking out and—"

"I'm so close, Priya," I told her earnestly. "Please. I don't think these emails were sent by any kind of Moriarty mastermind. Whoever it is completely forgot to sign out of their relay server, which is a rookie mistake. It's probably a kid or a befuddled incel or something. I can shut this shit down!"

She sighed. "Okay. Fine. I will try to buy you as much time as I can. But if you can't tie it all up by tonight, we're going to the police. We can't risk this stuff coming out on Election Day."

I took a deep breath, and since I was in the closet, that breath was full of mostly dust. "Twenty-four hours. Deal," I said, coughing.

• • •

WHEN I "WOKE UP" THE NEXT MORNING—A TERM I USE LOOSELY because I didn't go back to sleep—I felt like crap. It was Monday. The day before the election. (And one of the most *Monday* Mondays ever.) I brushed my teeth, washed my face, and debated peeling back my patch to check on my eye. It was starting to feel . . . leaky? And I couldn't be sure, but I thought it was burning a little more. They had given me some kind of drops to use when I left the ER. But I left them in Avery's car, and then he got his car detailed, and now I didn't know where they were. Pfff. Really needed to get this looked at by a professional.

My mom had asked me what the ophthalmologist said after my eye appointment last week. I didn't have the nerve to tell her that I blew off the appointment, so instead I just lied. "Everything's healing normally! Gonna be back to two eyes soon!" Lying to my parents was apparently an occupational hazard I couldn't avoid.

I was pretty sure this was also a rule #4 violation. I was definitely not taking care of myself. But there would be time for that after the election. Then I'd be able to take a big bath in Epsom salts or whatever you do when you're self-care-ing. (And for all of you keeping score at home, yes, I had now broken three out of my four rules. Which isn't great!) But it would all be over soon. I had a server location. Now all I had to figure out was who at Roosevelt would want to blackmail Shep Green.

Avery had graciously offered to drive me to school. So I went out to the Trinity Towers drop-off circle to wait for him. I was locked in my thoughts, cycling through all my fellow classmates—and teachers and school staff—trying to figure out who would want to hurt Shep. It made me wish I hadn't deleted the Register, my list of Roosevelt students and their habits that I had destroyed last year.

Avery tapped a gentle *beep* on the horn, and I finally noticed him waiting for me. When I got into the car, the first thing he said wasn't "Good morning," or even "Hey." It was "Are you okay?"

I looked down at myself. *What's the problem?* I was dressed. I'd even brushed my teeth.

"You didn't notice me until I beeped."

"I'm just distracted. Sorry!" I poked my index finger into my patch in an effort to scratch my now-itchy eye. But the patch made it impossible. It was like scratching an itch with a cotton ball.

Avery put his big, warm-but-not-sweaty hand on mine and drove. "I know. It's cool."

Holding his hand normally calmed me down. But right now I couldn't think straight. It was someone at Roosevelt. Literally everyone at my school was a suspect. And to my horror, I suddenly considered Avery.

"Avery, I have to ask you something," I said as I squirmed in my seat. I knew I should also tell him about Priya. But I decided not to. One thing at a time.

"Okay . . ." Avery finally said after a fretful pause.

"Your dad got another threatening email yesterday. And I figured out that it was sent from a computer at Roosevelt."

"Roosevelt? *What?*" he asked, flummoxed.

"And I just have to ask. It's not *you*, is it?"

He dropped my hand. "You think I'm trying to get my own dad to drop out of the race?"

"I don't!" I insisted. "I really don't. But look, I expected to trace the email to someone in the Lidori campaign or a rival business. But since it came from the school, I tried to think of anyone who has ties to your dad and . . . I mean, you have a tie?"

He gave me a look. A look that said, *No, I did not threaten my own father, why would I do that?* It was more disappointed than angry. Which somehow felt way worse.

"Okay. Sorry. I just felt like I had to ask." I picked at the toggle on my coat. "Because, honestly, I don't know who it could be. I mean, do you?"

He chewed his bottom lip. "No. I didn't think anyone cared about my dad. Let alone hated him enough to do something like this."

"I'm sure they don't hate him," I lied. "It's probably just politics. Or some weirdo with a vendetta because he didn't like the car Shep sold him or something."

Avery shook his head. "From our school? I don't know."

"Well, whoever it is, I have to find them in twenty-four hours, or Priya's going to turn the case over to the authorities. So either I'm going to figure it out today or . . . I'm not."

"That's not a lot of time," he said, then hesitated. Like he was going to say more but thought against it.

"What?" I asked.

"Nothing. It's just . . . if they took it to the FBI or whatever. And you stopped working for my dad. Would that be so bad?"

I sighed. I knew that Avery was beyond sick of this case. Of getting updates about his dad's extramarital dalliances. And I would've loved to tell him that he was right. That I could just walk away. But the truth was, I couldn't. I had to see this through. Whether it was right or wrong, I just had to. And all it took was a single glance for Avery to know that.

When we got into school, I went straight to the computer lab. The in-network computers were all located there or in the library. Most of the teachers brought their own laptops and didn't bother to connect to the school's network. Most, but not all. I'd seen Mr. Lumley on the lab computers. And sometimes Coach Powell.

There was a sign-in sheet in the lab that students were supposed to use, though most didn't bother and there was no one to enforce it. I scanned through the names anyway. Justin Chen, Olivia Hall, Chase Converse, Katie Travis, and more had all used the computer lab yesterday afternoon. Though it was very likely the blackmailer hadn't even signed in to the lab. If you're going to commit a crime, why leave your signature as evidence? Still, I started with the names I had. I scanned their SMs looking for anything political or pro-Lidori. Nothing. I ran the names by Avery to see if any of them had any connections to his dad.

AVERY: I don't think so. Chase has delivered pizza to our house? But I don't think my dad was home.

AVERY: And we always tip well.

I'd been to dinner with Avery enough to know that was true. He was generous. (Whereas my family always calculated *exactly* 18.5 percent.)

I skipped second and third periods, hunkering down in the lab instead. I looked at all the desktops, checking keystrokes, but I wasn't finding the exact computer that had sent that email.

After fourth, I went to the bathroom to take off my patch. It was itching so bad I couldn't stand it. When I did, I momentarily became queasy. Something was *not right* about my eye. It was weeping and puffy and honestly, a little yellow. Yikes. I tried to tape the patch back on, but the tape had lost its stick. *Just one more day*, I kept thinking to myself. *Gimme fourteen hours, ole lefty. We're almost there!* I went back to the computer lab to borrow some of the electrical tape they use to keep power cords wrangled. I was getting weird looks from people.

I headed to computer science fourth period because I'd already missed so many classes that Ms. Drexel was starting to give me shit. But I spent the entire time scrolling through my fellow students' Instagrams, looking for something, *anything*, to tie them to Shep Green.

I looked for anyone who might have a motive to blackmail Shep. Students like Ken Butler, who wore a M#GA hat to school, or Hayley Dunham, whose mom was voting for Susan Lidori because they both go to the same gym. But by the end of fourth, I needed a break. I swiped open Instagram, promising myself I'd only spend five minutes mindlessly scrolling before I returned to my search. But I soon found myself sucked into Ainsley's feed. I guess I'm a masochist, but I rarely went on IG without envy-scrolling her Stories. She's just so intimidatingly pretty, and every post makes her look carefree and cool. "Look, I'm eating a big messy sandwich, but I still look hot!" "I just hiked this mountain in sandals and a sundress!" "I found these clothes in a trash can but they all fit perfectly and look like high fashion!" I didn't expect to find anything useful on it. I was just killing time in a very unhealthy way. But then something caught my eye.

It was a close-up selfie with the caption **working girl! 1st day on the job!** But behind Ainsley's perfectly symmetrical face I could see the corner of a four-story glass building that I recognized instantly. She was standing in front of the offices of Forsythe and Mahn. *Did she work there?*

Ms. Drexel called on me to answer a question, but I told her I had to go to the nurse. She took one look at the electrical tape binding my eye and didn't question it.

I didn't go to the nurse though. I went to the stairwell and zoomed in on the photo of Ainsley, cross-referencing it with a Google image of the F&M offices. It was a match, I was pretty sure. So Ainsley worked in the building? Could she have accessed the safe? It was strange I never saw her on the company payroll. But maybe she'd been an unpaid intern or something? I would have to come out and ask her. Which would be awkward, given that she probably hated me for torpedoing her boyfriend's campaign. But what choice did I have?

THE BELL RANG AND I BOOKED IT TO THE CAF, HOPING TO CATCH Ainsley. I spotted her at a table near the windows where she was "sharing" a burger with P-Boy. And by "sharing" I mean watching him eat.

When I got to the table, they both looked up.

"Margot! Oh my god!" Ainsley said emphatically. "We've been looking for you."

Hm. Unexpected. Were they planning to beat me up? Or kidnap me? I shifted my weight and prepared to bolt.

"Margot, I know you probably won't believe me. But I promise you. I didn't hack your computer," P-Boy said with so much sincerity it made me wince.

"You . . . didn't?" I asked, trying (but not succeeding) to sound surprised.

"She doesn't believe me. Of course she doesn't," he whined to Ainsley, shaking his head.

"He didn't, Margot! I swear! He doesn't even know how to do that patch thing," Ainsley added, before grabbing my arm and leaning in to say quietly, "Margot. I think he was framed."

I looked at Ainsley, then back at P-Boy. His big doe eyes. And for the first time in my life, I actually felt sorry for him. Did he deserve what I did to him? Yes, he did. But also, in this moment, I felt like he didn't?

And then to my surprise, P-Boy asked, "Can I, like, hire you? To find out who did this?"

Oh boy. I didn't know how to even begin to answer that one. So instead I deflected. "Uh. Possibly. I'm kind of taking a break, but maybe?" Then I pivoted real hard.

"Ainsley, I actually wanted to ask you something. Did you ever work at Forsythe & Mahn?"

"No. I don't know what that is. Do they do those mud masks?" Ainsley asked. And unless she was a really good actress,[126] I believed her. Then she added, "I work at Slauder Jones. Part-time."

Huh. Not what I was expecting. Slauder Jones is a multilevel marketing scam that sells purportedly high-end "organic" face and body products. Anyone can sell it because you have to buy all your product up front first. That's how they get you.

"Slauder Jones?" I asked.

"Yeah. I sell it. You're supposed to be eighteen, but my aunt signed for me. She sells it too."

"Cool. That, uh, that sounds like a cool job." I tap danced. "So you've never heard of Forsythe & Mahn? The law firm?"

"Oh! Wait, yeah. They're on the fourth floor of our building, right? Slauder Jones is on two!" She beamed, happy to be connecting the dots for me. "Yeah, the only reason I know that is because that girl Abby used to work there? That's her name, right? Abby?"

"Yeah," concurred P-Boy, who evidently knew who she was talking about.

I froze. A high-pitched ringing filled my ears. But I managed to respond with, "Abby? Abby Durbin?"

"I think? I'm still learning names, honestly. She has brown hair. The girl who, like, walks really fast to class?"

"Abby Durbin doesn't work at Forsythe & Mahn," I corrected her. *Does she?*

"Oh. I don't know. I just ran into her in the parking lot, like,

---

126 Which she could be if she's actually Margot Robbie!

one time and she told me she worked there. But that was a while ago." I mumbled thanks and was about to leave the caf when Peter stopped me.

"Margot, I know you don't believe me. But I just need you to know that I didn't do this. I swear it on my sister. I swear. I'm not—"

The bell rang, and everyone got up from their tables to leave. I tried to ignore P-Boy's pleading face.

"I'll, uh . . . maybe I'll look into it," I said.

I followed the horde out of the caf, but I miscalculated where the middle divider in the double doors came down. I slammed into it with my shoulder and boob, and it pushed me backward.

I stepped back and sat my broken-ass body down on a plastic chair. My head was spinning even though I'd narrowly escaped hitting it on the door. *Abby worked for Forsythe & Mahn?* I'd looked at their damn payroll, and there was no mention of Abby!

I took out my phone and started stalking Abby's social. Abby didn't post to her grid often, but there were a few recent posts: seeing her sister off to college, a picture by the lake. She usually got a few dozen likes. (From Melanie, her mom, Ms. Gushman—Abby, unlike me, is a stellar Latin student.) But then I came across a particularly popular picture of hers (of a fancy-looking ice cream cone). I scrolled through the many likes and one name stuck out, even to a tired, woozy girl like me. Sylvia Mahn. Aka the Mahn in Forsythe & Mahn.

It took some more digging in Sylvia Mahn's Insta, but a month ago she posted a selfie with Abby and Abby's mom. The caption read: **Had a fabulous night with my amazing niece Abby**

and my adequate sister Dana. Sylvia Mahn was Abby's aunt. Holy. Shit. And didn't Karen Forsythe even say that she had a niece that went to Roosevelt?

But could Abby really mastermind a plan to blackmail a state senate candidate? It seemed unthinkable. This was the same person who couldn't bear being a second late to class. This was a rule-follower, a good girl, a tight-ass.

I texted Melanie, asking if we could talk. But she didn't respond. She was probably in class. Or she had figured out that I lied about P-Boy hacking me and would never talk to me again. Hopefully it wasn't the latter, but either way, it wasn't very helpful.

I went to the library and took a seat at one of the computer stations. I scoured Abby's grid and Stories to see if there were any clues as to why she would want to do this to Shep Green. But I wasn't finding anything. She just didn't post that often. And sometimes, like over the summer, there was practically nothing at all. She was friends with Avery. It didn't seem like they'd ever had beef. Why would she be doing this to his dad? *Come on, Abby,* I thought but didn't say out loud. *Why did you do this?*

"Find what you're looking for?" a voice asked softly.

I whipped my head around to find Abby looking over my shoulder.

CHAPTER 22

THE CONFESSION

I X-ed out of Instagram. My instinct was to make up some elaborate cover. But Abby was smart. I could see by her face that she knew what I was doing.

"DropOutShep," I said firmly. "It's you."

She took in a sudden breath. Like a gasp, but she wasn't surprised.

"The campaign hired me to find out who it was," I told her. "I know you had access to Tamika's flash drive. You work for your aunt at Forsythe & Mahn, right?"

She started to shake. Her lip quivered. Her eyes began to water. "I—I—"

"Are you okay?" I asked. And that was all it took. The tears started to trickle down her cheeks. One. Then three. Then . . .

"Are you going to arrest me or . . . I didn't— I don't know what I'm doing, Margot," she managed to blurt out before breaking down into sobs. Quiet but furious sobs.

"No. Abby. That's why they hired me. Because they don't want to go to the police. They just want the pictures back."

Abby nodded, some relief coming to her face that a swarm of agents weren't en route.

"It's going to be okay," I said, trying to be as soothing and re-assuring as possible. Even though I wasn't sure it *was*. What had possessed her to commit a crime like this? I put my hand on her shoulder and led her out of the library.

"It's not—it's not what you think. I wasn't trying to, like, blackmail him. I didn't mean to . . ." She continued to gasp for breath. "It all just kind of happened. I got the pictures and—I wanted him to drop out. If he just dropped out, I wasn't going to do anything. I wasn't going to tell anyone! I swear, Margot!"

The bell rang. *Thank god.* And I guided her out of the build-ing, not even stopping at our lockers. She was way too upset.

"So that's all you wanted? For him to drop out of the race?" I asked. "*Why?* I mean, I get that he cheated on his wife, but do you really think he should drop out because of that?"

She stared at me. She wasn't exactly crying, but her breath-ing was still really shallow.

"Shep didn't . . . He didn't tell you?"

"Tell me what?" I pressed. "Shep doesn't even know I'm working on this."

"About . . . about . . ." She started shaking her head back and forth. "I thought—I thought that was why you were . . ."

My ears felt hot. And my stomach turned over. Something was wrong, but I wasn't sure what. "Why I was what?"

"I thought you knew about me and Shep."

The phrase was innocuous enough. But when she said it, I knew that she didn't just mean *Me and Shep* like *Me and Shep went to the movies* or *Me and Shep both like the color blue.*

She went on, "That we had sex and stuff."

Her eyes found mine for the first time since she started crying. And I could tell right there, with all the pain and sincerity in her puffy face, that she was telling the truth.

The world became a blur. And my ears started ringing. The next thing I remember was falling toward the ground.

A FEW MOMENTS LATER I WAS REVIVED BY ONE OF THE CROSSING guards. I was given water and asked about my eye. But once I got my bearings, I insisted I was fine and excused myself. I needed to hear more from Abby. She had stopped crying long enough to look terrified.

"I thought you were having a seizure or something," she said.

I explained to her that I had fainted. And I tried to make a joke—something about being a Victorian lady. But neither of us laughed.

Somehow I persuaded Abby to join me at Greenbaum's. I had intended to treat her to some muffins, but when we got there I still felt really weak, so she went up to the counter. She got us herbal tea that she said helps with her migraines. I apologized profusely for passing out. I should have been the one comforting her. Instead, I was the damsel who passed out when she said "sex."

"I know I wasn't very cool back there. But . . . are you okay?

Do you need— What can I do to help you, Abby?"

She sighed, a little calmer now. "Nothing. I mean, I don't think there's anything anyone can do. I'm okay, I think. Or I will be." She looked down at her tea. "Maybe, just—could you not tell him it was me? Who sent the emails?"

"If you don't want me to, I won't," I assured her.

Abby looked confused. "Yeah, but you work for Shep. Isn't he going to—"

"Abby, if what you're saying is true, and as of right now I believe that it is, then I promise you I'm not working for Shep anymore. I'm working for you. And I want to help you in any way I can."

"Okay," Abby said, taking a sip of her tea. "So . . . should I just tell you the whole thing, then?"

Yes, the voice in my head shouted. But I put on my MCYF professional hat and calmly said, "Tell me whatever you're comfortable sharing."

"I mean, I've never talked about this to anyone. Not even Mel." She let out a big sigh. "But I honestly think it would be good. For me to just, like, tell someone."

Abby and I certainly weren't buds. In fact, she'd been extra prickly to me for weeks now. Which, in retrospect, makes sense. She'd been going through a lot. And she hadn't even told Melanie? She must have felt so alone.

"I started interning for Shep at the beginning of the summer. I was looking for something to put on my college résumé. My dad is in the chamber of commerce with Shep, so he recommended me. And at that point in the campaign, it was a really small group.

Like seven or eight people. And we were working out of his garage. He gave everyone his cell phone number, even the interns, because he said he wanted everyone to feel like, I don't know, we were a team, I guess. He said we were all equals. And I guess I took that to heart, because I texted him that night. Just to say thank you."

She paused. "I mean, I did text him first. So I guess I kinda started it." Her eyes welled up.

"You didn't start anything. Try not to blame yourself," I said calmly. "Did he text back?"

"Yeah. And I was honestly shocked. He texted back, like, right away. He was like, *I'm lucky to have you on the team.* Or something like that. And then, I don't know, we just started texting. I know it should've felt weird, but it honestly didn't. It was . . . nice."

Abby took a break to pick at the top of her paper cup. Ripping at the seam in the middle.

"It wasn't, like, sexual. At all. He asked me how the college search was going and if I wanted him to write me a recommendation. And he would sometimes tell me about his campaigning and how tiring it was. Like I was his friend. It was just nice. He was really smart and, like, impressive. It was interesting to hear his perspective on things. And he liked talking to me." She further dismantled her cup, then went on, "I think Shep is really easy to talk to. You probably noticed that."

I nodded. "Yeah. He's really . . . yeah," I said, biting the inside of my mouth.

"And I was going through some stuff. After the whole RB

thing, I felt kind of isolated. I love Mel, but she really didn't get what I was going through. And I didn't like talking to my parents about it. But Shep—he was always happy to talk. And he didn't want anything from me. He was just happy to listen."

I could taste blood in my mouth, but I couldn't stop biting down on the inside of my cheek. *He did want something from you,* I thought. *That fucker.*

Even though Shep was a conventionally attractive man, I had never, *ever* thought of him in any kind of romantic or sexual way. Maybe because I was so enamored with Avery. Or maybe older men don't really do it for me? But I tried to wrap my head around how she was feeling. She was lonely and traumatized. And dying for someone to listen to her awful, sad story. And then this powerful grown-ass man comes around and all he wants to do is listen to her. It must have been an amazing feeling. To be singled out like that. And finally heard.

"We got to texting kind of a lot. Like, we'd talk about some campaign event, and he'd share how insecure he felt. How nervous he was giving a speech or whatever. And how, like, every time he saw me in the back of the room, it always made him feel better. He said I was his anchor." Abby, having now mutilated the lid of her cup, pushed it away from her. "It's so stupid. 'Cause I wasn't his fucking anchor. I wasn't anything to him, probably. But at the time, I was starting to have feelings for him."

I just let her sit there for a minute. I really didn't want to push her. I tried to just breathe and not think about how bad this all was.

"Then in like July maybe? The texts got a little flirty. I can't remember when that started. Like, one text we were talking about colleges, and then about me staying in the dorms. And then he was like, *I wish I could hold you.* And then there was nothing else flirty for a while. And I thought I was crazy and had just imagined it. But then one day he was just like, *I can't stop thinking about you.* And then it got more, like, sexual. And, I don't know, suddenly it was everything. I was obsessed. I'd wait all day for his texts and every ping was . . . They made me, like, lose my mind."

"I get that," I said. I definitely felt that way when Avery texted me. Abby and I were both teenagers in love, after all. Which made what Shep—definitely not a teenager!—had done all the more abhorrent.

"It was so gradual. By the time we, you know, did it in his car, it didn't seem that weird. I mean, it was. But also it wasn't, if that makes sense."

I nodded. From her point of view, I was starting to understand how something like this could happen. It wasn't like Shep pounced on her the first night they met. He had been working at it for weeks.

"It was the night after my birthday. He drove me home from the campaign office—they had just moved into the new headquarters—and he gave me this bangle bracelet from Catbird. He remembered it was my birthday and got me a present? It was so . . ."

Devious? Premeditated? My nails dug into my palms. He waited until she was eighteen. Until she was "legal." Yet the grooming started long before? I was disgusted.

"He was my first," she said quietly. "I didn't think it would be a big deal. Like, I didn't want to be a virgin anymore anyway. But I don't know. It kinda messed me up."

"How did it end?" I asked, wondering how she got from car sex to sending a threatening email.

"Yeah. I mean, I was trying to find another time to meet up with him. I would've dropped anything I was doing. At that point I was, like, beyond obsessed with him. But then he got busy. With work and family stuff, he said. And then . . ."

More tears started to leak out of Abby's eyes. I gave her a napkin, which she used to dab harshly at her face.

"Then in August my parents made me go with them to Myrtle Beach for the week. And when I came back, he was done. He said the week apart gave him clarity. And that I should be focusing on my senior year because I have my whole life ahead of me. He said he was old and didn't deserve me. He cried, Margot. I felt so bad. Like *I* was doing it or like it was my idea or something. I felt guilty. Like, I just wanted him to feel better. And I would've done anything he said." She took a deep breath. "Which is why when he asked me to leave the campaign, I did. And when he told me to delete all my texts, I did that too. And when he asked to look at my phone to make sure I did it, I let him. I felt like it was the least I could do, because, you know, he was hurting so much. But later I realized how fucking manipulative that all was. Because now I can't even prove what happened. All those texts are gone."

More tears ran down her face. I held out another scratchy napkin to her.

"After that, I really spiraled. It had gone from this intense, personal, secret thing—that I thought was deep and mutual—to, like, silence. I went from having someone to talk to all the time to having no one. He wouldn't even *look* at me on my last day of interning. It really fucked with me. Honestly I think I took it worse than RB."

I hadn't really thought about how back-to-back traumas must be affecting her. Or if being on RB somehow led to her getting involved with Shep. The fact that Shep could have exploited that made the whole thing even more stomach-churning.

"What did you do?"

She hugged herself. "Well, I tried therapy. My mom definitely thought I was depressed. She made me go. And it was okay. But I never told my lady about Shep, because I knew that would've messed up his life."

I nodded. Trying not to show how furious I was. Shep had gotten so deep into Abby's brain that she felt like she couldn't talk to her therapist? Isn't that the one person you're supposed to be able to tell anything to?

"I honestly didn't want to get him in trouble. But the more distance between us, the more I started to second-guess everything. And to wonder why he was so totally fine after we broke up, even though I was a total mess. It made it seem like I had never mattered to him. How did I lose so much in our relationship, and he lost nothing?"

Abby shook her head and let out one rueful exhale that was almost like a laugh. Then she sat up a little straighter as she continued. She told me how she had been interning for her aunt at Forsythe & Mahn. And how when she saw Marion Briggs-Green come into the office, she eavesdropped outside the meeting. And when she heard that Marion had pictures of Shep's affair, Abby was terrified. She assumed they were pictures of her. So she figured out the safe's combo, repositioned the camera away from the safe, and grabbed the flash drive. But what she discovered wasn't illicit pictures of herself, but pictures of Shep with two other women. Yet another betrayal. And in her fit of rage and self-loathing, Abby copied the files to her own drive and sent the anonymous email.

"I didn't really have a plan. I was just furious. I thought he should drop out. I just didn't think a person like that should be elected to office. And . . . I don't know . . . I guess I was mad that what we had didn't actually mean anything to him."

We sat there for a moment. I was doing my best to process her story. And reconcile it with the Shep I had met. Passionate about change. Charismatic. Principled. My amazing boyfriend's amazing dad. How could that guy do something like this? And yet men do stuff like this all the time. Even when they have families. And especially when they have power.

"You don't believe me, do you?" Abby said.

"Trust me, I do. It's just . . . a lot to process," I said.

Abby nodded glumly. I felt sick. I was trying to be there for Abby. But my mind was spinning. Her revelation was about to blow up my life. The campaign I had been working on day and night? Kaboom. That was over. And Avery? My heart seized.

How was I supposed to tell him about *this* when I couldn't even tell him about Priya? And what would it do to him? I mean, how would he ever look at his dad again, knowing what he did to Abby?

I took a deep, centering breath. "Abby, look at me," I said firmly. "I believe you. And I'm going to do whatever you want. You want to blow up his campaign? You want to take this to the police? Or Caroline? I'll do it. Just tell me what you want."

"I don't know." She hesitated. "I kind of just want this to go away. Like, let him get elected or whatever. Just as long as he leaves me alone and I can get the fuck out of North Webster."

I nodded. And didn't say anything else. Which surprised me. Usually my sense of justice and vengeance would kick in, and I would beg her to go public. Maybe this was progress. Margot 2.0?

I wanted to support Abby's decision. I didn't want to force her to do a press conference if she didn't want to. And if I didn't say anything, she could just go on living her life.

But I also didn't want Shep to get away with this. Abby was seventeen when the grooming started. This wasn't just a scandalous affair. It was criminal. Even if technically legal. He should face a reckoning.

And yet, right now, all I did was nod in agreement.

"I don't know." She hesitated again. "If I had the texts, that would be one thing. But I don't have proof. And I know coming forward would be awful. Not just for me, but for my family too. I don't know, Margot. What do *you* think I should do?"

It made me furious we were even talking about proof. Why should Abby, after all she'd been through, have to also do the police's job? Because Shep was well-liked. And a businessman. And a politician. And he "just doesn't seem like the kind of guy to do a thing like that." So no one was going to believe Abby. Unless we made them believe.

"Well, it's not like you have to decide right now." I don't know what I was saying. The election was *tomorrow*. She really did need to decide. But I could just tell she was fragile. I didn't want to push her.

"Yeah. You're right, Margot. Thank you." She seemed like she was trying to hold herself together. But her hand was trembling. "I'm sorry I've been so mean to you. I've just been in such a dark place . . ." Her eyes teared up again.

"*Do not* apologize to me. I am fine," I assured her. "Do you want me to walk you home? Or you could call Melanie? Maybe she could pick you up?"

Abby liked that plan, and in a few mintues Melanie's car turned, slowing into the parking lot and, as usual, taking four attempts to park in an empty spot. I walked Abby out of Greenbaum's.

"Is it okay if I tell her? It feels weird that I never told her this stuff," Abby asked.

"It's your story, Abby," I told her. "You can tell whoever you want."

When I opened the door for Abby, Melanie looked shocked to see me. I guess things were still weird with us after all the election stuff. I gave a half shrug like, *Yup, it's me, sorry.* I'm not entirely sure my half shrug conveyed that, but Melanie sensed that Abby was in crisis. And that was all that mattered at the moment.

As Melanie drove Abby home, my phone buzzed. It was Avery. He was at the mall buying a gag gift for Greg Mayes's birthday and wanted to know which was funnier, a picture frame that says JESSICA or a cookie cake that says CONGRATULATIONS

ON YOUR RETIREMENT, with a picture of an old dog in frosting. I said old dog. Seeing his picture bubble in my text made my heart break. He was smiling, his arm over my shoulder. Happy. When he found out what happened—Abby—it was going to destroy him. Knowing your dad is a cheater is one thing. Knowing your dad is practically a statutory rapist is a whole new level of disgust. Once I told him, his life would never be the same.

He kept texting but I ignored him for now. I just couldn't handle it.

Still, I knew I needed to talk to someone. This Abby stuff was too big, and there were too many conflicting thoughts swirling around my brain. And only one person came to mind. Even though we had barely spoken to each other in months.

TWO HOURS LATER I TOOK A SEAT IN THE BACK BOOTH AT NICK'S and looked at the menu, even though I wasn't even remotely hungry. I just needed to do something with my hands.

"You've got something on your eye. Your left eye?" I heard a subdued voice say.

I put down my menu and looked at him. Sammi Santos. In the flesh. For the first time in five months. His hair was longer. And he was attempting to grow, I think, a mustache (or there was just a permanent shadow on his upper lip). But otherwise, it was the same old Sammi.

"I do?" I asked dryly.

"Yeah it's, like, big and it's covering your eye? You should probably get that looked at." He added, "You look weird."

"Thanks, Sammi," I said back. God. I was dying to just joke around with him like old times. And a big part of me was relieved that he was being silly. But I couldn't match his energy right now. I was too overwhelmed.

"Sorry. Are you okay? You're not going to, like, lose your eye, are you?"

"No. I don't think so? But to be honest, I haven't been following all of my doctor's instructions. So who knows?" I said.

"That seems about right," Sammi replied, picking up a dirty Nick's menu. "So what's up? I feel like whatever's going on with you, it must be pretty big. Are you trying to hack the Pentagon or something?"

"No, it's worse than that. I have a . . . moral dilemma," I said.

Sammi's eyes widened. "Are you sure you want my advice? I am the guy who built Roosevelt Bitches."

"I remember. Yeah," I told him earnestly as I played with my fork. "But I need a friend right now. And I guess I still think of you as that."

He gave me a half smile. "Oh yeah? So have I been upgraded from 'associate' or 'employee' or whatever?"

"I deserve that." I smiled, happy that Sammi was giving me shit.

Sammi then took out his phone and typed a quick text. "Sorry, I have to cancel a thing I have later. Seems like this might take a while."

"You have a thing?" I said, feeling bad. "It's not a date, is it?"

"It's no big deal," Sammi said, finishing the text and pocketing his phone.

"It's a date! Sammi! Go on the date! I'll figure my stuff out!"

"Trust me, it's cool. She's very laid-back. She's not, uh . . ." Sammi said, suddenly unsure of how to continue.

"Were you going to say, 'She's not like me'?" I inferred.

"Maybe. But I realized that sounded bad. And I actually don't want you to hate me for the rest of my life. So . . ." We both smiled.

WE ORDERED WAFFLES AND COFFEE, AND THROUGH SEVERAL generous refills I told him everything. Interning for Shep. My long and harrowing journey to find his blackmailer. And the horrible reveal that it was a classmate of ours. And how I wasn't sure what to do now. I didn't tell him Abby's name. I know she never asked me to keep it a secret, but I still felt like the less people who knew, the better off she was. So instead I just told Sammi it was someone he knew from Roosevelt. He didn't press it. Sammi was never nosy.

When I finished, Sammi took a big sip of coffee.

"Jesus, Margot. It's never easy with you, is it?"

"No. It's not," I said, swirling my now lukewarm coffee with a spoon.

"Fuck, man. I mean, Avery. That's his *dad*. He's gonna be so messed up." He offered, "And somebody from Roosevelt? Christ. I don't know what to tell you . . ." Sammi trailed off, unable to finish the horrible sentence.

"So what do you think? Do I help her make it all go away? Or do I push her to go public? Because if she comes out with this, Shep is ruined. And I know I shouldn't be thinking about

Avery, but this would destroy Avery's life. How can I do that to him? Especially when this girl would be more than happy to just bury it."

Sammi took the final bite of his waffle. Chewing thoroughly before saying, "Well, it's not like I can tell you what to do."

"Oh, great," I said, blowing the hair out of my face. "You do know that's the whole reason I asked you here—"

"Lemme finish," Sammi said, putting his fork down and wiping his hands clean. "I can't tell you what to do. But that doesn't matter. Because I know you're going to do the right thing. You're, like, physically incapable of doing anything else."

I gritted my teeth. "But that's the problem! There is no right thing! There's just a bunch of bad choices."

"Well, then figure out which one is the least bad and do that," he said, leaning back in his chair. "My guess is you already know what that is." Sammi threw his napkin on the table. There was something weirdly assertive about the way Sammi was being tonight. I guess college had given him a new confidence.

I huffed and ate the little orange slice garnish. He thinks he knows me *so* well just because sometimes he does. That jerk.

WE BULLSHITTED FOR A FEW MORE MINUTES, BUT SAMMI'S PHONE kept pinging. I assumed from his "laid-back" date who maybe wasn't as laid-back as Sammi thought. So I suggested we pay the check and go. But there was one last thing I wanted to ask him.

"Hey, Sammi. Before you go, I have to ask . . . Have you at least tried to apologize? For RB? Because it's one thing to feel bad and to be, like, trying to be a better person. But it's another to actually reach out to the people you hurt. And tell them that in person. It's something I can't fucking stand about P-Boy. That he's gone back to being popular again without really making amends."

Sammi sat back down, nodding nervously. "Um . . . I tried. I guess. I mean, I think."

"What does that mean?" I asked skeptically.

Sammi paused. Then drew in a big breath and mumbled, "I sent out a mass email to everyone on the site. Like, saying I was sorry and if anyone wanted to talk to me about it, I'd listen. I thought about texting them individually, but I don't want to, like, trigger them more. Anyway, I've heard from six of them. It wasn't fun. But, I'm doing it," he said, picking at his cuticles.

I wanted to say something cutting about how it's also "not fun" to be the victim of nonconsensual pornography, but I stopped myself. I didn't know what kicking him would do at this moment. Or what it was I even wanted from him. Probably for the whole thing to have never happened in the first place.

"Well, it's a good start," I said.

Sammi nodded before picking up his jacket and asking, "You coming?"

"Nah. I'm gonna sit here for a bit."

Sammi nodded, then gave a little wave as he left Nick's.

I knew my twenty-four-hour deadline was fast approaching and I didn't want Priya to go to the cops. But I also didn't want to go into all the details of what I learned. So I shot her a vague text saying essentially, **I found the blackmailer. I'm working on getting the photos back, but don't worry. They're not going to** spread. More soon. This seemed to pacify Priya's anxiety, and she sent me a flurry of GIFs and dancing emojis relaying her relief. I almost felt bad. She had no idea the bomb I was about to drop on her.

The waiter dropped off the check and for a moment I just sat there. Nick's was only half full, so I didn't feel bad taking up a slightly broken booth in the back. For a moment I just watched everyone. The cooks clanging around the kitchen. A group of college kids sharing pizza and dousing it in Nick Sauce. Over by the front entrance, a family of four was finishing up their dinner. The kids restless. The parents tired. I wondered if there was a world where I could ever just be normal like this. Enjoying a meal without a big "thing" hanging over my head.

I downed the rest of my coffee and picked up my coat. Time to make the least bad bad choice.

CHAPTER 23

ELECTION NIGHT EVE

I watched Avery's car pull into the parking lot. I saw him get out, check his phone, and then look up toward the picnic table where I was sitting, waiting for him. I'd asked him to meet me by the lake, since I knew there wouldn't be people around. On cold days, the lake was even colder than the rest of North Webster, and not too many people ventured out. There was something beautiful about it, but also unsettling—a quiet, freezing lake surrounded by shuttered ice cream stands and a carousel that closed for the season in September. It was a bitter-cold ghost town.

He jogged to meet me, but I found myself wishing he would walk slower. *Can't we just stay in this moment a little longer? Before I ruin your life?*

"Hey, sorry I'm late," he said, planting a kiss on my lips. "I got the cookie cake. I think you're right. The dog is funny. He has a pipe."

I tried to laugh. But instead I just stared straight ahead. My body couldn't even fake happiness at this point.

"Margot. Is everything okay?" He scanned my face for some sign of what was wrong.

"I'm . . . I'm fine," I tried to say, but clearly I was anything but fine.

Avery took a step back and quietly asked, "Are you breaking up with me?"

"No. No!" I insisted, pulling him closer to me. "That's the last thing I want. No, I just—I have some bad news. Sit." I gestured to the picnic table.

"Okay. It's not my dad again, is it?" Avery asked as he slumped down on the bench.

"Yes," I said, taking his hands. "He . . . Your dad did something bad. Like, really, really bad."

Avery leaned back and surveyed the lake. "Worse than sleeping with his employee?" He exhaled in disgust.

I nodded yes.

Avery paused. Then he lifted his hands out of mine. "Okay. Margot, you're starting to freak me out. Can you just—"

"Your dad had sex with Abby Durbin," I said, my jaw clenched so hard it felt fused shut. "She's the one who sent the emails."

He shook his head as if to say that was impossible. He was trying so hard to make sense of it. It was like he didn't know if he should come to his dad's defense or just be furious at him. "Margot, there's no way—"

"She told me everything. It happened when she was interning for the campaign," I said gently but firmly. I hoped I wasn't betraying Abby's trust by telling him. I just didn't know how to move forward without him knowing the truth. And I knew I could trust him not to tell anyone else.

Avery kept shaking his head. He seemed dazed and like he might not be hearing me. But I kept talking. "You know Abby. She's not a liar. Plus she was really detailed in what she said."

He finally looked at me, searching for a reason to doubt this news. "But, uh . . . I don't think—"

"There were texts too. Between her and your dad. Abby deleted them, but I'm going to try to recover them. To help her prove it." I knew of several ways to recover deleted texts. But I wasn't 100 percent confident in any of them. It all depended on how well Shep had covered his tracks. And my guess was, he covered them pretty well. "I'm sorry. I'm so sorry. But I have to help her if I can."

Avery nodded, his eyes darting back and forth like he was trying to read a book in a foreign language. And then he stumbled away from me, fell to his knees, and bent over to throw up.

"Oh my god! Avery!" I ran to him, putting my hand on his back. But the second my gloved hand touched his coat, he jolted away from me.

"Can you just . . . not, uh . . ." he said, his dark brown eyes looking lost and scared. I'd never seen that look from him before. He heaved again.

And now I felt nauseous too. I tried to comfort him again. "Sorry, I was just trying to—"

"I know. I know. Just— I can't right now, Margot." Plumes of air twisted from his mouth with every heavy breath. He stared out across the lake again, like he couldn't look at me. "Abby Durbin. *Abby Durbin?* She's our age."

I nodded from where I stood. I was dying to go to him, but he didn't want that. Everything was too awful.

"He just— There's something *wrong* with him, isn't there?" Avery's voice broke. "Like, something really wrong."

"Yeah," I said, backing away. Tears filled my eyes. "I'm so sorry, Avery, I—"

He turned around, his hands in fists at his sides. "I have to go. I think. I need to just . . . be alone for a bit."

All I wanted to do was hug him. To tell him that none of this was his fault and that he is nothing like his fucking predator of a father. But I didn't think anything I could say would help him. He seemed so lost and hurt and angry. So instead I said, "Of course. I'll give you some space."

Avery nodded, then started to stumble back to his car. And that's when I noticed my hand start to buzz. That weird numb, tingling thing I hadn't felt since last spring. Great.

Well, I told him. He knew now. But unfortunately, there was more I needed from Avery if I was going to find a way to help Abby.

"Wait—I need to get those texts," I called out to him, the words sounding wrong even as I said them. "And I might need to get on your dad's computer. Or his cloud if he—"

Avery laughed ruefully. "Right. Of course. You've still got to do your *job*." It wasn't exactly an attack, but there was some anger under it. The way he said *job*. "Nobody's home. It's Election Night Eve, remember?"

Ever since Abby's revelation, all the campaign stuff was blurry. Like it was happening far away in some other town, to people I didn't know.

"Here. Take my key," he said before tossing it to me. (I missed.) Then he turned, passed his car, and kept walking.

"Where are you going?"

"For a walk." He just kept going. Out of the parking lot. And for a while I just watched him and listened to the low churning of the waves that were rolling across the beach.

I DROVE AVERY'S TESLA FROM THE BEACH TO HIS HOUSE. EVERY moment of the ride was terrifying because his car was so different from the dry cleaning van, and I didn't know what the hell I was doing. (I mean, the touchscreen was playing a video game the whole time and I couldn't stop it. That doesn't seem safe?) When I finally got to Avery's house, it was almost ten. And while I knew his parents would be out late doing campaign events, I didn't know how long it would take to find Shep's backed-up texts. Assuming I could find them at all.

I parked (poorly) in the Green driveway and got out. And for a second, I just looked at the house. The columns and the uplighting. The giant circular driveway. I understand why rich people buy big houses. They're intimidating. The scale gives off the illusion that whoever owns the house should be respected. And maybe even feared.

Fuck that.

Once I got inside, I called Melanie to check on Abby. Melanie picked up in a hushed voice. Apparently after bringing her up to speed on everything, Abby passed out hard on Melanie's bed. Reliving your trauma twice in one day takes a toll, I guess.

"Well, we can take turns checking on her tomorrow. Right now I'm at Shep's trying to recover the texts he sent her."

"Does Abby know you're doing this? She just told me she's not ready to go public," Melanie warned.

"She told me she didn't know what she wanted to do. But if she ever decides to press charges, she'll need those texts," I countered. I dropped my bag in the foyer and headed up the stairs. "Look, I'm not going to do anything Abby doesn't want. I promise."

"Right. But you promised me that too. And then you went and framed P-Boy. So . . ."

For a moment I felt my throat seize up. Like it was blocking my ability to swallow.

"I'm sorry?" I managed to choke out. "I don't—"

"I'm not dumb, Margot," Melanie said. "I mean, either you framed him, or P-Boy, who's an idiot, somehow hacked you. And since you're the genius, why don't you tell me which makes more sense?"

My face felt hot. All I could think of to say was *SHUT UP!* But I knew that wouldn't be helpful.

Melanie let out a sigh. "Whatever. Just don't try to pull that shit with Abby. She might trust you, but I don't."

Her words were a brick to my sternum. But it was nothing I didn't deserve.

"I promise," I croaked. "I'll let Abby decide. If she doesn't want to come forward, I won't force it. And about P-Boy—"

"Abby's waking up. I gotta go."

She ended the call. I felt my eyes well up. I was so angry at myself that for the briefest of moments, I had the impulse to destroy something. But instead, I did the less dramatic gesture of stomping my foot on the floor several times. Then I moved on. I wasn't finished yet.

I quickly made my way through the upstairs hallway to Shep's office. I creaked open the door and surveyed the room. It was your typical midforties man's office. A big desk with glass paperweights and a bunch of phallic pens. Shelves of books by Doris Kearns Goodwin and Ta-Nehisi Coates. And framed photos of Shep with various "local celebrities" like Reggie Storm and Chuck Gravely. I took a seat and started combing through Shep's giant desktop computer. His phone was synced to his computer, so I could see all his texts. But there was nothing incriminating in any of them. It was almost impressive how well he had covered his tracks. He had meticulously erased anything he didn't want people to see. His phone didn't even recognize Abby's number. And not a single text mentioned her name, her address, or even her existence. I was starting to get a little worried.

Next I waded through his texts with Priya, just to see if there was any evidence of their affair. But while there were *a million of them*, they were all campaign-related. Priya had told me he sent her personal/sexual messages from his actual cell—he didn't have a burner or anything. But he had asked her to delete them after they ended things. So Priya went in and deleted all of their old messages from April and May. But Shep still had messages from that time period on his phone. Innocuous ones. He must have gone through them one by one and manually deleted the incriminating ones. That took a lot of effort.

I leaned back on his chair. Frustrated I wasn't able to uncover even the slightest digital trail to Abby's texts. I tried to think about what other devices he might have. A tablet for reading? An old Apple Watch? Anything he hadn't updated in a while? It was possible his texts could have synced to a device like that. *And* possible the texts could *still be there*, particularly if he hadn't used it in a few months (I know my dad has several old Kindle Fires collecting dust on his dresser). This was far from a sure thing, but it was the best idea I could come up with. I stood and started combing through his bookshelf when I heard a loud *smash*. Followed by a *thud*. Like a window was broken, followed by a body falling. Someone was in the house!

I quickly turned off the lights in the office and crouched down low. It was unlikely anyone would see me through Shep's office window, but still, it never hurts to make yourself small. I crawled to the door and slowly peeked my head out of the office. I didn't see anybody by the front door. But I heard noises coming from the kitchen. Moaning and someone shouting, "Aaaah! Come on. Stupid!" The speech was slurred but unmistakably familiar.

It was Avery.

I walked gingerly down the stairs and rounded the bannister to find Avery sitting on the floor next to a broken vodka bottle. He looked confused, and seemingly unconcerned that he was bleeding all over the kitchen floor. There was a large shard of glass embedded in his hand that he was looking at curiously.

"Avery?" I asked.

"I'm sorry," he slurred, his eyes half-open as I walked to him. I'd never seen him drunk before. It was jarring to see him so helpless and out of control. "I self-medicated."

"Just—don't move. I'll find a bandage or something."

"There's a first aid..." He trailed off, pointing to the bathroom.

I ducked in and found the first aid kit. The bathroom shelves were as pristine and well-organized as everything in the damn house. Then I did my best to take out the shard, disinfect his hand, and wrap it in gauze. I had seen my mom do this dozens of times. Despite the blood, Avery's cut wasn't too deep, so I didn't think he'd need stitches or anything. Avery insisted on going to sleep, so I helped him stumble from the kitchen to his bedroom. He leaned on me the whole time, apologized incoherently. Saying over and over again how this was all his fault.

"None of this is your fault, Avery," I said calmly.

"Yeah, but I should be fixing it. I'm the one who fixes ... My hand looks so big," Avery said, ping-ponging from thought to thought.

"Look, I get that you're not used to being the one who gets taken care of. But right now, that's what's going to happen. So just try and relax."

I made him drink a glass of water. Then helped him upstairs and into bed.

"Wait. Where is my phone?"

Avery then attempted to stand, which I quickly put a stop to by pushing him back down on the bed.

"I'll get it. Just, don't move and don't break any more glass," I commanded.

I ran downstairs and snatched his phone from the kitchen counter. I clicked it on to check the time, but what I saw made my lungs collapse. It was a missed text on the home screen. From Shep.

> **SHEP:** Hey bud. Leaving the party now, should be home in twenty minutes. Fingers crossed for tomorrow!

The text was sent fifteen minutes ago. Fuck. Double fuck. He'd be home any second.

I ran to give Avery his phone. He was already starting to drift. He looked so beautiful and peaceful. Almost like he wasn't having his entire life ruined by the monster he was dating. But there was no time to admire him. I raced back to the kitchen. There was glass and blood everywhere. And even though I had more pressing matters, I still had a strong compulsion to cover for Avery. He never would've gotten drunk if I hadn't told him about Abby. Or maybe I just didn't want anything to seem out of place. Whatever it was, I was doing a lightning-fast sweep of the kitchen when something on the shelf of cookbooks caught my eye. Stacked among the display of Yotam Ottolenghi and Alice Waters was the slim edge of an iPad. Weird spot for a device. *That felt promising.* There was even a thin layer of dust on the edge. When's the last time this baby synced to the cloud?

As I grabbed the tablet, headlights flooded the living room. A car was pulling into the driveway. Shit!

I tried to turn on the iPad, but it was dead. This was actually good news. It was possible that this iPad died in the window of time after Shep had texted with Priya and Abby and before he had gone through and deleted all the evidence. Which would make it a snapshot of that moment in time. With all those texts still on it.

I heard Shep's big Lexus SUV park in the garage, followed by the engine cutting off. Had to move.

Like a horror movie victim, I ran *up* the stairs, as quietly as I could. I reached the office and yanked the Wi-Fi router out of the wall. Internet down. Then I searched in the desk for a charger and found one in a drawer full of other random chargers, all neatly coiled and wrapped in rubber bands. I grabbed the iPad and charger and crawled into Avery's room, shutting the door behind me. I figured it would be less suspicious if Shep found me there. I should've just stayed put and pretended to sleep. But I couldn't wait to check the iPad. I plugged it in.

While I was waiting the interminable ninety seconds for the iPad to power up, I heard a jingle of keys followed by a door opening. Shep was on the phone, talking loudly to someone. Gail maybe? Or Priya?

Priya. Right. She was someone else I was going to have to talk to. Assuming I could get out of here without Shep catching me.

Finally the Apple logo lit up, and the iPad turned on. And as I heard Shep going over his latest polls, I placed it on airplane mode and opened up messages.

They were all there.

Messages to Priya. Sexual innuendo. Then pictures. Messages to Abby's number. A long, long thread that wasn't sexual at all—just him asking about her school day and offering advice. Only at the very end did the messages start to become more intense. Not sexual really. They were more, like, *romantic.* **I need you.**

Sometimes I think you're the only one who understands me. I dream about holding you. Somehow that was even *grosser* than the overtly sexual stuff he had texted to Priya.

I heard footsteps on the stairs. I stuffed the iPad in my bag and crawled into bed next to Avery. I closed my eyes just as the door cracked open and a shaft of light penetrated the room.

"Mr. Green!" I said, pretending to be groggy and embarrassed. Avery kept right on sleeping. "I'm so sorry. We were studying and we fell asleep, and—"

"It's okay, Margot. I was a teenager once." He laughed. "And it's *Shep*."

I shivered. I bet he made Abby call him "Shep" too.

"Don't you think your parents will be wondering where you are?" he asked.

I stumbled out of bed. "Yeah. They're probably freaking out."

"I'll wake up Avery to give you a ride home," he said, walking farther into the room.

"No!" I didn't want to admit that Avery had been drinking. I'm not sure why? Some sort of protective impulse as his girlfriend, I guess. "I think he's really tired."

I was sure Shep could smell vodka, but he didn't say anything. Instead he offered, "Well, then I'll give you a ride."

The thought sent chills down my spine. Alone in a car. With Shep? What if he saw the iPad in my bag? What if he did something worse, like made a pass at me? Or what if I couldn't control myself and I punched him in the ear for what he did to Abby? None of these seemed like great options.

"I can just call my mom. She's always happy to pick me up."

"Nonsense. Give your mom a break. She deserves it!" he said, ushering me out. A week ago I would've found this sort of thing charming. But tonight, it just felt threatening. Still, I couldn't think of a way out of it.

FOR A WHILE WE DROVE IN SILENCE. THEN SHEP STARTED fiddling with the radio, scrolling back and forth, I think to see if there was any coverage about his race.

"Margot, I . . ." Shep said, biting his lower lip. "Look, I'm gonna ask you something, but if you don't feel comfortable answering, you don't have to."

"Okay," I said, slinking into my seat. I had no idea where this was going, but I knew I didn't like it.

"Is Avery happy?" Shep finally asked. His eyes laser-focused on the road ahead.

"Um. Yeah," I answered. "I mean, you know, sometimes he gets down about stuff. But . . ."

"Like about me and his mom. I assume he told you about us?" Shep said, now looking over to me. There was pain in his eyes. He was genuinely worried about his son.

"I'm worried that the divorce, and my whole campaign, I worry that I'm screwing him up," Shep said, going back to the road. He wiped his eyes, in the way men do when even a hint of tear might be coming out. "And don't get me wrong. I'm proud of our campaign. And I think I could do a lot of good for North Webster if I got elected. But sometimes I just worry it isn't worth it. Or that maybe this whole thing is just an ego trip. I don't know . . ."

He was being *so* honest with me. I'd never heard an adult be that vulnerable. It made me *almost* feel sorry for him.

But then I thought, *Maybe that's how it happens?* He talks to you like you're his peer. And by being this vulnerable and open, he gets you to open up to him. To share things you wouldn't otherwise share. And once that happens, you feel like you could trust him with anything. I shivered.

"He'll be fine," I said coldly. "He's resilient. More than anybody I know."

Shep was taken aback by my blunt response.

"This is me," I said, pointing to Trinity Towers. Shep made a left into the parking circle, and I got out of the car. I didn't even thank him for the ride as I shut the door behind me. I was done with Shep Green.

CHAPTER 24

THE FIRST TUESDAY IN NOVEMBER

The next morning I woke to a call from Abby. She'd thought about it and decided to come forward. Not publicly, if it could be avoided, but she was willing to talk to the press if they'd use a pseudonym in their reporting.

"What changed your mind?" I asked.

She paused. "I . . . I just don't want him to do it to anybody else."

This was huge. A victim coming forward. *And* texts as proof. Shep was done. "Are you sure, Abby? You know even if they try to keep it secret, these things sometimes leak and—"

"I'm not being naive. I know what's going to happen." She sighed. "But I can't just do nothing."

So I made a call to Priya. And I told her that the man she had devoted her life to for the past six months was a serial cheater and basically a statutory rapist. It took her a minute or two to accept this. I could hear her straining the limits of her "believe women" mantra. And I felt for her. I knew all too well how it felt to be let down by a guy close to you. But Priya didn't fight me. She remembered Abby. And her story was detailed and plausible. Plus I had the texts as proof.

After she heard everything, Priya let out a primal scream. Then told me she was in. And ready to "burn Shep's whole operation to the fucking ground" (her words).

Before we ended the call, she grumbled, "Couldn't you have told me this before Election Day?"

I sighed. "Why? Is this inconvenient?"

I shot off a text to Avery to give him a heads-up. Letting him know that his life was going to change irrevocably just seemed like the kind thing to do. I told him I didn't expect him to respond. And he didn't.

By nine a.m., Priya was holding a hastily assembled press conference outside of HQ. She asked me to bring Abby, who was exhausted and so nervous she even pulled a Kevin Beane in the bathroom.[127]

"Abby was hoping to stay anonymous for now," I told Priya when we met in her office.

"Oh." Priya seemed surprised. She looked to Abby, who was somehow becoming even more pale. "I'm sorry. I misunderstood. I thought you said she was going to come forward—"

---

127 I should note that Kevin Beane, now a senior, hasn't thrown up since sophomore year. But his reputation as a chronic vomiter lives on.

"As an anonymous source, yes, but not to speak at a press conference."

"It's okay, Margot," Abby said, stepping toward us. "I can do it. I'll answer questions. What, um, do you think they're going to ask me?"

Convenient as it might have been in that moment to throw her to the press, I was hesitant. I didn't want to force Abby into something she wasn't ready to do. If she spoke to the press today, her face and name would be attached to every story about Shep dropping out. It would probably be national news. And while I appreciated that Abby was trying to be brave, I wasn't sure she'd had the time and space to think it all through.

Priya took one look at Abby, and I could see the gears clicking in her head. "Just, uh, why don't you two head out there and find a spot in the back?"

"Priya. I don't think—"

"Just find a spot," she said, waving me off. "It's all good!" I watched her cross to her purse, straighten her blazer, and apply a bold red lip, which I'd never seen her use before. Then we found a spot behind the scrum of reporters. A moment later Priya hopped onstage and announced she was quitting the campaign. Flanked by Gail, who she'd already filled in, she told the crowd she "no longer believed Shep was fit for office."

Abby kept squeezing my hand, waiting for the moment when Priya referred to her. When all the reporters' heads turned en masse to face us. Whoosh. But that moment didn't come. Priya explained that Shep was engaged in several extramarital affairs, including multiple sexual relationships with female staffers.

Including herself. This led to one of those moments that you see on TV where all the reporters just start screaming questions. But Priya never hinted at an affair with a high schooler. Instead she talked honestly about her own experience, and how, in retrospect, Shep's behavior reflected an error of judgment at best and an abuse of authority at worst.

Abby finally turned to me. "She's not going to make me get up there."

"I guess not," I said in awe.

And then we watched as Priya continued to take rapid-fire questions from the press. If I were in her shoes, I would've run away or screamed or put a bag over my head. But she just stood there, calmly waiting for the hubbub to die down before taking about a thousand more questions.

I asked her later why she torpedoed her own political career by admitting that to the press, instead of leading with the Abby stuff. Her affair with Shep hadn't been as egregious as the one with Abby. Now it was the first thing that popped up when you googled her. Priya told me she wasn't too worried about her "political career." And that she wasn't sure she even wanted one after this. "Besides," she told me, "this way Abby didn't have to get up there. And she's been through enough."

Damn, she was cool.

The last I heard from Priya, she was back at Cornell and had switched her major to public health. Which seems like a better major anyway. It was still hard to see her as anything but a hero. She always seemed so empowered. Plus, bold lip! Still, I wondered if any part of her felt like a victim, or rather *survivor* of

Shep's predation. Because now that I knew about Abby, it definitely made me think about the Priya thing differently. It was part of Shep's pattern. And the power differential made consent messy. I never asked her. But I always wondered.

After the press conference, I spent most of the morning being interviewed by a reporter Priya knew from the *North Webster Gazette*. In return for the major scoop I was giving her (including Shep's texts and the whole Abby story), she promised to keep Abby's name and personal information out of it, protecting her as a confidential source. Abby signed off on it. She spent her own morning giving a statement to the commissioner of the New York State Board of Elections.

Shep decided to punch back at the accusations by holding a few press conferences of his own. First, around ten a.m., he told reporters that the accusations weren't true. (Marion and Avery were conspicuously absent.) Then, by noon, as his staff and volunteers began to quit en masse, Shep announced that if he were elected, he would resign immediately. That he had "soul-searching" to do. And that the story was "becoming a distraction." Lidori, meanwhile, had a field day dunking on him and the Democrats. And I couldn't say I blamed her. If Lidori had screwed up this bad on Election Day, you bet I would've been torching her all over Twitter.

And all the while, people went to the polls. I wondered if any of them were following the saga at all. Would any of this matter?

We didn't get the results until 9:05 p.m., which made for a long, long day. I was actually surprised that a big part of me still really cared who won—even though I now knew both of the candidates were heinous monsters. (Although in very different ways: like Dracula and Frankenstein. But if Dracula were a statutory rapist and Frankenstein wanted to pass a bill discriminating against trans kids.) But I guess politics is kind of a weird addictive game that you can't look away from. Like LandBlast, but with real-world stakes.

In the end, Shep won. By something like fourteen hundred votes. September-me would have been thrilled. Melanie won. Shep won. I had gotten what I wanted. Yet I felt like a real loser.

It turns out that most people either didn't catch the warring Election Day news conferences, or were so disgusted by Susan Lidori they held their noses and voted for Shep anyway. Obviously Shep's sex scandal will prevent him from taking the office. New York State has already announced a special election to fill his seat. Which means North Webster's campaign season stretches on. I guess it's good? We'll have another chance at that seat. Which could mean another chance to pass § 245.01. But who knows?

Meanwhile instead of conceding, Lidori came out and cried fraud and demanded a recount. So that might be happening too. And in retaliation for her loss, someone on the Lidori team tweeted out Abby's personal info. So despite the *Gazette* reporter's best intentions, Abby's name is now out there. I tried to bury it for her. But conservative podcasts and fringe blogs (including *Nation Builders*) had picked it up, and there wasn't much I could do after that. Abby seemed weirdly fine about it though. She later told me that living with the aftermath was way easier than living with the secret. I should learn to embroider so I can put that on a cushion.

ALL THE WHILE, THE ONE PERSON I REALLY WANTED TO HEAR from had gone completely silent. I hadn't spoken to Avery since I had tucked him into bed. I texted him just after the results were announced to see if he was okay. And he wrote me back immediately.

> **AVERY:** Yes. I'm sorry. I meant to text you. I'm going to need some space for a little while. Hope that's okay.

I gave him space. I didn't text at all that night. Or the next day. Or the next week. I stayed away. I didn't want to make the same mistake I'd made with Beth, by texting all the time and putting undue pressure on him. This wasn't about me, it was about him.

So I filled my time. I did an extra-credit project for Latin. I went to Noodle Town so many times that I accumulated enough NoodlePointz for a free bowl. And I finally went to the ophthalmologist. (He was able to get my eye to stop leaking, but informed me I'd be wearing my favorite accessory for at least a few more months. Not ideal, but I had no one to blame but myself.)

I saw Avery in school a couple times. He always smiled and waved, and said hi if we were near enough to talk. One time he even said, "Thanks for this. For letting me have space."

"No prob," I said, willing myself not to reach up and touch him like I so desperately wanted to.

He wasn't in school much, though. I assumed that was because when he did come, everyone gawked at him, or asked him constantly if he was doing okay. I knew he was in hell, and that made it all the harder to be away from him. I wanted to comfort him. To be a salve for all the pain and confusion he must be going through. But he didn't seem to want that from me.

By the time two weeks had passed, I was really starting to worry. I hadn't seen him in school, and he wasn't posting on social. I started to wonder if he was depressed or if he had dropped out completely. I was about to do something drastic like call his mom when finally, mercifully, I received a text from him.

> **AVERY:** Hey Mertz. Sorry I've been ghosting you. I just needed to figure some stuff out. But I'm doing better now and I really want to tell you everything.

> **AVERY:** I've missed you. Would you be up for dinner tomorrow?

After a few practice texts, I wrote back with:

> **MARGOT:** Yes. I'd love dinner if you feel like you're ready. I love you.

This was much more sensible than *YESSS!!!!! OHMYGOD-IMISSEDYOU!!!!!!! LOVE!!!!!*

> **AVERY:** I love you too, Mertz.

We texted for a bit more, but then Avery said he was tired and wanted to go to bed. He suggested we go to Pomodoro. Pomodoro is pretty fancy, which I felt was a good sign. Italian food. Tablecloths. Those little knifey things they use to clear crumbs off said tablecloths. I didn't expect us to immediately get back to how we were before. I knew he was in crisis and would need a lot of support. But this felt like a good first step.

• • •

WHEN I ENTERED POMODORO, THE HOSTESS GREETED ME IMME-diately. I didn't even give her my name before she said, "Ms. Mertz! Your table is ready. Follow me." And then led me quickly to a secluded back room, where Avery was waiting for me. It was only later I realized she was trying to be as discreet as possible. Most of the press agreed it was poor form to stalk a teenager. But of course the more Lidori-friendly outlets continued to follow him and ask impertinent questions about his dad. I imagine it was pretty unnerving.

Avery stood up when I entered the room. Wearing a form-fitting brown blazer over a cream sweater, he was dressed more casually than I was, but still looked like he belonged at Pomodoro, whereas I was doing more of a cosplay version of a "fancy Pomodoro patron." I walked to him, ready to give him a big, tight hug. An *I'm here for you and I love you* embrace that would cut off his circulation. But Avery beat me to it, leaning over to kiss me on the cheek. It was dry and performative. And I knew that something was wrong. Then he gave me a gift, a small four-by-six box, but asked me not to open it until I got home.

I took a seat and tried to pretend none of this weirdness bothered me. I started talking, hoping that my rambling would make it a little less awkward. But loud awkward is just as awk-ward as quiet awkward.

"So this all looks so good! I've never had 'burrata' but I've been told, by my mom, that I have to try it. Do you like peas?" I asked, ripping off a piece of garlic bread.

"Margot," Avery blurted out, finally ungluing his eyes

from his menu. One of his hands was gripping the tablecloth as he said, "I'm sorry, I just have to tell you something. I'm . . . moving. To New York City."

I didn't respond. I just furrowed my brow and looked even harder at the menu.

"Sorry, did you hear what I said?" He continued, "I'm moving to New York City. With my mom."

"When?" I managed to say, still not looking at him.

"Like, soon. Before Christmas."

I put the menu down, then began fiddling with my fork as I said, "Okay. That's . . . soon. You're not even finishing your senior year at Roosevelt?"

"I know. It's weird, but . . ." he said quietly.

"Is that why you asked me out to a fancy dinner? To tell me that?" I asked, my mouth watering.

He shook his head. "I had this whole thing planned out. For how to tell you. I thought we could have a really good meal. And then, you know, at the end I'd tell you. But then seeing you, I—I don't know. I had to just spit it out."

I nodded. I was trying so damn hard to keep any tears from leaking out. My patch eye especially stung.

"So did your mom get that job or something? Is that why you're going?"

"Yeah. She wasn't going to take it. But then, with all the stuff about my dad, she thought it might be good to . . . relocate. For both of us."

I nodded. My heart was pounding. But everything else about me felt like it was going in slow motion. My hands. My breathing.

I blinked several times before saying, "She's probably right. I can't imagine living here after . . . what happened."

"Yeah," he said quietly.

"Have you talked to him . . . since . . ."

"No. I'm . . . No," Avery said, unable to say anything else. I'd never seen him look hopeless before. I felt actual, physical pain in my heart.

I reached out to take his hand, but he just let it hang limply in my grasp. I charged ahead anyway.

"Well, it's not like New York is *that* far away. And we have phones. We can FaceTime. And maybe I could even take the bus down sometime."

"Yeah. Maybe . . ." he whispered, his eyes cast down at his dinner plate.

"But I'm guessing you already thought of that. And that maybe the idea of still dating your girlfriend, from North Webster, makes you miserable. So . . ."

My tears were now fully making a run for it. But as I went to grab my napkin, his limp hand suddenly came to life, grabbing mine as he looked at me. His eyes now soft and sympathetic as he said, "Margot. I love you. I really do. But ever since all that stuff came out about my dad, I have been . . . either, like, volcanically angry. Like, punching-walls-in-my-house angry. Or seriously depressed. And the only thing that's brought me any sort of . . . I don't know, hope? Was when Mom brought up the idea of moving. Because in New York City, nobody's going to know who I am. And I think I need that. A clean break. You know, from . . . everything."

"Including me," I said, dabbing my good eye so hard I'd

probably need a second eye patch. "I get it. And I'm sorry if I—"

"You didn't do anything wrong, Margot," Avery said, leaning forward.

"Well, you didn't either," I said. "So why are we the ones being punished?"

I had probably known he was going to end things the second I saw him—his body language, all nerves and guilt. It was exactly how Beth had looked when she moved away. But I guess I just didn't want to believe it. Some part of me wouldn't accept it until I heard him say the words. We were over.

"Margot, I've never met anyone like you. And if there was a way to make this work, I would do it. But I'm just, like . . . not doing great. As a functioning person. And I . . . I don't know what else to do."

Avery started to rub his head. All of a sudden, he looked so incredibly fragile. And as much pain as I was in, and as much as I wanted to convince him to stay with me, to hold him and keep him and make him swear to visit me every weekend, I knew I couldn't. He was just trying to survive right now. And I guess somewhere deep down I wanted what was best for him, even if that meant I couldn't be with him. Which surprised me a little.

I grabbed his face and kissed him. The longest, saddest fucking kiss I'd ever given anyone. And when we pulled away, I looked at him deeply.

"I get it, Avery. I do," I said, wiping the tears from his cheeks. "And I hope you know that, deep down, I will always—"

But before I could dive into my whole painful confession of how much I loved him and how I'd wait for him to get over all this so we could be together, our waiter, Steven, arrived. And with no ability to read a goddamned room, Steven proceeded to ask us how we were feeling tonight.

Avery quietly ordered us drinks and tried to get him the hell out of there, but Steven insisted on telling us about the specials, and how the pasta was handmade. And how the cheese was imported from Italy. And how the wine menu won the coveted "Golden Grape" award from FingerLakesWineCountry.com. By the time we ordered appetizers and got rid of Steven, the moment was gone. All that was left was two heartbroken people. No longer a couple. Maybe not even friends. When the ravioli arrived, neither of us felt like eating.

AFTER AN EXCRUCIATINGLY LONG CAR RIDE HOME, WE SHARED A very awkward, very chaste peck on the cheek before I left his Tesla for the last time. He said, "Bye, Mertz." And it was more painful than if he ran me over with his car. I can't even remember if I said anything back.

Rule #1 had always been my most important rule. Don't lose friends over a job. I swear, with every choice I made in this case, I tried to do the right thing by Avery. To not do what I did last year, when I manipulated and took advantage of people and burned every meaningful friend-bridge I had. But here I was anyway. Once again losing my best friend.

And it's not like I could talk to Melanie about it. I was pretty sure that friendship had also sailed. Sadly, that one was purely my fault. I hadn't lost her in service of a job. Just in my own Ahab-esque quest to fell P-Boy. Which also felt terrible.

I didn't feel overly emotional as I walked into Trinity Towers after leaving Avery. It was more like my mind and body were just on autopilot. Like how when you have frostbite on your fingers and they hurt really bad and then weirdly they stop hurting and you're just like, meh? Well, I was feeling very meh.

I closed the door behind me, reached into my coat pocket, and took out Avery's parting gift. It was neatly wrapped in the blandest wrapping paper I've ever seen. And it didn't even have a note or a card. Just paper. I methodically took off the wrapping, revealing a small gold picture frame. In it was a scorecard from Gulf of Golf. From our first date, back when I was only pretending to like him. That sentimental goober kept it. Even after I broke up with him and he should've probably burned it.

I should've cried. I should've sobbed mad, theatrical sobs. But instead I just stared at the scorecard from the game I won. I would've traded that and all the other "wins" if it meant I didn't have to lose Avery.

Inside the apartment, my parents were engaged in an intense game of Scrabble. You can always tell because they're unusually quiet. Especially when it's my dad's turn. He's not a natural speller, and his turns take forever.

"How was the date?" my mom asked when I walked by.

"Fine," I said with no inflection.

"Does ointment have an 'a'?" my dad asked.

"No," I said, slipping the box back in my coat pocket.

"Okay. Is 'oint*mant*' a word?" my dad asked.

"No," my mom and I said in unison. I thought about heading

to the fridge to get something carby, but even that seemed like too much work.

"I'm gonna go to bed."

"All right, hun," my mom said, looking up from the board for the first time. Then she squinted at me before saying, "Are you okay?"

"Yeah. I'm just tired."

"Well, you deserve a break. After the couple of weeks you've had," my dad said, still glaring at his pieces. "What about 'tainment'?"

"No," my mom said without looking at him. Instead she got up and came over to me. "Margot, I know we've been butting heads a lot lately. But I just wanted to say that . . . I think I finally get it now. Why your work is so important to you. Because you're helping people who really need it. All those girls last year. And now Abby. I can't tell you how proud I am of you."

"It's really amazing," echoed my dad, finally looking up from his pending orthographical error. "I don't know how you do it. But I'm glad you're doing it."

"Okay. Uh, thanks," I said, no idea what to make of all this sudden positivity.

"So your dad and I talked, and we decided that if you want to spend your time working on this filth-cleaning stuff, we're going to stop getting in your way. You're an adult. So going forward, if space is what you need, then we're going to give you more space."

I felt my face get hot again. My eyes started to well. Because I was realizing space was exactly what I didn't want. Avery needed space. Melanie needed space. Beth had needed space. Everyone

I ever got close to came to the realization that they didn't want to be anywhere near me. And I know that's not what my parents were saying—I had told them to leave me alone so many times that they decided to do just that—but at this moment, I just wanted them to hug me. And shove brownies in my mouth. And tell me everything was going to be okay.

And they would. All I had to do was tell them how I felt. But for some reason I couldn't. Maybe it's because I'm not a kid anymore. I can't just run and tell Mommy and Daddy. Or maybe it's because I didn't think they could actually help me this time. Nothing they could say would bring Avery back to me. Or maybe I just didn't want to ruin their Scrabble game? But whatever the reason, I just said good night. And I went to bed surrounded by— and *drowning in*—the space everyone insisted on giving me.

CHAPTER 25

ANOTHER YEAR OLDER

More than a month later, I twisted my key into the mailbox and absentmindedly took out its crowded contents. A bunch of circulars, some kind of Spectrum ad, and a big envelope *from Stanford University*. I snatched it from our mailbox and barricaded myself in my room before my parents could see that it had arrived. They'd been nervously checking the mailbox for a week. But I'd known for nine days that I had gotten in. Ever since I logged on to the Stanford admissions portal. But for some reason, I just wasn't ready to let my parents know about it. I told myself I'd get excited about it when I finally got the letter in the mail. The packet was as impressive as I'd hoped it would be. There was a formal letter from the dean of admissions and a big, glossy folder with information about scheduling, housing, tuition, and more. It was everything I'd been working for since I was eight years old. The culmination of hours upon hours of studying and filth-cleaning and essay-writing. Here it finally was.

And as I held the letter in my hand, sitting on the very edge of my bed, my toes curled into a ball, I felt . . . fine. Good, I guess? But after working toward this goal for literally half my life, I guess I expected to feel something more. Fireworks? Spontaneous dancing? Mild—or not that mild—euphoria? But I didn't feel any of that. Somehow this didn't erase the fact that I missed Avery. Or that I had no friends. Or that something about my life was starting to feel a little dead.

Huh. That wasn't great.

I grabbed the envelope and headed outside for a walk. Maybe the frigid air and my feet stomping around in two inches of snow would snap me out of my funk. I put on my parka, my warm hat and gloves, and I braved the elements. I tried to keep the wind at my back. But it seemed to keep changing directions.

It was December twenty-second. Three days till Christmas. And also technically my birthday, even though I wasn't really observing. I was finally eighteen. An adult. I could get a tattoo, enlist in the army, donate blood, apply for a credit card, and play the lottery. I could legally have sex with literally anyone else over eighteen, regardless of their age. Meaning I could fuck a gross predator and it wouldn't be considered a crime! Hooray. Even if it were exploitative and damaging to me, it was now legal. Funny how they drew those lines.

As I walked alone, I thought of all the people in my life who had left me. The friends and cohorts who had once seemed so necessary to me, who had all drifted away somehow. Other than my parents, who bought me a cake, I didn't have anyone to celebrate my birthday with. I didn't know who to tell about Stanford.

I thought about Avery and wondered how he and his mom were settling into their swanky-looking apartment in Manhattan. How he was liking "The Hallton School," which is apparently very fancy and private. (I googled.) It even has a "film and media" class that he loves. (Per Instagram.) I wondered if he was actually as happy as his posts made him seem. And if he ever thought about me.

I thought about his dad. The district attorney had intimated that they were opening an investigation into Shep and the inappropriate texts he'd sent to a minor. Depending on what they were able to prove, Shep could even end up in jail, though Caroline thought jail time unlikely. I pictured him in his empty house, taking calls from consultants and high-priced lawyers. Planning his comeback, probably. Gross.

I thought about my parents, probably off on yet another date. They were true to their word, and since November they'd more or less left me alone. We even stopped having Family Time. And even though it made me a little lonely, it also made me happy to see them going on dates again. They deserved some Couple Time.

I thought about all the volunteers and underpaid staff I'd worked with on Shep's campaign. A few of them had started volunteering for the likely Democratic candidate, Michelle Tupper, who'd be running against Lidori in the special election. But more of them had stepped away from politics altogether and gone back to school or to their hobbies.

I thought about Abby. You'd think after everything she'd

been through that she'd be angry or depressed or, I don't know, crying all the time. But she honestly seemed like she was doing better than, well, than me. She posted on the Fury chat that she'd started going to therapy again. Maybe it was helping?

I thought about Caroline Goldstein, and how she was now lobbying the DCCC to make revenge porn legislation part of their statewide platform. I ran into her at Joe's Coffee a few weeks ago, and she told me once again, "You should've interned for me." This time I agreed with her.

I even thought about P-Boy. Fucking P-Boy, of all people. Out of everyone who had been swirling about my head, he was the one person I had actually seen recently. I ran into him at the mall while attempting to Christmas shop for my aunt Sarah (the woman has everything, she's impossible to buy for!). He was with Ainsley, volunteering as a bell ringer for the Salvation Army, probably in an attempt to rehabilitate his image.[128] He practically accosted me with his bell, repeating his claim that he didn't hack my computer. Insisting that he was really trying to be a better person. He was even auditioning for the spring musical. (As if that proved something?)

I still had my doubts. I'm just not sure people *can* actually change. And no amount of half-hearted bell ringing could convince me of that. After all, if I hadn't changed as much as I thought I had, how the fuck had P-Boy?

I bought Aunt Sarah a creamer shaped like a cow.

---

128 Ironically, Salvation Army is also trying to rehabilitate their image after a disastrous record of discrimination against LGBTQ+ people. Something tells me Ainsley and Peter don't know anything about this.

. . .

MY FEET TRUDGED THROUGH THE SNOW. MY BODY MOVED through space. More and more people kept invading my head. All living their lives. All not caring about what I did. Or what I would do.

I found an empty bench at the edge of Barnard Park. I took out my phone and started scrolling through my contacts. I thought about texting Avery. Or Sammi. For a fleeting moment, I thought maybe I should post something on Instagram about it being my birthday. You know, just to see if anyone would take the bait and like my post or send me a confetti emoji or some shit. But that felt so pathetic. And if I was looking to stave off a creeping depression, Instagram was the last place I should go.

And then my phone pinged. It was a text from Melanie. I hadn't heard from her since the night Abby confessed. Her last text to me had been about how disappointed she was in me. It was classy and very "high road," but the subtext had been clear: *We are not friends anymore. I don't like your shirt.*

So a text from Melanie was surprising.

> **MELANIE:** Abby's coming over for New Year's if you want to come.

I didn't respond right away. Mostly because I figured she had sent this text to the wrong person.

> **MELANIE:** I guess I should explain. I was and am pretty pissed at you for the whole P-Boy thing.

Yup. I mean, that tracks. I didn't know what to text back, so

I figured I would just thumbs-up her messages and call it a day. But then she sent another.

> **MELANIE:** But you are also a hero for how you helped Abby. So like the Endangered Species Act did for the Northern Spotted Owl when they declared their forest a "designated habitat," I'm giving you a second chance.

Well, okay, I thought. That's a good sign. It made me cautiously optimistic that I might be able to end my senior year with at least one to two friends? But even that wasn't giving me fireworks or spontaneous dancing. I still felt cold and confused and overwhelmed. I was about to text her back when I got another ping. A ping from someone I honestly hadn't thought about in weeks.

> **NICK:** Hey Margot. Random question. Are you still unretired? Cause I have a friend who would definitely hire you.

> **NICK:** If you don't help him, he's pretty fucked.

And then . . . fucking fireworks. My face flushed. At first I thought it was just because Nick was a boy. A boy who asked me out once. But then I realized it was something else. *Nick* wasn't getting my heart pumping and head buzzing. It was the job offer. The gig. Going back to what I knew I was good at. It felt like I was coming home.

My thumbs, as if they had a mind of their own, quickly typed out a response.

> **MARGOT:** I am unretired. Let's meet.

A FEW HOURS LATER, I WAS HUNKERED DOWN IN MY USUAL BOOTH at Petey O'Taverns. Two more of the pendant lights over the bar had gone out since I'd last been there, and I wondered if they'd ever replace them.

Nick was shooting darts and probably losing a fair bit of money to Big Dave, one of the regulars. But he didn't seem to mind. Nor did he seem to mind waiting for me while I met with his friend. Probably because he thought we were going to hook up later. And honestly, he wasn't wrong.

Back in fall, I'd gotten a few other DMs from potential clients. And on the way over to Petey's, I'd finally responded to all of them. I told them if they wanted my services, they should make their way there. No rules this time. No qualifiers. First come, first serve.

Soon they'd be perched on barstools between the familiar regulars or standing on the sticky floor by the jukebox, their feet making Velcro sounds every time they shifted their weight. And they would wait for me. Because they needed me. And I know this is a depressing thought—but maybe I needed them too.

Margot Mertz was open for business.

As Johnny Cash played on the jukebox, I felt like me again. Well, maybe not exactly *me*—my eye was still injured, and my left hand was doing that weird tingling thing—but I felt close to me. Or to the me I used to be. Which was better than feeling like nothing.

Ted swung by and handed me a club soda with lime. I thanked him with a nod, then brought my attention back to Nick's friend as he told me his story. About how he got drunk and emailed his professor a sex tape he made with his ex-girlfriend. I took a sip, and listened, and thought about all the ways I was going to help this sad, gross boy who probably didn't deserve a second chance. I was going to clean his filth. Even if it got me a little dirty in the process. Because at the end of the day, isn't that what I do?

Happy birthday to me.

ACKNOWLEDGMENTS

We'd like to thank Kelsey Murphy, our wonderful editor, who constantly pushes us to be better, to go deeper, and to make cuts. She is the reason our books are readable and not word salad.

Thank you as well to Alli Dyer at Temple Hill Publishing for helping this along. Alli is our cheerleader and often our tiebreaker, and we trust her instincts completely. And thank you to the rest of our team at Temple Hill Entertainment, Syndey Title and Julie Waters, for seeing possibilities in Margot. And to the team at Writers House working with Temple Hill, thank you, Simon Lipskar, Cecilia de la Campa, Alessandra Birch, and Sofia Bolido.

To everyone at Viking and Penguin Random House, thank you for working on our books! Thank you to Ken Wright and Tamar Brazis for leading us through the process. And to all who had a hand in designing this very cool-looking book: Monique Sterling, Ellice Lee, Maria Fazio, Kristin Boyle, Deborah Kaplan, and our brilliant cover artist, Katie Carey. And of course thank you to the sales and marketing teams who helped get this book actually read. And thank you to Ronni Davis for her insight and reflections on both Margot books. Her feedback made the book better and also made us grow as writers.

Carrie used to proofread as a side hustle. And Ian has spent most of his life as a proofreader's worst nightmare. Maybe that's why we are so enamored with our copyediting team. Thank you, Krista Ahlberg, Laura Blackwell, Alicia Balderrama, Marinda Valenti, and Sola Akinlana, for always knowing exactly what we were going for! And for catching so many mistakes! We love you for googling Spicy

Coconut flavored LaCroix, which is something we made up.

To our international team, we say merci, 감사합니다, obrigada, and thanks. That's La Martiniere, Moonhak Soochup, Eksmo, Nacional, and of course Hardie Grant. Seeing Margot cross international borders made us humbled and beyond grateful that you took a chance on us. And as soon as our son is vaccinated, we're coming to your bookstores!

Thank you to the team of people it takes for us to sound smart. We'll start with Jeff Roberts, a man who is far too cool given how much he knows about technology. You'd expect someone that gifted to be a little weird socially. Not the case with Jeff. You're a dream. And to our political operatives! This book required us to have a little better understanding of local campaigns than we could glean from *New Yorker* articles or *Game Change*. Thankfully, we had the help of Teale Fox and Steven Chlapecka, whose amazing anecdotes helped us paint a richer picture of upstate New York politics. Thank you too to our connectors, Tara Good and Melissa Foley, for putting us together. And to Matt Foley, who took the time to patiently explain focus group research to us. And to Karen McCrossen for outlining the disciplinary procedures of public school administration. Thank goodness our friends are so smart so we can remain so ignorant.

There's one other area where we constantly need authenticity help. Thank you to Sam Levy, Charlotte Sheffield, and Sophia and Gia Triassi for telling us how kids talk and for letting us know the ways in which high school is different now from when we went there in [REDACTED]. We text them random questions all the time and they text us back during school hours. Which, honestly, says a lot.

To our managers! Thank you Edna Cowan and Alex Platis for always having our backs! You are both wonderful and we always feel better after talking to you. And to *partner* Jay Patel at Peikoff-Mahan, our wonderful lawyer.

And thanks to a few other things that made our lives easier during our late-stage-pandemic work on this book. Thanks, cold Topo Chicos, takeout, first trimester afternoon naps, our therapists, and mostly, our friends in LA and NYC, who are all very nice and talented. It lowers our blood pressures to chat with you.

Also, thank you to all the readers of *Margot Mertz Takes It Down*! To our friends and family who read it out of obligation and politeness, and to the readers we've never met who must've read this of their own free will! And to everyone who shared positive feedback! We hope you like *For the Win*! Please still like us!

And finally, our biggest personal thanks go to our parents, Laurie, Karen, and Paul. They watch our son while we write. They make us dinner. The point is, they keep giving and we keep taking. Shouldn't we start caring for them at some point? You would think. To them, we say thank you for being the world's best parents and grandparents. Thank you for being our village and for encouraging us to write and make art and try stuff. God, we are lucky.

Thank you as well to Calvin. We would've dedicated one of these books to you, but it felt weird to dedicate a book about revenge porn to our three-year-old. But know that you are so important to us. Loving you is easy. And to the baby on the way, we'd like to say we're almost ready. Just sit tight. We love you already. And we're taking your kicks as positive feedback that we are on the right track creatively.